Sir Robert's Fortune by Margaret Oliphant

Margaret Oliphant Wilson was born on April 4th, 1828 to Francis W. Wilson, a clerk, and Margaret Oliphant, at Wallyford, near Musselburgh, East Lothian.

Her youth was spent in establishing a writing style and by 1849 she had her first novel published: Passages in the Life of Mrs. Margaret Maitland.

Two years later, in 1851 Caleb Field was published and also an invitation gained to contribute to Blackwood's Magazine; the beginning of a lifelong business relationship.

In May 1852, Margaret married her cousin, Frank Wilson Oliphant. Their marriage produced six children but, tragically, three died in infancy. When her husband developed signs of the dreaded consumption (tuberculosis) they moved to Florence, and then to Rome where, sadly, he died.

Margaret was naturally devastated but was also now left without support and only her income from writing to support the family. She returned to England and took up the burden of supporting her three remaining children by her literary activity.

Her incredible and prolific work rate increased both her commercial reputation and the size of her reading audience. Tragedy struck again in January 1864 when her only remaining daughter, Maggie, died.

In 1866 she settled at Windsor to be closer to her sons, who were being educated at near-by Eton School.

For more than thirty years she pursued a varied literary career but family life continued to bring problems. Cyril Francis, her eldest son, died in 1890. The younger son, Francis, who she nicknamed 'Cecco', died in 1894.

With the last of her children now lost to her, she had little further interest in life. Her health steadily and inexorably declined.

Margaret Oliphant Wilson Oliphant died at the age of 69 in Wimbledon on 20th June 1897. She is buried in Eton beside her sons.

Index of Contents

CHAPTER I

"We are to see each other no more."

These words were breathed rather than spoken in the dim recess of a window, hidden behind ample curtains, the deep recess in which the window was set leaving room enough for two figures standing close together. Without was a misty night, whitened rather than lighted by a pale moon.

"Who says so?"

"Alas! my uncle," said the white figure, which looked misty, like the night, in undistinguishable whiteness amid the darkness round.

The other figure was less distinguishable still, no more than a faint solidity in the atmosphere, but from it came a deeper whisper, the low sound of a man's voice. "Your uncle!" it said.

There was character in the voices enough to throw some light upon the speakers, even though they were unseen.

The woman's had a faint accentuation of feeling, not of anxiety, yet half defiance and half appeal. It seemed to announce a fact unchangeable, yet to look and hope for a contradiction. The man's had a tone of acceptance and dismay. The fiat which had gone forth was more real to him than to her, though she was in the position of asserting and he of opposing it.

"Yes," she said, "Ronald, my uncle—who has the strings of the purse and every thing else in his hands—"

There was a moment's pause, and then he said: "How does he mean to manage that?"

"I am to be sent off to-morrow—it's all settled—and if I had not contrived to get out to-night, you would never have known."

"But where? It all depends upon that," he said with a little impatience.

"To Dalrugas," she answered, with a sigh; and then: "It is miles and miles from anywhere—a moor and a lodge, and not even a cottage near. Dougal and his wife live there, and take care of the place; not a soul can come near it—it is the end of the world. Oh, Ronald, what shall I do? what shall I do?"

Once more in the passionate distress of the tone there was an appeal, and a sort of feverish hope.

"We must think; we must think," he said.

"What will thinking do? It will not change my uncle's heart, nor the distance, nor the dreadful solitude. What does he care if it kills me? or any body?" The last words came from her with a shriller tone of misery, as if it had become too much to bear.

"Hush, hush, for Heaven's sake; they will hear you!" he said.

On the other side of the curtain there was a merry crowd in full career of a reel, which in those days had not gone out of fashion as now. The wild measure of the music, now quickening to lightning speed, now dropping to sedater motion, with the feet of the dancers keeping time, filled the atmosphere—a shriek would scarcely have been heard above that mirthful din.

"Oh, why do you tell me to hush?" cried the girl impetuously. "Why should I mind who hears? It is not for duty or love that I obey him, but only because he has the money. Am I caring for his money? I could get my own living: it would not want much. Why do I let him do what he likes with me?"

"My darling," said the man's voice anxiously, "don't do anything rash, for God's sake! Think of our future. To displease him, to rebel, would spoil every thing. I see hope in the loneliness, for my part. Be patient, be patient, and let me work it out."

"Oh, your working out!" she cried. "What good has it done? I would cut the knot. It would be strange if we two could not get enough to live upon—or myself, if you are afraid."

He soothed her, coming closer, till the dark shadow and the white one seemed but one, and murmured caressing words in her ears: "Let us wait till the case is desperate, Lily. It is not desperate yet. I see chances in the moor and the wilderness. He is playing into our hands if he only knew it. Don't, don't spoil every thing by your impatience! Leave it to me, and you'll see good will come out of it."

"I would rather take it into my own hands!" she cried.

"No, dearest, no! I see—I see all sorts of good in it. Go quite cheerfully, as if you were pleased. No, your own way is best—don't let us awake any suspicions—go as if you were breaking your heart."

"There will be no feigning in that," she said; "I shall be breaking my heart."

"For a moment," he said. "'Weeping endureth for a night, but joy cometh in the morning.'"

"Don't, Ronald! I can't bear to hear you quoting Scripture."

"Why not? I am not the devil, I hope," he said, with a low laugh.

There was a question in the girl's hot, impatient heart, and then a quick revulsion of feeling. "I don't know what to do, or to think; I feel as if I could not bear it," she said, the quick tears dropping from her eyes.

He wiped them tenderly away with the flourish of a white handkerchief in the dark. "Trust to me," he said soothingly. "Be sure it is for our good, this. Listen: they are calling for you, Lily."

"Oh, what do I care? How can I go among them all, and dance as if I were as gay as the rest, when my heart is broken?"

"Not so badly broken but that it will mend," he whispered, as with a clever, swift movement he put aside the curtain and led her through. He was so clever: where any other man would have been lost in perplexity, or even despair, Ronald Lumsden always saw a way through. He was never at a loss for an expedient: even that way of getting back to the room out of the shadow of the curtains no one could have performed so easily, so naturally as he did. He met and entered into the procession of dancers going out of the room after the exertions of that reel as if he and his partner formed part of it, and had been dancing too. People did not "sit out" in those days, and Ronald was famous for his skill in the national dance. Nobody doubted that he had been exerting himself with the rest. Lily was half English—

that is, she had been sent to England for part of her education, and so far as reels were concerned, had lost some of her native skill, and was not so clever. She was not, indeed, supposed to be clever at all, though very nice, and pretty enough, and an heiress—at least she was likely to be an heiress, if she continued to please her uncle, who was not an easy man to please, and exacted absolute obedience. There were people who shook their heads over her chances, declaring that flesh and blood could not stand Sir Robert Ramsay's moods; but up to this time Lily had been more or less successful, and the stake being so great, she had, people said, "every encouragement" to persevere.

But Lily was by no means so strong as her lover, who joined the throng as if he had formed part of it, with a perfect air of enjoyment and light-heartedness. Lily could not look happy. It may be said that in his repeated assurance that all would be right, and that he would find a way out of it, she ought to have taken comfort, feeling in that a pledge of his fidelity and steadiness to his love. But there was something in this readiness of resource which discouraged, she could not have told why, instead of making her happy. It would have been so much simpler, so much more satisfactory, to have given up all thoughts of Sir Robert's money, and trusted to Providence and their own exertions to bring them through. Lily felt that she could make any sacrifice, live upon nothing, live anywhere, work her fingers to the bone, only to be independent, to be free of the bondage of the uncle and the consciousness that it was not for love but for his money that she had to accept all his caprices and yield him obedience. If Ronald would but have yielded, if he would have been imprudent, as so many young men were, how thankful she would have been! She would have been content with the poorest living anywhere to be free, to be with him whom she loved. She would have undertaken the conduct of their little ménage herself, without even thinking of servants; she would have cooked for him, cleaned the house for him, shrunk from nothing. But that, alas, was not Ronald's way of looking at the matter. He believed in keeping up appearances, in being rich at almost any cost, and, at best, in looking rich if he were not really so; and, above all and beyond all, in keeping well with the uncle, and retaining the fortune. He would not have any doubt thrown on the necessity of that. He was confident of his own powers of cheating the uncle, and managing so that Lily should have all she wanted, in spite of him, by throwing dust in his eyes. But Lily's soul revolted against throwing dust in any one's eyes. This was the great difference between them. I do not say that there was any great sin in circumventing a harsh old man, who never paused to think what he was doing, or admitted a question as to whether he was or was not absolutely in the right. He was one of the men who always know themselves to be absolutely right; therefore he was, as may be said, fair game. But Lily did not like it. She would have liked a lover who said: "Never mind, we shall be happy without him and his fortune." She had tried every thing she knew to bring young Lumsden to this point. But she was not able to do so: his opinion was that every thing must be done to preserve the fortune, and that, however hard it might be, there was nothing so hard but that it must be done to humor old Sir Robert, to prevent him from cutting his niece out of his will. Was not this right? Was it not prudent, wise, the best thing? If he, an advocate without a fee, a briefless barrister, living as best he could on chance windfalls and bits of journalism, had been as bold as she desired, and carried her off from the house in Moray Place to some garret of his own up among the roofs, would not every-body have said that he had taken advantage of her youth and inexperience, and deprived her of all the comforts and luxuries she was used to? That Lily cared nothing for those luxuries, and that she was of the mettle to adapt herself to any circumstances, so long as she had somebody to love and who loved her, was not a thing to reckon with public opinion about; and, indeed, Ronald Lumsden would have thought himself quite unjustified in reckoning with it at all. To tell the truth, he had no desire on his own part to give up such modest luxuries for himself as were to be had.

The day of clubs was not yet, at least in Edinburgh, to make life easy for young men, but yet to get along, as he was doing precariously, was easier for one than it would be for two. Even Lily, all hot for sacrifice and for ministering with her own hands to all the needs of life, had never contemplated the idea of doing without Robina, her maid, who had been with her so many years that it was impossible for either of them to realize what life would be if they were separated. Even if it should be a necessary reality, Robina was included as a matter of course. How it might be that Lily should require to scrub, and clean, and cook with her own hands, while she was attended by a lady's maid, was a thing she had never reasoned out. You may think that a lady's maid would probably be of less use than her mistress had such service been necessary; but this was not Robina's case, who was a very capable person all round, and prided herself on being able to "turn her hand" to anything. But then a runaway match was the last thing that was in Lumsden's thoughts.

It was a dance which every-body enjoyed that evening in the big, old-fashioned rooms in George Square. George Square has fallen out of knowledge in all the expansions of new Edinburgh, the Edinburgh that lies on the other side of the valley, and dates no farther back than last century. It also is of last century, but earlier than the Moray Places and Crescents; far earlier than the last developments, the Belgravia of the town. There Sir Walter once lived, in, I think, his father's house; and these substantial, ample, homely houses were the first outlet of the well-to-do, the upper classes, of Edinburgh out of the closes and high-up apartments, approached through the atrocities of a common stair, in which so refined and luxurious a sybarite as Lawyer Pleydell still lived in Sir Walter's own time. These mansions are severely plain outside—"undemonstrative," as Scotch pride arrogantly declares itself to be, aping humility with a pretence to which I, for one, feel disposed to allow no quarter; but they are large and pleasant inside, and the big square rooms the very thing to dance in or to feast in. They were full of a happy crowd, bright in color and lively in movement, with a larger share of golden hair and rosy cheeks than is to be seen in most assemblies, and, perhaps, a greater freedom of laughter and talk than would have been appropriate to a solemn ball in other localities. For Edinburgh was not so large then as now, and they all knew each other, and called each other by their Christian names—boy and girl alike—with a general sense of fraternity modified by almost as many love affairs as there were pairs of boys and girls present. There were mothers and aunts all round the wide walls, but this did not subdue the hilarity of the young ones, who knew each other's mothers and aunts almost as well as they knew their own, and counted upon their indulgence. Lily Ramsay was almost the only girl who had nobody of her own to turn to; but this only made her the more protected and surrounded, every-body feeling that the motherless girl had a special claim. They were by no means angels, these old-fashioned Edinburgh folk: sharper tongues could not be than were to be found among them, or more wicked wits; but there was a great deal of kindness under the terrible turbans which crowned the heads of the elder ladies and the scarfs which fell from their bare shoulders, and they all knew every one, and every one's father and mother for generations back. Their dress was queer, or rather, I should have said, it was queer before the present revival of the early Victorian or late Georgian style began. They wore puffed-out sleeves, with small feather pillows in them to keep them inflated; they had bare shoulders and ringlets; they had scarfs of lace or silk, carefully disposed so as not to cover anything, but considered very classical and graceful, drawn in over the elbows, by people who knew how to wear them, making manifest the slender waist (or often the outlines of a waist which had ceased to be slender) behind. And they had, as has been said, a dreadful particular, which it is to be hoped the blind fury of fashion will not bring up again—turbans upon their heads. Turbans such as no Indian or Bedouin ever wore, of all colors and every kind of savage decoration, such as may be seen in pictures of that alarming age.

When young Lumsden left his Lily, it was in the midst of a group of girls collected together in the interval between two dances, lamenting that the programme was nearly exhausted, and that mamma had made a point of not staying later than three o'clock. "Because it disturbs papa!" said one of them indignantly, "though we all know he would go on snoring if the Castle Rock were to fall!" They all said papa and mamma in those days.

"But mamma says there are so many parties going," said another: "a ball for almost every night next week; and what are we to do for dresses? Tarlatan's in rags with two, and even a silk slip is shameful to look at at the end of a week."

"Lily has nothing to do but to get another whenever she wants it," said Jeanie Scott.

"And throw away the old ones, she's such a grand lady," said Maggie Lauder.

"Hold all your tongues," said Bella Rutherford; "it does her this good, that she thinks less about it than any of us."

"She has other things to think of," cried another; and there was a laugh and a general chorus, "So have we all." "But, Lily! is Sir Robert as dour as ever?" one of the rosy creatures cried.

"I don't think I am going to any more of your balls," said Lily; "I'm tired of dancing. We just dance, dance, and think of nothing else."

"What else should we think about at our age?" said Mary Bell, opening wide a pair of round blue eyes.

"We'll have plenty other things to think about, mamma says, and that soon enough," said Alison Murray, who was just going to be married, with a sigh. "But there's the music striking up again, and who's my partner? for I'm sure I don't remember whether its Alick Scott, or Johnnie Beatoun, or Bob Murray. Oh! is it you, Bob?" she said with relief, putting her hand upon an outstretched arm. They were almost all in a similar perplexity, except, indeed, such as had their own special partner waiting. Lily was almost glad that it was not Ronald, but a big young Macgregor, who led her off to the top of the room to a sedate quadrille. The waltz existed in those days, but it was still an indulgence, and looked upon with but scant favor by the mothers. The elder folks were scandalized by the close contact, and even the girls liked best that it should be an accepted lover, or at the least a brother or cousin, whose arm encircled their waist. So they still preferred dances in which there were "figures," and took their pleasure occasionally in a riotous "Lancers" or a merry reel with great relief. Lily was young enough to forget herself and her troubles even in the slow movement of the quadrilles, with every-body else round chattering and beaming and forgetting when it was their turn to dance. But she said to herself that it was the last. Of all these dances of which they spoke she would see none. When the others gathered, delighted to enjoy themselves, she would be gazing across the dark moor, hearing nothing but the hum of insects and the cry of the curlew, or, perhaps, a watchful blackbird in the little clump of trees. Well! for to-night she would forget.

I need not say it was Lumsden who saw her to her own door on the other side of the square. No one there would have been such a spoil-sport as to interfere with his right whatever old Sir Robert might say. They stole out in a lull of the leave-taking, when the most of the people were gone, and others lingered for just this "one more" for which the girls pleaded. The misty moonlight filled the square, and made all the waiting carriages look like ghostly equipages bent upon some mystic journey in the middle of the night. They paused at the corner of the square, where the road led down to the pleasant Meadows, all white and indefinite in the mist, spreading out into the distance. Lumsden would fain have drawn her away into a little further discussion, wandering under the trees, where they would have met nobody at that hour; but Lily was not bold enough to walk in the Meadows between two and three in the morning. She was willing, however, to walk up and down a little on the other side of the square before she said good-night. Nobody saw them there, except some of the coachmen on the boxes, who were too sleepy to mind who passed, and Robina, who had silently opened the door and was waiting for her mistress. Robina was several years older than Lily, and had relinquished all thoughts of a sweetheart in her own person. She stood concealing herself in the doorway, ready, if any sound should be made within which denoted wakefulness on the part of Sir Robert, to snatch her young lady even from her lover's arms; and watching, with very mingled feelings, the pair half seen—the white figure congenial to the moonlight, and the dark one just visible, like a prop to a flower. "Lily's her name and Lily's her nature," said Robina to herself, with a little moisture in her kind eyes; "but, oh! is he worthy of her, is he worthy of her?" This was too deep a question to be solved by anything but time and proof, which are the last things to satisfy the heart. At last there was a lingering parting, and Lily stole, in her white wraps, all white from top to toe, into the dark and silent house.

CHAPTER II

Lily's room was faintly illuminated by a couple of candles, which, as it was a large room with gloomy furniture, made little more than darkness visible, except about the table on which they stood, the white cover of which, and the dressing-glass that stood upon it, diffused the light a little. It was not one of those dainty chambers in which our Lilys of the present day are housed. One side of the room was occupied by a large wardrobe of almost black mahogany, polished and gleaming with many years' manipulation, but out of reach of these little lights. The bed was a large four-post bed, which once had been hung with those moreen curtains which were the triumph of the bad taste of our fathers, and had their appropriate accompaniment in black hair-cloth sofas and chairs. Lily had been allowed to substitute for the moreen white dimity, which was almost as bad, and hung stiff as a board from the valance ornamented with bobs of cotton tassels. She could not help it if that was the best that could be done in her day. Every thing, except the bed, was dark, and the distance of the large room was black as night, except for the relief of an open door into a small dressing-room which Robina occupied, and in which a weird little dip candle with a long wick unsnuffed was burning feebly. Nobody can imagine nowadays what it was to have candles which required snuffing, and which, if not attended to, soon began to bend and topple over, with a small red column of consumed wick, in the midst of a black and smoking crust. A silver snuffer tray is quite a pretty article nowadays, and proves that its possessor had a grandfather; but then! The candles on the dressing-table, however, were carefully snuffed, and burned as brightly as was possible for them while Robina took off her young mistress's great white Indian mantle, with its silken embroideries, and undid her little pearl necklace. Lily had the milk-white skin of a Scotch girl, and the rose-tints; but she was brown in hair and eyes, as most people are in all countries, and had no glow of golden hair about her. She was tired and pale that night, and the tears were very near her eyes.

"Ye've been dancing more than ye should; these waltzes and new-fangled things are real exhaustin'," Robina said.

"I have been dancing very little," said Lily; "my heart was too heavy. How can you dance when you have got your sentence in your pocket, and the police coming for you to haul you away to the Grassmarket by skreigh of day?"

"Hoot, away with ye!" cried Robina, "what nonsense are ye talking? My bonnie dear, ye'll dance many a night yet at a' the assemblies, and go in on your ain man's airm—"

"It's you that's talking nonsense now. On whose arm? Have we not got our sentence, you and me, to be banished to Dalrugas to-morrow, and never to come back—unless—"

"Ay, Miss Lily, unless! but that's a big word."

"It is, perhaps, a big word; but it cannot touch me, that am not of the kind that breaks my word or changes my mind," said Lily, raising her head with a gesture full of pride.

"Oh, Miss Lily, my dear, I ken what the Ramsays are!" cried the faithful maid; "but there might be two meanings till it," and she breathed a half sigh over her young mistress's head.

"You think, I know—and maybe I once thought, too; but you may dismiss that from your mind, as I do," said the girl, with a shake of the head as if she were shaking something off. And then she added, clasping her hands together: "Oh, if I were strong enough just to say, 'I am not caring about your money. I am not afraid to be poor. I can work for my own living, and you can give your siller where you please!' Oh, Beenie, that is what I want to say!"

"No, my darlin', no; you must not say that. Oh, you must not say that!" Robina cried.

"And why? I must not do this or the other, and who are you that dares to say so? I am my mother's daughter as well as my father's, and if that's not as good blood, it has a better heart. I might go there— they would not refuse me."

"Without a penny," said Robina. "Can you think o't, Miss Lily? And is that no banishment too?"

Lily rose from her chair, shaking herself free from her maid, with her pretty hair all hanging about her shoulders. It was pretty hair, though it was brown like every-body else's, full of incipient curl, the crispness yet softness of much life. She shook it about her with her rapid movement, bringing out all the undertones of color, and its wavy freedom gave an additional sparkle to her eyes and animation to her look. "Without a penny!" she cried. "And who is caring about your pennies? You and the like of you, but not me, Beenie—not me! What do I care for the money, the filthy siller, the pound notes, all black with the hands they've come through! Am I minding about the grand dinners that are never done, and the parties, where you never see those you want to see, and the balls, where— Just a little cottage, a drink of milk, and a piece of cake off the girdle, and plenty to do: it's that that would please me!"

"Oh, my bonnie Miss Lily!" was all that Beenie said.

"And when I see," said the girl, pacing up and down the room, her hair swinging about her shoulders, her white under-garments all afloat about her in the energy of her movements, "that other folk think of that first. Whatever you do, you must not risk your fortune. Whatever you have to bear, you must not offend your uncle, for he has the purse-strings in his hand. Oh, my uncle, my uncle! It's not," she cried, "that I wouldn't be fond of him if he would let me, and care for what he said, and do what he wanted as far as I was able: but his money! I wish—oh, I wish his money—his money—was all at the bottom of the sea!"

"Whisht! whisht!" cried Beenie, with a movement of horror. "Oh, but that's a dreadful wish! You would, maybe, no like it yourself, Miss Lily, for all you think now; but what would auld Sir Robert be without his money? Instead of a grand gentleman, as he is, he would just be a miserable auld man. He couldna bide it; he would be shootin' himself or something terrible. His fine dinners and his house, and his made dishes and his wine that costs as much as would keep twa-three honest families! Oh, ye dinna mean it, ye dinna mean it, Miss Lily! You dinna ken what you are saying; ye wouldna like it yoursel', and, oh, to think o' him!"

Lily threw herself down in the big chair, which rose above her head with its high back and brought out all her whiteness against its sober cover. She was silenced—obviously by the thought thus suggested of Sir Robert as a poor man, which was an absurdity, and perhaps secretly, in that innermost seclusion of the heart, which even its possessor does not always realize, by a faint chill of wonder whether she would indeed and really like to be poor, as she protested she should. It was quite true that a drink of milk and a piece of oatcake appeared to her as much nourishment as any person of refinement need care for. In the novels of her day, which always affect the young mind, all the heroines lived upon such fare, and were much superior to beef and mutton. But there were undoubtedly other things—Robina, for instance; although no thought of parting from Robina had ever crossed Lily's mind as a necessary part of poverty. But she was silenced by these thoughts. She had not, indeed, ever confessed in so many words even to Robina, scarcely to herself, that it was Ronald who cared for the money, and that it was the want of any impulse on his part to do without it that carried so keen a pang to her heart. Had he cried, "A fig for the money!" then it might have been her part to temporize and be prudent. The impetuosity, the recklessness, should not, she felt, be on her side.

It was on the very next day that her decision was to be made, and it had not been till all other means had failed that Sir Robert had thus put the matter to the touch. He had opposed her in many gentler ways before it came to that. Sir Robert was not a brute or a tyrant—very far from it. He was an old gentleman of fine manners, pluming himself on his successes with "the other sex," and treating all women with a superfine courtesy which only one here and there divined to conceal contempt. Few men—one may say with confidence, no elderly man without wife or daughters—has much respect for women in general. It is curious, it is to some degree reciprocal, it is of course always subject to personal exceptions; yet it is the rule between the two sections of humanity which nevertheless have to live in such intimate intercourse with each other. In an old bachelor like Sir Robert, and one, too, who was conscious of having imposed upon many women, this prepossession was more strong than among men of more natural relationships. And Lily, who was only his niece, and had not lived with him until very lately, had not overcome all prejudices in his mind, as it is sometimes given to a daughter to do. He had thought first that he could easily separate her from the young man who did not please him, and bestow her, as he had a right to bestow his probable heiress, on whom he pleased. When this proved ineffectual, he cursed her obstinacy, but reflected that it was a feature in women, and therefore nothing to be surprised at. They were always taken in by fictitious qualities—who could know it better than he?—and considered it a glory to stick to a suitor unpalatable to their belongings. And then he had threatened her with the loss of the fortune which she had been brought up to expect. "See if this fine fellow you think so much of will have you without your money," he said. Lily had never in so many words put Lumsden to the trial, never proposed to him to defy Sir Robert; but she had made many an attempt to discover his thoughts, and even to push him to this rash solution, and, with an ache at her heart, had felt that there was at least a doubt whether the fine fellow would think so much of her if she were penniless. She had never put it to the test, partly because she dared not, though she had not been able to refrain from an occasional burst of defiance and hot entreaty to Sir Robert to keep his money to himself. And now she was to decide for herself—to give Ronald over forever, or to give over Edinburgh and the society in which she might meet him, and keep her love at the cost of martyrdom in her uncle's lonely shooting-box on the moors. There was, of course, a second alternative—that which she had so often thought of: to refuse, to leave Sir Robert's house, to seek refuge in some cottage, to live on milk and oatcake, and provide for herself. If the alternative had been to run away with her lover, to be married to him in humility and poverty, to keep his house and cook his dinners and iron his linen, Lily would not have hesitated for a moment. But he had not asked her to do this—had not dreamed of it, it seemed; and to run away alone and work for herself would be, Lily felt, to expose him to much animadversion as well as herself; and, most of all, it would betray fully to herself and to her uncle, with that sneer on his face, the certainty that Ronald would not risk having her without her money, that discovery which she held at arm's-length and would not consent to make herself sure of. All these thoughts were tumultuous in her mind as she opened her eyes to the light of a new day. This was the final moment, the turning-point of her life. She thought at first when she woke that it was still the same misty moonlight on which she had shut her eyes, and that there must still be some hours between her and the day. But it was only an easterly haar with which the air was full—a state of atmosphere not unknown in Edinburgh, and which wraps the landscape in a blinding shroud as of white wool, obliterating every feature in a place which has so many. Arthur's Seat and Salisbury Craigs and the Castle Rock had all disappeared in it from those who were in a position to see them; and here, in George Square, even the brown houses opposite had gone out of sight, and the trees in the garden loomed dimly like ghosts, a branch thrust out here and there. Lily asked herself, was it still night? And then her mind awoke to a state of the atmosphere not at all unusual, and a sense that the moment of her fate had arrived, and that every thing must be settled for her for good or for evil this day.

She was very quiet, and said scarcely anything even to Robina, who dressed her young mistress with the greatest care, bringing out a dress of which Sir Robert had expressed his approval, without consulting Lily, who indeed paid little attention to this important matter. Considering the visions of poverty and independence that ran in her mind, it was wonderful how peaceably she resigned herself to Robina's administration. Sometimes, when a fit of that independence seized her, she would push Robina away and do every thing for herself. Beenie much exaggerated the misfortunes of the result in such moments. "Her hair just a' come down tumbling about her shoulders in five minutes," she said, which was not true: though Lily did not deny that she was not equal to the elaborate braids which were in fashion at the moment, and could not herself plait her hair in anything more than three strands, while Beenie was capable of seven, or any number more.

But to-day she was quite passive, and took no interest in her appearance. Her hair was dressed in a sort of coronet, which was a mode only used on grand occasions. Ordinarily it was spread over the back of the head in woven coils and circles. There was not anything extraordinary in Lily's beauty. It was the beauty of youth and freshness and health, a good complexion, good eyes, and features not much to speak of. People did not follow her through the streets, nor stand aside to make way for her when she entered a room. In Edinburgh there were hundreds as pretty as she; and yet, when all was said, she was a pretty creature, good enough and fair enough to be a delight and pride to any one who loved her. She had innumerable faults, but she was all the sweeter for them, and impulses of temper, swift wrath, and indignation, and impatience, which proved her to be anything but perfect. Sometimes she would take you up at a word and misinterpret you altogether. In all things she was apt to be too quick, to run away with a meaning before you, if you were of slow movement, had got it half expressed. And this and many other things about her were highly provoking, and called forth answering impatience from others. But for all this she was a very lovable, and, as other girls said, nice, girl. She raised no jealousies; she entertained no spites. She was always natural and spontaneous, and did nothing from calculation, not even so much as the putting on of a dress. It did not occur to her even to think, to enquire whether she was looking her best when the hour had come at which she was to go to Sir Robert. Robina took her by the shoulders and turned her slowly round before the glass; but Lily did not know why. She gave her faithful servant a faint smile over her own shoulder in the mirror, but it did not enter into her mind that it was expedient to look her best when she went down stairs to her uncle. If any one had put it into words, she would have asked, what did he care? Would he so much as notice her dress? It was ridiculous to think of such a thing—an old man like Sir Robert, with his head full of different matters. Thus, without any thought on that subject, she went slowly down stairs—not flying, as was her wont—very sedately, as if she were counting every step; for was it not her fate and Ronald's which was to be settled to-day?

CHAPTER III

"So you are there, Lily," Sir Robert said.

"Yes, uncle, I am here."

"There is one thing about you," he said, with a laugh: "you never shirk. Now judicious shirking is not a bad thing. I might have forgotten all about it—"

"But I couldn't forget," said Lily firmly. These words, however, roused her to sudden self-reproach. If she had not been so exact, perhaps the crisis might have been tided over and nothing happened. It was just like her! Supposing her little affairs were of more importance than anything else in the world! This roused her from the half-passive condition in which she had spent the morning, the feeling that every thing depended on her uncle, and nothing on herself.

"Now that you are here," he said, not at all unkindly, "you may as well sit down. While you stand there I feel that you have come to scold me for some fault of mine, which is a reversal of the just position, don't you think?"

"No, uncle," replied Lily, "of course I have not come to scold you—that would be ridiculous; but I am not come to be scolded either, for I have not done anything wrong."

"We'll come to that presently. Sit down, sit down," he said with impatience. Lily placed herself on the chair he pushed toward her, and then there was a moment's silence. Sir Robert was an old man (in Lily's opinion) and she was a young girl, but they were antagonists not badly matched, and he had a certain respect for the pluck and firmness of this little person who was not afraid of him. They were indeed so evenly matched that there ensued a little pause as they both looked at each other in the milky-white daylight, full of mist and cold, which filled the great windows. Sir Robert had a fire, though fires had been given up in the house. It burned with a little red point, sultry and smouldering, as fires have a way of doing in summer. The room was large and sombre, with pale green walls hung with some full-length portraits, the furniture all large, heavy, and dark. A white bust of himself stood stern upon a black pedestal in a corner—so white that amid all the sober lines of the room it caught the eye constantly. And Sir Robert was not a handsome man. His features were blunt and his air homely; his head was not adapted for marble. In that hard material it looked frowning, severe, and merciless. The bust had lived in this room longer than Sir Robert had done, and Lily had derived her first impressions of him from its unyielding face. The irregularities of the real countenance leaned to humor and a shrewdness which was not unkindly; but there was no relenting in the marble head.

"Well," he said at last, "now we've met to have it out, Lily. You take me at my word, and it is best so. How old are you now?"

"I don't see," said Lily breathlessly, "what that can have to do with it, uncle! but I'm twenty-two—or at least I shall be on the 20th of August, and that is not far away."

"No, it is not far away. Twenty-two—and I am—well, sixty-two, we may say, with allowances. That is a great difference between people that meet to discuss an important question—on quite an equal footing, Lily, as you suppose."

"I never pretended—to be your equal, uncle!"

"No, I don't suppose so—not in words, not in experience, and such like—but in intention and all that, and in knowing what suits yourself."

Lily made no reply, but she looked at him—silent, not yielding, tapping her foot unconsciously on the carpet, nervous, yet firm, not disposed to give way a jot, though she recognized a certain truth in what he said.

"This gives you, you must see, a certain advantage to begin with," said Sir Robert, "for you are firmly fixed upon one thing, whatever I say or any one, and determined not to budge from your position; whereas I am quite willing to hear reason, if there is any reason to show."

"Uncle!" Lily said, and then closed her lips and returned to her silence. It was hard for her to keep silent with her disposition, and yet she suddenly perceived, with one of those flashes of understanding which sometimes came to her, that silence could not be controverted, whereas words under Sir Robert's skilful attack would probably topple over at once, like a house of cards.

"Well?" he said. While she, poor child, was panting and breathless, he was quite cool and collected. At present he rather enjoyed the sight of the little thing's tricks and devices, and was amused to watch how far her natural skill, and that intuitive cunning which such a man believes every woman to possess, would carry her. He was a little provoked that she did not follow that impetuous exclamation "Uncle!" with anything more.

"Well," he repeated, wooing her, as he hoped, to destruction, "what more? Unless you state your case how am I to find out whether there is any justice in it or not?"

"Uncle," said Lily, "I did not come to state my case, which would not become me. I came because you objected to me, to hear what you wanted me to do."

"By Jove!" said Sir Robert, with a laugh; and then he added, "To be so young you are a very cool hand, my dear."

"How am I a cool hand? I am not cool at all. I am very anxious. It does not matter much to you, Uncle Robert, what you do with me; but," said Lily, tears springing to her eyes, "it will matter a great deal to me."

"You little—" He could not find an epithet that suited, so left the adjective by itself, in sheer disability to express himself. He would have said hussy had he been an Englishman. He was tempted to say cutty, being a Scot—innocent epithets enough, both, but sufficient to make that little— flare up. "You mean," he said, "I suppose, that you have nothing to do with it, and that the whole affair is in my hands."

"Yes, uncle, I think it is," said Lily very sedately.

He looked at her again with another ejaculation on his lips, and then he laughed.

"Well, my dear," he said, "if that is the case, we can make short work of it—as you are in such a submissive frame of mind and have no will or intentions on your own part."

Here Lily's impatient spirit got the better of the hasty impulse of policy which she had taken up by sudden inspiration. "I never said that!" she cried.

"Then you will be so good as to explain to me what you did say, or rather what you meant, which is more important still," Sir Robert said.

"I meant—just what I have always meant," said Lily, drawing back her chair a little and fixing her eyes upon her foot, which beat the floor with a nervous movement.

"And what is that?" he asked.

Lily drew back a little more, her foot ceased to tap, her hands clasped each other. She looked up into his face with half-reproachful eyes full of meaning. "Oh, Uncle Robert, you know!"

Sir Robert jumped up from his chair, and then sat down again. Demonstrations of wrath were of no use. He felt inclined to cry, "You little cutty!" again, but did not. He puffed out a quick breath, which was a sign of great impatience, yet self-repression. "You mean, I suppose, that things are exactly as they were—that you mean to pay no attention to my representations, that you choose your own will above mine—notwithstanding that I have complete power over you, and can do with you what I will?"

"Nobody can do that," said Lily, only half aloud. "I am not a doll," she said, "Uncle Robert. You have the power—so that I don't like to disobey you."

"But do it all the same!" he cried.

"Not if I can help it. I would like to do it. I would like to be independent. It seems dreadful that one should be obliged to do, not what one wishes, but what another person wills. But you have the power—"

"Of the ways and means," he said; "I have the purse-strings in my hand."

It was Lily's turn now to start to her feet. "Oh, how mean of you, how base of you!" she said. "You, a great man and a soldier, and me only a girl. To threaten me with your purse-strings! As if I cared for your purse-strings. Give it all away from me; give it all—that's what I should like best. I will go away with Beenie, and we'll sew, or do something else for our living. I'm very fond of poultry—I could be a henwife; or there are many other things that I could do. Give it all away! Tie them up tight. I just hate your money and your purse-strings. I wish they were all at the bottom of the sea!"

"You would find things very different if they were, I can tell you," he said, with a snort.

"Oh, yes, very different. I would be free. I would take my own way. I would have nobody to tyrannize over me. Oh, uncle! forgive me! forgive me! I did not mean to say that! If you were poor, I would take care of you. I would remember you were next to my father, and I would do anything you could say."

He kept his eyes fixed on her as she stood thus, defiant yet compunctious, before him. "I don't doubt for a moment you would do every thing that was most senseless and imprudent," he said.

Then Lily dropped into her chair and cried a little—partly that she could not help it, partly that it was a weapon of war like another—and gained a little time. But Sir Robert was not moved by her crying; she had not, indeed, expected that he would be.

"I don't see what all this has to do with it," he said. "Consider this passage of arms over, and let us get to business, Lily. It was necessary there should be a flash in the pan to begin."

Lily dried her eyes; she set her little mouth much as Sir Robert set his, and then said in a small voice: "I am quite ready, Uncle Robert," looking not unlike the bust as she did so. He did not look at all like the bust, for there was a great deal of humor in his face. He thought he saw through all this little flash in the pan, and that it had been intended from the beginning as a preface of operations and by way of subduing him to her will. In all of which he was quite wrong.

"I am glad to hear it, Lily. Now I want you to be reasonable: the thunder is over and the air is clearer. You want to marry a man of whom I don't approve."

"One word," she said with great dignity. "I am wanting to marry—nobody. There is plenty of time."

"I accept the correction. You want to carry on a love affair which you prefer at this moment. It is more fun than marrying, and in that way you get all the advantages I can give you, and the advantage of a lover's attentions into the bargain. I congratulate you, my dear, on making the best, as the preacher says, of both worlds."

Lily flushed and clasped her hands together, and there came from her expanded nostrils what in Sir Robert's case we have called a snort of passion. Lily's nostrils were small and pretty and delicate. This was a puff of heated breath, and no more.

"Eh?" he said; but she mastered herself and said nothing, which made it more difficult for him to go on. Finally, however, he resumed.

"You think," he said, "that it will be more difficult for me to restrain you if you or your lover have no immediate intention of marrying. And probably he—for I do him the justice to say he is a very acute fellow—sees the advantage of that. But it will not do for me. I must have certainty one way or another. I am not going to give the comfort of my life over into your silly hands. No, I don't even say that you are sillier than most of your age—on the contrary; but I don't mean," he added deliberately, "to put my peace of mind into your hands. You will give me your word to give up the lad Lumsden, or else you will pack off without another word to Dalrugas. It is a comfortable house, and Dougal and his wife will be very attentive to you. What's in a locality? George Square is pleasant enough, but it's prose of the deepest dye for a lady in love. You'll find nothing but poetry on my moor. Poetry," he added, with a laugh, "sonnets such as you will rarely match, and moonlight nights, and all the rest of it; just the very thing for a lovelorn maiden: but very little else, I allow. And what do you want more? Plenty of time to think upon the happy man."

His laugh was fiendish, Lily thought, who held herself with both her hands to keep still and to retain command of herself. She made no answer, though the self-restraint was almost more than she could bear.

"Well," he said, after a pause, "is this what you are going to decide upon? There is something to balance all these advantages. While you are thinking of him he will probably not return the compliment. Out of sight, out of mind. He will most likely find another Lily not so closely guarded as you, and while you are out of the way he will transfer his attention to her. It will be quite natural. There are few men in the world that would not do the same. And while you are gazing over the moor, thinking of him, he will be taking the usual means to indemnify himself and forget you."

"I am not afraid," said Lily tersely.

"Oh, you are not afraid? It's little you know of men, my dear. Lumsden's a clever, ambitious young fellow. He perhaps believes he's fond of you. He is fond of anything that will help him on in the world and give him what he wants—which is a helping hand in life, and ease of mind, and money to tide him over till he makes himself known. Oh, he'll succeed in the end, there is little doubt of that; but he shall not succeed at my expense. Now, Lily, do not sit and glare, like a waxen image, but give me an answer like a sensible girl, as you can be if you like. Will you throw away your happy life, and society and variety and pleasure, and your balls and parties, all for the sake of a man that the moment your back is turned will think no more of you?"

"Uncle," said Lily, clearing her throat. But she could not raise her voice, which extreme irritation, indignation, and the strong effort of self-restraint seemed to have stifled. She made an effort, but produced nothing but a hoarse repetition of his name.

"I hope I have touched you," he said. "Come, my dear, be a sensible lassie, and be sure I am speaking for your good. There are more fish in the sea than ever came out in a net. I will find you a better man than Lumsden, and one with a good house to take you home to, and not a penniless—"

"Stop!" she cried, with an angry gesture. "Stop! Do you think I am wanting a man? Me! Just any man, perhaps, you think, no matter who? Oh, if I were only a laddie instead of a useless girl you would never, never dare, great man as you are, to speak like that to me!"

"Certainly I should not," he said, with a laugh, "for you would have more sense, and would not think any woman was worth going into exile for. But, girl as you are, Lily, the choice is in your own hands. You can have, not love in a cottage, but love on a moor, which soon will be unrequited love, and that, we all know, is the most tragic and interesting of all."

"Uncle," said Lily, slowly recovering herself, "do you think it is a fine thing for a man like you, a grand gentleman, and old, and that knows every thing, to make a jest and a mockery of one that is young like me, and has no words to make reply? Is it a joke to think of me breaking my heart, as you say, among all the bonnie sunsets and the moonlight nights and the lonely, lonely moor? I may have to do it if it's your will; but it's not for the like of you, that have your freedom and can do what you choose, to make a mock at those that are helpless like me."

"Helpless!" he said. "Nothing of the sort; it is all in your own hands."

And then there was again a pause. He thought she was making up her mind to submit to his will. And she was bursting with the effort to contain herself, and all her indignation and wrath. Her pride would not let her burst forth into cries and tears, but it was with the greatest watchfulness upon herself that she kept in these wild expressions of emotion, and the hot refusals that pressed to her lips—refusals to obey him, to be silenced by him, to be sentenced to unnatural confinement and banishment and dreary exile. Why should one human creature have such power of life and death over another? Her whole being revolted in a passion of restrained impatience and rage and fear.

"Well," he said lightly, "which is it to be? Don't trifle with your own comfort, Lily. Just give me the answer that you will see no more of young Lumsden. Give him no more encouragement; think of him no more. That is all I ask. Only give me your promise—I put faith in you. Think of him no more; that is all I ask."

"All you ask—only that!" said Lily in her fury. "Only that! Oh, it's not much, is it? not much—only that!" She laughed, too, with a sort of echo of his laugh; but somehow he did not find it to his mind.

"That is all," he said gravely; "and I don't think that it is very much to ask, considering that you owe every thing to me."

"It would have been better for me if I had owed you nothing, uncle," said Lily. "Why did you ever take any heed of me? I would have been earning my own bread and had my freedom and lived my own life if you had left me as I was."

"This is what one gets," he said, as if to himself, with a smile, "for taking care of other people's children. But we need not fall into general reflections, nor yet into recriminations. I would probably not do it again if I had it to do a second time; but the thing I want from you at the present moment is merely a yes or no."

"No!" Lily said almost inaudibly; but her tightly closed lips, her resolute face, said it for her without need of any sound.

"No?" he repeated, half incredulous; then, with a nod, flinging back his head: "Well, my dear, you must have your wilful way. Dalrugas will daily be growing bonnier and bonnier at this season of the year; and to-morrow you will get ready to go away."

CHAPTER IV

"I have been a fool," said Lily. "I have not said anything that I meant to say. I had a great many good reasons all ready, and I did not say one of them. I just said silly things. He played upon me like a fiddle;

he made me so angry I could not endure myself, and then I had either to hold my tongue or say things that were silly and that I ought not to have said."

"Oh, dear me, dear me," cried Robina, "I just thought you would do that. If I had only been behind the door to give ye a look, Miss Lily. Ye are too impetuous when you are left to yourself."

"I was not impetuous; I was just silly," Lily said. "He provoked me till I did not know what I was saying, and then I held my tongue at the wrong places. But it would just have come to the same whatever I had said. He'll not yield, and I'll not yield, and what can we do but clash? We're to start off for Dalrugas to-morrow, and that's all that we have to think of now."

"Oh, Miss Lily!" cried Robina. She wrung her hands, and, with a look of awe, added: "It's like thae poor Poles in 'Elizabeth' going off in chains to that place they call Siberée, where there's nothing but snow and ice and wild, wild forests. Oh, my bonnie lamb! I mind the woods up yonder where it's dark i' the mid of day. And are ye to be banished there, you that are just in your bloom, and every body at your feet? Oh, Miss Lily, it canna be, it canna be!"

"It will have to be," said Lily resolutely, "and we must make the best of it. Take all the working things you can think of; I've been idle, and spent my time in nothings. I'll learn all your bonnie lace stitches, Beenie, and how to make things and embroideries, like Mary, Queen of Scots. We'll be two prisoners, and Dougal will turn the key on us every night, and we'll make friends with somebody like Roland, the page, that will make false keys and let us down from the window, with horses waiting; and then we'll career across the country in the dead of night, and folk will take us for ghosts; and then—we'll maybe ride on broomsticks, and fly up to the moon!" cried Lily, with a burst of laughter, which ended in a torrent of tears.

"Oh, my bonnie dear! oh, my lamb!" cried Beenie, taking the girl's head upon her ample breast. It is not to be imagined that these were hysterics, though hysterics were the fashion of the time, and the young ladies of the day indulged in them freely at any contrariety. Lily was over-excited and worn out, and she had broken down for the moment. But in a few minutes she had raised her head, pushed Beenie away, and got up with bright eyes to meet her fate.

"Take books too," she cried, "as many as you can, and perhaps he'll let us keep our subscription to the library, and they can send us things by the coach. And take all my pencils and my colors. I'll maybe turn into a great artist on the moors that Uncle Robert says are so bonnie. He went on about his sunsets and his moonlights till he nearly drove me mad," cried Lily, "mocking! Oh, Beenie, what hard hearts they have, these old men!"

"I would just like," cried the faithful maid, "to have twa-three words with him. Oh, I should like to have twa-three words with him, just him and me by our twa sels!"

"And much good that would do! He would just turn you outside in with his little finger," said Lily in high scorn. But naturally Robina was not of that opinion. She was ready to go to the stake for her mistress, and facing Sir Robert in his den was not a bad version of going to the stake. It might procure her instant dismissal for anything Beenie knew; he might tell old Haygate, the old soldier-servant, who was now his butler, and an Englishman, consequently devoid of sympathy, to put her to the door; anyhow, he would scathe her with satirical words and that look which even Lily interpreted as mocking, and which is the most difficult of all things to bear. But Beenie had a great confidence that there were "twa-three things" that nobody could press upon Sir Robert's attention but herself. She thought of it during the morning hours to the exclusion of every thing else, and finally after luncheon was over, when Lily was occupied with some youthful visitors, Beenie, with a beating heart, put her plan into execution. Haygate was out of the way, too, the Lord be praised. He had started out upon some mission connected with the wine-cellar; and Thomas, the footman, was indigenous, had been Tommy to Robina from his boyhood, and was so, she said, like a boy of her own. He would never put her to the door, whatever Sir Robert might say. She went down accordingly to the dining-room, after the master of the house had enjoyed his good lunch and his moment of somnolence after it (which he would not for the world have admitted to be a nap), and tapped lightly, tremulously, with all her nerves in a twitter, at the door. To describe what was in Beenie's heart when she opened it in obedience to his call to come in was more than words are capable of: it was like going to the stake.

"Oh, Beenie! so it is you," the master said.

"'Deed, it's just me, Sir Robert. I thought if I might say a word—"

"Oh, say a dozen words if you like; but, mind, I am going out, and I have no time for more."

"Yes, Sir Robert." Beenie came inside the door, and closed it softly after her. She then took up the black silk apron which she wore, denoting her rank as lady's maid, to give her a countenance, and made an imaginary frill upon it with her hands. "I just thought," she said, with her head bent and her eyes fixed on this useful occupation, "that I would like to say twa-three words about Miss Lily, Sir Robert—"

"Oh," he said, "and what might you have to say about Miss Lily? You should know more about her, it is true, than any of us. Has she sent you to say that she has recovered her senses, and is going to behave like a girl of sense, as I always took her to be?"

Beenie raised her eyes from her fantastic occupation, and looked at Sir Robert. She shook her head. She formed her lips into a round "No," pushing them forth to emphasize the syllable. "Eh, Sir Robert," she said at last, "you're a clever man—you understand many a thing that's just Greek and Hebrew to the likes of us; but ye dinna understand a lassie's heart. How should ye?" said Beenie, compassionately shaking her head again.

Sir Robert's luncheon had been good; he had enjoyed his nap; he was altogether in a good humor. "Well," he said, "if you can enlighten me on that point, Beenie, fire away!"

"Weel, Sir Robert, do ye no think you're just forcing her more and more into it, to make her suffer for her lad, and to have nothing to do but think upon him and weary for him away yonder on yon solitary moor? Eh, it's like driving her to the wilderness, or away to Siberée, that awfu' place where they send the Poles, as ye will read in 'Elizabeth,' to make them forget their country, and where they just learn to think upon it more and more. Eh, Sir Robert, we're awfu' perverse in that way! I would have praised him up to her, and said there was no man like him in the world. I would have said he was just the one that cared nothing for siller, that would have taken her in her shift—begging your pardon for sic a common word; I would have hurried her on to fix the day, and made every thing as smooth as velvet; and then just as keen as she is for it now I would have looked to see her against it then."

"I allow," said Sir Robert, with a laugh, "that you have a cloud of witnesses on your side; but I am not quite sure that I put faith in them. If I were to hurry her on to fix the day, as you say, I would get rid, no doubt, of the trouble; but I am much afraid that Lily, instead of starting off on the other tack, would take me at my word."

"Sir," said Beenie in a lowered voice, coming a step nearer, "if we were to leave it to him to show her the contrary, it would be more effectual than anything you could say."

"So," said Sir Robert, with a long whistle of surprise, "you trust him no more than I do? I always thought you were a woman of sense."

"I am saying nothing about that, Sir Robert," Beenie replied.

"But don't ye see, you silly woman, that he would take my favor for granted in that case, and would not show her to the contrary, but would marry her in as great haste as we liked, feeling sure that I had committed myself, and would not then draw back?"

"He would do ye nae justice, Sir Robert, if he thought that."

"What do you mean, you libellous person? You think I would encourage her in her folly in the hope of changing her mind, and then deceive and abandon her when she had followed my advice? No," he said, "I am not so bad as that."

"You should ken best, Sir Robert," said Beenie, "but for me, I would not say. But if ye will just permit me one more word. Here she has plenty of things to think of: her parties and her dress, and her friends and her other partners—there's three young leddies up the stair at this moment talking a' the nonsense that comes into their heads—but there she would have no person—"

"Not a soul, except Dougal and his wife," said Sir Robert, with a chuckle.

"And nothing to think of but just—him. Oh, Sir Robert, think what ye are driving the bairn to! No diversions and no distractions, but just to think upon him night and day. There's things she finds to object to in him when he's by her side—just like you and me. But when she's there she'll think and think upon him till she makes him out to be an angel o' light. He will just get to be the only person in the world. He will write to her—"

"That he shall not do! Dougal shall have orders to stop every letter."

Beenie smiled a calm, superior smile. "And ye think Dougal—or any man in the world—can keep a lad and lass from communication. Eh, Sir Robert, you're a clever man! but just as ignorant, as ignorant as any bairn."

Sir Robert was much amused, but he began to get a little impatient. "If they can find means of communicating in spite of the solitude and the miles of moor and Dougal, then I really think they will deserve to be permitted to ruin all their prospects," he said.

"Sir Robert!"

"No more," he said. "I have already heard you with great patience, Beenie. I don't think you have thrown any new light on the subject. Go and pack your boxes; for the coach starts early to-morrow, and you should have every thing ready both for her and yourself to-night."

Beenie turned away to the door, and then she turned round again. She stood pinching the imaginary frill on her apron, with her head held on one side, as if to judge the effect. "Will that be your last word, Sir Robert?" she said. "She's your brother's bairn, and the only one in the family—and a tender bit thing, no used to unkindness, nor to be left all her lane as if there was naebody left in the world. Oh, think upon the bit thing sent into the wilderness! It is prophets and great men that are sent there in the way of Providence, and no a slip of a lassie. Oh, Sir Robert, think again! that's no your last word?"

"Would you like me to ring for Haygate and have you turned out of the house? If you stay another minute, that will be my last word."

"Na," said Beenie, "Haygate's out, Sir Robert, and Tommy's not the lad—"

"Will you go, you vixen?" Sir Robert shouted at the top of his voice.

"I'll go, since I cannot help it; but if it comes to harm, oh, Sir Robert! afore God the wyte will be on your head."

Beenie dried her eyes as she went sorrowfully upstairs. "The wyte will be on his head; but, oh, the sufferin' and the sorrow that will be on hers!" Beenie said to herself.

But it was evident there was no more to be said. As she went slowly upstairs with a melancholy countenance, she met at the door of the drawing-room the three young ladies who had been—according to her own description—"talking a' the nonsense that came into their heads," with Lily in the midst, who was taking leave of them. "Oh, there is Robina," they all cried out together. "Beenie will tell us what it means. What is the meaning of it all? She says she is going away. Beenie, Beenie, explain this moment! What does she mean about going away?"

"Eh, my bonnie misses," cried Beenie, "who am I that I should explain my mistress's dark sayings? I am just a servant, and ken nothing but what's said to me by the higher powers."

There was what Beenie afterward explained as "a cackle o' laughing" over these words, which were just like Beenie, the girls said. "But what do you know from the higher powers? And why, why is Lily to be snatched away?" they said. Robina softly pushed her way through them with the superior weight of her bigness. "Ye must just ask herself, for it is beyond me," she said.

Lily rushed after her as soon as the visitors were gone, pale with expectation. "Oh, Beenie, what did he say?" she cried.

"What did who say, Miss Lily? for I do not catch your meaning," said the faithful maid.

"Do you mean to say that you did not go down stairs—"

"Yes, Miss Lily, I went down the stairs."

"To see my uncle?" said the girl. "I know you saw my uncle. I heard your voice murmuring, though they all talked at once. Oh, Beenie, Beenie, what did he say?"

"Since you will have it, Miss Lily, I did just see Sir Robert. There was nobody but me in the way, and I saw your uncle. He was in a very good key after that grand dish of Scots collops. So I thought I would just ask him if it was true."

"And what did he say?"

Beenie shook her head and said, "No," in dumb show with her pursed-out lips. "He just said it was your own doing, and not his," she added, after this impressive pantomime.

"Oh, how did he dare to say so! It was none of my doing—how could he say it was my doing? Was I likely to want to be banished away to Dalrugas moor, and never see a living soul?"

"He said you wouldna yield, and he wouldna yield; and in that case, Miss Lily, I ask you what could the like of me do?"

"I would not yield," said Lily. "Oh, what a story! what a story! What have I got to yield? It was just him, him, his own self, and nobody else. He thinks more of his own will than of all the world."

"He said you would not give up your love—I am meaning young Mr. Lumsden—no, for anything he could say."

"And what would I give him up for?" cried Lily, changing in a moment from pale to red. "What do I ever see of Sir Robert, Beenie? He's not up in the morning, and he's late at night. I have heard you say yourself about that club— I see him at his lunch, and that's all, and how can you talk and make great friends when your mouth is full, and him so pleased with a good dish and angry when it's not to his mind? Would I give up Ronald, that is all I have, for Sir Robert with his mouth full? And how does he dare to ask me—him that will not do a thing for me?"

"That is just it," said Beenie, shaking her head; "you think a' the reason's on your side, and he thinks a' the reason is on his; and he'll have his own gate and you'll have your will, and there is no telling what is to be done between you. Oh, Miss Lily, my bonnie dear, you are but a young thing. It's more reasonable Sir Robert should have his will than you. He's gone through a great deal of fighting and battles and troubles, and what have you ever gone through but the measles and the king-cough, that couldna be helped? It's mair becoming that you should yield to him than he should yield to you."

"And am I not yielding to him?" said Lily. "I just do whatever he tells me. If he says, 'You are to come out with me to dinner,' though I know how wearisome it will be, and though I had the nicest party in the world and all my own friends, I just give in to him without a word. I wear that yellow gown he gave me, though it's terrible to behold, just to please him. I sit and listen to all his old gentlemen grumbling, and to him paying his compliments to all his old ladies, and never laugh. Oh, Beenie, if you could hear him!" and here Lily burst into the laugh which she had previously denied herself. "But when he comes and tells me to give up Ronald for the sake of his nasty, filthy siller—"

"Miss Lily, that's no Mr. Ronald's opinion."

"Oh!" cried Lily, stamping her foot upon the ground, while hot tears rushed to her eyes, "as if that did not make it a hundred times worse!" she cried.

And then there was a pause, and Beenie, with great deliberation, began to take out a pile of dresses from the wardrobe, which she opened out and folded one after another, patting them with her plump hands upon the bed. Lily watched her for some moments in silence, and then she said with a faltering voice: "Do you really think, then, that there is no hope?"

Robina answered in her usual way, pursing out her lips to form the "No" which she did not utter audibly. "Unless you will yield," she said.

"Yield—to give up Ronald? To meet him and never speak to him? To let him think I'm a false woman, and mansworn? I will never do that," Lily said.

"But you'll no marry him, my lamb, without your uncle's consent?"

"He'll not ask me!" cried Lily, desperate. "Why do you torment me when you know that is just the worst of all? Oh, if he would try me! And who is wanting to marry him—or any man? Certainly not me!"

"If you were to give your uncle your word—if you were to say, 'We'll just meet at kirk and market and say good-even and good-morrow,' but nae mair. Oh, Miss Lily, that is not much to yield to an old man."

"I said as good as that, but he made no answer. Beenie, pack up the things and let us go quietly away, for there is no help for us in any man."

"A' the same, if I were you, I would try," said Robina, taking the last word.

Lily said nothing in reply; but that night, when she was returning with Sir Robert from a solemn party to which she had accompanied him, she made in the darkness some faltering essay at submission. "I would have to speak to him when we meet," she said, "and I would have to tell him there was to be no more—for the present. And I would not take any step without asking you, Uncle Robert."

Sir Robert nearly sprang from his carriage in indignation at this halting obedience. "If you call that giving up your will to mine, I don't call it so!" he cried. "'Tell him there is to be no more—for the present!' That is a bonnie kind of submission to me, that will have none of him at all."

"It is all I can give," said Lily with spirit, drawing into her own corner of the carriage. Her heart was very full, but not to save her life could she have said more.

"Very well," said Sir Robert; "Haygate has his orders, and will see you off to-morrow. Mind you are in good time, for a coach will wait for no man, nor woman either; and I'll bid you good-by now and a better disposition to you, and a good journey. Good-night."

And at seven o'clock next morning, in the freshness of the new day, the North mail sure enough carried Lily and Robina away.

CHAPTER V

A highland moor is in itself a beautiful thing. When it is in full bloom of purple heather, with all those breaks and edges of emerald green which betray the bog below, with the sweet-scented gale sending forth its odor as it is crushed underfoot, and the yellow gorse rising in broken lines of gold, and here and there a half-grown rowan, with its red berries, and here and there a gleam of clear dark water, nothing can be more full of variety and the charm of wild and abounding life. But when the sky is gray and the weather bleak, and the heather is still in the green, or dry with the gray and rustling husks of last year's bloom; when there is little color, and none of those effects of light and shade which make a drama of shifting interest upon the Highland hills and lochs, all this is very different, and the long sweep of wild and broken ground, under a low and dark sky, becomes an image of desolation instead of the fresh and blooming and fragrant moor of early autumn. Dalrugas was a tall, pinched house, with a high gable cut in those rectangular lines which are called crow steps in Scotland, rising straight up from the edge of the moor. The height and form of this gave a parsimonious and niggardly look—though the rooms were by no means contemptible within—which was increased by the small windows pierced high up in the wall. There was no garden on that side, not so much as the little plot to which even a cottage has a right. Embedded within the high, sharp-cornered walls behind was a kitchen-garden or kale-yard, where the commonest vegetables were grown with a border of gooseberries and a few plants of sweet-william and appleringie; but this was not visible to give any softness to the prospect. The heather came up uncompromisingly, with a little hillock of green turf here and there, to the very walls, which had once been whitewashed, and still in their forlorn dinginess lent a little variety to the landscape; but this did but add to the cold, pinched, and resistant character of the house. It looked like a prim ancient lady, very spare, and holding her skirts close round her in the pride of penury and evil fortune. The door was in the outstanding gable, and admitted directly into a low passage from which a spiral stair mounted to the rooms above. On the ground-floor there was a low, dark-pannelled dining-room and library full of ancient books, but these rooms were used only when Sir Robert came for shooting, which happened very rarely. The drawing-room upstairs was bare also, but yet had some lingerings of old-fashioned grace. From the small, deep-set, high windows there was a wide, unbroken view over the moor. The moor stretched everywhere, miles of it, gray as the low sky which hung over it, a canopy of clouds. The only relief was a bush of gorse here and there half in blossom, for the gorse is never wholly out of blossom, as every-body knows, and the dark gleam of the water in a cutting, black as the bog which it was meant to drain. The dreary moorland road which skirted the edge passed in front of the house, but was only visible from these windows at a corner, where it emerged for a moment from a group of blighted firs before disappearing between the banks of heather and whin, which had been cut to give it passage. This was the only relief from the monotony of the moor.

It was in this house that Lily and her maid arrived after a journey which had not been so uncheerful as they anticipated. A journey by stage-coach through a beautiful country can scarcely be dreary in the worst of circumstances. The arrivals, the changes, the villages and towns passed through, the contact with one's fellow-creatures which is inevitable, shake off more or less the most sullen discontent; and Lily was not sullen, while Beenie was one of the most open-hearted of human creatures, ready to interest herself in every one she met, and to talk to them and give her advice upon their circumstances. The pair met all sorts of people on their journey, and they made almost as many friendships, and thus partially forgot the penitential object of their own travels, and that they were being sent off to the ends of the earth.

It was only when "the gig" met them at the village, where the coach stopped on its northern route, that their destination began to oppress either the mistress or the maid. This was on the afternoon of a day which had been partially bright and partially wet, the best development of weather to be hoped for in the North. The village was a small collection of cottages, partly with tiled roofs, making a welcome gleam of color, but subdued by a number of those respectable stone houses with blue tiles, which were and are the ideal of comfortable sobriety, which, in defiance of all the necessities of the landscape, the Scotch middle class has unfortunately fixed upon. The church stood in the midst—a respectable oblong barn, with a sort of long extinguisher in the shape of a steeple attached to it. On the outskirts the cottages became less comfortable and more picturesque, thatched, and covered with lichens. It was a well-to-do village. The "merchant," as he was called, i. e., the keeper of the "general" shop, was a Lowland Scot, very contemptuous of "thae Highlanders," and there was a writer or solicitor in the place, and a doctor, besides the minister, who formed a little aristocracy. The English minister so called, that is, the Episcopalian, came occasionally—once in two or three Sundays—to officiate in a smaller barn, without any extinguisher, which held itself a little apart in a corner, not to mingle with the common people who did not possess Apostolical Succession; though, indeed, in those days there was little controversy, the Episcopalians being generally of that ritual by birth, and unpolemical, making no pretensions to superiority over the native Kirk.

The gig that met the travellers at Kinloch-Rugas was a tall vehicle on two wheels, which had once been painted yellow, but which was scarcely trim enough to represent that type of respectability which a certain young Thomas Carlyle, pursuing the vague trade of a literary man in Edinburgh, had declared it to be. It was followed closely by a rough cart, in which Beenie and the boxes were packed away. They were not large boxes. One, called "the hair trunk," contained Lily's every-day dresses, but no provision for anything beyond the most ordinary needs, for there was no society nor any occasion for decorative garments on the moors. Beenie's box was smaller, as became a serving-woman. These accessories were all in the fashion of their time, which was (like Waverley, yet, ah, so unlike!) sixty years since or thereabout—in the age before railways, or at least before they had penetrated to the distant portions of the country. The driver of the gig was a middle-aged countryman, very decent in a suit of gray "plaidin"—what we now call tweed—with a head of sandy hair grizzled and considerably blown about by the wind across the moor. His face was ruddy and wrinkled, of the color of a winter apple, in fine shades of red and brown, his shaggy eyebrows a little drawn together—by the "knitting of his brows under the glaring sun," and the setting of his teeth against the breeze. He said, "Hey, Beenie!" as his salutation to the party before he doffed his bonnet to the young lady. Lily was not sure that it was quite respectful, but Dougal meant no disrespect. He was a little shy of her, being unfamiliar with her grown-up aspect, and reverential of her young ladyhood; but he was at his ease with Robina, who was a native of the parish, the daughter of the late blacksmith, and "weel connectit" among the rustic folk. It would have been an ease to Dougal to have had the maid beside him instead of the mistress, and it was to Beenie he addressed his first remarks over his shoulder, from pure shyness and want of confidence in his own powers of entertaining a lady. "Ye'll have had a long journey," he said. "The coach she's aye late. She's like a thriftless lass, Beenie, my woman. She just dallies, dallies at the first, and is like to break her neck at the end."

"But she showed no desire to break her neck, I assure you," said Lily. "She was in no hurry. We have just taken it very easy up hill and down dale."

"Ay, ay!" he said, "we ken the ways o' them." With a glance over his shoulder: "Are you sure you're weel happit up, Beenie, for there's a cauld wind crossing the moor?"

"And how is Katrin, Dougal?" Lily asked, fastening her cloak up to her throat.

"Oh, she's weel eneuch; you'll see little differ since ye left us last. We're a wee dried up with the peat-reck, and a wee blawn aboot by the wind. But ye'll mind that fine, Beenie woman, and get used to't like her and me."

Lily laid impatient fingers on the reins, pulling Dougal's hand, as if he had been the unsteady rough pony he drove. "Speak to me," she said, "you rude person, and not to Beenie. Do you think I am nobody, or that I cannot understand?"

"Bless us all! No such a thought was in my head. Beenie, are ye sitting straight? for when the powny's first started whiles he lets out."

"Let me drive him!" Lily cried. "I'll like it all the better if he lets out; and you can go behind if you like and talk to Beenie at your ease."

"Na, na," said Dougal, with a grin. "He kens wha's driving him. A bit light hand like yours would have very sma' effect upon Rory. Hey, laddies! get out of my powny's way!"

Rory carried out the prognostics of his driver by tossing his shaggy head in the air, and making a dash forward, scattering the children who had gathered about to stare at the new arrivals; though before he got to the end of the village street he had settled into his steady pace, which was quite uninfluenced by any skill in driving on Dougal's part, but was entirely the desire and meaning of that very characteristic member of society—himself. The day had settled into an afternoon serenity and unusual quietness of light. The mountains stood high in the even air, without any dramatic changes, Schehallion, with his conical crest, dominating the lesser hills, and wearing soberly his mantle of purple, subdued by gray. The road lay for a few miles through broken ground, diversified with clumps of wood, wind-blown firs, and beeches tossing their feathery branches in the air, crossing by a little bridge a brown and lively trout stream, which went brawling through the village, but afterward fell into deeper shadows, penetrating between close fir-woods, before it reached the edge of the moor, round which it ran its lonely way. Lily's spirits began to rise. The sense of novelty, the pleasant feeling of arrival, and of all the possibilities which relieve the unknown, rose in her breast. Something would surely happen; something would certainly be found to make the exile less heavy, and to bring back a little hope. The little river greeted her like an old friend. "Oh, I remember the Rugas," she cried. "What a cheery little water! Will they let me fish in it, Dougal? Look how it sparkles! I think it must remember me."

"It's just a natural objick," said Dougal. "It minds naebody; and what would you do—a bit lady thing—fishing troot? Hoots! a crookit pin in a burn would set ye better, a little miss like you."

In those days there were no ladies who were salmon fishers. Such a thing would have seemed to Dougal an outrage upon every law.

"Don't be contemptuous," said Lily, with a laugh. "You'll find I am not at all a little miss. Just give me the reins and let me wake Rory up. I mean to ride him about the moor."

"I'm doubting if you'll do that," said Dougal, with politeness, but reserve.

"Why shouldn't I do it? Perhaps you think I don't know how to ride. Oh, you can trust Rory to me, or a better than Rory."

"There's few better in these parts," said Dougal with some solemnity. "He's a beast that has a great deal of judgment. He kens well what's his duty in this life. I'm no thinking you'll find it that easy to put him to a new kind of work. He has plenty of his ain work to do."

"We'll see about that," said Lily.

"Ah," replied Dougal cautiously, "we'll just see about that. We must na come to any hasty judgment. Cheer up, lad! Yon's the half of the road."

"Is this only the half of the road?" said Lily, with a shudder. They were coming out of the deep shade of the woods, and now before them, in its full width and silence, stretched the long levels of the moor. It was even now, in these days before the heather, a beautiful sight, with the mountains towering in the background, and the bushes of the ling, which later in the year would be glorious with blossoms, coming down, mingled with the feathery plumes of the seeding grass, to the very edge of the road: beautiful, wild, alive with sounds of insects, and that thrill of the air which we call silence—silence that could be heard. The wide space, the boundless sky, the freedom of the pure air, gave a certain exaltation to Lily's soul, but at the same time overwhelmed her with a sense of the great loneliness and separation from all human interests which this great vacancy made. "Only half-way," she repeated, with a gasp.

"It's a gey lang road, but it's a very good road, with few bad bits. An accustomed person need have nae fear by night or day. There was an ill place, where ye cross the Rugas again, at the head of the Black Scaur; but it's been mended up just uncommon careful, and ye need have nae apprehension; besides that, there's me that ken every step, and Rory that is maist as clever as me."

"But it's the end of the world," Lily said.

"No that, nor even the end of the parish, let alone the countryside," said Dougal. "It's just ignorance, a' that. It's the end o' naething but your journey, and a bonnie place when you're there; and a good dinner waiting for ye; and a grand soft bed, and your grandmither's ain cha'lmer, that was one of the grandest leddies in the North Country. Na, na, missy, it's no the end of the world. If ye look far ahead, yonder by the east, as soon as we come to the turn of the road, ye'll maybe, if it's clear, see the tower. That's just a landmark over half the parish. Ye'll mind it, Beenie? It's lang or ye've seen so bonnie a sight."

"Oh, ay, I mind it," said Beenie, subdued. She had once thought, with Dougal, that the tower of Dalrugas was a fine sight. But she had tasted the waters of civilization, and the long level of the moor filled her breast, like that of her mistress, with dismay; though, indeed, it was with the eyes of Lily, rather than her own, that the kind woman saw this scene. For herself things would not be so bad. Dougal and Katrin in the kitchen would form a not uncongenial society for Robina. She did not anticipate for herself much difficulty in fitting in again to a familiar place; and she would always have her young mistress to pet and console, and to take care of. But Lily—where would Lily find anything to take her out of herself? Beenie realized, by force of sympathy, the weary gazing from the windows, the vacant landscape, through which no one ever would come, the loneliness indescribable of the great solitary moor; not one of her young companions to come lightly over the heather; neither a lad nor lass in whom the girl would find a playfellow. "Ay, I mind it," said Beenie, shaking her head, with big tears filling her eyes.

Lily, for her part, did not feel disposed to shed any tears; her mind was full of indignation and harsher thoughts. Who could have any right to banish her here beyond sight or meeting of her kind? And it was not less but more bitter to reflect that the domestic tyrant who had banished her was scarcely so much to blame as the lover who would risk nothing to save her. If he had but stood by her—held out his hand—what to Lily would have been poverty or humbleness? She would have been content with any bare lodging in the old town, high among the roofs. She would have worked her fingers to the bone—at least Beenie would have done so, which was the same thing. That was a sacrifice she would have made willingly; but this that was demanded—who had any right to exact it? and for what was it to be exacted? For money, miserable money, the penny siller that could never buy happiness. Lily's eyes burned like coal. Her cheeks scorched and blazed. Oh, how hard was fate, and how undeserved! For what had she done? Nothing, nothing to bring it upon herself.

It was another long hour before the gig turned the corner by the trees, where there was a momentary view of Dalrugas, and plunged again between the rising banks, where the road ran in a deep cutting, ascending the last slopes. "We'll be at the house in five minutes," Dougal said.

CHAPTER VI

Katrin stood under the doorway, looking out for the party: a spare, little, active woman, in that native dress of the place, which consisted of a dark woollen skirt and pink "shortgown," a garment not unlike the blouse of to-day, bound in by the band of her white apron round a sufficiently trim waist. She was of an age when any vanity of personal appearance, if ever sanctioned at all, is considered, by her grave race, to be entirely out of place; but yet was trim and neat by effect of nature, and wore the shortgown with a consciousness that it became her. A gleam of sunshine had come out as the two vehicles approached in a little procession; and Katrin had put up her hand to her eyes to shade them from that faint gleam of sun as she looked down the road. The less of sun there is the more particular people are in shielding themselves from it; which is a mystery, like so many other things in life, small as well as great. Katrin thought the dazzle was overwhelming as she stood looking out under the shadow of her curved hand. The doorway was rather small, and very dark behind her, and the strong gleam of light concentrated in her pink shortgown, and made a brilliant spot of the white cap on her head. And to Katrin the two vehicles climbing the road were as a crowd, and the arrival an event of great excitement, making an era in life. She was interested, perhaps, like her husband, most particularly in Robina, who would be an acquisition to their own society, with all her experience of the grand life of the South; but she bore a warm heart also to the little lady who had been at Dalrugas as a child, and of whose beauty, and specially of whose accomplishments, there had been great reports from the servants in town to the servants on the moor. She hastened forward to place a stool on which Miss Lily could step down, and held out both her hands to help, an offer which was made quite unnecessary by the sudden spring which the girl made, alighting "like a bird" by Katrin's side. "Eh, I didna mind how light a lassie is at your age," cried the housekeeper, startled by that quick descent. "And are ye very wearied? and have ye had an awfu' journey? and, eh, yonder's Beenie, just the same as ever! I'm as glad to see ye as if I had come into a fortune. Let me take your bit bag, my bonnie lady. Give the things to me."

"Yes, Beenie is just the same as ever—and you also, Katrin, and the moor," said Lily, with a look that embraced them all. She had subdued herself, with a natural instinct of that politeness which comes from the heart, not to show these humble people, on her first arrival, how little she liked her banishment. It was not their fault; they were eager to do their utmost for her, and welcomed her with a kindness which was as near love as any inferior sentiment could be—if it was, indeed, an inferior sentiment at all. But when she stood before the dark doorway, which seemed the end of all things, it was impossible not to betray a little of the loneliness she felt. "And the moor," she repeated. But Katrin heard the words in another sense.

"Ay, my bonnie lamb! the moor, that is the finest sight of a'. It's just beautiful when there's a fine sunset, as we're going to have the night to welcome ye hame. Come away ben, my dear; come away in to your ain auld house. Oh! but I'm thankful and satisfied to have ye here!"

"Not my house, Katrin. My uncle would not like to hear you say so."

"Hoot, away! Sir Robert's bark is waur than his bite. What would he have sent such orders for, to make every thing sae comfortable, if there had been any doubt that it was your very ain house, and you his chosen heir? If Dougal were to let ye see the letter, a' full of loving kindness, and that he wanted a safe hame for his bit lassie while he was away. Oh, Miss Lily, he's an auld man to be marching forth again at the head of his troop to the wars."

"He is not going to the wars," said Lily. She could not but laugh at the droll supposition. Sir Robert, that lover of comfort and luxury, marching forth on any expedition, unless it were an expedition of pleasure! "There are no wars," she added. "We are at peace with all the world, so far as I can hear."

"Weel, I was wondering," said Katrin. "Dougal, he says, that reads the papers, that there's nae fighting neither in France nor what they ca'ed the Peninshula in our young days. But he says there are aye wars and rumor of wars in India, and such like places. So we thought it might, maybe, be that. Weel, I'm real content to hear that Sir Robert, that's an old man, is no driven to boot and saddle at his age."

"He is going, perhaps, to London," Lily said.

"Weel, weel, and that's no muckle better than a fight, from a' we hear—an awfu' place, full of a' the scum of the earth. Puir auld gentleman! It maun be the king's business, or else something very important of his ain, that takes him there. Anyway, he's that particular about you, my bonnie lady, as never was. You're to have a riding-horse when ye please, and Dougal to follow you whenever he can spare the time; and there's a new pianny-fortey come in from Perth, and a box full of books, and I canna tell you all what. And here am I keeping you at the door, havering all the time. You'll mind the old stair, and the broken step three from the top; or maybe you will like to come into the dining-room first and have a morsel to stay your stomach till the dinner's served; or maybe you would like a drink of milk; or maybe— Lord bless us! she's up the stair like a fire flaught and paying no attention; and, oh, Beenie, my woman, is this you?"

Beenie was more willing to be entertained than her mistress, whose sudden flight upstairs left Katrin stranded in the full tide of her eloquence. She was glad to be set down to a cup of tea and the nice scones, fresh from the girdle, with which the housekeeper had intended to tempt Lily. "I'll cover them up with the napkin to keep them warm, and when ye have ta'en your cup o' tea, ye'll carry some up to her on a tray, or I'll do it mysel', with good will; but I mind ye are aye fondest of taking care of your bonnie miss yoursel'."

"We'll gie her a wee moment to settle down," said Robina: "to take a good greet," was what she said to herself. She swallowed her tea, always with an ear intent on the sounds upstairs. She had seen by Lily's countenance that she was able for no more, and that a moment's interval was necessary; and there she sat consuming her heart, yet perhaps comforted a little by having the good scones to consume, too.

"Oh," she said, "ye get nothing like this in Edinburgh; ae scone's very different from another. I have not tasted the like of this for many a year."

"Ye see," said Katrin, with conscious success, "a drop of skim-milk like what ye get in a town is very different from the haill cream of a milking; and I'm no a woman to spare pains ony mair than stuff. She's a bonnie, bonnie creature, your young lady, Beenie—a wee like her mother, as far as I mind, that was nothing very much in the way of blood, ye ken, but a bonnie, bonnie young woman as ever stood. The auld leddy and Sir Robert were real mad against Mr. Randall for making such a poor match; but now there's nobody but her bairn to stand atween the house and its end. He'll be rael fond of her, Sir Robert—his bonny wee heir!"

"Ay," said Beenie, "in his ain way."

"Weel, it wasna likely to be in a woman's way like yours or mine. The men they've aye their ain ways of looking at things. I'll warrant there's plenty of lads after her, a bonnie creature like that; and the name of Sir Robert's siller and a'."

"Oh, ay! she hasna wanted for lads," Beenie said.

"And what'll be the reason, Beenie, since the auld gentleman's no going to the wars, as Dougal and me thought—what'll be the reason, are ye thinkin', for the young leddy coming here? He said it was to be safe at hame while he was away."

"Maybe he would be right if that's what he says."

"Oh, Beenie, woman," cried Katrin, "you're secret, secret! Do you think we are no just as keen as you to please our young leddy and make her comfortable? or as taken up to ken why she's been sent away from a' her parties and pleasurings to bide here?"

"There's no many parties nor pleasurings here for her," said Dougal, joining the two women in the low but airy kitchen, where the big fire was pleasant to look upon, and the brick floor very red, and the hearthstone very white. The door, which stood always open, afforded a glimpse of the universal background, the everywhere-extending moor, and the air came in keen, though the day was a day in June. Dougal pushed his bonnet to one side to scratch his grizzled head. In these regions, as indeed in many others, it is not necessary to take off one's headgear when one comes indoors. "There's neither lad to run after her nor leddies to keep her company. If she's light-headed, or the like of that, there canna be a better place than oor moor."

"Light-headed!" said Robina in high scorn. "It just shows how little you ken. And where would I be, a discreet person, if my young leddy was light-headed? She's just as modest and as guid as ever set foot on the heather. My bonnie wee woman! And as innocent as the babe new-born."

Dougal pushed his cap to the other side of his head, as if that might afford enlightenment. "Then a' I can say is that it's very queer." And he added after an interval: "I never pretend to understand Sir Robert; he's an awfu' funny man."

"He might play off his fun better than upon Miss Lily," said his wife in anxious tones.

"And that minds me that I'm just havering here when I should be carrying up the tray," said Beenie. "Some of those cream scones—they're the nicest; and that fine apple jelly is the best I've tasted for long. And now the wee bit teapot, and a good jug of your nice fresh milk that she will, maybe, like better than the tea."

"And my fine eggs—with a yolk like gold, and white that is just like curds and cream."

"Na," said Beenie, waving them away, "that would just be too much; let me alone with the scones, and the milk and the tea."

She went up the spiral stairs, making a cheerful noise with her cups and her tray. A noise was pleasant in this quiet place. Beenie understood, without knowing how, that the little clatter, the sound of some one coming, was essential to this new life; and though her arm was very steady by nature, she made every thing ring with a little tinkle of cheerfulness and "company." The drawing-room of the house, which opened direct from the stairs with little more than a broadened step for a landing, was a large room occupying all the breadth of the tall gable, which was called the tower. It was not high, and the windows were small, set in deep recesses, with spare and dingy curtains. The carpet was of design unconjecturable, and of dark color worn by use to a deep dinginess of mingled black and brown. The only cheerful thing in the room was a rug before the fireplace, made of strips of colored cloth, which was Katrin's winter work to beguile the long evenings, and in which the instinct of self-preservation had woven many bits of red, relics or patterns of soldiers' coats. The eye caught that one spot of color instinctively. Beenie looked at it as she put down her tray, and Lily had already turned to it a dozen times, as if there was something good to be got there. The walls were painted in panels of dirty green, and hung with a few pictures, which made the dinginess hideous—staring portraits executed by some country artist, or, older relics still, faces which had sunk altogether into the gloom. Three of the windows looked out on the moor, one in a corner upon the yard, where Rory and his companion were stabled, and where there was an audible cackle of fowls, and sometimes Katrin's voice coming and going "as if a door were shut between you and the sound." Lily had been roaming about, as was evident by the cloak flung in one corner, the hat in another, the gloves on the table, the little bag upon the floor. She had gravitated, however, as imaginative creatures do, to the window, and sat there when Beenie entered as if she had been sitting there all her life, gazing out upon the monotonous blank of the landscape and already unconscious of what she saw.

"Well, Miss Lily," said Robina cheerfully, "here we are at last; and thankfu' I am to think that I can sit still the day, and get up in peace the morn without either coach or boat to make me jump. And here's your tea, my bonnie dear—and cream scones, Katrin's best, that I have not seen the like of since I left Kinloch-Rugas. Edinburgh's a grand place, and many a bonnie thing is there; and maybe we'll whiles wish ourselves back; but nothing like Katrin's scones have ye put within your lips for many a day. My dear bonnie bairn, come and sit down comfortable at this nice little table and get your tea."

"Tea!" said Lily; her lips were quivering, so that a laugh was the only escape—or else the other thing. "You mind nothing," she cried, "so long as you have your tea."

"Weel, it makes up for manythings, that's true," said Beenie, eager to adopt her young mistress's tone. "Bless me, Miss Lily, it's no the moment to take to that weary window and just stare across the moor when ye ken well there is nothing to be seen. It will be time enough when we're wearied waiting, or when there's any reasonable prospect—"

"What do you mean?" cried Lily, springing up from her seat. "Reasonable prospect—of what, I would like to know? and weary waiting—for whom? How dare you say such silly words to me? I am waiting for nobody!" cried Lily, in her exasperation clapping her hands together, "and there is no reasonable prospect—if it were not to fall from the top of the tower, or sink into the peat-moss some lucky day."

"You're awfu' confident, Miss Lily," said the maid, "but I'm a great deal older than you are, and it would be a strange thing if I had not mair sense. I just tell you there's no saying; and if the Queen of Sheba was here, she could utter no more."

"You would make a grand Queen of Sheba," said Lily, with eyes sparkling and cheeks burning; "and what is it your Majesty tells me? for I cannot make head nor tail of it for my part."

"I just tell you, there's no saying," Beenie repeated very deliberately, looking the young lady in the face.

Poor Lily! her face was glowing with sudden hope, her slight fingers trembled. What did the woman mean who knew every thing? "When we're wearied waiting—when there's no reasonable prospect." Oh, what, what did the woman mean? Had there been something said to her that could not be said to Lily? Were there feet already on the road, marching hither, hither, bringing love and bringing joy? "There's no saying." A woman like Robina would not say that without some reason. It was enigmatical; but what could it mean but something good? and what good could happen but one thing? Beenie, in fact, meant nothing but the vaguest of consolations—she had no comfort to give; but it was not in a woman's heart to shut out imagination and confess that hope was over. Who would venture to say that there was no hope, any day, any moment, in a young life, of something happening which would make all right again? No oracle could have said less; and yet it meant every thing. Lily, in the light of possibility that suddenly sprang up around her, illuminating the moor better than the pale sunshine, and making this bare and cold room into a habitable place, took heart to return to the happy ordinary of existence, and remembered that she was hungry and that Katrin's scones were very good and the apple jelly beautiful to behold. It was a prosaic result, you may say, but yet it was a happy one, for she was very tired, and had great need of refreshment and support. She took her simple meal which was so pretty to look at—never an inconsiderable matter on a woman's table; the scones wrapped in their white napkin, the jug of creamy milk, the glass dish with its clear pink jelly. She ate and drank with much satisfaction, and then, with Beenie at her side, went wandering over the house to see if there was any furniture to be found more cheerful than the curtains and carpets in the drawing-room. The days of "taste" had not arisen—no fans from Japan had yet been seen in England, far less upon the moors; but yet the natural instinct existed to attempt a little improvement in the stiff dulness of the place. Lily was soon running over all the house with a song on her lips—commoner in those days when music was not so carefully cultivated—and a skipping measure in the patter of her feet. "Hear till her," said Dougal to Katrin; "our peace and quiet's done." "Hear till her indeed, ye auld crabbit body! It's the blessing o' the Lord come to the house," said Katrin to Dougal. He pushed his cap now to one side, now to the other, with a scratch of impartial consultation what was to come of it—but also a secret pleasure that brought out a little moisture under his shaggy eyebrows. The old pair sat up a full half-hour later, out of pure pleasure in the consciousness of the new inmate under that roof where they had so long abode in silence. And Lily rushed upstairs and downstairs, and thrilled the old floor with her hurried feet, but kept always saying over to herself those words which were the fountain of contentment—or rather expectation, which is better: "There's no saying—there's no saying!" If Beenie knew nothing in which there was a reasonable hope, how could she have suffered herself to speak?

CHAPTER VII

When Lily got up next morning, it was to the cheerful sounds of the yard, the clucking of fowls, the voices of the kitchen calling to each other, Katrin darting out a sentence as she came to the door, Dougal growling a bass order to the boy, the sounds of whose hissing and movement over his stable-work were as steady as if Rory were being groomed like a racer till his coat shone. It is not pleasant to be disturbed by Chanticleer and his handmaidens in the middle of one's morning sleep, nor to hear the swing of the stable pails, and the hoofs of the horses, and the shouts to each other of the outdoor servants. I should not like to have even one window of my bedchamber exposed to these noises. But Lily sprang up and ran to the window, cheered by this rustic Babel, and looked out with keen pleasure upon the rush of the fowls to Katrin's feet as she stood with her apron filled with grain, flinging it out in handfuls, and upon the prospect through the stable of the boy hissing and rubbing down Rory, who clattered with his impatient hoofs and would not stand still to have his toilet made. Dougal was engaged in the byre, in some more important operations with the cow, whose present hope and representative—a weak-kneed, staggering calf—looked out from the door with that solemn stare of wondering imbecility which is often so pathetic. Lily did not think of pathos. She was cheered beyond measure to look out on all this active life instead of the silent moor. The world was continuing to go round all the same, the creatures had to be fed, the new day had begun—notwithstanding that she was banished to the end of the world; and this was no end of the world after all, but just a corner of the country, where life kept going on all the same, whether a foolish little girl had been to a ball overnight, or had arrived in solitude and tears at the scene of her exile. A healthful nature has always some spring in it at the opening of a new day.

She went over the place under Katrin's guidance, when she had dressed and breakfasted, and was as ready to be amused and diverted as if she had found every thing going her own way; which shows that Lily was no young lady heroine, but an honest girl of twenty-two following the impulses of nature. The little establishment at Dalrugas was not a farm. It had none of the fluctuations, none of the anxieties, which befall a humble agriculturist who has to make his living out of a few not very friendly acres, good year and bad year together. Dougal loved, indeed, to grumble when any harm came over the potatoes, or when his hay was spoiled, as it generally was, by the rain. He liked to pose as an unfortunate farmer, persecuted by the elements; but the steady wages which Sir Robert paid, with the utmost regularity, were as a rock at the back of this careful couple, whose little harvest was for the sustenance of their little household, and did not require to be sold to produce the ready money of which they stood so very little in need. Therefore all was prosperous in the little place. The eggs, indeed, produced so plentifully, were not much profit in a place where every-body else produced eggs in their own barnyards; but a sitting from Katrin's fowls was much esteemed in the countryside, and brought her honor and sometimes a pleasant present in kind, which was to the advantage both of her comfort and self-esteem. But a calf was a thing which brought in a little money; and the milk formed a great part of the living of the house in various forms, and when there was any over, did good to the poor folk who are always with us, on the banks of the Rugas as in other places. Dougal would talk big by times about his losses—a farmer, however small, is nothing without them; but his loss sat very lightly on his shoulders, and his comfort was great and his little gains very secure. The little steading which lurked behind Sir Robert's gray house, and was a quite unthought-of adjunct to it, did very well in all its small traffic and barter under such conditions. The mission of Dougal and his wife was to be there, always ready to receive the master when he chose to "come North," as they called it, with the shooting-party, for whom Katrin always kept her best sheets well aired. But Sir Robert had no mind to trust himself in the chilly North: that was all very well when a man was strong and active, and liked nothing so much as to tramp the moor all day, and keep his friends at heck and manger. But a man's friends get fewer as he gets old, and other kinds of pleasure attract him. It was perhaps a dozen years since he had visited his spare paternal house. And Dougal and Katrin had come to think the place was theirs, and the cocks and the hens, and the cows and ponies, the chief interest in it. But they were no niggards; they would have been glad to see Sir Robert himself had he come to pay them a visit; they were still more glad to see Lily, and to make her feel herself the princess, or it might be altogether more correct to say the suzerain, under whom they reigned. They did not expect her to interfere, which made her welcome all the more warm. As for Sir Robert, he might perhaps have interfered; but even in the face of that doubt Dougal and Katrin would have acted as became them, and received him with a kindly welcome.

"Ye see, this is where I keep the fowls," said Katrin. "It was a kind of a gun-room once; but it's a place where a shootin' gentleman never sets his fit, and there's no a gun fired but Dougal's auld carabeen. What's the use of keeping up thae empty places, gaun to rack and ruin, with grand names till them? The sitting hens are just awfu' comfortable in here; and as for Cockmaleerie, he mairches in and mairches out, like Mr. Smeaton, the school-master, that has five daughters, besides his wife, and takes his walks at the head of them. A cock is wonderful like a man. If you just saw the way auld Smeaton turns his head, and flings a word now and then at the chattering creatures after him! We've put the pig-sty out here. It's no just the place, perhaps, so near the house; but it's real convenient; and as the wind is maistly from the east, ye never get any smell to speak of. Besides, that's no the kind of smell that does harm. The black powny he's away to the moor for peat; but there's Rory, aye taking another rug at his provender. He's an auld farrant beast. He's just said to himself, as you or me might do: 'Here's a stranger come, and I am the carriage-horse; and let's just make the most of it.'"

"He must be very conceited if he thinks himself a carriage-horse," said Lily, with a laugh.

"'Deed, and he's the only ane; and no a bad substitute. As our auld minister said the day yon young lad was preaching: 'No a bad substitute.' I trow no, seeing he's now the assistant and successor, and very well likit; and if it could only be settled between him and Miss Eelen there could be naething more to be desired. But that's no the question. About Rory, Miss Lily—"

"I would much rather hear about Miss Helen. Who is Miss Helen? Is it the minister's little girl that used to come out to Dalrugas to play with me?"

"She's a good ten years older than you, Miss Lily."

"I don't think so. I was—how old?—nine; and I am sure she was not grown up, nor anything like it. And so she can't make up her mind to take the assistant and successor? Tell me, Katrin, tell me! I want to hear all the story. It is something to find a story here."

"There are plenty of stories," said Katrin; "and I'll tell you every one of them. But about Miss Eelen. She's a very little thing. You at nine were bigger than she was—let us say—at sixteen. There maun be five years atween you, and now she'll be six-and-twenty. No, it's no auld, and she's but a bairn to look at, and she will just be a fine friend for you, Miss Lily; for though they're plain folk, she has been real well brought up, and away at the school in Edinburgh, and plays the pianny, and a' that kind of thing. I have mair opinion mysel' of a good seam; but we canna expect every-body to have that sense."

"And why will she have nothing to say to the assistant and successor? and what is his name?"

"His name is Douglas, James Douglas, of a westland family, and no that ill-looking, and well likit. Eh, but you're keen of a story, Miss Lily, like a' your kind. But I never said she would have naething to say to him. She is just great friends with him. They are aye plotting thegether for the poor folk, as if there was nothing needed but a minister and twa-three guid words to make heaven on earth. Oh, my bonnie lady, if it could be done as easy as that! There's that drunken body, Johnny Wright, that keeps the merchant's shop." Katrin was a well-educated woman in her way, and never put f for w, which is the custom of her district; but she said chop for shop, an etymology which it is unnecessary to follow here. "But it's a good intention—a good intention. They are aye plotting how they are to mend their neighbors; and the strange thing is— But, dear, bless us! what are we to be havering about other folk's weakness when nae doubt we have plenty of our ain?"

"I am not to be cheated out of my story, Katrin. Do you mean that the young minister is not a good man himself?"

"Bless us, no! that's not what I mean. He's just as pious a lad and as weel living— It's no that—it's no that. It's just one o' thae mysteries that you're far o'er-young to understand. She's been keen to mend other folk, poor lass; and that the minister should speak to them, and show them the error o' their ways! But the dreadful thing is that her poor bit heart is just bound up in a lad—a ne'er-do-weel, that is the worst of them all. Oh, dinna speak of it, Miss Lily, dinna speak of it! I'll tell you anither time; or, maybe, I'll no tell ye at all. Come in and see the kye. They're honest creatures. There's nothing o' the deevil and his dreadful ways in them."

"I wouldna be ower sure of that," said Dougal, who came to meet them to the door of the byre, his cap hanging on to the side of his head, upon one grizzled lock, so many pushes and scratches had it received in the heat of his exertions. "There's Crummie, just as little open to raison as if she were a wuman. No a step will she budge, though it's clean strae and soft lying that I'm offering till her. Gang ben, and try what ye can do. She's just furious. I canna tell what she thinks, bucking at me, and butting at me, as if I was gaun to carry her off to the butcher instead of just setting her bed in comfort for her trouble. None of the deil in them! What d'ye say to Rory? He's a deil a'thegether, from the crown of his head to his off leg, the little evil spirit! And what's that muckle cock ye're so proud o'? Just Satan incarnate, that's my opinion, stampin' out his ain progeny when they're o' the same sect as himsel'. Dinna you trust to what she says, Miss Lily. There's nae place in this world where he is not gaun about like a roarin' lion, seekin', as the Scripture saith, whom he may devour."

"Eh, man," said his wife, coming out a little red, yet triumphant, "but you're a poor hand with your doctrines and your opinions! A wheen soft words in poor Crummie's ear, and a clap upon her bonnie broad back, poor woman, and she's as quiet as a lamb. Ye've been tugging at her, and swearing at her, though I aye tell ye no. Fleeching is aye better than fechting, if ye would only believe me—whether it's a woman or a bairn or a poor timorsome coo."

"Ye're a' alike," said Dougal, with a grunt, returning to his work. "I'm thinking," he said, pausing to deliver his broadside, "that, saving your presence, Miss Lily, weemen are just what ye may call the head of the irrational creation. It's men that's a little lower than the angels; we're them that are made in the image of God. But when ye speak o' the whole creation that groaneth and travaileth, I'm thinking—"

"Ye'll just think at your work, and haud your ill tongue before the young lady," cried his wife in high wrath. But she, too, added as he swung away with a big laugh: "Onyway, by your ain comparison, we're at the head and you're at the tail. Come away, Miss Lily, and see the bonnie doos. There is nae ill speaking among them. I'm no so sure," she added, however, when out of hearing of her husband, "I've heard yon muckle cushat, the one with the grand ruff about his neck, swearin' at his bonnie wifie, or else I'm sair mista'en. It's just in the nature o' the men-kind. They like ye weel enough, but they maun aye be gibing at ye, and jeerin' at ye—but, bless me, a bit young thing like you, it's no to be expeckit ye could understand."

The pigeons were very tame, and alighted not only on Katrin's capacious shoulders, who "shoo'd" them off, but on Lily's, who liked the sentiment, and to find herself so familiarly accosted by creatures so highly elevated above mere cocks and hens—"the bonnie creatures," as Katrin said, who sidl'd and bridl'd about her, with mincing steps and graceful movements. "The doocot" was an old gray tower, standing apart from the barnyard, in a small field, the traditional appendage of every old Scotch house of any importance. To come upon Rory afterward, dragging after him the boy, by name Sandy, and not unlike, either in complexion or shape, to the superior animal whom he was supposed to be taking out for exercise, brought back, if not the former discussion on the prevalence of evil, at least a practical instance of "the deevil" that was in the pony, and was an additional amusement. Lily made instant trial of the feminine ministrations which had been so effective with the cow, whispering in Rory's ear, and stroking his impatient nose, without, however, any marked effect.

"He'll soon get used to ye," Katrin said consolingly, "and then you'll can ride him down to the town, and make your bit visits, and get anything that strikes your fancy at the shop. Oh, you'll find there's plenty to divert ye, my bonnie leddy, when once ye are settled down."

Would it be so? Lily felt, in the courage of the morning, that it might be possible. She resolved to be good, as a child resolves; there should be no silly despair, no brooding nor making the worst of things. She would interest herself in the beasts and the birds, in Rory, the pony, and Crummie, the cow. She would always have something to do. Her little school accomplishment of drawing, in which she had made some progress according to the drawing-master, she would take that up again. The kind of drawing Lily had learned consisted in little more than copying other drawings; but that, when it had been carefully done, had been thought a great deal of at school. And then there was the fine fancy-work which had been taught her—the wonderful things in Berlin wool, which was adapted to so many purposes, and occupied so large a share of feminine lives. Miss Martineau, that strong-minded politician and philosopher, amused her leisure with it, and why should not Lily? But Berlin patterns, and all the beautiful shades of the wool, could not, alas! be had on Dalrugas moor. Lily decided bravely that she would knit stockings at least, and that practice would soon overcome that difficulty about turning the heel which had damped her early efforts. She would knit warm stockings for Sir Robert—warm and soft as he liked them—ribbed so as to cling close to his handsome old leg, and show its proportions, and so, perhaps, touch his heart. And then there would, no doubt, turn up, from time to time, something to do for the poor folk. Surely, surely there would be employment enough to "keep her heart." Then she would go to Kinloch-Rugas and see "Miss Eelen," Helen Blythe, the minister's daughter, whom she remembered well, with the admiration of a little girl for one much older than herself. Here was something that would interest her and occupy her mind, and prevent her from thinking. And then there were the old books in the library, in which she feared there would be little amusement, but probably a great many good books that she had not read, and what a fine opportunity for her to improve her mind! Her present circumstances were quite usual features in the novels before the age of Sir Walter: a residence in an old castle or other lonely house, where a persecuted heroine had the best of reading, and emerged quite an accomplished woman, was the commonest situation. She said to herself that there would be plenty to do, that she would not leave a moment without employment, that her life would be too busy and too full to leave any time for gazing out at that window, watching the little bit of road, and looking, looking for some one who never came. Having drawn up this useful programme, and decided how she was to spend every day, Lily, poor Lily, all alone—even Beenie having gone down stairs for a long talk with Katrin—seated herself, quite unconsciously, at the window, and gazed and gazed, without intermission, at the little corner of the road that climbed the brae, and across the long level of the unbroken moor.

CHAPTER VIII

The days that succeeded were very much like this first day. In the morning Lily went out "among the beasts," and visited, with all the interest she could manage to excite in herself, the byre and the stable, the ponies and the cows. She persuaded herself into a certain amusement in contrasting the very different characters of Rory, the spoiled and superior, with that little sturdy performer of duty without vagary, who had not even a name to bless himself with, but was to all and sundry the black powny and no more. Poor little black powny, he supported Rory's airs without a word; he gave in to the fact that he was the servant and his stable companion the gentleman. He went to the moor for peat, and to the howe for potatoes, and to the town for whatever was wanted, without so much as a toss of his shaggy head. Nothing tired the black powny, any more than anything ever tired the "buoy" who drove and fed and groomed him, as much grooming as he ever had. Sandy was the "buoy," just as his charge was the black powny. They went everywhere together, lived together, it was thought even slept together; and though the "buoy" in reality occupied the room above the stable, which was entered by a ladder—the loft, in common parlance—the two shaggy creatures were as one. All these particulars Lily learned, and tried to find a little fun, a little diversion in them. But it was a thin vein and soon exhausted, at least by her preoccupied mind.

The post came seldom to this place at the end of the world. It never indeed came at all. When there were other errands to do in the village, the buoy and the black powny called at the post-office to ask for letters—when they remembered; but very often Sandy did not mind, i. e., recollect, to do this, and it did not matter much. Sir Robert, indeed, had made known his will that there were to be no letters, and correspondence was sluggish in those days. Lily had not bowed her spirit to the point of promising that she would not write to whomsoever she pleased, but she was too proud to be the first to do so, and, save a few girl epistles for which, poor child, she did not care, and which secured her only a succession of disappointments, nothing came to lighten her solitude. No, she would not write first, she would not tell him her address. He could soon find that out if he wanted to find it. Sir Robert Ramsay was not nobody, that there should be any trouble in finding out where his house was, however far off it might be. Poor Lily, when she said this to herself, did not really entertain a doubt that Ronald would manage to write to her. But he did not do so. The post came in at intervals, the powny and the boy went to the town, and minded or did not mind to call for the letters: but what did it matter when no letters ever came? Ah, one from Sir Robert, hoping she found the air of the moor beneficial; one from a light-hearted school-fellow, narrating all the dances there had been since Lily went away, and the last new fashion, and how like Alice Scott it was to be the first to appear in it. But no more. This foolish little epistle, at first dashed on the ground in her disappointment, Lily went over again, through every line, to see whether somewhere in a corner there did not lurk the name which she was sick with longing to see. It might so easily have been here: "I danced with Ronald Lumsden and he was telling me," or, "Ronald Lumsden called and was asking about you." Such a crumb of refreshment as that Lily would have been glad of; but it never came.

Yet she struggled bravely to keep up her heart. One of those early days, after sundry attempts on the moor, where she gradually vanquished him, Lily rode Rory into Kinloch-Rugas with only a few controversies on the way. She was light and she was quiet, making no clattering at his heels as the gig did, and by degrees Rory habituated himself to the light burden and the moderate amount of control which she exercised over him. It amused him after a while to see the whisk of her habit, which proved to be no unknown drag or other mechanism, but really a harmless thing, not heavy at all, and as she gave him much of his own way and lumps of sugar and no whip to speak of, he became very soon docile—as docile as his nature permitted—and gave her only as much trouble as amused Lily. They went all the way to the toun together, an incongruous but friendly pair, he pausing occasionally when a very tempting mouthful of emerald-green grass appeared among the bunches of ling, she addressing him with amiable remonstrances as Dougal did, and eventually touching his point of honor or sense of shame, so that he made a little burst of unaccustomed speed, and got over a good deal of ground in the stimulus thus applied. He was not like the trim and glossy steeds on which, with her long habit reaching half-way to the ground, and a careful groom behind, Lily had ridden out with Sir Robert in the days of her grandeur, which already seemed so far off. But she was, perhaps, quite as comfortable in the tweed skirt, in which she could spring unfettered from Rory's back and move about easily without yards of heavy cloth to carry. The long habit and the sleek steed and the groom turned out to perfection would have been out of place on the moor; but Rory, jogging along with his rough coat, and his young mistress in homespun were entirely appropriate to the landscape.

It required a good many efforts, however, before the final code of amity was established between them, the rule of bearing and forbearing, which encouraged Lily to so long a ride. When she slipped off his back at the Manse door, Rory tossed his shaggy head with an air of relief, and looked as if he might have set off home immediately to save himself further trouble; but he thought better of it after a moment and a few lumps of sugar, and was soon in the careful hands of the minister's man, who was an old and intimate friend, and on the frankest terms of remonstrance and advice. Lily was not by any means so familiar in the minister's house. She went through the little ragged shrubbery where the big straggling lilac bushes were all bare and brown, and the berries of the rowan-trees beginning to redden, but every thing unkempt and ungracious, the stems burned, and the leaves blown away before their time by an unfriendly wind. The monthly rose upon the house made a good show with its delicate blossoms, looking far too fragile for such a place, yet triumphant in its weakness over more robust flowers; and a still more fragile-looking but tenacious and indestructible plant, the great white bindweed or wild convolvulus, covered the little porch with its graceful trails of green, and delicate flowers, which last so short a time, yet form so common a decoration of the humblest Highland cottages. Lily paused to look through the light lines of the climbing verdure as she knocked at the Manse door. It was so unlike anything that could be expected to bloom and flourish in the keen northern air. It gave her a sort of consoling sense that other things as unlike the sternness of the surroundings might be awaiting her, even here, at the end of the world.

And nothing could have been more like the monthly rose on the dark gray wall of the Manse than Helen Blythe, who came out of the homely parlor to greet Lily when she heard who the visitor was. "Miss Eelen" was Lily's senior by even more than had been supposed, but she did not show any sign of mature years. She was very light of figure and quick of movement, with a clear little morning face extremely delicate in color, mild brown eyes that looked full of dew and freshness, and soft brown hair. She came out eagerly, her "seam" in her hand, a mass of whiteness against her dark dress, saying, "Miss Ramsay, Dalrugas?" with a quick interrogative note, and then Helen threw down her work and held out both her hands. "Oh, my bonnie little Lily," she cried in sweet familiar tones. "And is it you? and is it really you?"

"I think I should have known you anywhere," said Lily. "You are not changed, not changed a bit; but I am not little Lily any longer. I am a great deal bigger than you."

"You always were, I think," said Helen, "though you were only a bairn and me a little, little woman, nearly a woman, when you were here last. Come ben, my dear, come ben and see papa. He does not move about much or he would have come to welcome you. But wait a moment till I get my seam, and till I find my thimble; it's fallen off my finger in the fulness of my heart, for I could not bide to think about that when I saw it was you. And, oh, stand still, my dear, or you'll tramp upon it! and it's my silver thimble and not another nearer than Aberdeen."

"I've got one," cried Lily, "and you shall have it, Helen, for I fear, I fear it is not so very much use to me."

"Oh, whisht, my dear. You must not tell me you don't like your seam. How would the house go on, and what would folk do without somebody to sew? For my part I could not live without my seam. Canny, canny, my bonnie woman, there it is! They are just dreadful things for running into corners—almost as bad as a ring. But there is a mischief about a ring that is not in a thimble," said Helen, rising, with her soft cheeks flushed, having rescued the errant thimble from the floor.

"And are you always at your seam," said Lily, "just as you were when I was little, and you used to come to Dalrugas to play?"

"I don't think you were ever so little as me," said Helen with her rustic idiom and accent, her low voice and her sweet look, both as fresh as the air upon the moor. She did not reach much higher than Lily's shoulder. She had the most serene and smiling face, full, one would have said, of genuine ease of heart. Was this so? or was her mind full, as Katrin had said, of unhappy love and anxious thoughts? But it was impossible to believe so, looking at this soft countenance, the mouth which had not a line, and the eyes which had not a care.

Nowadays the humblest dwelling which boasts two rooms to sit in possesses a dining-room and drawing-room, but at that period drawing-rooms were for grand houses only, and the parlor was the name of the family dwelling-place. It was very dingy, if truth must be told. The furniture was of heavy mahogany, with black hair-cloth. Though it was still high summer, there was a fire in the old-fashioned black grate, and close beside, in his black easy chair, was the minister, a heavy old man with a bad leg, who was no longer able to get about, and indeed did very little save criticise the actions of his assistant and successor, a man of new-fangled ways and ideas unlike his own. He had an old plaid over his shoulders, for he was chilly, and a good deal of snuff hanging about the lapels of his coat. His countenance was large and fresh-colored, and his hair white. In those days it was not the fashion to wear a beard.

"So that's Miss Lily from the town," he said. "Come away ben, come ben. Set a chair by the fire for the young lady, Eelen, for she'll be cold coming off the moor. It's always a cold bit, the moor. Many a cough I've catched there when I was more about the countryside than I am now. Old age and a meeserable body are sore hindrances to getting about. Ye know neither of them, my young friend, and I hope you'll never know."

"Well, papa, it is to be hoped Lily will live to be old, for most folk desires it," said Helen. Papaw, a harsh reporter would have considered her to say, but it was not so broad as a w; it was more like two a's—papaa—which she really said. She smiled very benignantly upon the old gentleman and the young creature whom he accosted. The name of gout was never mentioned, was, indeed, considered an unholy thing, the product of port-wine and made dishes, and not to be laid to the account of a clergyman. But Mr. Blythe contemplated with emotion, supported on his footstool, the dimensions of a much swollen toe.

"Well," said he, "I hope she'll never live to have the rose in her foot, or any other ailment of the kind. And how's Sir Robert, my dear? Him and me are neighbor-like; there is not very much between us. Is he coming North this year to have a pop at the birds, or is he thinking like me, I wonder, that a good easy chair by the fire is the best thing for an auld man? and a brace of grouse well cooked and laid upon a toast more admirable than any number of them on the moor?"

"I don't think he is coming for the shooting," said Lily, doubtful. Sir Robert was in many respects what was then called a dandy, and anything more unlike the exquisite arrangements for his comfort, carried out by his valet, than the old clergyman's black cushion and footstool and smouldering fire could not be.

"You'll have had an illness yourself," said the minister, "though you do not look like it, I must say. Does she, now, Eelen, with a color like that? But your uncle would have done better, my dear, to take you travelling, or some place where ye would have seen a little society and young persons like yourself, than to send you here. He'll maybe have forgotten what a quiet place it is, and no fit for the like of you. But I'll let him know, I'll let him know as soon as he comes up among us, which no doubt he will soon do now."

"Now, papa," said Helen, "you will just let Sir Robert alone, and no plot with him to carry Lily away from me: for I am counting very much upon her for company, and it will do her no harm to get the air of the moor for a while and forget all the dissipations of Edinburgh. You will have to tell me all about them, Lily, for I'm the country mouse that has never been away from home. Eh," said Helen, "I have no doubt every thing is far grander when you're far off from it than when you're near. I dare say you were tired of the Edinburgh parties, and I would just give a great deal to see one of them. And most likely you thought the Tower would be delightful, while we are only thinking how dull it will be for you. That is aye the way; what we have we think little of, and what we have not we desire."

"I was not tired," said Lily, "except sometimes of the grand dinners that Uncle Robert is so fond of, and I cannot say that I expected the Tower to be delightful; but you know I have no father of my own, and I must just do what I am told."

"My dear," said the old minister, "I see you have a fine judgment; for if you had a father of your own, like Eelen there, you would just turn him round your little finger; and I'm much surprised you don't do the same, a fine creature like you, with your uncle too."

"Whisht, papa," said Helen; "we'll have in the tea, which you know you're always fond of to get a cup when you can, and it'll be a refreshment to Lily after her ride. And in the meantime you can tell her some of your stories to make her laugh, for a laugh's a fine thing for a young creature whatsoever it's about, if it's only havers."

"Which my auld stories are, ye think?" said the minister. "Go away, go away and mask your tea. Miss Lily and me will get on very well without you. I'll tell ye no stories. They are all very old, and the most of them are printed. If I were to entertain ye with my anecdotes of auld ministers and beadles and the like, ye would perhaps find them again in a book, and ye would say to yourself, 'Eh, there's the story Mr.

Blythe told me, as if it was out of his own head,' and you would never believe in me more. But for all that it's no test being in a book; most of mine are in books, and yet they are mine, and it was me that put them together all the same. But I have remarked that our own concerns are more interesting to us than the best of stories, and I'm a kind of spiritual father to you, my dear. If I did not christen you, I christened your father. Tell me, now that Eelen's out of the way, what is it that brought ye here? Is it something about a bonnie lad, my bonnie young lass? for that's the commonest cause of banishment, and as it cannot be carried out with the young man, it's the poor wee lassies that have the brunt to bear—"

"I never said," cried Lily, angry tears coming to her eyes, "that there was any reason or that it was for punishment. I just came here because—because Uncle Robert wanted me to come," she added in a little burst of indignation, yet dignity; "and nobody that I know has a right to say a word."

"Just so," said Mr. Blythe; "he wanted you, no doubt, to give an eye to Dougal and Katrin, who might be taking in lodgers or shooting the moors for their own profit for anything that he can tell. He's an auld-farrant chield, Sir Robert. He would not say a word to you, but he would reckon that you would find out."

"Mr. Blythe," cried Lily with fresh indignation, "if you think my uncle sent me here for a spy, to find out things that do not exist—"

"No, my dear, I don't, I don't," said the minister. "I am satisfied he has a mind above that, and you too. But he's not without a thread of suspicion in him; indeed, he's like most men of his years and experience, and believes in nobody. No, no, Dougal does not put the moor to profit, which might be a temptation to many men; but he has plenty of sport himself in a canny way, and there's a great deal of good game just wasted. You may tell Sir Robert that from his old friend. Just a great deal of good game wasted. He should come and bring a few nice lads to divert you, and shoot the moor himself."

"That's just one of papa's crazes," said Helen, returning with her teapot in her hand, the tray, with all its jingling cups and saucers, having been put on the table in the meantime. "He thinks the gentlemen should come back from wherever they are, or whatever they may be doing, to shoot the moors. It would certainly be far more cheery for the countryside, but very likely Sir Robert cares nothing about the moor, and is just content with the few brace of grouse that Dougal sends him. I believe it's considered a luxury and something grand to put on the table in other places, but we have just too much of it here. Now draw to the table and take your tea. The scones are just made, and I can recommend the shortbread, and you must be wanting something after your ride. I have told John to give the powny a feed, and you will feel all the better, the two of you, for a little rest and refreshment. Draw in to the table, my bonnie dear."

These were before the days of afternoon tea; but the institution existed more or less, though not in name, and "the tea" was administered before its proper time or repeated with a sense of guilt in many houses, where the long afternoon was the portion of the day which it was least easy to get through— when life was most languid, and occupation at a lull. Lily ate her shortbread with a girl's appetite, and took pleasure in her visit. When she mounted Rory again and set forth on her return, she asked herself with great wonder whether it was possible that there could be anything under that soft aspect of Helen Blythe, her serene countenance and delicate color, which could in any way correspond with the trouble and commotion in her own young bosom? Helen had, indeed, her father to care for, she was at home, and had, no doubt, friends; but was it possible that a thought of some one who was not there lay at the bottom of all?

Lily confessed to Robina when she got home that she had been much enlivened by her visit, and that Helen was coming to see her, and that all would go well; but when Beenie, much cheered, went down stairs to her tea, Lily unconsciously drew once more to that window, that watchtower, from which nobody was ever visible. The moor lay in all the glory of the evening, already beginning to warm and glow with the heather, every bud of which awoke to brightness in the long rays of the setting sun. It was as if it came to life as the summer days wore toward autumn. The mountains stood round, blue and purple, in their unbroken veil of distance and visionary greatness, but the moor was becoming alive and full of color, warming out of all bleakness and grayness into life and light. The corner of the road under the trees showed like a peep into a real world, not a dreary vacancy from which no one came. There was a cart slowly toiling its way up the slope, its homely sound as it came on informing the silence of something moving, neighborly, living. Lily smiled unconsciously as if it had been a friend. And when the cart had passed, there appeared a figure, alone, walking quickly, not with the slow wading, as if among the heather, of the rare, ordinary passer-by. Lily's interest quickened in spite of herself as she saw the wayfarer breasting the hill. Who could he be, she wondered. Some sportsman, come for the grouse—some gentleman, trained not only to moorland walking, but to quick progress over smoother roads. He skimmed along under the fir-trees at the corner, up the little visible ascent. Lily almost thought she could hear his steps sounding so lightly, like a half-forgotten music that she was glad, glad to hear again; but he disappeared soon under the rising bank, as every thing did, and she was once more alone in the world. The sun sank, the horizon turned gray, the moor became once more a wilderness in which no life or movement was.

No!—what a jump her heart gave!—it was no wilderness: there was the same figure again, stepping out on the moor. It had left the road, it was coming on with springs and leaps over the heather toward the house. Who was it? Who was it? And then he, he! held up his hand and beckoned, beckoned to Lily in the wilderness. Who was he? Nobody—a wandering traveller, a sportsman, a stranger. Her heart beat so wildly that the whole house seemed to shake with it. And there he stood among the heather, his hat off, waving it, and beckoning to her with his hand.

CHAPTER IX

The situation of Ronald Lumsden, for whom Lily felt herself to have sacrificed so much, and who showed, as she felt at the bottom of her heart, so little inclination to sacrifice anything for her, was, in reality, a difficult one. It would have been false to say that he did not love her, that her loss was no grief to him, or that he could make himself comfortable without her—which was what various persons thought and said, and he was not unaware of the fact. Neither was he unaware that Lily herself had a half grudge, a whole consciousness, that the way out of the difficulty was a simple one; and that he should have been ready to offer her a home, even though it would not be wealthy, and the protection of a husband's name and care against all or any uncles in the world. He knew that she was quite willing to share his poverty, that she had no objection to what is metaphorically called a garret—and would really have resembled one more than is common in such cases: a little flat, high up under the roofs of an Edinburgh house—and to make it into a happy and smiling little home. And as a matter of fact that garret would not have been inappropriate, or have involved any social downfall either on his side or Lily's. Young Edinburgh advocates in those days set up their household gods in such lofty habitations without either shame or reluctance. Not so very long before the man whom we and all the world know as Lord Jeffrey set out in the world on that elevation and made his garret the centre of a new kind of empire. There was nothing derogatory in it: invitations from the best houses in Edinburgh would have found their way there as freely as to George Square; and Lily's friends and his own friends would have filled the rooms as much as if the young pair had been lodged in a palace. He could not even say to himself that there would have been privations which she did not comprehend in such a life; for, little though they had, it would have been enough for their modest wants, and there was a prospect of more if he continued to succeed as he had begun to do. Many a young man in Edinburgh had married rashly on as little and had done very well indeed. All this Ronald knew as well as any one, and the truth of it rankled in his mind and made him unhappy. And yet on the other side there was, he felt, so much to be said! Sir Robert Ramsay's fortune was not a thing to be thrown away, and to compare the interest, weight, and importance of that with the suffering involved to young people who were sure of each other in merely waiting for a year or two was absurd. According to all laws of experience and life it was absurd. Lily was very little over twenty; there was surely no hurry, no need to bring affairs to a climax, to insist on marrying when it would no doubt be better even for her to wait. This was what Lumsden said to himself. He would rather, as a matter of preference, marry at once, secure the girl he loved for his life-companion, and do the best he could for her. But when all things were considered, would it be sensible, would it be right, would it be fair?

This was how he conversed with himself during many a lonely walk, and the discussion would break out in the midst of very different thoughts, even on the pavement of the Parliament House as he paced up and down. Sir Robert's fortune—that was a tangible thing. It meant in the future, probably in the near future, for Sir Robert was a self-indulgent old man, a most excellent position in the world, safety from all pecuniary disasters, every comfort and luxury for Lily, who would then be a great lady in comparison with the struggling Edinburgh advocate. And the cost of this was nothing but a year's, a few years', waiting for a girl of twenty-two and a young man of twenty-eight. How preposterous, indeed, to discuss the question at all! If Lily had any feeling of wrong in that her lover did not carry her off, did not in a moment arrange some makeshift of a poor life, the prelude to a continual, never-ending struggle, it could only be girlish folly on Lily's part, want of power to perceive the differences and the expediencies. Could anything be more just than this reasoning? There is no one in his senses who would not agree in it. To wait a year or two at Lily's age—what more natural, more beneficial? He would have felt that he was taking advantage of her inexperience if he had urged her to marry him at such a cost. And waiting cost nothing, at least to him.

Not very long after Lily left Edinburgh Lumsden had encountered Sir Robert one evening at one of the big dinner-parties which were the old gentleman's chief pleasure, and he had taken an opportunity to address the young fellow on the subject which could not be forgotten between them. He warned Lumsden that he would permit no nonsense, no clandestine correspondence, and that it was a thing which could not be done, as his faithful servants at Dalrugas kept him acquainted with every thing that passed, and he would rather carry his niece away to England or even abroad (that word of fear and mystery) than allow her to make a silly and unequal marriage. "You are sensible enough to understand the position," the old man had said. "From all I hear of you you are no hot-headed young fool. What you would gain yourself would be only a wife quite unused to shifts and stress of weather, and probably a mere burden upon you, with her waiting-woman serving her hand and foot, and her fine-lady ways—not the useful helpmate a struggling man requires."

"I should not be afraid of that," said Lumsden, with a pale smile, for no lover, however feeble-hearted, likes to hear such an account of his love, and no youth on the verge of successful life can be anything but impatient to hear himself described as a struggling man. "I expect to make my way in my profession, and I have reason to expect so. And Lily—"

"Miss Ramsay, if you please. She is a fine lady to the tips of her fingers. She can neither dress nor eat nor move a step without Robina at her tail. She is not fitted, I tell you, for the wife of a struggling man."

"But suppose I tell you," cried Lumsden with spirit, "that I shall be a struggling man only for a little while, and that she is in every way fitted to be my wife?"

"Dismiss it from your mind, sir; dismiss it from your mind," said Sir Robert. "What will the world say? and what the world says is of great consequence to a man that has to struggle, even if it is only at the beginning. They will say that you've worked upon a girl's inexperience and beguiled her to poverty. They will say that she did not know what she was doing, but you did. They will say you were a fool for your own sake, and they will say you took advantage of her."

"All which things will be untrue," said Lumsden hotly.

But then they were disturbed and no more was said. This conversation, though so brief, was enough to fill a man's mind with misgivings, at least a reasonable man's, prone to think before and not after the event. Lumsden was not one that is carried away by impulse. The first effect was that he did not write, as he had intended, to Lily. What was the use of writing if Sir Robert's faithful servants would intercept the letters? Why run any risk when there lay behind the greater danger of having her carried off to England or "abroad," where she might be lost and never heard of more? Ronald pondered all these things much, but his pondering was in different circumstances from Lily's. She had nothing to divert her mind; he had a great deal. Society had ended for her, but it was in full circulation, and he had his full share in every thing, where he was. The pressure is very different in cases so unlike. The girl had nothing to break the monotony of hour after hour, and day after day. The young man had a full and busy life: so long in the Parliament House, so long in his chambers; a consultation; a hard piece of mental work to make out a case; a cheerful dinner in the evening with some one; a wavering circle of other men always more or less surrounding him. The difficulty was not having too much time to think, but how to have time enough; and the season of occupation and company and events hurried on so that when he looked back upon a week it appeared to him like a day. And he had no way of knowing how it lingered with Lily. He wondered a little and felt it a grievance that she did not write to him, which would have been so very easy. There were no faithful servants on his side to intercept letters. She might have at least sent him a line to announce her safe arrival, and tell him how the land lay. He on his side could quite endure till the Vacation, when he had made up his mind to do something, to have news of her somehow. Even this determination made it more easy for him to defer writing, to make no attempt at communication; for why warn Sir Robert's servants and himself of what he intended to do, so that they might concert means to balk him? whereas it was so very doubtful whether anything he sent would reach Lily. Thus he reasoned with himself, with always the refrain that a year or two of waiting at his own age and Lily's could do no one any harm.

Yet Ronald was but mortal, though he was so wise. Sir Robert left Edinburgh, going to pay his round of visits before he went abroad, which he invariably did every autumn. There was no Monte Carlo in those days, and old gentlemen had not acquired the habit of sunning themselves on the Riviera; but, on the other hand, there was much more to attract them at the German baths, which had many of the attractions now concentrated at Monte Carlo; and Florence possessed a court and society where life went on in that round of entertainment and congregation which is essential to old persons of the world.

Sir Robert disappeared some time before the circles of the Parliament House broke up, and young Lumsden was thus freed from the disagreeable consciousness of being more or less under the personal observation of his enemy. And he loved Lily, though he was willing to wait and to be temporarily separated from her in the interests of their future comfort and Sir Robert's fortune. So that, when he was released from his work, and free to direct his movements for a time as he pleased, an attraction which he could not resist led him to the place of his lady's exile. All the good reasons which his ever-working mind brought forth against this were, I am happy to say, ineffectual. He said to himself that it was a foolish thing; that if reported to Sir Robert—and how could it fail to be reported to Sir Robert, since his servants were so faithful, and it would be impossible to keep them in the dark?—would only precipitate every thing and lead to Lily's transfer to a safer hiding-place. He repeated to himself that to wait for a year or two at twenty-two and at twenty-eight was no real hardship: it was rather an advantage. But none of these wise considerations affected his mind as they ought to have done. He had a hunger and thirst upon him to see the girl he loved. He wanted to make sure that she was there, that there was a Lily in the world, that eventually she would be his and share his life. It was plus fort que lui.

He went home, however, as in duty bound, to the spare old house on the edge of the Highlands, where he and all his brothers and sisters had been born and bred; where there was a little shooting, soon exhausted by reason of the many guns brought to bear upon it, and a good deal of company in a homely way, impromptu dances almost every night, as is the fashion in a large family, which attracts young people round it far and near. But in all this simple jollity Ronald only felt more the absence of his love, and the vacant place in the world which could only be filled by her; though what, perhaps, had as great an effect upon him as anything else was that his favorite sister, whom, next to her, perhaps he liked best in the world, knew about Lily, having been taken into his confidence before he had realized all the difficulties, and talked to him perpetually about her, disapproving of his inactivity and much compassionating the lonely girl. "Oh, if I were only near enough, I would go and see her and keep up her heart!" Janet Lumsden would cry, while her brother was fast getting into the condition of mind in which to see her, to make sure of her existence, was a necessity. In this condition the old house at home, with all its simple gayeties and tumult, became intolerable to him. He could have kicked the brother who demanded his sympathy in his engagement to a young lady with a fortune, neither the young lady nor the fortune being worthy to be compared to Lily, though the family was delighted by such a piece of good luck for Rob. And it set all his nerves wrong to see the flirtations that went on around him, though they were frank and simple affairs, the inevitable preferences which one boy and girl among so many would naturally show for each other. All this seemed vulgar, common, intolerable, and in the worst taste to Ronald. It was not that he was really more refined than his brothers, but that his own affairs had gone (temporarily) so wrong, and his own chosen one was so far out of the way. All the jolly, hearty winter life at home jarred on him and upset his nerves, those artificial things which did not exist in Perthshire at that period, whatever they may do now.

At last, when he could not endure it any longer, he announced that he was going a-fishing up toward the North. He was not a great fisherman, and the brothers laughed at Ronald setting out with his rod; but he had the natural gift, common to all Scotsmen of good blood, of knowing most people throughout his native country, or at least one part of his native country, and being sure of a welcome in a hundred houses in which a son of Lumsden of Pontalloch was a known and recognizable person, though Lumsden of Pontalloch himself was by no means a rich or important man. This is an advantage which the roturier never acquires until at least he has passed through three or four generations. Ronald Lumsden knew that he would never be at a loss, that if rejected in one city he could flee into another, and that if any impertinent questions were put to him by Sir Robert's own faithful servants, he could always say that he was going to stay at any of the known houses within twenty miles. This hospitality perhaps exists no longer, for many of these houses now, probably the greater part of them, are let to strangers and foreigners, to whom even the native names are strange and the condition of the country means nothing. But it was so still in those days.

He set out thus, more or less at his ease, and lingered a little on his way. Then he bethought himself, or so he said, of the Rugas, in which he had fished once as a boy, and which justified him in getting off the coach at the little inn, not much better than a village public-house, where a bare room and a hard bed were to be had, and a right to fish could be negotiated for. He had a day's fishing to give himself a countenance, enquiring into the history generally of the country, and which houses were occupied, and which lairds "up for the shooting."

"Sir Robert here? Na, Sir Robert's not here. Bless us a', what would bring him here, an auld man like that, that just adores his creature comforts, and never touches a gun, good season or bad. No, he's no here, nor he hasna been here this dozen years. But I'll tell you wha's here, and that's a greater ferlie: his bonnie wee niece, Maister James's daughter, Miss Lily, as they call her. And it's no for the shooting, there's nae need to say, nor for the fishing either, poor bit thing. But what it is for is more than I can tell ye. It's just a black, burning shame—"

"Why is it a shame? Is the house haunted, or what's the matter?" Ronald said, averting his face.

"Haunted! that's a pack of havers. I'm not minding about haunted. But I tell ye what, sir, that bit lassie (and a bonnie bit lassie she is) is all her lane there, like a lily flower in the wilderness; for Lily she's called, and Lily she is—a bit willowy slender creature, bowing her head like a flower on the stalk." The landlord, who was short and red and stout, leaned his own head to one side to simulate the young lady's attitude. "She's there and never sees a single soul, and it's mair than her life's worth if ye take my opinion. If there was any body to keep her company, or even a lot of sportsmen coming and going, it would be something; but there she is, all her lane."

"Miss Ramsay! I have met her in Edinburgh," Ronald said.

"Then, if I were you, I would just take my foot in my hand and gang ower the moor and pay her a visit. She will have a grand tocher and she is a bonnie lass, and nowadays ye canna pick up an heiress at every roadside. It would be just a charity to give the poor thing a little diversion and make a fool o' yon old sneck-drawer to his very beard. Lord! but I wouldna waste a meenit if I were a young man."

Ronald laughed, but put on a virtuous mien. He said he had come for the fishing, not to pay visits, and to the fishing he would go. But when he had spent the morning on the river, it occurred to him that he might take "a look at the moor"; and this was how it was that he stole under the shadow of the bank when the last rays of the sunset were fading, and suddenly came out upon the heather under Dalrugas Tower.

CHAPTER X

Lily could not believe her eyes. That it was Ronald who approached the house, leaping over the big bushes of ling, seeking none of the little paths that ran here and there across the moor, did not occur to her. She was afraid that it was some stranger or traveller, probably an Englishman, who, seeing a woman's head at a window, thought it an appropriate occasion for impertinently attempting to attract her attention. It was considered in those days that Englishmen and wanderers unknown in the district were disposed to be jocularly uncivil when they had a chance, and indeed the excellent Beenie, who had but few personal attractions, had rarely gone out alone in Edinburgh, as Lily had often been told, without being followed by some adventurous person eager to make her acquaintance. Lily's first thought was that here must be one of Beenie's many anonymous admirers, and after having watched breathlessly up to a certain point she withdrew with a sense of offence, somewhat haughtily, surprised that she, even at this height and distance, could be taken for Beenie, or that any such methods should be adopted to approach herself. But her heart had begun to beat, she knew not why, and after a few minutes' interval she returned cautiously to the window. She did not see any one at first, and with a sigh of relief but disappointment said to herself that it was nobody, not even a lover of Beenie, who might have furnished her with a laugh, but only some passer-by pursuing his indifferent way. Then she ventured to put out her head to see where the passing figure had gone; and lo, at the foot of the tower, immediately below the window, stood he whom she believed to be so far away. There was a mutual cry of "Ronald" and "Lily," and then he cried, "Hush, hush!" in a thrilling whisper, and begged her to come out. "Only for a moment, only for a word," he cried through the pale air of the twilight. "Has anything happened?" cried Lily, bewildered. She had no habit of the clandestine. She forgot that there was any sentence against their meeting, and felt only that when he did not come to her, but called to her to go to him, there must be something wrong.

But presently the sense of the position came back to her. Dougal and Katrin had given no sign of consciousness that any restraint was to be exercised, they had not opposed any desire of hers, or attempted to prevent her from going out as she pleased; therefore the thought that they were now themselves at supper and fully occupied, though it came into her mind, did not affect her, nor did she feel it necessary to whisper back in return. But he beckoned so eagerly that Lily yielded to his urgency. She ran down stairs, catching up a plaid as she went, and in a moment was on the moor and by Ronald's side. "At last," he said, "at last!" when the first emotion of the meeting was over.

"Oh, it is me that should say 'at last,'" said the girl; "it is not you that have been alone for weeks and weeks, banished from every thing you know: not a kent face, not a kind word, and not a letter by the post."

"I gave a promise I would not write. Indeed, I wanted to give them no handle against us, but to come the first moment I could without exciting suspicion."

"You are very feared of exciting suspicion," she said, shaking her head.

"Have I not cause? Your uncle upbraided me that I was taking advantage of your inexperience, persuading you to do things you would repent after. Can I do this, Lily? Can I lay myself open to such a reproach? Indeed, I do know the facts of things better than you."

"I don't know what you call the facts of things," she said. "Do you know the facts of this—the moor and nothing but the moor, and the two-three servants, and the beasts? Could you contrive to get your diversion out of the ways of a pony, and the cackle of the cocks and hens? Not but they are very diverting sometimes," said Lily, her heart rising. She was impatient with him. She was even angry with him. He it was who was to blame for her banishment, and he had been long, long in doing anything to enliven it; but still he was here, and the world was changed. Her heart rose instinctively; even while she complained the things she complained of grew attractive in her eyes. The pony's humors brought smiles to her face, the moor grew fair, the diversion which she had almost resented when it was all she had now appeared to her in a happy glow of amusement; though she was complaining in this same breath of the colorlessness of her life, it now seemed to her colorless no more.

He drew her arm more closely through his. "And do you think I had more diversion?" he asked, "feeling every street a desert and my rooms more vacant than the moor? But that's over, my Lily, Heaven be praised. I'm thought to be fishing, and fish I will, hereaway and thereaway, to give myself a countenance, but always within reach. And the moor will be paradise when you and I meet here every day."

"Oh, Ronald, if we can keep it up," Lily murmured in spite of herself.

"Why shouldn't we keep it up, as long, at least, as the Vacation lasts? After that, it is true, I'll have to go back to work; but it is a long time before that, and I will go back with a light heart to do my best, to make it possible to carry you off one day and laugh at Sir Robert, for that is what it must come to, Lily. You may have objections, but you must learn to get over them. If he stands out and will not give in to us, we must just take it in our own hands. It must come to that. I would not hurry or press a thing so displeasing if other means will do. And in the meantime we'll be very patient and try to get over your uncle by fair means. But if he is obstinate, dear, that's what it will have to come to. No need to hurry you; we're young enough. But you must prepare your mind for it, Lily, for that is what will have to come if he does not give way."

Lily clung to her lover's arm in a bewilderment of pleasure which was yet confusion of thought, as if the world had suddenly turned upside down. This was her own sentiment, which Ronald had never shared: how in a moment had it become his, changing every thing, making the present delightful and the future all hope and light? Sir Robert's fortune had, then, begun to appear to him what it had been to her, so secondary a matter! and Sir Robert himself only a relative worthy of consideration and deference, but not a tyrant obstructing all the developments of life. She could not say: "This is how I have felt all through," for, indeed, it had never been possible to her to say to him: "Take me; let us live poorly, but together," as she had always felt. Was it he who had felt this all through and not she at all? Lily was bewildered, her standing-ground seemed to have changed, the whole position was transformed. Surely it must have been she who held back, who wanted to delay and temporize, not the lover, to whom the bolder way was more natural. She did not seem to feel the ground beneath her, all had so twisted and changed. "That is what it must come to; you must prepare your mind for it, Lily." Had that solid ground been cut from under her? was she walking upon air? Her head felt a little giddy and sick in the change of the world; yet what a change! all blessedness and happiness and consolation, with no trouble in it at all.

"I have thought so sometimes myself," she said in the great bewilderment of her mind.

"But in the meantime we must be patient a little," he said. "Of course I am going to take my vacation here where we can be together. What kind of people are those servants? Do they send him word about every thing and spy upon all your movements? Never mind, I'll find a way to baffle them; I am here for the fishing, you know, and after a little while I'll find a lodging nearer, so that we may be the most of the time together while pretending to fish. If we keep up in this direction, we will be out of the reach of the windows, and you can set Beenie to keep watch and ward. For I suppose you still tell Beenie every thing, and she is as faithful to you as Sir Robert's servants are to him?"

"I have no doubt they are faithful," said Lily, a little chilled by this speech, "but they are not spies at all. They never meddle with me. I am sure they never write to him about what I am doing; besides, Sir Robert is a gentleman; he would never spy upon a girl like me."

"We must not be too sure of that. He sent you here to be spied upon, at least to be kept out of everybody's sight. I would not trust him, nor yet his servants. And I am nearer to you than Sir Robert, Lily. I am your husband that is going to be. It might be wrong for you to meet any other man, which you would never think of doing, but there's nothing wrong in meeting me."

"I never thought so," said Lily, subdued. "I am very, very glad to have you here. It will make every thing different. Only there is no need to be alarmed about Dougal and Katrin. I think they are fonder of me than of Uncle Robert. They are not hard upon me, they are sorry for me. But never mind about that. Will you really, really give up your vacation and your shooting, and all your pleasure at home, to come here and bide with me?"

"That and a great deal more," said Ronald fervently. He felt at that moment that he could give every thing up for Lily. He was very much pleased, elevated, gratified by what he himself had said. He had taken the burden of the matter on his own shoulders, as it was fit that a man should do. He had felt when they last parted that in some way, he could not exactly say what, he had not come up to what was expected of him. He had not reached the height of Lily's ideal. But now every thing was different. He had spoken out, he had assumed a virtue of which he had not been quite sure whether he had it or not; but now he was sure. He would not forsake her, he would never ask her to wait unduly or to suffer for him now. To be sure, they would have to wait—they were young enough, there was no harm in that—but not longer than was fit, not to make her suffer. He drew her arm within his, leading her along through the intricacies of the firm turf that formed a green network of softness amid the heather. It was not for her to stumble among the big bushes of ling or spring over the tufts. His business was to guard her from all that, to lead her by the grassy paths, where her soft footsteps should find no obstacle. There is a moment in a young man's life when he thinks of this mission of his with a certain enthusiasm. Whatever else he might do, this was certainly his, to keep a woman's foot from stumbling, to smooth the way for her, to find out the easiest road. The more he did it the more he felt sure that it was his to do, and should be, through all the following years.

Lily was a long time out of doors that night. Robina came upstairs from the lengthened supper, which was one of the pleasantest moments of the day down stairs, when all the work was done, and all were free to talk and linger without any thought of the beasts or the poultry. The cows and the ponies were all suppered and put to bed. All the chickens, mothers and children, had their heads under their wings. The watchfullest of cocks was buried in sleep, the dogs were quiet on the hearthstone. Then was the time for those "cracks" which the little party loved. Beenie told her thrice-told tale of the wonders of Sir Robert's kitchen, and the goings on of Edinburgh servants, while Katrin gave forth the chronicles of the countryside, and Dougal, not to be outdone, poured forth rival recollections of things which he had seen when the laird's man, following his master afar, and of the tragedy of Mr. James, Lily's father, who had died far from home. They would sometimes talk all together without observing it, carrying on each in his various strain. And as there was nobody to interrupt, supper-time was long, and full of varied interest. Sandy, the boy, sat at the foot of the table with round and wondering eyes. But though he laid up many an image for future admiration, his interest flagged after a while, and an oft-repeated access of sleep made him the safest of listeners. "G'y way to your bed, laddie," Katrin would say, not without kindness. "Lord bless us!" cried Dougal, giving his kick of dismissal under the table. "D'ye no hear what the mistress tells ye?" But this was the only thing that disturbed the little party. And Beenie usually came upstairs to find Lily with her pale face, she who had no cronies, nor any one with whom to forget herself in talk, "wearying" for her sole attendant.

But on this night Beenie found no one there when she came upstairs, running, and a little guilty to think of the solitude of her little mistress. For a moment Beenie had a great throb of terror in her breast: the window was open, a faint and misty moon was shining forlorn over the moor, there were no candles lighted, nor sign of any living thing. Beenie coming in with her light was like a searcher for some dreadful thing, entering a place of mystery to find she knew not what. She held up her candle and cast a wild glance round the room, as if Lily might have been lying in a heap in some corner; then, with a suppressed scream, rushed into the adjacent bedroom, where the door stood open and all was emptiness. Not there, not there! The distracted woman flew to the open window with a wild apprehension that Lily, in her despair, might have thrown herself over. "Oh, Miss Lily, Miss Lily!" she cried, setting down her light and wringing her hands. Every horrible thing that could have happened rushed through Beenie's mind. "And what will they say to me, that let her bide her lane and break her heart?" she moaned within herself. And so strong was the certainty in her mind that something dreadful had happened that when a sound struck her ear, and she turned sharp round to see the little mistress, whom she had in imagination seen laid out white and still upon her last bed, standing all radiant in life and happiness behind her, the scream which burst forth from Beenie's lips was wilder than ever. Was it Lily who stood there, smiling and shining, her eyes full of the dew of light, and every line of her countenance beaming? or was it rather Lily's glorified ghost, the spirit that had overcome all troubles of the flesh? It was the mischievous look in Lily's eyes that convinced her faithful servant that this last hypothesis could not be the explanation. For mischief surely will not shine in glorified eyes, or the blessed amuse themselves with the consternation of mortals. And Beenie's soul, so suddenly relieved of its terrors, burst out in an "Oh, Miss Lily!" the perennial remonstrance with which the elder woman had all her life protested against, yet condoned and permitted, the wayward humors of the girl.

"Well, Beenie! and how long do you think you will take to your supper another time?" Lily said.

"Oh, Miss Lily, and where have you been? I've had a fright that will make me need no more suppers as long as I live. Supper, did ye say? Me that thought that you were out of the window, lying cauld and stark at the foot of the tower. Oh, my bonnie dear, my heart's beating like a muckle drum. Where have ye been?"

"I have been on the moor," said Lily dreamily. "I've had a fine walk, half the way to the town, while you have been taken up with your bannocks and your cheese and your cracks. I had a great mind to come round to the window and put something white over my head and give you a good fright, sitting there telling stories and thinking nothing of me."

"Eh, I wasna telling stories—no me!"

Why Beenie made this asseveration I cannot tell, for she did nothing but tell stories all the time that Dougal, Katrin, and she were together; but it was natural to deny instinctively whatever accusation of neglect was brought against her. "And eh," she cried, with natural art, turning the tables, "what a time of night to be out on that weary moor, a young lady like you. Your feet will be wet with the dew, and no a thing upon your shoulders to keep you from the cold. Eh, Miss Lily, Miss Lily!" cried Robina, with all the fictitious indignation of a counter accusation, "them that has to look after you and keep you out of mischief has hard ado."

"Perhaps you will get me a little supper now that you have had plenty for yourself," said Lily, keeping up the advantage on her side. But she was another Lily from that pale flower which had looked so sadly over the moor before Robina went down stairs to her prolonged meal, a radiant creature with joy in every movement. What could it be that had happened to Lily while her faithful woman was down stairs?

CHAPTER XI

Lily kept the secret to herself as long as it was in mortal power to do so. She sent Beenie off to bed, entirely mystified and unable to explain to herself the transformation which had taken place, while she herself lay down under the canopies of the "best bed" and watched the misty moonlight on the moor, and pictured to herself that Ronald would be only now arriving, after his long walk, at his homely lodging. But what did it matter to him to be late, to walk so far, to traverse, mile after mile in the dark, that lonesome road? He was a man, and it was right and fit for him. If he had been walking half the night, it would have been just what the rural lads do, proud of their sweethearts, for whom they sacrifice half their rest.

"I'll take my plaid and out I'll steal,
And o'er the hills to Nannie O."

That was the sentiment for the man, and Lily felt her heart swell with the pride of it and the satisfaction. She had thought—had she really thought it?—that he was too careful, too prudent, more concerned about her fortune than her happiness, but how false that had all been! or how different he was now! "To carry you off some day and laugh at Sir Robert, for that is what it must come to, Lily." Ah, she had always known that this was what it must come to; but he had not seen it, or at least she had thought he did not see it in the Edinburgh days. He had learned it, however, since then, or else, which was most likely, it had always been in him, only mistaken by her or undeveloped; for it takes some time, she said to herself, before a man like Ronald, full of faith in his fellow-creatures, could believe in a tyranny like Sir Robert's, or think that it was anything but momentary. To think that the heartless old man should send a girl here, and then go away and probably forget all about her, leaving her to pine away in the wilderness—that was a thing that never would have entered into Ronald's young and wholesome mind. But now he saw it all, and that passiveness which had chilled and disappointed Lily was gone. That was what it must come to. Ah, yes, it was this it must come to: independence, no waiting on an old man's caprices, no dreadful calculations about a fortune which was not theirs, which Lily did not grudge Sir Robert, which she was willing, contemptuously, that he should do what he pleased with, which she would never buy at the cost of the happiness of her young life. And now Ronald thought so too. The little flat high up under the tiles of a tall old Edinburgh house began to appear again, looming in the air over the wild moor. What a home it would be, what a nest of love and happiness! Ronald never should repent, oh, never, never should he repent that he had chosen Lily's love rather than Sir Robert's fortune. How happy they would be, looking out over all the lights and shadows with the great town at their feet and all their friends around! Lily fell asleep in this beatitude of thought, and in the same awakened, wondering at herself for one moment why she should feel so happy, and then remembering with a rush of delightful retrospection. Was it possible that all the world had thus changed in a moment, that the clouds had all fled away, that these moors were no longer the wilderness, but a little outlying land of paradise, where happiness was, and every thing that was good was yet to be?

Beenie found her young mistress radiant in the morning as she had left her radiant when she went to bed. The young girl's countenance could not contain her smiles; they seemed to ripple over, to mingle with the light, to make sunshine where there was none. What could have happened to her in that social hour when Robina was at supper with her friends, usually one of the dullest of the twenty-four to lonely Lily? Whom could she have seen, what could she have heard, to light those lamps of happiness in her eyes? But Robina could not divine what it was, and Lily laughed and flouted, and reproached her with smiles always running over. "You were so busy with your supper you never looked what might be happening to me. You and Katrin and Dougal were so full of your cracks you had no eyes for a poor lassie. I might have been lost upon the moor and you would never have found it out. But I was not lost, you see, only wonderfully diverted, and spent a happy evening, and you never knew."

"Miss Lily," said Beenie, with tears, "never more, if I should starve, will I go down to my supper again!"

"You will just go down to your supper to-night and every night, and have your cracks with Dougal and Katrin, and be as happy as you can, for I am happy too. I am lonely no more. I am just the Lily I used to be before trouble came—oh, better! for it's finer to be happy again after trouble than when you are just innocent and never have learned what it is."

"The Lord bless us all!" cried Beenie solemnly, "the bairn speaks as if she had gone, like Eve, into the thickest of the gairden and eaten of the tree—"

"So I have," said Lily. "I once was just happy like the bairn you call me, and then I was miserable. And now I know the difference, for I'm happy again, and so I will always be."

"Oh, Miss Lily," said Beenie, "to say you will always be is just flying in the face of Providence, for there is nobody in this world that is always happy. We would be mair than mortal if we could be sure of that."

"But I am sure of it," said Lily, "for what made me miserable was just misjudging a person. I thought I understood, and I didn't understand. And now I do; and if I were to live to a hundred, I would never make that mistake again. And it lies at the bottom of every thing. I may be ill, I may be poor, I may have other troubles, but I can never, never," said Lily, placing piously her hands together, "have that unhappiness which is the one that gives bitterness to all the rest—again."

"My bonnie lady! I wish I knew what you were meaning," Beenie said.

Lily kept her hands clasped and her head raised a little, as if she were saying a prayer. And then she turned with a graver countenance to her wondering maid. "Do you think," she said, "that Dougal or Katrin—but I don't think Katrin—writes to Uncle Robert and tells him every thing I do?"

"Dougal or Katrin write to Sir Robert? But what would they do that for?" said Beenie, with wide-open eyes.

"Well, I don't know—yes, I do know. I know what has been said, but I don't believe it. They say that Sir Robert's servants write every thing to him and tell all I do."

"You do nothing, Miss Lily. What should they write? What do they ken? They ken nothing. Miss Lily, Sir Robert, he's a gentleman. Do you think he would set a watch on a bit young creature like you? He may be a hard man, and no considerate, but he is not a man like that."

"That's what I said!" cried Lily; "but tell me one thing more. Do they know—did he tell them why—what for he sent me here?"

A blush and a cloud came over her sensitive face, and then a smile broke forth like the sunshine, and chased the momentary trouble away.

"Not a word, Miss Lily, not a word. Was he likely to expose himsel' and you, that are his nearest kin? No such thing. Many, many a wonder they have taken, and many a time they have tried to get it out of me; but I say it was just because of having no fit home for a young lady, and him aye going away to take his waters, and to play himself at divers places that were not fit for the like of you. They dinna just believe me, but they just give each other a bit look and never say a word. And it's my opinion, Miss Lily, that they're just far fonder of you, Mr. James's daughter, than they are of Sir Robert, for Dougal was Mr. James's ain man, and to betray you to your uncle, even if there was anything to tell—which there is not, and I'm hoping never will be—is what they would not do. You said yourself you did not believe that Katrin would ever tell upon you; and I'm just as sure of Dougal, that is very fond of you, though he mayna show it. And then there's the grand security of a', Miss Lily, that there is nothing to tell."

"To be sure, that is, as you say, the grand security of all!" Then Lily's face burst into smiles, and she flung discretion to the winds. "Beenie," she said, "you would never guess. I was very lonely at the window last night, wondering and wondering if I would just bide there all my life, and never see any body coming over the moor, when, in a moment, I saw somebody! He was standing among the heather at the foot of the tower."

"Miss Lily!"

"Just so," said the girl, nodding her head in the delight of her heart, "it was just—him. When every thing was at the darkest, and my heart was broken. Oh, Beenie! and it's quite different from what I thought. I thought he was more for saving Uncle Robert's fortune than for making me happy. I was just a fool for my pains. 'If he stands out, we must just take it in our own hands; it must come to that; you must just prepare your mind for it, Lily.' That was what he said, and me misjudging and making myself miserable all the time. That is why I say I will never be miserable again, for I will misjudge Ronald no more."

"Eh, Miss Lily!" Beenie said again. Her mind was in a confusion even greater than that of her young mistress; and she did not know what to say. If Lily had misjudged him, so had she, and worse, and worse, she said to herself! Beenie had not been made miserable, however, by the mistake as Lily had been, and she was not uplifted by the discovery, if it was a discovery; a cold doubt still hovered about her heart.

"I will tell you the truth. I will not hide anything from you," said Lily. "He is at Kinloch-Rugas; he is staying in the very town itself. He has come here for the fishing. He'll maybe not catch many fish, but we'll both be happy, which is of more importance. Be as long as you like at your supper, Beenie, for then I will slip out and take my walk upon the moor, and Dougal and Katrin need never know anything except that I am, as they think already, a silly lassie keeping daft-like hours. If they write that to Uncle Robert, what will it matter? To go out on the moor at the sunset is not silly; it is the right thing to do. And the weather is just like heaven, you know it is, one day rising after another, and never a cloud."

"'Deed, there are plenty of clouds," said Beenie, "and soon we'll have rain, and you cannot wander upon the moor then, not if he were the finest man in all the world."

"We'll wait till that time comes, and then we'll think what's best to do; but at present it is just the loveliest weather that ever was seen. Look at that sky," said Lily, pointing to the vault of heavenly blue, which, indeed, was not cloudless, but better, flushed with beatific specks of white like the wings of angels. And then the girl sprang out of bed and threw herself into Robina's arms. "Oh, I've been faithless, faithless!" she cried; "I've thought nothing but harm and ill. And I was mistaken, mistaken all the time! I could hide my face in the dust for shame, and then I could lift it up to the skies for joy. For there's nothing matters in this world so long as them you care for are good and true and care for you. Nothing, nothing, whether it's wealth or poverty, whether it's parting or meeting. I thought he was thinking more of the siller than of true love. The more shame to me in my ignorance, the silly, silly thing I was. And all the time it was just the contrary, and true love was what he was thinking of, though it was only for an unworthy creature like me."

"I wouldna be so humble as that, my bonnie dear. Ye are nane unworthy; you're one that any person might be proud of to have for their ain. I'm saying nothing against Mr. Ronald, wha is a fine young man and just suits ye very well if every thing was according. Weel, weel, you need not take off my head. Ye can say what you like, but he would just be very suitable if he had a little more siller or a little more heart. Oh, I am not undoubting his heart in that kind of a way. He's fond enough of you, I make no doubt of that. It's courage is what he wants, and the heart to take things into his own hands."

"Beenie," said the young mistress with dignity, "when the like of you takes a stupid fit, there is nothing like your stupidity. Oh! it's worse than that—it is a determination not to understand that takes the patience out of one. But I will not argue; I might have held my tongue and kept it all to myself, but I would not, for I've got a bad habit of telling you every thing. Ah! it's a very bad habit, when you set yourself like a stone wall, and refuse to understand. Go away now, you dull woman, and leave me alone; and if you like to betray me and him to those folk in the kitchen, you will just have to do it, for I cannot stop you; but it will be the death of me."

"I betray you!" said Beenie with such a tone of injured feeling as all Lily's caresses, suddenly bestowed in a flood, could not calm; but peace was made after a while, and Robina went forth to the world as represented by Katrin and Dougal with an increase of dignity and self-importance which these simple people could not understand.

"Bless me, you will have been hearing some grand news or other," said Katrin.

"Me! How could I hear any news, good or bad, and me the same as in prison?" said Beenie, upon which both her companions burst into derisive laughter.

"An easy prison," said Katrin, "where you can come and gang at your pleasure and nobody to say, 'Where are ye gaun?'"

"You're on your parole, Beenie," said Dougal, "like one of the officers in the time of the war."

"That is just it," said Robina; "you never said a truer word. I'm just on my parole. I can go where I please, but no go away. And I can do what I please, but no what I want to do. That's harder than stone walls and iron bars."

"But what can ye be wanting to do sae out of the ordinary?" said Katrin. "Me, I thought we were such good friends just living very peaceable, and you content, Beenie, more or less, as weel as a middle-aged woman with nothing happening to her is like to be."

"I wasna consulting you about my age or what I expected," Beenie replied with quick indignation. It was a taunt that made the tears steal to her eyes. If Katrin thought it was such a great thing to be married, and that she, Robina, had not had her chance like another! But she drew herself up and added grandly: "It is my young lady that is in prison, poor thing, shut out from all her own kind. And how do I ken that you two are not just two jailers over her, keeping the poor thing fast that she should never make a step, nor see a face, but what Sir Robert would have to know?"

The two guardians of Dalrugas consulted each other with a glance. "Oh, is that hit?" said Katrin. It is seldom, very seldom, that a Scotch speaker makes any havoc with the letter h, but there is an occasional exception to this rule for the sake of emphasis. "Is that hit" is a stronger expression than "is that it." It isolates the pronoun and gives it force. Dougal for his part pushed his cap off his head till it hung on by one hair. It had been Robina's object to keep them in the dark; but her attempt was not successful. It diverted rather a stream of light upon a point which they had not yet taken into consideration at all. Many had been the wonderings at first over Lily's arrival, and Sir Robert's reason for sending her here, but no guidance had been afforded to the curious couple, and their speculations had died a natural death.

But Robina's unguarded speech woke again all the echoes. "It will just be a lad, after a'," Katrin said to her spouse, when Robina, perceiving her mistake, retired.

"I wouldna say but what it was," answered Dougal.

"And eh, man," said his wife, "you and me, that just stable our beasts real peaceable together, would not be the ones to make any outcry if it was a bonnie lad and one that was well meaning."

"If the lad's bonnie or not is naething to you or me," said the husband.

"I'm no speaking of features, you coof, and that ye ken weel; but one that means weel and would take the poor bit motherless lassie to a hame of her ain: eh, Dougal man!" said Katrin, with the moisture in her eyes.

"How do we ken," said Dougal, "if there is a lad—which is no way proved, but weemen's thoughts are aye upon that kind of thing—that he is no just after Sir Robert's fortune, and thinking very little of the bonnie lass herself?"

"Eh, but men are ill-thinking creatures," said Katrin. "Ye ken by yourselves, and mind all the worldly meanings ye had, when a poor lass was thinking but of love and kindness. And what for should the gentleman be thinking of Sir Robert's fortune? He has, maybe, as good a one of his ain."

"No likely," said Dougal, shaking his head. But he added: "I'll no play false to Maister James's daughter whatever, and you'll no let me hear any clashes out of your head," he said, with magisterial action striding away.

"When it was me that was standing up for her a' the time!" Katrin cried with an indignation that was not without justice.

CHAPTER XII

Next night the supper was much prolonged in the kitchen at Dalrugas. The three convives—for Sandy tumbled off to sleep and was hustled off to bed at an early hour—told stories against each other with devotion, Katrin adding notes and elucidations to every anecdote slowly worked out by her husband, and meeting every wonder of Beenie's by a more extraordinary tale. But while they thus occupied themselves with a strong intention and meaning that Lily's freedom should be complete, the thrill of consciousness about all three was unmistakable. How it came about that they knew this to be the moment when Lily desired to be unwatched and free neither Dougal nor Katrin could have told. Lily had been roaming about the moor for a great part of the day, sometimes with Beenie, sometimes alone; but they had taken no more notice than usual. Perhaps they thought of the country custom which brings the wooer at nightfall; perhaps something magnetic was in the air. At all events this was the effect produced. They sat down in the early twilight, which had not yet quite lost its prolonged midsummer sweetness, and the moon was shining, whitening the great breadth of the moor, before they rose. They had neither heard nor seen anything of Lily on the previous evening, though she had gone out with more haste and less precaution than now; but her movements to-night seemed to send the thrill of a pulse beating all through the gaunt, high house. Each of them heard her flit down stairs, though her step was so light. The husband and wife gave each other a glance when they heard the sound, though it was no more than the softest touch, of the big hall-door as she drew it behind her; and Beenie raised her voice instinctively to drown the noise, as if it had been something loud and violent. They all thought they heard her step upon the grass, which was impossible, and the sound of another step meeting hers. They were all conscious to their finger-tips of what poor little Lily was about, or what they thought she was about; though, indeed, Lily had flown forth like a dove, making no noise at all, even in her own excited ears.

And as for any sound of their steps upon the mossy greenness of the grass that intersected the heather, and made so soft a background for the big hummocks of the ling, there was no such thing that any but fairy ears could have heard. Ronald was standing in the same place, at the foot of the tower, when Lily flew out noiseless, with the plaid over her arm. He had brought a basket of fish, which he placed softly within the hall-door.

"You see, I am not, after all, a fisher for nothing," he whispered, as he put the soft plaid about her shoulders.

"Whisht! don't say anything," said Lily, "till we are further off the house."

"You don't trust them, then?" he said.

"Oh, I trust them! but it's a little dreadful to think one has to trust any body and to be afraid of what a servant will say."

"So it is," he agreed, "but that is one of the minor evils we must just put up with, Lily. We would not if we could help it. Still, when your uncle compels you and me to proceedings like this, he must bear the guilt of it, if there is any guilt."

"'Guilt' is a big word," said Lily; and then she added: "I suppose it is what a great many do and think no shame."

"Shame!" he said, "for two lovers to meet that are kept apart for no reason in the world! If we were to meet Sir Robert face to face, I hope my Lily would not blush, and certainly there would be no shame in me. He dared us to it when he sent you away, and I don't see how he can expect anything different. I would be a poor creature if, when I was free myself, I let my bonnie Lily droop alone."

"A poor Lily you would have found me if it had lasted much longer," she said, "but, oh, Ronald! never think of that now. Here we are together, and we believe in each other, which is all we want. To doubt, that is the dreadful thing—to think that perhaps there are other thoughts not like your own in his mind, and that however you may meet, and however near you may be, you never know what he may be thinking." Lily shuddered a little, notwithstanding that he had put the plaid so closely round her, and that her arm was within his.

"Yes," said Ronald, "and don't you think there might be the same dread in him? that his Lily was doubting him, not trusting, perhaps turning away to other—"

"Don't say that, Ronald, for it is not possible. You could not ever have doubted me. Don't say that, or I'll never speak to you again."

"And why not I as well as you?" said Ronald. "There is just as much occasion. I believe there is no occasion, Lily. Don't mistake me again, but just as much occasion."

She looked at him for a moment with her face changing as he repeated: "Just as much occasion." And then, with a happy sigh: "Which is none," she said.

"On either side. The one the same as the other. Promise me you will always keep to that, and never change your mind."

She only smiled in reply; words did not seem necessary. They understood each other without any such foolish formula. And how was it possible she should change her mind? how ever go beyond that moment, which was eternity, which held all time within the bliss of its content? The entreaty to keep to that seemed to Lily to be without meaning. This was always; this was forever. Her mind could no more change than the great blue peak of Schiehallion could change, standing up against the lovely evening sky. She had recognized her mistake, with what pride and joy! and that was over forever. It was a chapter never to be opened again.

The lingering sunset died over the moor, with every shade of color that the imagination could conceive. The heather flamed now pink, now rose, now crimson, now purple; little clouds of light detached themselves from the pageant of the sunset and floated all over the blue, like rose-leaves scattered and floating on a heavenly breeze; the air over the hills thrilled with a vibration more delicate than that of the heat, but in a similar confusion, like water, above the blue edges of the mountains. Then the evening slowly dimmed, the colors going out upon the moor, tint by tint, though they still lingered in the sky;

then in the east, which had grown gray and wistful, came up all at once the white glory of the moon. It was such an evening as only belongs to the North, an enchanted hour, neither night nor day, bound by no vulgar conditions, lasting forever, like Lily's mood, no limits or boundaries to it, floating in infinite vastness and stillness between heaven and earth. The two who, being together, perfected this spotless period, wandered over all the moor, not thinking where they were going, winding out and in among the bushes of the heather, wherever the spongy turf would bear a footstep. They forgot that they were afraid of being seen: but, indeed, there was nobody to see them, not a soul on the high-road nor on the moor. They forgot all chances of betrayal, all doubts about Sir Robert's servants, every thing, indeed, except that they were together and had a thousand things to say to each other, or nothing at all to say to each other, as happened, the silence being as sweet as the talk, and the pair changing from one to the other as caprice dictated: now all still breathing like one being, now garrulous as the morning birds. They forgot themselves so far that, after two or three false partings, Ronald taking Lily home, then Lily accompanying Ronald back again to the edge of the moor, he walked with her at last to the very foot of the tower, from whence he had first called her, though there were audible voices just round the corner, clearly denoting that the other inmates were taking a breath of air after their supper at the ha'-door. There was almost a pleasure in the risk, in coming close up to those by-standers, yet unseen, and whispering the last good-night almost within reach of their ears.

"I do not see why I should carry on the farce of fishing all day long," said Ronald, "and see you only in the evening. You can get out as easily in the afternoon as in the evening, Lily."

"Oh, yes, quite as easy. Nobody minds me where I go."

"Then come down to the waterside. It is not too far for you to walk. I will be by way of fishing up the stream; and I will bring my lunch in my pocket and we will have a little picnic together, you and me."

"I will do that, Ronald; but the evening is the bonnie time. The afternoon is just vulgar day, and this is the enchanted time. It is all poetry now."

"It is you that are the poetry, Lily. Me, I'm only common flesh and blood."

"It is the two of us that make the poetry," said Lily; "but the afternoon will be fine, too, and I will come. I will allow you to catch no fish—little bonnie things, why should they not be happy in the water, like us on the bank?"

"I like very well to see them in the basket, and to feel I have been so clever as to catch them," said Ronald.

"And so do I," cried Lily, with a laugh so frank that they were both startled into silence, feeling that the audience round the corner had stopped their talk to listen. This, the reader will see not all protestations, not all sighs of sentiment, was the manner of their talk before they finally parted, Ronald making a long circuit so as to emerge unseen and lower down upon the high-road, on the other side of the moor. Was it necessary to make any such make-believe? Lily walked round the corner, with a blush yet a smile, holding her head high, looking her possible critics in the face. It was Dougal and Katrin, who had come out of doors to breathe the air after their supper, and to see the bonnie moor. Within, in the shadow of the stairs, was a vision of Beenie, very nervous, her eyes round and shining with eagerness and suspense. Lily coming in view, all radiant in the glory of her youth, full of happiness, full of life, too completely inspired and lighted up with the occasion to take any precautions of concealment, was like a revelation. She was youth and joy and love impersonified, coming out upon the lower level of common life, which was all these good people knew, like a star out of the sky. Katrin, arrested in the question on her lips, gazed at her with a woman's ready perception of the new and wonderful atmosphere about her. Dougal, half as much impressed, but not knowing why, pushed his cap on one side as usual, inserting an interrogative finger among the masses of his grizzled hair.

"So you've been taking your walk, Miss Lily," said Katrin, subdued out of the greater vigor of remark which she had been about to use.

"Yes, Katrin, while you have been having your supper. Your voices sound very nice down stairs when you are having your cracks, but they make me feel all the more lonely by myself. It's more company on the moor," Lily said, with an irrestrainable laugh. She meant, I suppose, to deceive—that is, she had no desire to betray herself to those people who might betray her—but she was so unused to any kind of falsehood that she brought out her ambiguous phrase so as to make it imply, if not express, the truth.

"I am glad you should find it company, Miss Lily. It's awfu' bonnie and fresh and full of fine smells, the gale under your foot, and the wholesome heather, and a' thae bonnie little flowers."

"Losh me! I would find them puir company for my part," said Dougal; "but there is, maybe—"

"Hold your peace, you coof. Do ye think the like of you can faddom a young leddy that is just close kin to every thing that's bonnie? You, an auld gillie, a Highland tyke, a—"

"Don't abuse Dougal, though you have paid me the prettiest compliment. Could I have the powny to-morrow, Dougal, to go down the water a bit? and I will take a piece with me, Katrin, in case I should be late; and then you need never fash your heads about me whether I come in to dinner or not."

"My bonnie leddy, I like every-body to come in to their denner," said Katrin, with a cloud upon her face.

"So do I, in a usual way. But I have been here a long time. How long, Beenie? A whole month, fancy that! and they tell me there is a very bonnie glen down by the old bridge that people go to see."

"So there is, a real bonnie bit. I'll take ye there some day mysel', and Beenie, she can come in the cairt with the black powny gin she likes. She'll mind it well; a' the bairns are keen to gang in the vacance to the Fairy Glen."

"I'll not wait for Beenie this time, or you either, Dougal," said Lily, again with a laugh. "I will just take Rory for my guide and find it out for myself. I think," she added, with a deeper blush and a faltering voice, "that Miss Helen from the Manse—"

She did not get far enough to tell that faltering fib. "Oh, if you are to be with Miss Eelen! Miss Eelen knows every corner of the Fairy Glen. I will be very easy in my mind," said Katrin, "if Miss Eelen's there; and I'll put up that cold chicken in a basket, and ye shall have a nice lunch as ever two such nice creatures could sit down to. But ye'll mind not to wet your feet, nor climb up the broken arch of the auld brig yonder. Eh, but that's an exploit for a stirring boy, and no a diversion for leddies. And ye'll just give the powny a good feed, and take him out a while in the morning, Dougal, that he mayna be too fresh."

"I'm just thinking," said Dougal, "there's a dale to do the morn; but if ye were to wait till the day after, I could spare the time, Miss Lily, to take you mysel'."

"And if it's just preceesely the morn that Miss Eelen's coming!" cried Katrin, with great and solid effect, while Lily, alarmed, began to explain and deprecate, pleading that she could find the way herself so easily, and would not disturb Dougal for the world. She hurried in after this little episode to avoid any further dangers, to be met by Beenie's round eyes and troubled face in the dark under the stair. "Oh, Miss Lily!" Beenie cried, putting a hand of remonstrance on her arm, which Lily shook off and flew upstairs, very happy, it must be allowed, in her first attempt at deceit. Robina looked more scared and serious than ever when she appeared with a lighted candle in the drawing-room, shaking her solemn head. Her eyes were so round, and her look so solemn, that she looked not unlike a large white owl in the imperfect light, and so Lily told her with a tremulous laugh, to avert, if possible, the coming storm. But Beenie's storm, though confused and full of much vague rumble of ineffectual thunder, was not to be averted. She repeated her undefined but powerful remonstrance, "Oh, Miss Lily!" as she set down the one small candle in the midst of the darkness, with much shaking of her head.

"Well, what is it? Stop shaking your head, or you will shake it off, and you and me will break our backs looking for it on the floor, and speak out your mind and be done with it!" cried Lily, stamping her foot upon the carpet. Robina made a solemn pause, before she repeated, still more emphatically, her "Oh, Miss Lily!" again.

"To bring in Miss Eelen's name, puir thing, puir thing, that has nothing to do with such vanities, just to give ye a countenance and be a screen to you, and you going to meet your lad, and no leddy near ye at a'."

"Don't speak so loud!" cried Lily with an affectation of alarm; and then she added: "I never said Helen was coming; I only—"

"Put it so that Katrin thought that was what you meant. Oh, I ken fine! It's no a falsehood, you say, but it's a falsehood you put into folk's heads. And, 'deed, Katrin was a great fool to take heed for a moment of what you said, when it was just written plain in your eyes and every line of your countenance, and the very gown on your back, that you had come from a meeting with your lad!"

"I wish you would not use such common words, Beenie! as if I were the house-maid meeting my lad!"

"I fail to see where the difference lies," said Beenie with dignity; "the thing's just the same. You're maybe no running the risks a poor lass runs, that has naebody to take care of her. But this is no more than the second time he's come, and lo! there's a wall of lees rising round your feet already, trippin' ye up at every step. What will ye say to Katrin, Miss Lily, the morn's night when ye come hame? Will ye keep it up and pretend till her that Miss Eelen's met ye at the auld brig? or will ye invent some waur story to account for her no coming? or what, I ask ye, will ye do?"

"Katrin," said Lily, with burning cheeks, but a haughty elevation of the head, "has no right to cross-question me."

"Nor me either, Miss Lily, ye will be thinking?"

"It does not matter what I'm thinking. She is one thing and you are another. I have told you— Oh, Beenie, Beenie," cried the girl suddenly, "why do you begin to make objections so soon? What am I doing more than other girls do? Who is it I am deceiving? Nobody! Uncle Robert wanted to make me promise I would give him up, but I would not promise. I never said I would not see him and speak to him and make him welcome if he came to me; there was never a word of that between us. And as for Katrin!" cried Lily with scorn. "Why, Grace Scott met Robbie Burns out at Duddingston, and told her mother she had only been walking with her cousin, and you just laughed when you told me. And her mother! very different, very different from Katrin. You said what an ill lassie! but you laughed and you said Mrs. Scott was wrong to force them to it. That was all the remark you made, Robina, my dear woman," said Lily, recovering her spirit; "so I am not going to put up with any criticism from you."

"Oh, Miss Lily!" Robina said. But what could she add to this mild remonstrance, having thus been convicted of a sympathy with the vagaries of lovers which she did not, indeed, deny? And it cannot be said that poor Lily's suggested falsehood did much harm. Katrin, for her part, had very little faith in Miss Eelen as the companion of the young lady's ramble. She too shook her head as she packed her basket. "I see now," she said, "the meaning o't, which is aye a satisfaction. It's some fine lad that hasna siller enough to please Sir Robert. And he's come after her, and they're counting on a wheen walks and cracks together, poor young things. Maybe if she had had a mother it would have been different, or if poor Mr. James had lived, poor man, to take care of his ain bit bairn. Sir Robert's a dour auld carl; he's not one I would put such a charge upon. What does he ken about a young leddy's heart, poor thing? But they shall have a good lunch whatever," the good woman said.

And when the sun was high over the moor and every thing shining, not too hot nor too bright, the tempered and still-breathing noon of the North, Lily set out upon her pony with the basket by her saddle, and all the world smiling and inviting before her. Never had such a daring and delightful holiday dawned upon her before. Almost a whole day to spend together, Ronald all that she dreamed, and not an inquisitive or unkindly eye to look upon them, not even Beenie to disturb their absorption in each other. She waved her whip in salutation to the others behind as they stood watching her set out. "A bonnie day to ye, Miss Lily," cried Katrin. "And you'll no be late?" said anxious Beenie. "'Od," cried Dougal, with his cap on his ear, "I wish I had just put off thae potataies and gone with her mysel'—" "Ye fuil!" said his wife, and said no further word. And Lily rode away in heavenly content and expectation over the moor.

CHAPTER XIII

The day was one of those Highland days which are a dream of freshness and beauty and delight. I do not claim that they are very frequent, but sometimes they will occur in a cluster, two or three together, like a special benediction out of heaven. The sun has a purity, a clearness, an ecstasy of light which it has nowhere else. It looks, as it were, with a heavenly compunction upon earth and sky, as if to make up for the many days when it is absent, expanding over mountain and moor with a smiling which seems personal and full of intention. The air is life itself, uncontaminated with any evil emanation, full of the warmth of the sun, and the odor of the fir-trees and heather, and the murmur of all the living things about. The damp and dew which linger in the shady places disappear as if by magic. No unkindly creature, no venomous thing, is abroad; no noise, no jar of living, though every thing lives and grows and makes progress with such silent and smiling vigor. The two lovers in the midst of this incense-breathing nature, so still, yet so strong, so peaceful, yet so vigorous, felt that the scene was made for them, that no surroundings could have been more fitly prepared and tempered for the group which was as the group in Eden before trouble came. They wandered about together through the glen, and by the side of the shining brown trout stream, which glowed and smiled among the rocks, reflecting every ray and every cloud as it hurried and sparkled along, always in haste, yet always at leisure. They lingered here and there, in a spot which was still more beautiful than all the others, though not so beautiful as the next, which tempted them a little further on. Sometimes Ronald's rod was taken out and screwed together; sometimes even flung over a dark pool, where there were driftings and leapings of trout, but pulled in again before, as Lily said, any harm was done. "For why should any peaceful creature get a sharp hook in its jaw because you and me are happy?" she said. "That's no reason." Ronald, but for the pride of having something to carry back in his basket, was much of her opinion. He was not a devoted fisherman. Their happiness was no reason, clearly, for interfering with that of the meanest thing that lived. And they talked about every thing in heaven and earth, not only of their own affairs, though they were interesting enough. Lily, who for a month had spoken to nobody except Beenie, save for that one visit to the Manse, had such an accumulation of remark and observation to get through on her side, and so much to demand from him, that the moments, and, indeed, the hours, flew. It is astonishing, even without the impulse of a long parting and sudden meeting, what wells of conversation flow forth between two young persons in their circumstances. Perhaps it would not sound very wise or witty if any cool spectator listened, but it is always delightful to the people concerned, and Lily was not the first comer, so to speak. She was full of variety, full of whim and fancy, no heaviness or monotony in her. Perhaps this matters less at such a moment of life than at any other. The dullest pair find the art of entertaining each other, of keeping up their mutual interest. And now that the cold chill of doubt in respect to Ronald was removed from her mind Lily flowed like the trout stream, as dauntless and as gay, reflecting every gleam of light.

"The worst thing is," Ronald said, "that the Vacation will come to an end, not now or soon, Heaven be praised; but the time will come when I shall have to go back and pace the Parliament House, as of old, and my Lily will be left alone in the wilderness."

"Not alone, as I was before," said Lily—"never that any more; for now I have something to remember, and something to look forward to. You've been here, Ronald; nothing can take that from us. I will come and sit on this stone, and say to myself: 'Here we spent the day; and here we had our picnic; and this was what he said.' And I will laugh at all your jokes over again."

"Ah!" he said, "it's but a grim entertainment that. I went and stood behind those curtains in that window, do you remember? in George Square, and said to myself: 'Here my Lily was; and here she said—' But, instead of laughing, I was much more near crying. You will not find much good in that."

"You crying!" she said, with the water in her eyes, and a little soft reproving blow of her fingers upon his cheek. "I do not believe it. But I dare say I shall cry and then laugh. What does it matter which? They are just the same for a girl. And then I shall say to myself: 'At the New Year he is coming back again, and then—'"

"What shall we do at the New Year?" he said. "No days like this then. How can I take my Lily out on the moor among the snow?"

"If I am a Lily, I am one that can bloom anywhere—in the snow as well as the sun."

"And so you are, my dearest, making a sunshine in a shady place. But still we must think of that. Winter and summer are two different things. Cannot we find a friend to take us in?"

"I will tell you where we shall find a friend. You'll come to the Tower with your boldest face as if it was the first time you had been near. And you will ask: 'Does Miss Ramsay live here?' And Katrin will say: "Deed does she, sir. Here and no other place.' And you will smite your thigh in your surprise, and say: 'I thought I had heard that! I am a friend from Edinburgh, and I just stopped on the road to [here say any name you please] to say "Good-day" to the young lady, if she was here.' And then you will look about, and you will say: 'It is rather a lonesome place.'"

"Go on," said Ronald, laughing; "I like the dialogue—though whether we should trust your keepers so far as that—"

"My keepers! They are my best of friends! Well, Katrin will look round too, and she will say, as if considering the subject for the first time: 'In winter it is, maybe, a wee lonesome—for a young leddy. Ye'll maybe be a friend of Sir Robert's, too?' And you will say: 'Oh, yes, I am a great friend of Sir Robert's.' And she will open the door wide and say: 'Come ben, sir, come ben. It will be a great divert to our young leddy to see a visitor. And you're kindly welcome.' That's what she will say."

"Will she say all that, and shall I say all that? Perhaps I shall, including that specious phrase about being a friend of Sir Robert's, which would surprise Sir Robert very much."

"Well, you know him, surely, and you are not unfriends. It strikes me that, to be a lawyer, Ronald, you are full of scruples."

"What a testimonial to my virtue!" he said, with a laugh. "But it is not scruples; it is pure cowardice, Lily. Are they to be trusted? If Sir Robert were to be written to, and I to be forbidden the door, and my Lily carried off to a worse wilderness, abroad, as he threatened!"

"I will tell you one thing: I will not go!" said Lily, "not if Sir Robert were ten times my uncle. But you need not fear for Katrin. She likes me better than Sir Robert. You may think that singular, but so it is. And I am much more fun," cried Lily, "far more interesting! I include you, and you and me together, we are a story, we are a romance! And Katrin will like us better than one of the Waverley novels, and she will be true to us to the last drop of her blood."

"These Highlanders, you never can be sure of them," said Ronald, shaking his head. He spoke the sentiment of his time and district, which was too near the Highland line to put much confidence in the Celt.

"But she is not a Highlander. She is Aberdeen," cried Lily. "Beenie is a Highlander, if you call Kinloch-Rugas Highland, and she is as true as steel. Oh, you are a person of prejudices, Ronald; but I trust all the world," she cried, lifting her fine and shining face to the shining sky.

"And so do I," he cried, "to-day!" And they paused amid all considerations of the past and future to remember the glory of the present hour, and how sweet it was above every thing that it should be to-day.

Thus the afternoon fled. They made their little table in the sunshine, for shade is not as desirable in a Highland glen as in a Southern valley, and ate their luncheon merrily together, Lily recounting, with a little shame, how it had been intended for Helen Blythe instead of Ronald Lumsden. "I was very near telling a fib," she said compunctiously, "but I did not do it. I left it to Katrin's imagination."

"Helen Blythe must have a robust appetite if all this was for her," he said. "Is this an effort of imagination too? But come, Lily, we must do our duty by the view. There is the old brig to climb, and all the Fairy Glen to see."

"I promised not to climb the old brig," she said. "But that promise, I suppose, was only to hold in case it was Helen Blythe that was with me, for she could give little help if I slipped, whereas you—"

"I? I hope I can take care of my Lily," said the young man; and after they had packed their basket, and put it ready to be tied once more to Rory's saddle, who was picnicking too on the grass in one continuous and delicate meal, they wandered off together to make the necessary pilgrimage, though the old brig and the Fairy Glen attracted but little of the attention of the pair, so fully engrossed in each other. They climbed the broken arch, however, which was half embedded in the slope of the bank, and overgrown with every kind of green and flourishing thing, arm in arm, Ronald swinging his companion lightly over the dangerous bits, for love, while Lily, for love, consented to be aided, though little needing the aid. And how it happened will never be known, but their happy progress came to a sudden pause on an innocent bit of turf where no peril was. If it were Ronald who stepped false, or Lily, neither of them could tell, but in a moment calamity came. He disengaged himself from her, almost roughly, pushing her away, and thus, instead of dragging her with him, crashed down alone through the briers and bushes, with a noise which, to Lily, filled the air like thunder. When she had slipped and stumbled in her fright and anxiety after him, she found him lying, trying to laugh, but with his face contorted with pain, among the nettles and weeds at the bottom. "What has happened? What has happened?" she cried.

"What an ass I am," said he, "and what a nuisance for you, Lily! I believe I have sprained my ankle, of all the silly things to do! and at this time, of all others, betraying you!"

Lily, I need not say, was for a moment at her wit's end. There were no ambulance classes in those days, nor attempts to train young ladies in the means of first help. But there is always the light of nature, a thing much to be trusted to, all the same. Lily took his handkerchief, because it was the largest, and bound up his foot, as far as that was possible, cutting open the boot with his knife; and then they held a brief council of war. Ronald wished to be left there while she went for help, but there was no likelihood of obtaining help nearer than Kinloch-Rugas, and finally it was decided that, in some way or other, he should struggle on to Rory's back, and so be led to the Manse, where a welcome and aid were sure to be found. It was a terrible business getting this accomplished, but with patience, and a good deal of pain, it was done at last, the injured foot supported tant bien que mal in the stirrup, and a woful little group set forth on the way to the village. But I do wrong to say it was a woful group, for, though the pain made Ronald faint, and though Lily's heart was full of anguish and anxiety, they both exerted themselves to the utmost, each for the sake of the other. Lily led the reluctant pony along, sometimes running by his side, sometimes dragging him with both her hands, too much occupied for thought. What would people think did not occur to her yet. People might think what they liked so long as she got him safe to the Manse. She knew that they would be kind to him there. But what an end it was to the loveliest of days: and the sun was beginning to get low, and the road so long.

"Oh, Rory, man!" cried poor Lily, apostrophizing the pony after the manner of Dougal. "If you would only go steady and go soft to-day! To-morrow you may throw me if you like, and I will never mind; but, oh, go canny, if there is any heart in you, to-day!" I think that Rory felt the appeal by some magnetism in her touch if not by her words, on which point I cannot say anything positively; but he did at least overcome his flightiness, and accomplished the last half of the road at a steady trot, which gave Ronald exquisite pain, and kept Lily running, but shortened considerably the period of their suffering. They were received with a great outcry of sympathy and compassion at the Manse, where Ronald was laid out at once on the big hair-cloth sofa, and his foot relieved as much as Helen's skill, which was not inconsiderable, could do. It was he who made the necessary explanations, Lily, in her trouble, having quite forgot the necessity for them.

"I was so happy," he said, "so fortunate as to be seen by Miss Ramsay, who knew me—the only creature hereabouts who does; and you see what she has done for me: helped me to struggle up, put me on her pony, and brought me here—a perfect good Samaritan."

"Oh, don't, don't speak like that!" said Lily in her distress. She felt she could not at this moment bear the lie. Nobody had ever seen Lily Ramsay so dishevelled before: her hair shaken out by her run, her skirt torn where she had caught her foot in it in her struggles to help Ronald, and covered with the dust of the road.

"She would just be that," said Helen Blythe, receiving the narrative with faith undoubting, "and what a good thing it was you, my dear, that knew the gentleman, and not a strange person! And what a grand thing that you were riding upon Rory! Just lie as quiet as you can; the hot bathing will relieve the pain, and now the boot's off ye'll be easier; and the doctor will come in to see you as soon as he comes home. Don't ye make a movement, sir, that ye can help. Just lie quiet, lie quiet! that is the chief remedy of all."

"He is Mr. Lumsden, Helen," said Lily, composed, "a friend of my uncle's, from Edinburgh. Oh, I am glad he is in your hands. He had slipped down the broken arch at the old brig, where all the tourists go; and I had ridden there to-day just to see it."

"Eh, my dear, how thankful you must be," was all Helen's reply; but it seemed to Lily that the old minister in his big chair by the fireside gave her a glance which was not so all-believing as Helen's.

"It was just an extraordinary piece of good luck for the young man," the minister said. "Things seldom happen so pat in real life. But a young lady like you, Miss Lily, likes the part of the good Samaritan."

She could not look him full in the face, and the laugh with which he ended his speech seemed the most cruel of mocking sounds to poor Lily. She put up her hands to her tumbled hair.

"May I go to your room and make myself tidy?" she said to Helen. "I had to run most of the way with Rory, and my skirt so long for riding. I don't know what sort of dreadful person they must have thought me in the town."

"Nobody but will think all the better of you for your kindness," said Helen, "and we'll soon mend your skirt, for there's really little harm done. And I think you should have the gig from the inn to drive you back, my dear, for your nerves are shaken, and the afternoon's getting late, and you must not stir from here till you have got a good rest and a cup of tea."

"The gig may perhaps take me back to the inn first," said Ronald, "for it is there I am staying—for the fishing," he added, unable to keep out of his eyes a half-comic glance at the companion of his trouble.

"Indeed, you are going back to no inn," said Helen; "you are just going to stay at the Manse, where you will be much better attended to; and Lily, my dear, you'll come and see Mr. Lumsden, that owes so much to you already, and that will help to make him feel at home here."

But when Lily came down stairs, smoothed and brushed, with her hair trim, and the flush dying off her cheeks, and her skirt mended, though in many ways the accident had ended most fortunately, she could not meet the smile in the old minister's eyes.

CHAPTER XIV

There was great excitement in the Tower when the gig from "the toun" was seen slowly climbing the brae. Almost every-body in the house was in commotion, and Beenie, half crazy with anxiety, had been at the window for hours watching for Lily's return, and indulging in visions and conjectures which her companions knew nothing of. All that Dougal and Katrin thought of was an accident. Though, as they assured each other, Rory's bark was worse than his bite, it was yet quite possible that in one of his cantrips he might have thrown the inexperienced rider in her long skirt; and even if she was not hurt, she might have found it impossible to catch him again and might have to toil home on foot, which would account for the lateness of the hour. Or she might have sprained her ankle or even broken her arm as she fell, and been unable to move. When these fears began to take shape, the boy had been sent off flying on the black pony to the scene of the picnic, the only argument against this hypothesis being that, had any such accident happened, Rory by this time would in all probability have reached home by himself. Beenie, I need not say, was tormented by other fears. Was it possible that they had fled together, these two who had now fully discovered that they could not live without each other? Had he carried her away, as it had been on the cards he should have done three months ago? and a far better solution than any other of the problem. These ideas alternated in Robina's mind with the suggestion of an accident. She did not believe in an accident. Lily had always been masterful, able to manage anything that came in her way, "beast or bird," as Beenie said, and was it likely she would be beaten by Rory, a little Highland pony, when she had ridden big horses by Sir Robert's side, and never stumbled? Na. "She'll just have gone away with him," Beenie said to herself, and though she felt wounded that the plan had not been revealed to her, she was not sorry, only very anxious, feeling that Lily would certainly find some opportunity of sending her a word, and telling her where to join them. "It is, maybe, the best way out of it," she said over and over again to herself, and accordingly she was less moved by Katrin's wailings than that good woman could understand. Katrin and Dougal were out upon the road, while Beenie kept her station at the window. And Dougal's fears for the young lady were increased by alarms about his pony, an older and dearer friend than Lily. "If the poor beast has broken his knees, I'll ne'er forgive myself for letting that bit lassie have the charge of him alone."

"The charge of him!" said his wife in high indignation, "and her that has, maybe, twisted her ankle, or broken her bonnie airm, the darlin', and a' the fault of that ill-willy beast. And it's us that has the chairge of her."

This argument silenced Dougal for the moment, but he still continued to think quite as much of Rory as of the young lady, whichever of the two was responsible for the trouble which had occurred. When the boy came back to report that there was nothing to be found at the old brig but great marks on the ruin, as if somebody had "slithered down," branches torn away, and the herbage crushed at the bottom, the alarm in the house rose high. And Dougal had fixed his cap firmly on the top of his head, as a man prepared for any emergency, and taken his staff in his hand to take the short cut across the moor, and find out for himself what the catastrophe had been, when a shout from Sandy on the top of the bank, and Beenie at the window, stopped further proceedings. There was Lily, pale, but smiling, in the gig from the inn, and Rory, tossing his red head, very indignant at the undignified position in which he found himself, tied to that shabby equipage. "The puir beast, just nickering with joy at the sight of home, but red with rage to be trailed at the tail of an inn geeg," Dougal said, hurrying to loose the rope and lead the sufferer in. He was not without concern for Lily, but she was evidently none the worse, and he asked no more.

"I have had such an adventure," she said, as soon as she was within hearing, "but I am not hurt, and nothing has happened to me. Such an adventure! What do you think, Beenie? A gentleman climbed up the old brig while we were there, and slipped and fell; and when I ran to see, who should it be but Mr. Lumsden, Ronald Lumsden, whom we used to see so much in Edinburgh." Here Lily's countenance bloomed so suddenly red out of her paleness that Katrin had a shock of understanding, and saw it all in a moment, if not more than there was to see. "And he had sprained his ankle," Lily said, a paleness following the flush; "he couldn't move. You may fancy what a state we were in."

"Eh," said Katrin, with her eyes fixed on Lily's face, "what a good thing Miss Eelen was with you, for she kens as much about that sort o' thing as the doctor himsel'."

"I got him on the pony at last," said Lily, "and we bound up his foot, and then we took him to the Manse. It was the nearest, and the doctor just at their door. But, oh, what a race I had with the pony, leading him, and sometimes he led me till I had to run; and I put my foot through my skirt, see? We mended it up a little at the Manse, and drew it out of the gathers. But look here: a job for you, Beenie. And my hair came down about my shoulders, and if you had seen the figure I was, running along the road—"

"But Miss Eelen with ye made a' right," said Katrin. "Ah, what a blessing that Miss Eelen was with ye."

Lily was getting out of the gig, from the high seat of which she had hastened to make her first explanations. It was not an easy thing getting out of a high gig in those days, and "the geeg from the inn" was, naturally, without any of the latest improvements. She had to turn her back to the spectators as she clambered down, and if her laugh sounded a little unsteady, that was quite natural. "She is, indeed, as good as the doctor," she said; "if you had seen how she cut open the boot and made him comfortable! And Rory behaved very well, too," she said. "I spoke to him in his ear as you do, Dougal. I said: 'Rory, Rory, my bonnie man, go canny to-day; you can throw me to-morrow, if you like, an I'll never mind, but, oh, go canny to-day.' And you did, Rory, you dear little fellow, and dragged me, with my hair flying like a wild creature, along the road," she added, with a laugh, taking the rough and tossing head into her hands, and aiming a kiss at Rory's shaggy forehead. But the pony was not used to such dainties and tossed himself out of her hands.

"You're awfu' tired, Miss Lily, though you're putting so good a face upon it, and awfu' shaken with the excitement, and a' that. And to think o' you being the one to find him—just the right person, the one that knew him—and to think of him being here, Maister Lumsden, touring or shooting or something, I suppose."

Beenie's speech ended spasmodically in a fierce grip of the arm with which Lily checked her as she went upstairs.

"What need have you," said the young lady in an angry whisper, "to burden your mind with lies? Say I have to do it, and, oh, I hate it! but you have no need. Hold your tongue and keep your conscience free."

"Eh, Miss Lily," said Beenie in the same tone, "I'm no wanting to be better than you. If ye tell a lee, and it's but an innocent lee, I'll tell one too. If you're punished for it, what am I that I shouldna take my share with my mistress? But about the spraining o' the ankle, my bonnie dear: that's a' true?"

Lily answered with a laugh to the sudden doubt in Robina's eyes. She was very much excited, too much so to feel how tired she was, and capable of nothing without either laughter or tears. "Oh, yes, it's quite true; and, oh, Beenie, he is badly hurt and suffering a great deal of pain. Poor Ronald! But he will be safe in Helen's hands. If he were only out of pain! Perhaps it is a good thing, Beenie. That is what he whispered when I came away. Oh, how hard it was to come away and leave him there ill, and his foot so bad! but I am to go down to-morrow, and it will be a duty to stay as long as I can to cheer him up and to save Helen trouble, who has so many other things to do. I am not hard-hearted; but he says himself, if he were only out of pain, perhaps it's a good thing."

Here Lily stopped and cried, and murmured among her tears: "If it had only been me! It's easier for a girl to bear pain than a man."

"But if it had been you, Miss Lily, it would have been no advantage. You can go to him at the Manse, but he could not have come to you here."

"That is true," cried Lily, laughing; "you are a clever Beenie to think of that. But how am I to live till to-morrow, all the long night through, and all the morning without news?"

"A young gentleman doesna die of a sprained ankle," said Beenie sedately, "and if you are a good bairn, and will go early to bed, and take care of yourself, I'll see that the boy goes into the toun the first thing in the morning to hear how he is."

"You are a kind Beenie," cried Lily, clasping her arms about her maid's neck. But it was a long time before Robina succeeded in quieting the girl's excitement. She had to hear the story again half-a-dozen times over, now in its full reality, now in the form which it had to bear for the outside world, with all the tears and laughter which accompanied it. "And he grew so white, so white, I thought he was going to faint," said Lily, herself growing pale.

"I'm thankful ye were spared that. It is very distressing to see a person faint, Miss Lily."

"And then he cheered up and gave a grin in the middle of his pain: I will not call it a smile, for it was no more than a grin, half fun and half torture. Poor Ronald! oh, my poor lad, my poor lad!"

"He was a lucky lad to get you to do all that for him, Miss Lily."

"Me! What did it matter if it was me or you or a fishwife," said Lily, "when a man is in such dreadful pain?"

They discussed it over and over again from every point of view, until Lily fell asleep from sheer weariness in the hundredth repetition of the story. Beenie, for her part, was exceedingly discreet at supper that evening. Indeed, she was altogether too discreet to be successful with a quick observer like Katrin, who saw, by the extreme precautions of her friend, and the close-shut lips with which Beenie minced and bridled, and made little remarks about nothing in particular, that there was something to conceal. Katrin was very near to penetrating the mystery even now, but she said nothing except those somewhat ostentatious congratulations to all parties on the fact that Miss Eelen was there, which were designed to show the growing conviction that Miss Eelen was not there at all. Beenie was quite quick enough to perceive this, but she exercised much control over herself, and made no signs before Dougal. He was chiefly occupied by the address to Rory which Lily had made, which struck him as an excellent joke, and which he repeated to himself from time to time, with a laugh which came from the depths of his being. "She said till him: 'Ye can throw me the morn, and welcome, if ye'll go canny the day.' Losh, what a spirit she has, that lassie, and the fun in her! 'Go canny the day, and ye can throw me, if ye like, the morn.' And Rory to take it a' in like a Christian!" He laughed till he held his sides, and then he said feebly: "It'll be the death of me."

The joke did not strike the women as so brilliant. "I hope he'll no take her at her word," said Beenie.

"Na, na, he'll no take her at her word: he's ower much of a gentleman; but if he does, you'll see she'll stand it and never a word in her head. That's what I call real spirit, feared at nothing. 'Go canny the day, and you can throw me, if you like, the morn.' I think I never heard anything so funny in a' my born days."

"You're easy pleased," said his wife, though she was quite inclined to consider Lily's speeches as brilliant, and herself as the flower of human kind, but to let a man suppose that he was the discoverer of all this was not to be thought of. She communicated, however, some of her suspicions to Dougal, for want of any other confidant, when they were alone in the stillness of their chamber. "I have my doubts," said Katrin, "that it was nae surprise to her at a' to find the gentleman, and that it was him that was the Miss Eelen that met her at the auld brig."

"Him that was Miss Eelen? And how could he be Miss Eelen, a muckle man?" said Dougal.

"Oh, ye gowk!" said his wife, and she put back her discoveries into her bosom, and said no more.

Lily was very restless next day until she was able to get away on her charitable mission. "I must go now," she said, "to help to take care of him, or Helen will have no time for her other business, and she has so much to do."

"You maun take care and no find another gentleman with a broken foot," said Katrin; "you mightn't be able to manage Rory so well a second time."

"Oh, I am not afraid of Rory," the girl cried. "I just speak to him, as Dougal does, in his ear."

"Mind you what you've promised him, Miss Lily," said that authority, chuckling; "he is to cowp you over his head, if he likes, the day."

"He'll not do that!" cried Lily confidently, waving her hand to the assembled household, who were standing outside the door to see her start. What a diversion she was, with her comings and goings, her adventures and mishaps, to that good pair! How dull it must have been for them before Lily came to excite their curiosity and brighten their sense of humor. Dougal returned to his work, shaking once more with a laugh that went down to his boots and thrilled him all over, saying to himself: "He's ower much of a gentleman to take her at her word;" while Katrin stood shading her eyes with her hand, and looking wistfully after the young creature in her confidence and gayety of youth. "Eh, but I hope the lad's worthy of her," was what Katrin said.

Ronald was lying once more upon the big hair-cloth sofa, as she had left him. He would not stay in bed, Helen lamented, though it would have been so much better for him. "But a simple sprain," she said, "no complication. If I could have persuaded him to bide quiet in his bed, he would have been well at the end of the week; but nothing would please him but to be down here, limping down stairs, at the risk of a fall, with two sticks and only one foot. My heart was in my mouth at every step."

"But he is none the worse," cried Lily, "and I can understand Mr. Lumsden, Helen. It is far, far more cheery here, where he can see every thing that is going on, and have you and Mr. Blythe to talk to. A sprain makes your ankle bad, but not your mind."

"That is true," said Ronald, "and what I have been laboring to say, but had not the wit. My ankle is bad, but not my mind. I am in no such hurry to get well as Miss Blythe thinks. Don't you see," he said, looking up in Lily's face, as she stood beside him, "in what clover I am here?"

Lily answered the look, but not the words. A tremulous sense of ease and happiness arose in her being. The moor was sweet when he was there, and to look for that hour in the evening had been enough for the first days to make her happy. But to start out to meet him, nobody knowing, glad as she had been to do it, cost Lily a pang. There are some people to whom the stolen joys are the most sweet, but Lily was not one of these. The clandestine wounded her sense of delicacy, if not her conscience. She was doing no wrong, she had said to herself, but yet it felt like wrong so long as it was secret, so long as a certain amount of deception was necessary to procure it. She was like the house-maid, stealing out to meet her lover. To the house-maid there was nothing unbecoming in that, but there was to Lily. She had suffered even while she was happy. But now the clandestine was all over. The constant presence of the old minister, who regarded them with eyes in which there was too much insight and satire for Lily's peace of mind, was troublesome, but it was protection; it set her heart at rest. The accident restored all at once the ease of nature. "It is the best thing that could have happened," Ronald said, when Helen left them alone, and Mr. Blythe had hidden himself behind the large, broad sheet of The Scotsman, the new clever Whig paper which had lately begun to bring the luxury of news twice a week to the most distant corners of the land. "I don't mean to get better at the end of the week. It was a dreadful business yesterday, but I see the advantage of it now."

"Was it so dreadful yesterday, poor Ronald?" she said in the voice of a dove, cooing at his ear.

"It was not delightful yesterday, though I had the sweetest Lily. But now I warn you, Lily, I mean to keep ill as long as I can. You will come and stay with me; it is your duty, for nobody knows me at Kinloch-Rugas but only you, and you are the good Samaritan. You put me on your own beast, and brought me to the inn."

"Oh, do not speak like that, do not put me in mind that we are both deceivers! I have forgotten it, now that we are here."

"We are no deceivers," he said. "It is all quite true; you put me on your own beast. And where did you get all that strength, Lily? You must have almost lifted me in your arms, you slender little thing, a heavy fellow like me!"

"Oh, you did very well on your one foot," said Lily, trying to laugh; but she shuddered and the tears came into her eyes. She was aching still with the strain that necessity had put upon her, but he did not think of that—he only thought how strong she was.

"Here, you two," said the minister, "I'm going to read you a bit out of the paper. It is just full of stories, as good as if I had told them myself."

"Oh, never heed with your stories, father," said Helen; "keep them till Lily goes away, for she has a wonderful way with her, and keeps things going. Our patient will not be dull while Lily is here."

Was that all she meant, or did Helen, too, suspect something? The two lovers interchanged a glance, half of alarm, half of laughter, but Helen went and came, unconscious, sometimes pausing to turn the cushion under the bad foot, or to suggest a more comfortable position, with nothing but kindness in her mild eyes.

CHAPTER XV

Ronald was, as he had prophesied, a long time getting well. Even Helen was a little puzzled, she who thought no evil, at the persistency of his suffering; at the end of the second week he could, indeed, stumble about with his two sticks, but still complained of great pain when he tried to walk. The prolonged presence of the visitor began at last to become a little trouble, even to the hospitable Manse, where strangers were entertained so kindly, but where there was but one maid-of-all-work, with the occasional services, chiefly outdoors, of the minister's man; and an invalid of Ronald's robust character, whose presence necessitated better fare and gave a great deal of additional work, was a serious addition both to the expenses and labors of the house. It would have been much against the traditions of the Manse to betray this in any way; but there was no doubt that the minister was a little more sharp in his speeches, and apt to throw a secret dart, in the disguise of a jest, at the guest whose convalescence was so prolonged. Lily rode down from Dalrugas every day to help to nurse the patient, that Helen might not have the whole burden of his helplessness on her shoulders; but Lily, too, became aware that, delightful though this freedom of meeting was, and the long hours of intercourse which were made legitimate as being a form of duty, they were beginning to last too long and awaken uneasy thoughts. Helen, who was so tender to her at first, became a little wistful as the days went on. The gentle creature could think no harm, but perhaps it was her father's remarks which put it into her head that the two young people were making a convenience of her hospitality, and that all was not honest in the tale which had brought so unlooked-for a visitor under the shelter of her roof. And then the village, as was inevitable, made many remarks. "Bless me, but the young leddy at Dalrugas is an awfu' constant visitor, Miss Eelen. She comes just as if she was coming to her lessons every morning at the same hour." "She is the kindest heart in the world," said Helen. "You see, this gentleman that sprained his foot is a friend of her uncle's, and she could not take him to Dalrugas, where there is nobody but servants; and she will not let me have all the trouble of him. A man, when he is ill, takes a great deal of attendance," said the minister's daughter, with a smile.

"Losh! I would just let him attend upon himsel'," said one.

"He should send for a sister, or somebody belonging to him," said another.

"Oh, not that," said Helen—"I could not put up a lady, there is but little room in the Manse—and with Miss Lily's help we can pull through."

"He should get an easy post-chaise from Aberdeen—there's plenty easy carriages to be got there nowadays—and go back to his ain folk. He's a son of Lumsden of Pontalloch, they tell me; that's not so far but that he might get there in a day."

"I have no doubt he will do that as soon as he is well enough," said Helen; but all these remarks made her uneasy. Impossible for Scotch hospitality to give a hint, to intimate a thought, that the visitor had overstayed his welcome—and a man that had been hurt and was, perhaps, still suffering! "No, no," she said, shaking her head. But it troubled her gentle mind that Lily's visits should be so remarked, and it was strange—or was it only the village gossip that made her feel that it was strange? Lily perceived all this with an uneasy perception of new elements in the air.

"Ronald," she said one day, when they were alone for a few minutes, "you could put your foot to the ground without hurting when you try. You will have to go away."

"Why should I go away?" he said, with a laugh. "I am very comfortable. It is not luxury, but it does very well when I see my Lily every day—"

"But, oh," she cried, the color coming to her cheeks, which had been growing pale these few days, "there are things of more consequence than Lily! The Manse people are not rich—"

"You need not tell me that," he said, looking round at the shabby furniture with a smile.

"But, oh, Ronald, you don't see! They try to get nice things for you, they spend a great deal of trouble upon you, and they were glad at first—but it is now a fortnight."

"Lily, my love," he said quickly, "if you have ceased to care for this chance of meeting every day—if you want me to go away, of course I will go."

"Do you think it likely I should have ceased to care?" she said, with tears in her eyes. "But we must think of other people, too."

"Thinking of other people is generally a mistake. We all know how to take care of ourselves best—unless it is here and there some one like you, if there is any one like my Lily. But, dear, I give very little trouble. What is there to do for me? Another bed to make, another knife and fork—or spoon, I should say, for we have broth, broth, and nothing but broth—and a little grouse now and then, sent to them by somebody, and therefore costing nothing."

"It is ungenerous to say that!" Lily cried.

"My dearest, you will tell me what present I can send them when at last I am forced to tear myself away. A good present that will make up to them—a chest of tea, or a barrel of wine, or— But I don't want to go away, Lily; I would rather stay here and see you every day until I am forced to go back to my work."

"Oh, and so would I!" cried Lily; "but," she added, with a sigh, "we must think of them. Mr. Blythe sits always, always in this room. It is the sunny room in the house, and he likes it best. But you see he has gone into his little study this day or two—which is very dreary—all because we are here."

"Very considerate of him," said Ronald, with a laugh, "if that is a reason for going away, that they now leave us sometimes alone. I fear it will not move me, Lily; you must find a better than that."

"Oh, Ronald, will you not see?" cried Lily in distress. But what could a girl do? She could not put understanding into his eyes nor consideration into his heart. He was willing to take advantage of these good people, and the inducement was strong. She spoke against her own heart when she urged him to go away, and she was glad to be laughed out of her scruples, to be told of the "good present" that would make up for every thing, of the gratitude that he would always feel, and his conviction that he gave very little trouble, and added next to nothing to their expenses. "Broth is not expensive," he said, "and the grouse, you know, Lily, the grouse!" Lily turned her head away, sick at heart. Oh, it was not how he should speak of the people who were so kind to him; but still, when she mounted Rory—now quite docile and accustomed to trot every day into Kinloch-Rugas—in the afternoon, she could not but be glad to think that she might still come to-morrow, that there was at least another day.

One of these afternoons the parlor was full of people, under whose eyes Lily could not continue to sit by the side of the sofa and minister to the robust invalid's wants. There was the doctor, who gave him a little slap on his leg and said: "I congratulate ye on a perfect cure. You can get up and walk when you like, like the man in the Bible." And the school-master's wife, who said: "Eh, what a good thing for you, Mr. Lumsden, and you been on your back so long." And there was the assistant and successor, Mr. Douglas, who was visibly anxious to get rid of all interlopers and speak a word to Helen. Oh, why did he not follow Helen when she went out to open the door for her visitors, and leave Lily free to say once more to Ronald, but more energetically: "You must go!"

"I was wanting to say, sir," said Mr. Douglas, "and I may add that I have Miss Eelen's opinion all on my side, that I would like very much if you would say a parting word to the lads that are going out to Canada. We have taken a great deal of trouble with them, and a word from the minister—"

"You are the minister yourself, Douglas; they know more of you than they do of me."

"Not so, Mr. Blythe. I am your assistant, and Miss Eelen she is your daughter and the best friend they ever had; but it's your blessing the callants want, and a word from you—"

"My blessing!" the old man said, with an uneasy laugh. "You're forgetting, my young man, that there's no sacerdotal pretensions in the auld Kirk."

"You blessed them when they were christened, sir, and you blessed them and gave them the right hand of fellowship when they came to the Lord's table. I'm thinking nothing of sacerdotalism. I'm thinking of human nature. We have no bishops, but while we have ordained ministers we must always have fathers in God."

Mr. Blythe had never been of this new-fangled type of devotion. He had been an old Moderate, very shy of overmuch religion, and relying upon habit and tradition and a good deal of wholesome neglect. But the young man's earnestness, backed as it was by the serious light in Helen's eyes, brought a color to his old face. He was a little ashamed of the importance given to him, and half angry at the young people's high-flown notions. "I am not sure," he said, "that I go with you, Douglas, nor with Eelen either, in your dealings with these lads. You just cultivate a kind of forced religion in them, that makes a fine show for a moment; it's the seed that fell by the wayside and sprang up quickly, but had no root in itself."

"We can never tell that, sir," said the assistant; "it may help them when they have no ordinances to mind them of their duty. If they remember their Creator in the days of their youth—"

"'Deed," said the old minister, "it is just as often as not to forget every thing all the quicker when they come to man's estate. Solomon knew mainy things, but not the lads in a parish so near the Highlant line."

"Anyway, father, it will be kindly like, and them going so far, far away."

"That is just it," said Mr. Blythe: "why should they go far, far away? Why couldn't ye let them jog on as their fathers did before them? I'm not an advocate for emigration. There are plenty of things the lads could do without leaving their own country. Let them go to Glasgow, where there's work for every-body, or to the South. You think you can do every thing with your arrangements and your exhortations, and looking after more than ye were ever asked to look after. I have never approved of all these meetings and things, and your classes and your lessons, and all the fyke you make about a few country callants. Let them alone to their fathers' advice and their mothers'. You may be sure the women will all warn them to keep off the drink—and much good it will do, whatever you may say, either them or you."

"But just a word of farewell, sir," pleaded the assistant; "we ask no more."

"And that is just a great deal too much in present circumstances," cried the old minister. "Where would ye have me speak to them—a dozen big country lads, like colts out of the stable? I cannot go out to the cold vestry at night, me that seldom leaves the house at all. And the dining-room is too small, and what other room have we free? Eelen, you know that as well as me. I cannot have them up in my bedchalmer, and the kitchen, with lasses in it, would be no place for such a ceremonial. No, no; we have no room, that is true."

"I hope, sir," said Ronald from his sofa, "you are not saying this from consideration for me. I'd like nothing better than to see the boys, and hear your address to them. It would be good, I am sure, and I am as much in need of good advice as any of them can be."

"You are very considerate, Mr. Lumsden," said the minister, after a pause. "It is a great thing to have an inmate that takes so much thought. But how can I tell that it would not be bad for you in your delicate state, with your nurses at your side all the day?"

"Delicate! I am not delicate!" cried Ronald, with a flush. "It is only, you know, this confounded foot."

"Well, Douglas," said the minister, "between Mr. Lumsden's confoondit foot and your confoondit pertinacity, what am I to do? Since your patient, Eelen, is so kind and permits the use of our best parlor, have them in, have ben your callants. I must not be less gracious than my own guest," the old man said.

Lily went away trembling after this scene, giving Ronald a beseeching glance, but she had no opportunity for a word. Next day, still tremulous, she returned, to find him still there, a little defiant, not to be driven out. But a short time after, when she was again preparing to go into the "toun"—without any pleasant looks now from her household, or complaisance on the part of Dougal, who openly bemoaned his pony—the whole population of Dalrugas turned out to see the inn "geeg" once more climbing the brae. It contained Ronald and his portmanteau, speeding off to catch the coach, but incapable, as he said, in the hearing of every-body, of going away without thanking and saying farewell to his kind nurse. "Do you know what this young lady did for me?" he said to the little company, which included Rory, ready saddled, and the black pony harnessed, with the boy at his head. "She lifted me, I think, from where I lay, and put me on her own beast, like the good Samaritan. She was more than the good Samaritan to me. Look at her, like a fairy princess, and me a heavy lump, almost fainting, and with but one foot. That is what charity can do."

"Well, it was a wonderful thing," Katrin allowed, "but maist more than that was riding down ance errand to the town to take care of ye every day."

"Ah, that was for Miss Blythe's sake and not mine," he said. "May I come in, Miss Ramsay, to give you her message? Oh, Robina, I am glad to see you here. I can carry the last news to Sir Robert, and tell him how both mistress and maid are thriving on the moor."

It was all false, false, as false as words that were true enough in themselves could be. Lily ran up the spiral stair, while Beenie helped him to follow. The girl's heart was beating high with more sensations than she could discriminate. This was the parting, then, after so long a time together; the farewell, which was more dreadful than words could say—and yet she was glad he was going. He was her own true-love, and nobody was like him in the world, and yet Lily's mind revolted against every word he said.

"Why did you say all that?" she cried, breathless, when they were alone. "It was not wanted, surely, here!"

"Necessary fibs," he said. "You are too particular, Lily, for me that am only carrying out my rôle. You see, I am obeying you and going away at last."

"Oh, Ronald, it was not that I wanted you to go away."

"No, if I could have gone away, yet stayed all the same. But one can't do two opposite things at the same time. And, Lily, it must be good-by now—for a little while. You will look out for me at the New Year."

"Do you call it just a little while to the New Year?" she cried, with the tears in her eyes.

"Three months, or a little more. I shall not come to Kinloch-Rugas; I'll find a lodging in some little farm. And in the meantime you will write to me, Lily, and I will write to you."

"Yes, Ronald," she said, giving him both her hands. Was this to be all? It was not for her to ask; it was for him to say:

"My bonnie Lily! If I could but carry you off, never to part more! But if nothing happens to release you, if Sir Robert does not relent, mind, my dearest, we must make up our minds and take it into our own hands. He is not to keep us apart forever. You will let me know all that goes on, and whether those people down stairs have reported the matter; and I, for my part, will take my measures. When we meet again, every thing will be clearer. And, Lily, on your side, you will tell me every thing, that we may see our way."

"There will be nothing to tell you, Ronald. There will be no report sent; Uncle Robert, I think, has forgotten my existence. There will be nothing, nothing to say but that it is weary living alone here on the moor."

"Not more weary than my life in Edinburgh, pacing up and down the Parliament House, and looking out for work. But we'll see what is going to happen before the New Year; and I will send the present to those good Manse folk, and you will keep up with them, for they may be very useful friends. Is it time for me to go? Well, I will go if I must; and good-by for the present, my darling, good-by till the New Year!"

Was it possible that he was gone, that it was all over, and Lily left again alone on the moor? She ran to Beenie's room, which was on the other side of the house, to watch the inn "geeg" as long as it was in sight. Nothing is ever said of what is intended to be said in a hasty last meeting like this. It was worse than no meeting at all, leaving all the ravelled ends of parting. And was it true that all was over, and Ronald gone and nothing more to be done or said?

CHAPTER XVI

The dead calm into which Lily fell after all the agitations of this wonderful period was like death itself, she thought, after the tumult and commotion of a climax of life. Those days during which she had trotted down to the village on Rory, the mountain breezes in her face, and all the warmest emotions stirred in her breast, days full of anxiety and expectation, sometimes of more painful feelings, agitations of all kinds, but threaded through and through with the consciousness that for hours to come she would be with her lover, ministering to his wants, hearing him speak, going over and over with him, in the low-voiced talk to which the old minister behind his newspaper gave, or was supposed to give, no heed, their own prospects and hopes, their plans for the future—all those things that are more engrossing and delightful to talk of than any other subjects in heaven or earth—were different from all the days that had passed over her before. Her youthful existence was like a dream, thrown back into the distance by the superior force and meaning of all that had happened since: both the loneliness and the society, the bitter time of self-experience and solitude, the joy of the reunion, the love so crossed and mingled which had grown with greater intensity with every chance. The little simple Lily who had "fallen in love," as she thought, with Ronald Lumsden, as she might have fallen in love with any one of a half-dozen of young men, was very, very different from the Lily who had been torn out of her natural life on his account, who had doubted him and found him wanting, who had been converted into the faith of an enthusiast in him, and conviction that it was she, and not he, that was in the wrong. Their stolen meetings on the moor, which had startled her back into the joy of existence, which had been so few, yet so sweet; their little meal together, which was like a high ceremony and sacrament of a deeper love and union; the tremendous excitement of the accident, and the agitated chapter of constant yet disturbed intercourse which followed (disturbed at last by a renewed creeping in of the old doubts, and anxiety to push him forward, to make him act, to make him think not always of himself, as he was so apt to do)—

all these things had formed an epoch in her life, behind which every thing was childish and vague. She herself was not the same. It happens often in a woman's life that the change from youth and its lighter atmosphere of natural, simple things comes before the mind is developed, before the character is able to bear that wonderful transformation. Lily at first had been essentially in this condition. Her trial came to her before she had strength for it, and every new point of progress was marked, so to speak, with a new wound, quickly healed over, as became her youth, yet leaving a scar, as all internal wounds do. Even when the thrill of happiness had been in her young frame and mind it had been intensified by a thrill of pain: the pang of secrecy, the sharp sting of falsehood—falsehood which was abhorrent to Lily's nature. She had laughed as other girls laugh at the stratagems of lovers, their devices to escape the observation of jealous parents, the evils that are said to be legitimate in love and war. Nobody is so severe as to judge harshly these aberrations from duty. Even the sternest parent smiles at them when they are not directed against himself. But when it came to inventing a story day by day; when it came to deceiving Katrin, with her sharp eyes, at one end, and Helen's unsuspicious soul at the other—then Lily could not bear the tangled web in which she had wound herself. She had to go on; it was too late to tell the truth now, she had said to herself, day by day, her heart aching from those thanks which Helen showered upon her for her kind attendance upon the unexpected guest. "If it had not been for you, Lily, what could I have done?" the minister's daughter had said, again and again; and Lily's heart had grown sick in the midst of her strained and painful happiness at Ronald's side.

Now this was over and another phase come. She had urged him to go, feeling the position untenable any longer in a way which his robust self-confidence had not felt; but when suddenly he had taken the step she urged, Lily felt herself flung back upon herself, the words taken out of her mouth, and the meaning from her mind. All her little fabric of life tumbled down about her. Those habits which are formed so quickly, which a few days suffice to bind upon the soul like iron, dropped from her, and she felt as if the framework by which she was sustained had broken down, and she could no longer hold herself erect. Her life seemed suddenly to have lost all its meaning, all its occupations. There was no sense in going on, no reason for its continuance merely to eat meals, to take walks, to go to bed and to get up again. She looked behind her, to the immediate past, with a pang, and before her, to the immediate future, with a blank sense of vacancy which was almost despair. When the "geeg" that carried him away was gone quite out of sight, Lily went slowly back to the drawing-room, and seated herself at the window from which she had first seen him appearing across the moor. It had been then all ablaze with the heather, which now had died away into rustling bunches of dead flowers, all dried like husks upon the stalks, gray and dreary, like the dull evening of a glowing day. Her heart beat dull with the reverberation of all those convulsions that had gone through it. And now they were all over, like the glow of the heather—and what was before her? The winter creeping on, with its short days and long nights; storm and rain, when even Rory would not face the keen wind; solitude unbroken for weeks and months; and beyond that what was there to look forward to? Oh, if it had been but poverty—the little flat under the roofs in a tall Edinburgh house, and to work her fingers to the bone! Poor Lily, who knew so little what working your fingers to the bone meant! who thought that would be blessedness beside one you loved, and in the world where you were born! So, no doubt, it would have been; but yet, in all probability, though she did not intend it so, it would have been Robina's fingers, not hers, that were worked to the bone.

I would not have the reader think that, translated into ordinary parlance, all this meant the vulgar fact that Lily was longing to be married, and would not accept the counsels of patience and wait, though she was only twenty-three, and had so many, many years before her. Had Ronald been an eager lover, ready to brave fortune for her sake, and consider that, for love, the world were well lost, she would no doubt have taken the other side of the question, and preached patience to him, and borne her own part of the burden with a smile. But it is very different when it is the lover who is prudent, and when the girl, with an unsatisfied heart, has to wait and know that her happiness, her society, her life, are of less value to him than the fortune which he hopes, by patience, to secure along with her; also that she can do nothing to emancipate herself, nothing to escape from whatever painful circumstances may surround her, till he gives the word, which he shows no inclination to give, and which womanly pride and feeling forbid her even to suggest; also, and above all, that in his hesitation, in his prudence and delay, he is falling short of the ideal which every lover should fulfil or lose his place and power. This was the worst of all: not only that Ronald was acting so, but that it was so far, far different from the manner in which Ronald, had he been the Ronald she thought, would have acted. This gave the bitterness under which Lily's heart sank. Again, she did not know what he meant to do, or if he meant to do anything, or if she were to remain as she was, perhaps for long years, consuming her heart in loneliness and vacancy, diversified by moments of clandestine meeting and unlovely happiness, bought by deceit. She could not again yield to that, she said to herself, with passionate tears. Though her heart were to break, she would not heal it at the cost of lies. It might not have given Lily many compunctions, perhaps, to have deceived her uncle; but to deceive Helen, to deceive kind Katrin and Dougal, to give false accounts of the simplest circumstances—oh! no, no; never again, never again! She said this to herself, with passionate tears falling like rain, as she sat at her lonely window on many a dreary day, straining her eyes across the moor, where the rain so often fell to double the effect of those tears. Let them give each other up mutually; let them part and be done with it if he chose; but to deceive every-body and meet secretly, or meet openly upon the falsest of pretences—oh! no, no, Lily said to herself, never more!

But how these decisions melted when, in the heart of the winter, there began to dawn the promise of the New Year, it is easy to imagine, and I do not need to say. Lily, it must be remembered, had no one but Ronald to represent to her happiness and life. She had never had many people to love. Her father and mother had both died before she was old enough to know them. She had no aunt, though that is often an unsatisfactory relation, not even cousins whom she knew, which is strange to think of in Scotland—nobody to take her part or whom she could repose her heart upon but Beenie, her maid, to whom Lily's concerns were her own sublimated, and who could only agree in and intensify Lily's own natural impulses and thoughts. Ronald was all she had, the only one who could help her, the sole deliverer possible, and opener to her of the gates of life. To be sure, she might have renounced him and so returned to her uncle, to be dragged about in a back seat of his chariot, if not at its wheels; though, indeed, even this was problematical, for Sir Robert was a selfish old man, who was, on the whole, very glad to have got rid of the burden of a young woman to take about with him, and considered that she would do very well at the old Tower, and might be quite content with such a quiet and comfortable home, a good cook (which Katrin was), a pony to ride upon, and the run of the moor. He had half forgotten her existence by this time, as Lily divined, and was absent "abroad" in that vague and wide world of which stayers at home in Scotland knew so much less then than every-body knows now. And as the time approached for Ronald's return, Lily, in her longing for him, added to her longing for something, for some one, for society, emancipation, something that was life, began to forget all her old aches and troubles of mind; the doubts flew away; she remembered only that Ronald was coming, that he was coming, that the sun was about to shine again, that there was happiness in prospect, love and company and talk and sympathy, and all that is good in youth and life. This time she must manage so that the deceit of old would be necessary no longer. Helen should know that the two who had met so often in the Manse parlor had come to love each other. What so natural, what so fitting, seeing they had spent so much time together under her own wing and her own mild eyes? And Katrin and Dougal should be permitted to see what Lily was very sure they had divined already, that the poor gentleman whom Lily had nursed so faithfully was more to her than any other gentleman in the world. He should come to Dalrugas to see her, and be with her openly as her lover in the sight of all men. If Sir Robert heard of it, why, then she must escape, she must fly; the pair must at last take it, as Ronald had said, into their own hands—and Lily did not feel that she would be very sorry if this took place. At all events now every thing should be open and honest, clandestine no more.

It seemed as if he had come to the same decision when he arrived on the night which was then called in Scotland, and is perhaps still to some extent, Hogmanay—why I do not know, nor I believe does any one—the last night of the year. He came in the early twilight, when the short, dark day was ending, and the long, cheerful evening about to begin. What a cheerful evening it was! the fire so bright, the candles twinkling, the curtains drawn, and from the kitchen the sound of the children singing who had come out in a band all the way from the village to call upon Katrin:

"Get up, gudewife, and shake your feathers,
And dinna think that we are beggars,
For we are bairns, come out to play;
Get up and gie's our Hogmanay."

Lily was about to go down, flying down the spiral stairs, her heart beating loud with expectation, wondering breathlessly when he would come, how he would come, who alone could bring the Hogmanay cheer to her, and in the meantime ready, for pure excitement, and to keep herself still, to join the women in the kitchen, and fill the children's wallets with cakes, cakes par excellence, the oatmeal cakes to wit, which are still what is meant in Scotland by that word, baked thin and crisp, and fresh from the girdle, making a pleasant smell; and over and above these with shortbread, in fine, brown farls, the true New Year's dainty, and great pieces of bun, the Scotch bun, which is something between a plum-pudding and the Pan Giallo of the Romans, a mass of fruit held together by flour and water. Great provision of these delights was in the kitchen, which was all "redd up" and shining for the festival, with Katrin in her best cap, and Beenie in a silk gown and muslin apron, a resplendent figure. A band of "guisards" had accompanied the children, ready to enact some scene of the primitive drama of prehistoric tradition. Lily was hastening down to join this party, in a white dress which she too had put on in honor of the occasion. The kitchen was very noisy, full of these visitors, and nobody but she heard the summons at the big hall-door. Lily hesitated for a moment, her heart giving a bound as loud as the knock—then opened it. And there he stood—the hero and the centre of all!

"And, eh, what a lucky thing to come this night that Miss Lily may have her ploy too! You will just stop and eat your bit dinner with her, Maister Lumsden!" Katrin cried.

"Will it be a ploy for Miss Lily? I would like to be sure of that."

"Eh, nae need to pit it in words," said Katrin: "look at her bonnie e'en; and reason good, seeing that she has never spoken to one of her own kind, and least of all to a young gentleman, since the day ye gaed away."

"I am staying at Tam the shepherd's, on the other side of the moor," said Ronald.

"Losh me! at Tam the shepherd's, for the shootin'?" she asked in a tone of consternation.

"Well," he said, with a laugh, "you can judge, Katrin, for yourself."

"Ay, ay," she said, brightening all over, "I judge for mysel', sir, and I see it's just the auld story. Tam the shepherd's an awfu' haverel, but his wife's an honest woman, and clean," she added, "as far as she kens. But you shall have a good dinner with Miss Lily, I promise you, for once in a way."

Lily only half listened, but she heard all that was said. And her heart danced to see his open look, and the words in which there was no pretence of shooting, or any reason, save the evident one, for his presence there. The excuses were all over; there was to be no more deception. Honestly he came as her lover, endeavoring to throw no dust in the eyes of her humble guardians. If they had been noble guardians, holding her fate in their hands, Lily could not have been more happy. They were not to be deceived. Openness and honesty were to be around her in the house which was her home. What was wanted but this to make her the happiest girl that ever piled shortbread into a child's wallet in honor of Hogmanay, and the New Year which was coming to-morrow? A new year, a new life, a different world! Katrin came up to her with half-affected horror and tender kindness, grasping her arm. "Eh, Miss Lily," she cried, "you'll just ruin the family, and we'll no have a single farl of shortbread left for our ain use; and the morn's the New Year! Ye are giving every thing away. Na, na, we must mind oursel's a wee. No more for you, my wee man. Miss Lily's just ower good to you. Run up the stairs, my bonnie leddy, for Beenie is setting the table, and you'll get your dinner, you and the gentleman, before the guisards begin."

"The gentleman!" Lily felt her countenance flame, as she laughed and turned away. "How kind you are, Katrin," she said, "to provide me with company, too, me that never sees any body."

"Am I no kind," cried Katrin in triumph, "and him for coming just at the right moment? I am awfu' pleased that you have a pairty of your ain to bring in a good New Year."

How strange, how delightful it was to sit down opposite to him at the table, to eat Katrin's excellent dinner, which, though it was almost impromptu, was so good—trout and game, the Highland luxuries, which were, indeed, almost daily bread on the edge of the moor, but not to Ronald, who amid all their happiness was man enough to like his dinner and praise it. "This is how we shall sit at our own table, and laugh at all our little troubles when they are over," he said.

"Oh, Ronald!" said Lily, with a little cloud in the midst of joy. They might be little troubles to him, but not to her, all lonely in the wilderness.

"At all events they will soon be over," he said. His eyes were bright and his tones assured; there was no longer any doubt in his look, which she examined in the moments when he was not looking at her with an anxious criticism. "And tell me about the good folk at the Manse, and kind Miss Eelen and her assistant and successor. Is he to be her assistant, too, as well as her father's? I had a famous letter from the old gentleman about the wine I sent him. And, Lily, I think that with very little trouble I will get him to do all we want as soon as you can make up your mind to it. After all this time we must not have any more delay."

"To do all we want?" she said, looking up at him with surprise. The dinner was over by this time, and they had left the table and were standing by the fire.

"Yes," he said. "What do we want but to belong to each other, Lily? You don't need grand gowns or all the world at your wedding. Oh, yes, I should have liked to see my Lily with all her friends about her, and none so sweet as herself. But since we cannot do that, why should we mind it, when the old minister here can make every thing right in half an hour?"

"Ronald," she said, with a gasp, "you take away my breath!"

"Why," he cried, "is not this what has been in our minds for ever so long? Have you not promised, however poor I was, in whatever straits—"

"Yes, yes, there is no question of that."

"And why, then, should it take away your breath? My bonnie Lily, is it not an old bargain now? We have waited and waited, but nothing has come of waiting. And Providence has put us in a quiet place, with nothing but friends round, and a good old minister, a kind old fellow, who likes a good glass of wine and knows what he's drinking!" He laughed at this as he drew her closer toward him. "Lily, with every thing in our favor, you will not put me off and make a hesitation now?"

Oh, this was not quite the way, not the way she looked for! Yet she drew her breath hard, that breath which fluttered in spite of herself, and put both her hands in his. No, after so long waiting why should she make a hesitation now? And then they went down to the kitchen together, arm in arm, Lily yielding to the delightful consciousness that there was no need for concealment, to see the guisards act their primitive drama, and to bring in the New Year.

Oh, the New Year! which was coming in amid that rustic mirth among those true, kind, humble friends to whom the young pair were as gods in the glory of their love and youth. Lily trembled in her joy: what bride does not? What would it bring to them, that New Year?

CHAPTER XVII

This New Year's Eve remained, amid all the experiences of Lily, a thing apart. It became painful to her to think of it in after times, but in the present it was like a completion and climax of life, still all in the visionary stage, yet so close on the verge of the real that she became herself like an instrument, thrilling to every touch, answering every air that blew, every word that was said, in each and all of which there were meanings hidden of which none was aware but herself. There was the little dinner first, so carefully prepared by Katrin, so tenderly served by Beenie, the two young people sitting on either side of the table as if at their bridal banquet, while the sound of the festivities going on in the kitchen came up by times when the door was opened: a squeak of the fiddle, the sound of the stamping of the guisards as they performed their little archaic drama, adding a franker note of laughter to the keen supreme pleasure that reigned above. Beenie went and came, always bringing with her along with every new dish that little gust of laughter and voices from below, to which she kept open half an ear, while with the other she attended to what her little mistress said.

"You maun come down, Miss Lily, to do them a grace: they a' say they'll no steer till they've seen the young leddy; and they're decent lads just come out to play, as the bairns say in their sang, neither beggars nor yet stravaigers, but lads from the town, to please ye with their bit performance; and I ken a' their mothers!" Beenie cried with a little outburst of affectionate emotion.

When Lily went down accordingly, followed closely by her lover, the little primitive drama was repeated, with more stamping and shouting than ever; and then there was an endless reel, to the sound of the squeaking fiddle, in which Lily danced as long as she could hold out, and Beenie held out, as it seemed, forever, wearing out all the lads.

"Eh! I was a grand dancer in my time," she admitted, when she had breath enough, while the fiddle squeaked on and on.

And then, as was right, Ronald said good-night as the rural band streamed away from the door. The curious group of the guisards, some of them in white shirts outside their garments, some in breastplates of tin, with an iron pot on their heads by way of helmet, "set him home" with much respectful kindness. "But I wuss ye were coming with us to the toun, for Tam the shepherd's is no a howff for a gentleman," they said.

"Any hole will do for me," said Ronald in the exhilaration of the evening; and all the house came out of doors to speed the parting guests. The moon shone mistily over the long stretch of the moor, throwing up a sinister gleam here and there from the deep cuttings, and flinging a veil as of gossamer over the great breadth of the country. The air was fresh, not over-cold, "saft," as Dougal called it, with the suggestion of rain, and the sudden irruption of voices and steps into the supreme and brooding silence made the strangest effect in the middle of the night. Lily stood watching them as they streamed away, Ronald so distinct from them all as they streamed down under the shadow of the bank, to show again, chiefly by reason of their disguises, upon the road a little way down. Lily lingered until a speck of white in the distance was all that was visible. She was wrapped in a plaid which Ronald had put round her, drawing the soft green and checkered folds closely around her face, and as warm physically as she was at heart. Now he was himself; he had flung all prudences and fancies to the wind; he had forgotten Sir Robert and his fortune, and every other common thing that could come between. Lily danced up the spiral staircase with a heart that sang still more than her lips did as she "turned" the tune to which they had been dancing. No one can keep still to whom "Tullochgoram" is sung or played. She danced up the stairs, keeping time faster and faster to the mad melody—the essence unadulterated of reckless fun and drollery.

"Eh, my bonnie leddy!" Beenie cried, who had gone before with the candles; while Katrin stood looking after her, and Dougal locked and bolted the great hall-door. Katrin shook her head a little: she was much experienced. "Eh, if he be but worthy of her!" she sighed.

"It's late, late at nicht, and the New Year well begun," said Robina. "Eh, Miss Lily, you'll never forget this New Year?"

"Why should I forget it?" said Lily. "You had better wait till it is past before you say that. But maybe you are right, after all, for there never was a Hogmanay like this; and to think that the morn will come, and that it will be no more like the other days than this has been! Beenie, did you ever hear that folk might be as feared for joy as for trouble? or is it only me that am so timorsome, and cannot tell which it is going to be?"

"'Deed, and I've heard o' that many's the day. It's just the common way, my bonnie dear. Many a bonnie lassie would fain flee to the ends of the earth the day before her bridal that is just pleased enough when a's said and done. You mustna lose heart."

"I'm not losing heart," said Lily. "The day before my bridal! Is that what it is? I will just be happy to-night and never think of the morn; for when I begin to think, it takes so manythings to be satisfied, and I would like to be satisfied just for once, and take no thought."

Robina had a great deal to do in Lily's room that night. She kept moving to and fro, softly opening and shutting drawers and presses, laying away her mistress's things with a care that was scarcely necessary, and meant only restlessness and excitement and an incapacity to keep still. Long before she had done moving about the half-lighted room Lily was fast asleep, her excitement, though presumably greater, not being enough to keep sleep from the eyes which were dazzled with the sudden gleam of something so new and strange in her life, as well as tired with an unusual vigil. Lily slept as soundly as a child till the clear, somewhat shrill daylight, touched with frost, shone upon her late in the wintry morning and called her up much more effectually than the wavering call of Beenie, who was hanging over her in the morning, as she had been at night, the first to meet her eyes.

"Eh, Miss Lily, what a grand sleep ye have had!" Beenie cried. She had slept but little herself, her head full of the new situation and all the strange things that might be to come. The house in general had a sense of excitement breathing through it, not visible, indeed, in Dougal, who was, as usual, wrestling with the powny outside, but very apparent in Katrin, who went about her morning work with an extremely serious face, as if all the cares of the world were on her shoulders. Robina and she had various stolen moments of communication through the day, indeed, which testified to a degree of confidence between them, and a mutual preoccupation.

"I'm no to say a word to her; but how am I to keep my tongue in my head when Dauvit himself says that when he was musin' the fire burnt!"

"Losh," cried Katrin, "if it was naething but haudin' your tongue! but what I've to think of is mair than that. Eh, I'm doing that for Miss Lily I would do for none of my kin, no, nor Dougal himself; and I wish I was just clean out of it, for I'm no fond of secrets—they are uncanny things."

"Eh, woman! ye wouldna betray them?" Beenie cried.

"Betray them? Am I a person to betray what's trusted to me? But I wish there were nae secrets in this world. It's just aye cheating somebody. Ye canna be straichtforward, do what ye will, when ye've got other folks' secrets to keep, let alone them that are your ain."

"I'm no sae particular," said Beenie, with a little toss of her head, "and there will be no stress upon ye for long. It's just the ae step."

"I have my doubts," said Katrin, shaking her head.

"Ye have your doubts? And what doubts would ye have? It will a' be plain when ance it's done. There are nae mair secrets after that! It's just as I said, the ae step. Eh me, I could have likit it far better in Sir Robert's grand house in George Square, and a' Edinburgh there, and the Principal himself to join their hands thegether, and my bonnie Miss Lily in the white satin, and the auld lady's grand necklace about her bonnie white neck. But we canna have every thing our ain gate. The Manse parlor is just a' that can be desired in the circumstances we're noo in; and when it's done, it will just be done and naething more to say."

But Katrin still shook her head. She was a far-seeing woman. "I'm no just sure we will be out of it sae easy as that," she said.

This talk was not completed at once, but came in on various occasions, a few words here and there, as opportunity secured; and the two women, though both were excited and disturbed, did no doubt enjoy the rôle of conspirator, more or less, and felt that those secret consultations added a zest to life. Beenie, whose lips were sealed in the presence of her mistress, and Katrin, who had to maintain an aspect of absolute calm in the sight of Dougal, could not but feel a consciousness of superiority, which consoled them for much that was uncomfortable. But, indeed, it was exasperatingly easy to deceive Dougal. He suspected nothing; secrets or mysteries had never come his way. Life meant to him his daily work, his daily parritch, the comfort of a crack now and then with his friends, a glass of toddy on an occasion, and the prevailing consciousness of being well done for at all times, with a clean hearthstone, and the parritch and the broth both well boiled and appetizing, more than fell to the lot of ordinary men. If he had known even that Katrin was keeping a secret from him, it is doubtful whether he would have been at all moved. He would have thought it some whigmaleerie of the wife's, and would have remained perfectly easy in his mind, in the conviction that she would tell him if it was anything he had to do with, and if not, wha was minding? Nothing that she did or said roused his curiosity to any great degree. There had need to be something more serious than Dougal to account for the little contraction over Katrin's eyes.

This was, perhaps, more visible, however, after the conversation she had with Mr. Lumsden on the afternoon of New Year's Day. I cannot tell what he said to her, but there was something in it additional to what he had said on the evening before, when he had told her and Beenie what their parts were to be in the little drama for which he had not yet fully prepared the chief actor of all. Lily waited for him at the window with a heart that beat high in her breast on that frosty morning, when all the stretches of the moor were crisp and white, and every little rowan-tree and bush of withered heather shone like something of frosted silver across the gray surface, tinged with a lower tone of whiteness. Lily saw him almost before he had come within the range of mortal vision, so far off that the road itself could not be seen, and only a faint speck that moved was distinguishable in the chill and frozen silence. The speck moved on, disappeared, came out again till it grew into absolute sight and knowledge, near enough to be recognized from the window, and hastily met at the door with a sweep of flying feet and hands outstretched. "My bonnie Lily! the only flower that's not frosted!" he said. The change that had taken place between them was made plain by this: that he came quite openly to the door, and that Lily flew to meet him. There was no longer any occasion for the supposed accident of meetings on the moor. How this change came about Lily did not stop to enquire. It was, and that was enough; and she was too happy in it ever to wonder what could have been said or done underneath to make the lover's appearance now a thing expected, and which it was unnecessary to attempt to conceal.

"It will perhaps be for to-morrow and perhaps for the day after; I am not certain yet," Ronald said.

"What will perhaps be for to-morrow?" Lily cried, with a sudden flush on her cheek.

"We are not going to make any fuss about it, Lily. You promised me you would not desire that. It's very easy to be married in our country. If we were to call Dougal up and Katrin, and say we were man and wife, we would be married just as fast as by all the ministers in the world."

"Ronald!" cried Lily, growing pale.

"I am not suggesting such a thing. Do you think that I would put a scorn on my bonnie Lily with a marriage like that? Not I! What I cannot bear is that you should be stinted of one thing you would like—though, for my part, the less the better, I say, and the most agreeable to me. But no; I am not that kind of man. I like the sanction of the Kirk. I like every thing done decently and in order. That is why I say to-morrow or the next day, for I have not yet seen Mr. Blythe."

"And is it to be so soon as that?" said Lily with awe.

"My darling, what object have we in waiting? The vacation is short enough anyway. We must not lose a day. You promised to be ready at a moment's warning. Well, I'm giving you a day's warning. If every thing had been right, it would have been you to fix the time, and all your fancies consulted. But we're past that, Lily. You know you put yourself into my hands to have it done as soon as was possible."

"Did I?" said Lily, confused; and then she added: "I know. I am not one to make a trouble. It is best to be done when we can—and as soon as we can—and end this dreary life."

"That is what I knew you would say. No certainty, no ground to stand on, and not knowing what might happen at any moment. No, Lily, it is no time for scruples now."

"Still," said Lily, "I would have liked to have heard all your plans and what we are to do. It is fine planning. It is aye a pleasure, even when it comes to nothing. And now, when it must come to something—"

"That's the difference, I suppose, between man and woman," said Ronald, with a laugh. "I have no thought of anything but one thing. I care nothing about plans. You, that are all made up of imagination, you shoot past and begin again. But me, I think only of getting my Lily, of having her for my own. I have neither plots nor plans in my head."

"It is a good thing, then, that women think of them, for we can't do without them," Lily said. But she was soothed and pleased that her bridegroom should have no thought but for herself. Perhaps this was what was most fit for the man. The woman had the outset to think of, the new house to live in, and every thing else that was involved. The reverse thought gives pleasure in other circumstances. There is no consistency in the reasonings of this period of life.

"Let us go out now," said Ronald; "the frost is hard, and it's fine dry walking; we'll get a turn round the moor, and then I will be off to the 'toun' to see the minister, and to-night I'll come back and tell you all about it. Wrap up well, for it's cold, but so bright that it does the heart good. But it is the day itself, and because it is the day, that does the heart most good," he said, once more wrapping Lily up, close round her pretty throat, with the soft, voluminous folds of the plaid. The two faces so close together, the light in her eyes, the contagious happiness in his face, took every shadow from Lily's heart. There had been no shadows, only a faint sort of floating gossamer, which had no meaning, and now it melted all away.

The ramble round the moor filled all the bright noon of the wintry day. It was not possible to wander among the ling bushes, or by the soft, meandering lines of turf. All was crisp with the curling whiteness of the frost, except here and there where a prominent point had been melted and darkened by the sun. They went along the road, which crackled under their feet, with small ice crystals in every fissure. The mountains stood blue in a faint haze that seemed to breathe into the still air, and the moor stretched white, like a piece of crisp embroidery, under the shining of the light. How wintry the air was, and how exhilarating, tightening the nerves and stimulating every force! Toward the north the sky was heavy and spoke of snow, but there were soft breaks of blue and lines of yellow light in the brighter quarter. They walked now quickly as they faced the wind, now slowly as they turned their backs upon it, and, wrapped in their soft plaids, felt the soft glow and warmth mount to their youthful cheeks. I doubt if any summer ramble, in the sweetest air and among the flowers, was more full of pleasure. They talked to each other incessantly, but perhaps not very much that would bear repeating; yet there was a little veiled conflict certainly going on all the time, scarcely conscious, hidden in innocent questions and suggestions, in innocent seeming evasions. Lily wanted to ask so much, but half feared to put a direct question lest it should be an offence, while he wanted to keep every question at arm's-length, but did not dare to do so lest it should excite suspicion. There was an occasional flash of the rapiers, soon covered up in the softest tones and touches, but still they kept their distinct parts: she anxious to see a little beyond, he eager to keep her within the limits of the day. He parried all her thrusts with this pretence: that his thoughts could not stray beyond to-morrow. "Sufficient unto the day is the happiness thereof," he said.

Then they went in and had their mid-day meal together, once more attended by Beenie, with a world of meaning in every glance. "They are just twa bonnie doos crooning on a branch," she said to Katrin, as she came down stairs for another dish. "Doos!" cried Katrin; "they have a very good will to their meat, that's a' that I can say." "They are like twa bonnie squirrels in a wood," cried Beenie, at her next dive into the kitchen, "givin' aye a look the one to the ither." "Squirrels, my certy! but I wouldna like to gether the nits for them a' the year through," said Katrin. But when Beenie came back for the pudding, and declared that "they were like twa bonnie fishes side by side in the burn, the ane mair silvery and golden than the other," Katrin's amazement and ridicule, and the excitement underneath, found vent in a shriek which brought Dougal hurrying in from the barn. "Losh, woman! are ye burnt in the fire, or have ye spilt the boiling pot upon ye, or what have ye done?" "I'll gie you the boiling pot yourself, and a dishclout to pin to your tail, and that will learn ye to ask fule questions!" Katrin said.

CHAPTER XVIII

Ronald walked into Kinloch-Rugas after the plentiful lunch upon which Katrin had made so many remarks. His head was buzzing and his bosom thrilling with the excitement natural at that period of existence. He loved Lily—as well as he was capable of loving—with all the mingled sentiment and passion, the emotions high and low, the very human and half divine, which are involved in that condition of mind. He was a healthy, vigorous, and in no way vicious young man. If he had not the highest ideal, he had not at all the lowered standard of a man whose mind has been debased by evil communications. He was, in his way, a true lover, at the climax of life which is attained by a bridegroom. His thoughts were set to a kind of rhythmic measure of "Lily, Lily," as he walked swiftly and strongly down the long road toward the village. If his mind had been laid bare by a touch of the angel's spear, it would not, I fear, have satisfied Lily, nor any one who loved her, but it sufficiently satisfied himself. He did not want to look beyond the next step, which, he had convinced himself, was the right step to take; what was to follow was, he tried to assure himself, in the providence of God; or, if that was too serious (but Ronald was a serious man, willingly conceding to God the right to influence human affairs), it was open to all the developments, chances even, if you like to say so, of natural events. Who could say what would happen on the morrow? In the meantime a reasonable man's concern was with the events of the day. And though he was not a highly strung person by nature, he was to-day all lyrical, and thrilling with the emotions of a bridegroom. He was not unworthy of the position. His very foot acknowledged that thrill, and struck the ground in measure, as if the iron strings of frost had been those of a harp. The passer-by, plodding along with head down and nose half sheltered from the cutting wind, took that member half out of the folds of his plaid to see what it was that was so bye-ordinary in the man he met. He did not sound like a common man going into the town on common business, nor look like it when the spectator turned to breathe the softer way of the wind for a moment and look after the stranger. Neither did Ronald feel like any one else on that wintry afternoon. He was a bridegroom, and the thrill of it was in all his veins.

It was nearly dark when he came in sight of the lights, chiefly twinkling lights in windows, for there was no gas as yet to illuminate every little place as we have it now. In the Manse, with its larger windows, it was still light enough, and the soft yellow and pink of the frosty evening sky lent color, as well as light, to the calm of the parlor, facing toward the west, where Mr. Blythe sat alone. It was the minister's musing time. Sometimes he had a doze; sometimes he sat by the fire, but with his chair turned to the sunset, and indulged in his own thoughts. These were confessedly, in many cases, his old stories, over which he would go from time to time, with a choke of a laugh in the stillness over this and that: perhaps there were moments in which his musings were more solemn, but of these history bears no record. The Manse parlor had no feature of beauty. It was a very humdrum room; but to the minister it was the abode of comfort and peace. He wanted nothing more than was to be found within its four walls; life was quite bounded to him by these walls, and I think he had no wish for any future that went beyond them: his Scotsman, which lasted him from one day to another, till the next (bi-weekly) number came in; his books, chiefly volumes of old history or Reminiscences, sometimes a Scots (occasionally printed Scott's) novel—but that was a rare treat, and not to be calculated upon; a bout of story-telling now and then with another clerical brother or old elder whose memory stretched back to those cheerful, jovial, legendary days, where all the stories come from: these filled up existence happily enough for the old minister. His work was over, and I fear that perhaps he had never put very much of his heart into that, and he had his daughter to serve him "hand and foot," as the maids said. He did not need even to take the trouble of finding his spectacles (which, like most other people, he was always losing) for himself. "Eelen, where's my specs?" he said, without moving. Such was this old Scotch presbyter and sybarite, and though a paradise of black hair-cloth and mahogany does not much commend itself to us nowadays, I think Mr. Blythe would gladly have compounded for the deprivation of pearly gates and golden streets could he have secured the permanence of this.

He was very glad to see Ronald, notwithstanding that he had become very anxious to get rid of him during his stay at the Manse. A visitor of any kind was a godsend in the middle of winter, and at this time of the year, and especially a visitor from Edinburgh, with news to tell, and perhaps a fresh story or two of the humors of the courts and the jokes of the judges, things that did not get in even to The Scotsman. "And what's a' your news, Mr. Lumsden?" he said eagerly. Ronald, who had had many opportunities of understanding the old minister, had come provided with a scrap or two piquant enough to please him, and what with the jokes, and what with the politics, made a very good impression in the first half-hour of his visit. Then came the turn of more personal things.

"Yon was a fine glass of wine, Mr. Lumsden," said the minister, with a slight smack of his lips.

"I am very glad you liked it, sir; it was chosen by one of my friends who is learned in such matters. I would not trust it to a poor judge like myself."

"Better for you, Mr. Lumsden, better for you at your age not to be too good a judge. Look not upon the wine when it is red, says the prophet, which is just when it's best, many persons think. I am strongly of his opinion when your blood's hot in your veins, like the most of you young lads; but when a man begins to go down the hill, and when he's well exercised in moderation, and to use without abusing, then a grand jorum of wine like yon makes glad the heart, as is to be found in one rather mysterious scripture, of God and man."

"I hoped it would give you a charitable thought of one that was rather a sorner, as I remember you said, upon your hospitality."

"That was never meant, that was never meant," said the minister, waving his large flabby hands. Ronald had risen from his seat and was now standing by the fire, leaning his arm on the mantel-piece. The slow twilight was waning, and though the daffodil sky still shone in the window, the fire had begun to tell, especially in the shadow of the half-lit room.

"You see, sir," said Ronald, with a leap of his heart into his throat, and of the voice which accompanied it, coming forth with sudden energy, "there was more in that than met the eye."

"Ay, do ye say so?" said Mr. Blythe, also with a quickened throb of curiosity in his voice.

"Miss Ramsay and I—had met in Edinburgh," said Ronald, clearing his throat, "we had seen—a great deal of each other. We had, in short—"

"I always said it, I always said it!" said the minister. "I told Eelen the very first night. I've seen much in my day. 'These two are troth-plighted,' I said to my daughter, before ye had been in my house a single night."

"I thought it was vain to attempt deceiving your clever eyes," said Ronald; "I told Lily so; but ladies, you know, are never so sure—they think they can conceal things."

"Thrust their heads into the sand like the ostriches, silly things, and think nobody can see them!" said the minister. "I know them well; that's just what they all do."

"Well, so it was, at least," said Ronald. "You will not, perhaps, wonder now that I stayed as long as I could, outstaying my welcome, I fear, and wearing out even your hospitality; but it was a question of seeing Lily, without exciting any suspicion, in a natural, easy way."

"I will not say much about that last, for it was more than suspicion on my part."

"Ah, but every-body is not like you; neither your experience nor your powers of observation are common," said Ronald. He paused a moment, to let this compliment sink in, and then resumed. "Mr. Blythe, I will admit to you that Sir Robert is not content, and that, in short, Lily was banished here to take her away from me."

"I cannot think it a great banishment to be sent to Dalrugas, which is a fine house in its way, though maybe old-fashioned, and servants to be at her call night and day," said the minister, "but you may easily see it from another point of view. Proceed, proceed," he added, with another wave of his hand.

"Well, sir, I can but repeat: Sir Robert does not think me rich enough for his niece. She is his only kin; he would like her to marry a rich man; he would sacrifice her, my bonnie Lily, to an old man with a yellow face and bags of money."

"Well, well, that's no so unnatural as you think. I would like my Eelen to have a warm down-sitting if I could help her to it, to go no further than myself."

"I understand that, sir; my Lily is worthy of a prince, if there could be a prince that loved her as well as I do. But it is me she has chosen and nobody else, and she is not one to change if she were shut up in Dalrugas Tower all her life."

"Eh, I would not lippen to that," said the minister; "she is but a young thing. Keep you out of the gate, and let her neither hear from you or see you, and her bit heart, at that age, will come round."

"Thank you for the warning, sir," said Ronald, with a laugh that was forced and uncomfortable; "that's what Sir Robert thought, I suppose. But you may believe there is no pleasure to me in thinking so. And besides, it would never happen with Lily, for Lily is true as steel." He paused for a moment, with a little access of feeling. It remained to be seen whether he was true as steel himself, and perhaps he was not quite assured on that point; yet he was capable, so far, of understanding the matter that he was sure of it in Lily, and the conviction expanded his breast with pride and pleasure. He paused with natural sentiment, and partly with the quickening of his breath, to take the full good of that sensation; and then he resumed:

"I am not rich, you will easily understand; we are a lot of sons at home, and my share will not be great. But I have a good profession, and in a few years, so far as I can see, I may be doing with the best. As far as family is concerned, there can be no question between any Ramsay and my name."

The minister waved his hand soothingly over this contention. It was not to be gainsaid, nor was any comparison of races to be attempted. He said: "In that case, my young friend, if it's but a few years to wait and you will be doing so well, and both young, with plenty of time before ye, so far as I can see ye can well afford to wait."

"I might afford to wait, that am kept to my work, and little enough time to think, but Lily, Mr. Blythe. Here is Lily alone in the wilderness, as she says. I'm forbidden to see her, forbidden to write to her."

"Restrictions which ye have broken in both cases."

"Yes," cried Ronald. "How could we let ourselves be separated, how could I leave her to languish alone? I tried as long as I could. I did not write to her. I did not come near her, but flesh and blood could not bear it. And then when I saw how glad she was to see me, and how her bonnie countenance changed—" Here he nearly broke down, his voice trembled, so genuine and true was his feeling. "We cannot do it," he said faintly, "and that's all that's to be said. Mr. Blythe, you are the minister, you have the power in your hands—"

"Eh, man! but I'm only the auld minister nowadays," cried the old gentleman, with a sudden outburst of natural bitterness to which he very seldom gave vent. He was delighted to have nothing to do, but did not love his supplanter any more on that account. "Ye must ask nothing from me; go your ways to my assistant and successor—he is your man."

"I will go to nobody but you!" cried Ronald, with all the fervor of a temptation resisted. "Mr. Blythe, will you marry Lily to me?"

Mr. Blythe made a long pause. "If ye are rightly cried in the kirk, I have no choice but to marry ye," he said.

"But I want it done at once, and very private, without any crying in the kirk."

"That would be very irregular, Mr. Lumsden."

"I know it would, but not so irregular as calling up Beenie and Dougal and Katrin, and saying before them: 'This is my wife.'"

"No," said the minister, "not just so bad as that, but very irregular. Do ye know, young man, I would be subject to censure by the Presbytery, and I canna tell what pains and penalties? And why should I do such a thing, to save you a month or two, or a year or two's waiting, that is nothing, nothing at your age?"

"It is a great deal when people are in our circumstances," cried Ronald. "Lily so lonely, not a creature near her, no pleasure in her life, no certainty about anything: for Sir Robert might hear I had been seen about, and might just sweep her away, abroad, to the ends of the earth. You say she would forget, but she does not want to forget, nor do I, you may be sure, whereas, if you will just do this for us, you will make us both sure of each other forever, and I can never be taken from her, nor she from me."

"Young man," said the minister impressively, "I got my kirk from the Ramsays; they're patrons o' this parish, and I was a young man with little influence. I was tutor to Mr. James, but I had little chance of anything grander than a parish school, where I might have just flourished as a stickit minister all my days, and it was the Ramsays that made me a placed minister, and set me above them a': that was the old laird before Sir Robert's days. But Sir Robert has been very ceevil the times he has been here. He has asked me whiles to my dinner, and other whiles he has sent me just as many grouse and paitricks as I could set my face to. Would it be a just return, think ye, to marry away his bonnie niece to a landless lad as ye confess ye are, with nothing but fees at the best, and not too many of them coming in?"

"Mr. Blythe," cried Ronald, "if it was Mr. James you were tutor to, it is to Mr. James you owe all this, and Mr. James, had he been living, would never have gone against the happiness of his only child!"

"Eh! but who can tell that?" cried the minister. "Little was he thinking of that or of any kind of child. He was a young fellow, maybe as heedless, maybe more than ye are yourself. Na, there was no thought neither of wife nor bairn in his head."

"But," cried Ronald, "you must feel you have a double duty to one that is his child, and his only one, little as he knew of it at the time."

"A double duty: and what is that?" said the minister, shaking his head. "The duty to keep her from any rash step, puir young unfriended thing, or to let her work out her silly will, which, maybe, in a year's time she would rather have put her hand in the fire than have done?"

"You give a bonnie character of me," Ronald said, with a harsh laugh.

"I am giving no character of you. I am thinking nothing of you. I am thinking of the bit lassie. It is her I am bound to protect, both for her father's sake and her own. Most marriages that are made in haste are, as the proverb says, repented of at leisure. She might be heart-grieved at me that helped her to her will to-day when she knows more of life and what it means. Na, na, my young friend, take you your time and wait. Waiting is aye a salutary process. It brings out many a hidden virtue, it consolidates the character, and if you are diligent in your business it brings ye your reward, which ye enjoy more than if you had snatched it before your time."

"I tell you, minister," cried Ronald, "that we cannot wait, that it's a matter of life and death to us, both to Lily and me!"

"What is that you are saying? I am hoping there is no meaning in it, but only words," the old man said sharply in an altered tone.

The room had grown almost quite dark, the daffodil color had all faded away, and the heavy curtain of the coming snow was stretching over the last faint streak of light. The fire was smouldering and added little to the room, which lay in a ruddy dark, warmed rather than lighted up. Ronald stood with his elbow on the mantel-piece close to the old minister, whose face had been suddenly raised toward him with an expression of keen command and alarm. And who can tell what devil had stolen in with the dark to put words of shame into the mouth of the young man who had come down the frosty moorland road like a song of joy and youth? It was rapid as a dart. He stooped down and said something in the old minister's ear.

The shameful lie! the shameful, shameful lie! The temptation, the fall, was so instantaneous that Ronald himself was scarcely conscious of it, or of what he had done in his haste. The old gentleman uttered into the darkness a sort of moan. And then he spoke briefly and sharply, with a keen tone of scorn in his words which stung his companion even through the confusion of the time.

"If that's so, ye're a disgraceful blackguard! but it's not my part to speak. Be here at this house the morn, with her and your witnesses; I insist upon the witnesses, two of them, to sign the lines. I will send Eelen out of the way. Come before it's dark, as ye came to-day; I am always alone at this hour. That's enough, man, I hope. What are you wanting more?"

"I want only to say that you judge me very hastily, Mr. Blythe."

"It's a case in which least said is soonest mended," said the minister. "To-morrow, just before the darkening, and, thank the Lord, there need not be another word said between you and me!"

CHAPTER XIX

Ronald started back on his way to Dalrugas in the beginning of the wintry night in a condition very different from that in which he came. His head was dazed and swimming; something had happened to him; he had taken a step such as he had never contemplated taking, a step which, did Lily ever know or suspect it, would, he knew, open such a gulf between them as nothing could ever bridge over. He was in a hundred minds to turn back, to confess his sin before he had passed the last house in the village. We do not call that a temptation when we are impelled to do right, but it is the same thing, only the temptations to do right are somehow less potent than those to do wrong. He was torn by a strong impulse to go back and remedy what he had done: the temptation to commit that fault had been momentary, but overwhelming; the temptation to go back and confess was continuous, but evidently feeble, for he went straight on through all its tuggings, and did not walk more slowly. But yet it would have done him much good and probably no harm had he done so: the minister would have forgiven a fault so soon repented of; he would probably, in the natural feeling toward a penitent sinner, have acceded to his wishes all the same. These thoughts went through Ronald's head without ever stopping his steady and quick walk into the dark. He repented, if that had been enough, in sackcloth and ashes; he was so deeply ashamed of what he had done that he felt his countenance flame in the darkness where nobody could by any possibility see. But he did not turn back. And presently by repetition the impulse weakened a little, his brain cleared, and the world became steady once again. The thing was done; it could not be undone. There was no possibility that Lily should ever hear of it; nobody would ever know of it but old Blythe and himself, and old Blythe would die. It would be a recollection which, in the depth of the night, in moments of solitude, or when awakened by a sudden touch of the past, would go on stinging him like a serpent all the days of his life, but it would be otherwise innocuous. Lily would never hear of it, that was the great thing; there was no chance that she could ever hear. The old minister's lips were sealed. It would be contrary to every rule of honor if he were to betray what had been said to him. Ronald said to himself that he must accept the stinging of that recollection, which he would never get rid of all his life, as his punishment; but no one else would suffer, Lily least of all.

These feelings were hot and strong in his mind as he set out; but a walk of four miles against a cold wind, and with the snow threatening to come down every moment, is a very good thing for dispersing troublous thoughts: they gradually blew away as he went on, and the bridegroom's state of triumph and rapture came back, dimly at first, and as if he dared not indulge it, but gaining strength every moment, until, before he reached Dalrugas, from the first moment when he saw his love's light in her window shining far over the moor, it came back in full force, driving every thing else away. He saw, first, the little star of light hanging midway between earth and sky, and then the shape of the window, and then Lily's figure or shadow coming from time to time to look out; and no lover's heart could have risen higher or beat more warmly. He entirely forgot how he had wronged her in the glory of having her, of knowing her to be there waiting for him, and that she would be his wife to-morrow. She came to the top of the stairs to meet him, while he rushed up three steps at a time, rubbing against the narrow spiral of the stair with such passion and force of feeling as the best man in the world could not have surpassed. One does not require, it is evident, to be the best man in the world, or even a true man at all, to love truly and fervently, and with all the force of one's being. One might say that it was selfishness on Ronald's part to appropriate at any cost the girl he loved; but the fact remained, a fact far deeper than any explanation, that he did love her as deeply, as warmly, as sincerely as any man could. Their meeting was a moment of joy to both, like a poem, like a song; their hearts beat as high as if it had been a first meeting after years of absence, and yet it would have been less complete had they been parted for more than the two or three hours which was its real period. I need not go any further into this record. It did not matter what they said; words are of little account at such moments. It is only to note that a man who had just told a disgraceful lie, and put upon his bride a stigma of the most false and cruel kind, and whose mind was already shaping thoughts which were destined to work her woe, was at the moment when he met her with the news that their marriage was to take place next day as much, as tenderly in love with her as heart could desire. The problem is one which I have no power to explain.

Next day being still one of the daft days, bright with the reflection of the New Year, and the day of the weekly market in Kinloch-Rugas, Katrin announced early her intention of going in to the toun in the course of the day, an expedition which Beenie, with much modesty and reference to Miss Lily, proposed to share. "I havena been in the toun, no to say in the toun, ither than at the kirk, which is a different thing, since I came to Dalrugas. I'll maybe get ye a fairing, laddie, for the sake of the New Year—"

"If he gangs very canny with the powny, and tak's care of a' our bundles," Katrin said.

"And me, I'm to be left my lane, to keep the hoose," said Dougal, "like Joan Tamson's man."

"Weel," said Katrin, "ye're in there mony a day and me at hame; it would be a funny thing if I couldna gang to the market once at the New Year."

"I'm saying nothing against you and your market. And here's Miss Lily away to her tea at the Manse, and maun have Rory no less to drive her in the geeg with that lad from Edinburgh. I wish there was less of that lad from Edinburgh; he's nae ways agreeable to me."

"Losh, man! it's no you he's running after," cried Katrin, "nor me neither. But he's a fine lad for all that."

"Fine or foul, I would like to see the back of him," said Dougal; and the women in their guilty consciences trembled. They had both been brought to Ronald's side. Both of them had a soft heart for true love, and the fact of stealing a march upon Sir Robert was as pleasant to Katrin as if she had been ten times his housekeeper. The house was full of subdued excitement, hidden words exchanged between the women on the stairs and in dark corners, as if they were conspirators or lovers. "Has he any suspicion, do ye think?" Beenie whispered in Katrin's ear. "Him!" cried Katrin. "If it was put under his nose in black and white, he would bring it to me to spell it out till him." "Eh, but sometimes these simple folks discern a thing when others that are wiser see nothing." "Wha said my man was simple? There's no a simple bit about him; but he knows I'm a woman to be trusted, and he'll no gang a step without Katrin!" It was not, perhaps, a moment when an anxious enquirer could feel this trust justified. "Eh, Katrin," cried Robina, "tell me just what's the worst that could happen to them if it was found out." "The worst is just that he would have to take his bride away, Beenie." "Eh! she would no be minding! That's just what she wants most." "And lose her uncle's siller," Katrin added, with a deeper gravity of tone. "That wouldna trouble her either," said Beenie, shaking her head as over a weakness of her mistress which she could not deny. "But I am feared, feared," said Katrin solemnly, with that repetition which makes an utterance emphatic, "that it would be a sore trouble to him." "Anyway, it's a' settled now, and we'll have to stick to them," said Beenie doubtfully. "Oh, I'll stick to them as long as I can stand," Katrin said with vigor; and this was the last word.

It was clear enough that something was going to take place at the tower of Dalrugas on that Thursday; but this was sufficiently accounted for by the fact that Katrin was going to the market, a thing that did not happen above twice or thrice a year. There were a great many arrangements to make, and the black powny had begun his toilet, and the little cart had been scrubbed and brushed before the sun was well up in the sky to receive the two substantial forms, which, on their side, were arrayed in their best gowns before the early dinner to which they sat down, each with her heart in her mouth in all the excitement of the ripe conspiracy. Only an hour or two now, and the signal would be given, the cord would be pulled, and the great scene would open upon them. "Will you and me ever forget this day, Katrin?" Beenie gasped, unable to control herself. Katrin gave her a push with her shoulder, and took her own place soberly at the board to dispense the dinner as usual. "There's an awfu' fine piece of beef in the pot," she said, "ower good for the like of us; but it'll mind ye, Dougal, of the day ye keepit the house, and I gaed to the toun."

"It's no the first day I've keepit the house, and you been the one to gang to the toun."

"No, maybe, ye've done it four times since you and me were marriet. If ye ever got better broth than thae broth, it's no me that made them. They're that well boiled they just melt in your mouth with goodness, with a piece of meat in them fit for the laird's table. Have ye taken up some of my broth, Beenie, to the young lady and her friend up the stair?"

"You're no taking much of them yourself," said Dougal, "nor Beenie either. Bless the women, your heads are just turned with the grand ploy o' going to the market. Me, I gang to the market and say naething about it, nor ever lose a bite of a bannock on that account. But you're queer creatures, no to be faddomed by man. Are ye going to spend a lot o' siller that ye're in siccan a state? Beenie, now, she'll be wanting a new gown."

"If ye think that I, that am used to a' the grand shops in Edinburgh, would buy a gown at Kinloch-Rugas—"

"Oh, when ye can get nae better, it's aye grand to tak' what ye can get," said Dougal. "As for Katrin, I canna tell what's come over her. Her hand's shaking—"

"My hand's no shakin'!" cried Katrin vehemently. "I'm just as steady as any person. But I've been awfu' busy this mornin' putting every thing in order, and I've very little appetite. I'm no a great eater at any time."

"Nor me," said Beenie, "and I'm tired too. I've just been turning over and over Miss Lily's things."

"Ye had very little to do," said Katrin, resenting the adoption of her own argument. "Miss Lily's things could easy wait. Sup up your broth, and dinna keep us all waiting. Sandy, here's a grand slice for you. It's seldom you've tasted the like of that. And as soon as you're done, laddie, hurry and put in the pony, for we must have a good sight o' the market, Beenie and me, before it gets dark."

Dougal came out to the door to see them off, with his bonnet hanging upon the side of his head by a hair. He felt the presence of something in the atmosphere for which he could not account. What was it? It was some "ploy" among the women, probably not worth a man's trouble to enquire into. And, as soon as they were off, he had Rory to put in, and await the pleasure of "thae twa" upstairs. He could not refuse Lily anything, nor, indeed, had he any right to refuse to Sir Robert's niece the use of Rory, on whom she had already ridden about so often. But the lad from Edinburgh was a trial to Dougal. He had an uneasy feeling that it would not please his master to hear of this visitor, and that a strange man about the house was not to be desired. "If it had but been a lassie," he said, in that case he would have been glad that Miss Lily had some company to amuse her; but a gentleman, and a gentleman too that was a stranger, not even of the same county—a lawyer lad from the Parliament House. He did not willingly trust a long-leggit loon like that to drive Rory. He was mair fit to carry Rory than Rory to carry him. So that Dougal's countenance was entirely overcast.

There had been some snow in the morning, a sprinkling just enough to cover the ground more softly and deeply than the hoar frost, but that was but preliminary—there was a great deal more to come. Dougal stood when the pony was ready, pushing his cap from side to side and staring at the sky. "Ye'll do weel to bide but very short time, Miss Lily," he said; "the tea at the Manse is, maybe, very good, but the snow will be coming down in handfu's before you get hame."

"We shall not stay long, Dougal, I promise you," Lily said. There was a tremble in her voice as there had been in Katrin's and in Robina's. "The women are all clean gyte!" Dougal said to himself. He watched them go away, criticising bitterly the pose of Ronald as he drove. "A man with thae long legs has no mortal need for a pony," he said; "they're just a yard longer than they ought to be. I'm about the figure of a man, or just a thought too tall, for driving a sensitive beast like our Rory. Puir beast, but he has come to base uses," said Dougal. I don't know where he had picked up this phrase, but he was pleased with it, and repeated it, chuckling to himself.

That evening, just before the darkening, when once more the sunset sky was flushed with all kinds of color, and shone in graduated tints of rose pink darkening to crimson, and blue melting into green, through the Manse window, one homely figure after another stole into the Manse parlor. Katrin had brought the minister a dozen of her own fresh eggs, and what could he do less than call her in and say, "How is a' with ye?" at New Year's time, when everybody had a word of good wishes to say? "And this is Robina," he added, with a touch of reserve and severity in his tone. Beenie could not understand how to her, always so regular at the kirk and known for a weel-living woman, the minister should be severe; but it was easy to understand that on such an occasion he had a great deal on his mind. There was a chair at either end of the great sofa that stood against the wall; for in these days furniture was arranged symmetrically, and it was not permitted that anything should be without its proper balance. The two women placed themselves there modestly one at each end; the great arms of the sofa half hid them in the slowly growing twilight. Katrin, who was nearest the door, was blotted out altogether. Beenie, who was at the end nearest the window, showed like a shadow against the light.

And then there was a pause; it was a very solemn pause indeed, like the silence in church. The minister sat in his big chair in the darkest part of the room, with the red glow of a low fire just marking that there was something there, but not a word, not a movement, disturbing the dark. The room after a while seemed to turn round to the two watchers, it was so motionless. When Mr. Blythe drew a long breath, a sort of suppressed scream came from both of them. Was it rather a death than a marriage they had come to witness? They had never seen any living thing so still, and the awe of the old man's presence was overwhelming enough in itself.

"What's the matter with you," he said almost roughly. "Can I not draw my breath in my own house?"

"Oh, sir, I beg your pardon," cried Katrin, thankful to recover her voice. "It was just so awfu' quiet, and we're no used to that. In our bit houses there's nobody but says whatever comes into his head, and we're awfu' steering folk up at Dalrugas Tower."

"Just in the way o' kindness, and giving back an answer when you're spoken to," said Beenie deferentially, in her soft, half-apologetic voice. It was a great comfort to them in the circumstance, which was very unusual and full of responsibility, to hear themselves speak.

"Ye must just try and possess your souls in patience till ye get back again," the minister said out of his dark corner. It was just a grand lesson, both thought, and the kind of thing that the minister ought to say. And the silence fell again with a slow diminution of the light, and gradual fading of the yellow sky. To sit there without moving, without breathing, with always the consciousness of the minister unseen, fixing a penetrating look upon them, which probably showed him, so clever a man, the very recesses of their hearts, became moment by moment more than Katrin or Robina could bear.

"The young fools; I'll throw it all up if they dinna put in an appearance before that clock strikes!" cried Mr. Blythe at last. "Look out of the window, one of you women, and see if ye can see them."

"There's nothing, minister, nothing, but a wheen country carts going from the market," said Beenie in the rôle of Sister Anne.

"The idiots!" said Mr. Blythe again with that force of language peculiar to his country. "Not for their ain purposes, and them all but unlawful, can they keep their time."

"Oh, sir, ye mustna be hard upon them at siccan a moment!" cried Katrin, rocking herself to and fro in anxiety.

"Eh, but I see the powny!" cried Beenie from the window; "there's a wee laddie holding Rory. And will I run and open the door no to disturb Marget in the kitchen?" she said, not waiting for an answer. The spell of the quiet had so gained upon Robina, and the still rising tide of excitement, that she swept almost noiselessly into the narrow hall, and opened the door mysteriously to the two other shadows who stole in, as it seemed, out of the yellow light that filled up the doorway behind into a darkness which, turning from that wistful illumination, seemed complete.

CHAPTER XX

It was all like a dream, a scene without light or sound, shadows moving in the faint twilight, at first not a word said. Beenie remained at the door, holding the handle to guard the entrance. Katrin had risen up too, and stood against the wall, trembling very much, but not betraying it in this faint light. These two were in the light side of the room, the half made visible by the window with its fading sunset glimmer. The other two passed into the darker side and were all but lost to sight. A sudden flicker of the fire caught the color of Lily's dress and revealed her outline for the moment. She had taken off her hat, not knowing why, and the soft beaver with its feather was hanging down by her side in her hand. Katrin made a step forward and relieved her of it, trembling lest some dreadful voice should come to her ears out of the darkness, though not seeing the minister's eyes, which shot upon her a fiery glance. Then he broke that strange haunted silence, in which so many thoughts and passions were hidden, by his voice suddenly rising harsh, sounding as if it were loud: it was not at all loud, it was, indeed, a soft voice on ordinary occasions, only in the circumstances and in the intense quiet it had a strange tone. To Ronald it sounded menacing, to Lily only half alarming, as she knew no reason why it should be less kind than usual; the women were so awe-stricken already that to them it was as the voice of fate. The brief little ceremony was as simple as could be conceived. The troth was not given, as in other rites, by the individuals themselves, but simply said by the old minister's deepening voice, which he was at pains to subdue after the shock of the first words, and assented to by the bride and bridegroom, Lily, to the half horror of the two women, who gripped each other wildly in their excitement at the sound, giving an audible murmur of assent, while Ronald bowed, which was the usual form. "Yon'll be the English way," Katrin whispered to Beenie. "Oh, whisht, whisht!" said the other. And then in the darkness there ensued a few rolling words of prayer, the long vowels solemnly drawn out, the long words following each other slowly and with a certain grandeur of diction in their absolute simplicity, and the formula common to all: "Whom God hath joined together let no man put asunder." And then there was a little stir in the darkness and all was over.

"But there's just this to say to you, young man," came out of the gloom from the old voice, quavering a little with feeling or fatigue: "Forasmuch as ye have been wanting before, so much the more are ye pledged now to be all a man ought to be to this young creature that has trusted herself to you. If ever I hear an ill word of your conduct or your care, and me living, you will have one to answer to that will have it in his power to do you an ill turn, and will not refrain. Mind you this: if I am in the land of the living, and know of any hairm to this poor lassie, I will not refrain; and ye know what I mean, and that I am one that will do what I say."

"If you think I require to be frightened into loving and cherishing my bonnie wife—" said Ronald, confused and alarmed, but attempting to take a high tone.

"Oh, Mr. Blythe!" cried Lily, "how little you know!" She could speak in the dark, where no one could see, though the light would have reduced her to silence and blushes. She put her hand with a pretty gesture within Ronald's arm.

"I, maybe, know more than I'm thought to do," he said gruffly; "light that candle that you'll find on the mantel-piece, and let us get our work done." The candle brought suddenly to light the confused scene, all the party standing except the figure of the minister, large and shapeless in his big chair. And there was a moment of commotion, while one by one they signed the necessary papers, the young pair quickly, the women with a grotesqueness of awe and difficulty which might have transferred the whole scene at once to the regions of the burlesque. Both to Katrin and Robina it was a very solemn business, slowly accomplished with much contortion both of countenance and figure. "Women, can ye not despatch?" Mr. Blythe said sternly. "My daughter may be here any minute, the time of my supposed rest is over, and this sederunt should be over too. Marget will be in from the kitchen with the lamp."

"Oh, Beenie, be quick, quick!" murmured Lily. She had feared to be entreated with the constant hospitality of the Manse to wait until Helen came, and to take tea. It gave her a curious wound to feel that this was not likely to be the case, even though she was most anxious to escape. She was indeed a little frightened for Marget and the lamp, and for Helen and the tea; but it hurt her that the minister who had just made her Ronald's wife should have any hesitation. Feelings are not generally so fine in rural places. A bride is one to be eagerly embraced, not kept out of sight. Though, indeed, she did not want to see Helen or any one, she said almost indignantly to herself.

"And now there are your lines, Mistress Lumsden," the minister said. "Keep them safe and never let them out of your own hands, and I wish ye all that is good. If it's been a hasty step or an unconsidered, it's you that will probably have to bear the wyte of it. I will not deceive you with smooth things; but if there has been error at the beginning—"

"Excuse me," said Ronald in a low fierce voice, "but there is snow in the sky, and it's already dark, and I must take my wife away."

"Don't you interrupt me," said the old minister, "or I will, maybe, say more than I meant to say. If there's been error at the beginning, my poor lassie, take you care to be all the more heedful in time to come. Do nothing ye cannot acknowledge in the face of day. And God bless you and keep you and lift up the light of his countenance upon you," he said, lifting up his arms. The familiar action, the familiar words, subdued all the group in a moment. He had not meant with these words to bless the bride that had been brought before him as poor Lily had been, but it had been drawn from him phrase by phrase.

And then the door opened, and Lily found herself once more outside in the keen air touched with the foretaste of snow which is so distinct in the North. The sky was heavy with it for half the circle from north to south, but in the west was something of that golden radiance still, and a clear blueness above, and one or two stars sparkling through the frost. She lifted her eyes to these with relief, with a feeling of consolation. Was that the light of His countenance that was to shine upon her? But below all things were dark and dreary. To the hurry of excitement which had possessed her before something vexing, troublous, had come in. She had wished, and was eager to hurry away, to escape Helen, but why had she been hurried away, made to perceive that she was not intended to see Helen? It was more fantastic than could be put into words. And Ronald too was in so great a hurry, eager to get her beyond the observation of the people coming from the market, almost to hide her in a sheltered corner, while he himself went to get the pony. "Nobody will see you here," he said. She wished that nobody should see her, but yet an uncalled-for tear came to Lily's eyes as she stood and waited. It looked almost as if it was a path into heaven, the narrow way which was spoken of in the Bible, that strip of golden light with the stars shining above. But it was not to heaven she wanted to go in the joy of her espousals, on her wedding day. She wanted the life that was before her—the human, the natural, the life that other women had; to be taken to the home her husband had made for her, to be free of the bonds of her girlhood and the loneliness of her previous days. But Lily did not know, not even a step of the path before her. It rushed upon her now that he had never said a word, never one definite word. She did not know what was going to happen to-morrow. To-night it was too late, certainly too late, to go further than Dalrugas, but to-morrow! She remembered now suddenly, clearly, that to all her questions and imaginings what they were to do he had never made one distinct reply. He had allowed her to talk and to imagine what was going to be, but he had said not a word. There seemed nothing, nothing clear in all the world but that one golden path leading up into the sky. "Lift up the light of His countenance upon you." That did not mean, Lily thought, half pagan as the youthful thinker so often is, the blessing that is life and joy, but rather that which is consolation and calm. And it was not consolation or calm she wanted, but happiness and delight. She wanted to be able to go out upon the world with her arm in her husband's and her head high, and to shape her new life as other young women did—a separate thing, a new thing, individual to themselves, not any repetition or going back. Standing there in the dark corner, hidden till he could find the pony and take her up secretly out of sight, hurrying away not to be seen by any one—Lily's heart revolted at these precautions, even though it had been to a certain extent her own desire they should be taken. But, oh! it was so different, her own desire! that was only the bridal instinct to hide its shy happiness, its tremor of novelty and wonder. It was not concealment she had wanted, but withdrawal from the gaze of the crowd; but it was concealment that was in Ronald's thought, a thing always shameful, not modest, not maidenly, but an expedient of guilt.

Perhaps Ronald was just a little too long getting the pony; but he was not very long. He had her safely in the little geeg, with all her wraps carefully round her, before fifteen minutes had passed; but fifteen minutes in some circumstances are more than as many hours in others. Lily was very silent at first, and he had hard ado to rouse her from the reflections that had seized upon her. "What are we going to do?" she said out of the heaviness of these reflections, when all that found its way to his lips was the babble of love at its climax. Was it that she loved him less than he loved her? He whispered this in her ear, with one arm holding her close, while Rory made his way vigorously along the road, scenting his stable, and also the snow that was coming. Lily made no answer to the suggestion. Certainly that murmur of love did not seem to satisfy her. She was overcome by it now and then, and sat silent, feeling the pressure of his arm, and the consciousness that there was nobody but him and herself in the world, with the seductive bewilderment of emotion shared and intensified, yet from time to time awoke sharply to feel the force over again of that question: "What are we going to do?" Oh, why had she not insisted on an answer to it before? The night grew darker, the snow began to fall in large flakes. They were more and more isolated from the world which was invisible round them, nothing but Rory tossing his shaggy ears and snorting at the snow that melted into his nostrils. By the time they reached the Tower, discovering vaguely, all at once, the glimmer of the lights and the voice of Dougal calling to the pony to moderate the impatience of his delight at sight of his own stable, they were so covered with snow that it was difficult for Lily to shake herself clear of it as she stumbled down at the great door. "Bide a moment, bide a moment; just take the plaid off her bodily. It's mair snaw than plaiden!" cried Dougal. "Ye little deevil, stand still, will ye? Ye'll get neither bite nor sup till your time comes. Have ye no seen the ithers on the road? Silly taupies to bide so long, and maybe be stormsted in the end!"

"They're on the road, Dougal," cried Lily, with humility, remembering that she had never once thought of Katrin and Beenie. "I am sure they're on the road."

"They had better be that," he said angrily. "What keepit them, I'm asking? Sir, if ye'll be advised by me, ye'll just bid good-by to the young leddy and make your way to Tam's as fast as ye can, for every half-hour will make it waur. It's on for a night and a day, or I have nae knowledge of the weather."

"Half-an-hour can't make much difference, Dougal," said Ronald, with a laugh.

"Oh, can it no? It's easy to see ye ken little of our moor. And the e'en will be as black as midnicht, and the snaw bewildering, so that ye'll just turn round and round about, and likely lie down in a whin bush, and never wake more."

A half shriek came from Lily in the doorway, while Ronald's laugh rang out into the night. "It will be no worse in half-an-hour," he said.

"Ay, will it! There's a wee bit light in the west the noo, but there will be nane then. Heigh! is't you? Weel, that's aye something," Dougal said, as the other little vehicle, with its weight of snow-covered figures, came suddenly into the light; and in the bustle of the second arrival, which was much more complicated than the first, nothing more was said. Katrin and Beenie had shaken off the awe of their conspiracy. They were full of spirits and laughter, and their little cart crowded with parcels of every kind. They had found time to buy half the market, as Dougal said, and they occupied him so completely with their talk, and the bustle of getting them and their cargo safely deposited indoors, that the young couple stole upstairs unnoticed. "Tam may whistle for me to-night," Ronald said, "and Dougal growl till he's tired, and the snow fall as much as it pleases. I'm safe of my shelter, Lily. A friend in court is worth many a year's fee."

"Who is your friend in court?" she said, shivering a little. The cold and the agitation had been a little too much for Lily. Her teeth chattered, the light swam in her eyes.

It was Katrin who was the Providence of the young people. She it was who ordained peremptorily, not letting Dougal say a word, that to send Mr. Lumsden off to Tam's cottage on such a night was such a thing as had never been heard of.

"I wouldna turn out a dog," she cried, "to find its way, poor beast, across the moor."

"I warned the lad," said Dougal; "I tell'd him every half-hour would make it waur. It is his ain fault if he is late. What have you and me to do harboring a' the young callants in the country, or out of it, that may come here after Miss Lily? You've just got some nonsense about true love in your head."

"Am I the person," said Katrin, "to have true love cast in my face, me that have been married upon you, Dougal, these thirty year? Na, na! I'm no that kind of woman; but I have peety in my heart, and there's a dozen empty rooms in this house. I think it's just a shame when I think of the poor bodies that are about, maybe sleepin' out on the cauld moor. I'll not take the life of this young lad, turning him away, and neither shall you, my man, if you want to have any comfort in your ain life."

"I warned him," said Dougal; "if he didna take my warning, it's his ain wyte."

"It shanna be mine nor yours either," said Katrin, and, indeed, even Dougal, when he looked out, perceived that there was nothing to be said. The snow had fallen so continuously since their arrival that already every trace, either of wheels or hoofs, was filled up. The whiteness lay unbroken in the court-yard and up to the very door, as if no one had come near the house for days. Sandy was in the stable with his lantern, hissing over the little black pony as he rubbed him down; but even Sandy's steps to the stable were wiped out by the snow-storm. It covered every thing, fair things and foul, and, above all, every trace of a path or road.

"I'm no easy in my mind about what Sir Robert would say," he muttered, pushing his cap to his other ear.

"And what would Sir Robert say? If it had been a lad on the tramp, a gangrel person or selling prins about the road, he would never have grudged him a bed, or at the worst a pickle straw in the stable, on such a night. And this is a young gentleman of the family of the Lumsdens of Pontalloch, kent folk, and as much thought of as any person. Is't a pickle straw the laird would have offered to a gentleman's son like that? He's just biding here till the storm's over, if it was a week or a fortnicht, and I'll answer for it to the laird!" Katrin cried.

Dougal looked at her in consternation. "A week or a fortnight! It's no decent for the young leddy," he said.

"It's just a grand chance for the young lady—company to pass the time till her, and her all her lane. If he will bide—but maybe he will not bide," said Katrin, with a sigh. Katrin, too, was a little anxious, as Lily was, for what to-morrow would bring forth. She had but taken the bull by the horns, in Dougal's person, saying the worst that could be said. "But it's my hope, Beenie," she said afterward, with an anxious countenance, "that he'll just take his bonnie wife away to his ain house as soon as the snaw's awa'."

"Oh, ay! ye needna have any doubt of that," said Beenie, with a broad smile of content.

"Then you'll just take off your grand gown and serve them with their dinner. I have naething but the birds to put to the fire, and that will take little time; and if they never had a good dinner before nor after, they shall have one that any prince might eat, between you and me, Robina, poor things, on their wedding night."

CHAPTER XXI

The snow-storm lasted for about a week, day after day, with an occasional interval, with winds that drifted it, and dreadful nights of frost that made it shrink, but covered it over with sparkling crystals, and with occasional movements of a more genial temperature, that touched the surface only to make it freeze again more fiercely when that relenting was over. The whole landscape was turned to whiteness, and the moor, with all its irregular lines, rounded as if a heavy white blanket had been laid over the hummocks of the ling and the hollows and deep cuttings. The hills were white, too, but showing great seams and crevasses of darkness, from which all the magical color had been taken by the absence of light. Black and white was what every thing was reduced to, like the winter Alps, with a gray sky overhead still heavy with inexhaustible snow. This snow-storm was "a special providence" to the inhabitants of Dalrugas—at least to most of them. Dougal grumbled, and suggested various ways in which it might be possible for the lad from Edinburgh to get away. He might walk two miles north, to a village on the main road, where the coach was bound to pass every lawful day, whether it snowed or whether it blew; or he might get the geeg from the inn at Kinloch-Rugas to carry him south, and strike the route of another coach also bound to travel on every lawful day. But Dougal talked to the air, and nobody gave him heed: not to say that the gentleman from Edinburgh found means to conciliate him by degrees, and that, at last, a crack with Mr. Lumsden became a great relief to Dougal from the unmitigated chatter of the womankind by which he was surrounded night and day.

This week of snow flew as if on wings. They were shut off from all intrusion, and even from every invading question, by the impossibility of overstepping that barrier which nature had placed around them; they lived as in a dream, which circumstances had thus made possible without any strain of nature. Nobody could turn a stranger out into the snow, not Sir Robert himself. Had he been there, however little he liked his visitor, he would have been compelled to keep him in his house, and treat him like a favored guest. Not even an enemy's dog could have been turned out into the snow. It made every thing legitimate, every thing simple and natural. I don't know that Lily required this thought to support her, for, indeed, she was not at that time aware that any secret was made of the marriage, that it was concealed from any one in the house, even Dougal, or that Helen Blythe at the Manse, for instance, had not been made aware of it by that time. She had never clearly entered into the question why Helen Blythe had not been present, why the ceremony had been performed in the darkening, and so much mystery had surrounded it, except by the natural reason that no observation which could be avoided should be drawn upon the bride, and that, indeed, all possibility of vulgar remark should be guarded against. The question, what was to be done next? had filled Lily's mind on that day; but the snow had silenced it and covered it over like the ling bushes and the burn, which no longer made its usual trill of running remark, but was also hushed and bound by the new conditions which modified all the life of this portion of the earth. The moor and all its surroundings hung between heaven and earth in a great silence during this period. The gray sky hung low, so that it seemed as if an unwary wayfarer, if he went far enough against that heavy horizon, might strike against it, blinded as he must have been by the whirling flakes that danced and fluttered down, sometimes quickening in pace like the variations of a swift strathspey, sometimes falling large and deliberate like those dilated flakes of fire that fell on the burning sands in the Inferno. There were no images, however different in sentiment, that might not have been applied to that constant falling. It was snow, always snow, and yet there was in it all the variety of poetry when you looked at it, so to speak, from within, looking through it upon an empty world in which no other life or variety seemed to be left.

Sometimes, however, the pair sallied forth, notwithstanding the snow, to breathe the crisp and frosty air, and to feel with delight the great atmosphere and outdoor world around them instead of four walls. Lily wore a great camlet cloak, rough, but a protection against both wet and chill, with a large silver clasp under her chin, and her head and shoulders warmly hooded and wrapped in her plaid of the Ramsay color, which she wore as fair Ramsays did in Allan Ramsay's verse. Lily's eyes sparkled under the tartan screen, and not to risk the chilling of a hand which it would have been necessary to put forth to clasp his arm, Ronald in his big coat walked with his arm round her, to steady her on the snow; for every path was obliterated, and they never knew when they might not stumble over a stifled burn or among the heathery hillocks of the moor. These walks were not long, but they were delightful in the stillness and loneliness, the white flakes clothing them all over in another coat, lighting upon Lily's hair and Ronald's beard, getting into their eyes, half blinding them with the sudden moisture, and the laughter that followed. I will not attempt to give any account of the talk with which they beguiled both these devious rambles and the long companionship indoors in the warm room from which they looked out with so much comfort on the white and solitary world. It harmonized and made every thing legitimate, that lucky snow. One could not ask: "What shall we do to-morrow?" in the sight of the absolute impossibility of doing anything. It was not the bridegroom but Nature herself who had arranged this honeymoon. If it would but last! But then it was in the nature of things that it could not last.

The frost began to break up a little on the eighth day, or rather it was not the frost that broke up, but the sky that cleared. In the evening instead of the heavy gray there came a break which the sky looked through, and in it a star or two, which somehow changed altogether the aspect of affairs. That evening, as she stood looking out at the break so welcome to every-body, but which she was not so sure of welcoming as other people were, Lily felt the question again stir, like a bird in its nest, in the hushed happiness of her heart. In the morning, when she looked out upon a world that had again become light, with blue overhead, and a faint promise of sun, and no snow falling, it came back more strongly, this time like a secret ache. The women and Dougal and Sandy and even the ponies were full of delight in the end of the storm. "What a bonnie morning!" they shouted to each other, waking Lily from her sleep. A bonnie morning! There was color again on the hills and color in the sky. The distance was no longer shut out, as by a door, by the heavy firmament: it was remote, it was full of air, it led away into the world, into worlds unseen. As Lily gazed a golden ray came out of it and struck along the snow in a fine line. Oh, it was bonnie! as they called to each other in the yard, as Rory snorted in his stable, and all the chickens cackled, gathering about Katrin's feet. The snow was over! The storm was over! In a little while the whiteness would disappear and the moor would be green again. "What are we going to do?" All nature seemed to ask the question.

"I wish," said Ronald, "those fowls would cease their rejoicings about the end of the snow. I wish the snow could have lasted another fortnight, Lily; though perhaps I should not say that, for I could not have taken advantage of it. I should need to have invented some means of getting away."

"Because you were tired of it, Ronald?" she said, with a smile; but the smile was not so bright as it had been. It was not Lily's snow-smile, all light and radiance; it was one into which the question had come, a little wistful, a little anxious. Ronald saw, and his heart grieved at the change.

"That's the likely reason!" he said, with a laugh; "but, oh, Lily, my bonnie love, here is the Parliament House all astir again, the judges sitting, and all the work begun."

"Well," she said, that smile of hers shooting out a pure beam of fire upon him, "I am ready, Ronald, I am ready, too."

"Ready to speed the parting husband, and to wish me good luck?" he said with a faint quiver in his voice. He was not a coward by nature, but Ronald this time was afraid. He had not forgotten the question: "What are we going to do?" which had been expressed in every line of Lily's face, in every tone of her voice, before the evening of the marriage. He knew it had come again, but he did not know how he was to meet it. He plunged into the inevitable conflict with his heart in his mouth.

"To speed the parting— Are you going, Ronald, are you thinking of going, without me?"

"My dearest," he said, spreading out his hands in deprecation, "it's like rending me asunder; it is like tearing my heart out of my bosom."

"I am not asking you what it is like!" cried Lily. "What I am asking is your meaning. Were you thinking of going without me?"

"Lily, Lily!" he said, "don't be so dreadfully hard upon me! What am I to do? I know nothing else that I can do."

"Oh, if it's only that," she said, "I can tell you, and very easy, what to do. You will just take me down to Kinloch-Rugas, or to that other place where the coach stops, and wrap me well in my camlet cloak and in my tartan plaid, and I'll not feel the cold, not so much as you will, for women's blood is warm, and when we get to Edinburgh we will take the topmost story of a house, and make it as warm as a nest, and get the first sunshine and the bonnie view away to Fife and the north. And Beenie will follow us with my things and her own; but we'll just be all alone for the first day or two, and I will make you your dinner with my own hands," said Lily, holding up those useful implements with a look of triumph, which was, alas! too bright, which was like the sun when a storm is coming: brilliant with alarm and a sense of something very different to come.

"They don't look very fit for it, those bits of white hands," he said, eager, if possible, by any means to divert her from the more important question, and he took her hands in his and kissed them; but Lily was not to be diverted in this way.

"You may think what you like of how they look, but they are just a very useful pair of hands, and can cook you a Scots collop or a chicken or fish in sauce as well as any person. I know what I have undertaken, and if you think I will break down, you are mistaken, Ronald Lumsden, in me."

"I am not mistaken in you, Lily. I know there is nothing you could not do if you were to try; but am I to be the one to make a drudge of my Lily—I that would like her to eat of the fat and drink of the sweet, as the ministers say, and have no trouble all her days?"

"It depends upon what you call trouble," said Lily, still holding up her flag. "Trouble I suppose we shall have, sooner or later, or we'll be more than mortal; but to serve you your dinner is what I would like to do. You'll go out to the Parliament House and work to get the siller, for it must be allowed that between us we have not much of the siller, and you cannot buy either collops or chuckies without it, nor scarcely even a haddie or a herring out of the sea. But that's the man's share. And then I will buy it and clean it, and put it on in the pot, and you will eat of your wife's cooking and your heart will be glad. Do you think I want to go back to George Square, or a fine house in one of the new Crescents, and sit with my hands before me? Not me, not me!"

"My bonnie Lily," he cried, "it's a bonnie dream, and like yourself, and if you only cooked a crust, it would be better than all the grand French kickshaws in the world or the English puddings to me."

"You need not be so humble, sir," said Lily; "I will cook no crust. It will be savory meat, such as thy soul loveth; though I'll not cheat you as that designing woman Rebekah did."

"My bonnie Lily, you'll always do more for me, and better for me, than I deserve," he cried. "Is that the postman for the first time coming up the road from the town?"

They went to the window to look out at this remarkable phenomenon, and there he kept her, pointing out already the break of the snow upon the side of the moor, revealing the little current of the burn, and something of the edge of the road, along which, wonderful sight! that solitary figure was making its way. "But it will not be passable, I think, till to-morrow for any wheeled thing, so we will make ourselves happy for another day," Ronald said; and this was all the answer he gave her. He was very full of caresses, of fond speeches, and lover's talk all day. He scarcely left an opening for anything more serious. If Lily began again with her question, he always found some way of stopping her mouth. Perhaps she was not unwilling, in a natural shrinking from conflict, to have her mouth stopped. But there rose between them an uneasy sense of something to be explained, something to be unravelled, a desire on one side which was to encounter on the other resistance not to be overcome.

Ronald went out to Dougal after dinner and stood by him while he suppered the pony. "I think the roads will be clear to-morrow, Dougal," he said.

"I wouldna wonder," said Dougal. His opinion was that the lad from Edinburgh would just sorn on there forever eating Sir Robert's good meat and would never more go away.

"Which do you think would be best? to lend me Rory and the little cart to take me in to Kinloch-Rugas, or to send for the geeg from the inn to catch the coach on the South Road at Inverlochers?"

"I could scarcely gie an opinion," said Dougal. "A stoot gentleman o' your age might maybe just as easy walk."

When Dougal said "a stoot gentleman" he did not mean to imply that Ronald was corpulent, but that he was a strong fellow and wanted no pony to take him four miles.

"That's true enough," said Ronald; "but there's my portmanteau, which is rather heavy to carry."

"As grand as you—" Dougal began, but then he stopped and reflected that he was, so to speak, on his own doorstep (in the absence of Sir Robert), and that it was a betrayal of all the traditions of hospitality to be rude to a guest, especially to one who was about to take himself away. "Weel," he added quickly, with a push to his bonnet, "I canna spare you Rory—the young leddy might be wanting a ride; but Sandy and the black powny will take in the bit box if ye're sure that you've made up your mind—at last."

"I dare say you thought I was never going to do that," Ronald said, with a laugh.

And then Dougal melted too. "Oh," he said, "I just thought you knew when you were in good quarters," in a more friendly voice.

"And did not you think I was a sensible fellow," said the amiable guest, "to lie warm and feed well instead of fighting two or three days, or maybe more, through the snow? But now the courts are opened, and the judges sitting, and every-body waiting for me. I would much rather bide where I am, but I must go."

"If it's for your ain interest," said Dougal; "and I wudna wonder but ye're a wee tired of seeing naebody and doing naething, no even a gun on your shoulder. I'll bid the laddie be ready, I'll say, at sax of the clock."

"Six o'clock!" said Ronald in dismay; "the coach does not leave till ten."

"Weel, I'll say aicht if you like. You should be down in good time. Whiles there are a heap of passengers, and mair especial after a storm like this, that has shut up a' the roads."

"I shall be very much obliged to you, Dougal. I have been obliged to you all the time. I will explain the circumstances to Sir Robert if he is in Edinburgh in the spring, and I will tell him that Katrin and you have been more than kind."

"'Deed, and if I were you," said Dougal, "I would just keep a calm sough and say naething to Sir Robert. He might wonder how ye got here; he would maybe no think that our young leddy— I'm wanting no certificate frae any strange gentleman," said Dougal, "and least said is soonest mended. There are folk that canna bide to hear their ain house spoke of by a stranger, nor friends collecting about it that might maybe no just be approved. No, no, haud you your tongue and keep your ain counsel; and so far as things have gaen, you'll hear nae more about it frae Katrin or me."

Ronald was confounded by this speech. "So far as things have gaen." Had this rough fellow any idea how far they had gone? Had his wife told him what happened in the Manse parlor? Had his suspicions penetrated the whole story? But Dougal turned back to the pony with a preference so unaffected, and whistled "Charlie is my darling" with so distinct an intention of dismissing his interlocutor, that Ronald could not imagine him to see in the least into the millstone of this involved affair. Dougal was much more occupied with his own affairs than either those of Lily or those so very little known to him of the strange gentleman who had kept Lily company during the daft days, the saturnalia of the year. He proceeded with his work, pausing sometimes to swing his arms and smite his breast for cold, clanking out and in through the warm atmosphere of the stable to the wildly cold and sharp air outside, absorbed more than was at all necessary in the meal and the toilet of Rory, and taking no further heed of the guest.

CHAPTER XXII

"At last," said Ronald, coming upstairs with his light-springing foot three steps at a time, "at last, Lily, I have settled with Dougal, and I am starting to-morrow morning: at eight, he says, but nine will do. And this for a little while, my darling, will be my last night in the nest."

The room had undergone a wonderful change since it had first been Lily's bower. It had changed much while she was there alone, but the change was much greater within the last week than all that had happened before. It had become a home: there were two chairs by the fire, there was an indefinable consciousness in every thing of two minds, two people, the union and conjunction which make society. It was all warm, social, breathing of life, no suggestion in it of loneliness or longing, or unsatisfied thought, or the solitude which breathes a chill through every comfort. Lily, sitting alone, had been, it was very clear, left but for a moment. This sentiment cannot, indeed, expand stone walls, yet the once dull and chilly drawing-room, with its deep small windows, seemed to possess a widened circle, a fuller atmosphere. Into this already had there pushed a care or two, the reflection of the diversities of two minds as well as their union? If so, it only helped to widen the sphere still further, to make it more representative of the world. Lily looked up from the book she had taken up in her husband's absence with a change of countenance and sudden exclamation.

"You are going to-morrow? Not we?" she cried.

"My bonnie Lily, you were always reasonable—how could it be we? I'm thankful, though, that you meant it to be we, for it was not a happy thought that my own lassie, my wife of a week old, was pushing me away, back with the first loosening of the frosts, into the world."

"You never thought that, you never could have thought that!" cried Lily, divided between indignation and a tumult of new feeling that rose in her. And then she covered her face with her hands. "Are you going to leave me here, Ronald, my lane, my lane?" she cried, with a tone of anguish in her voice.

He was behind her, drawing her head upon his shoulder, soothing her in every way he knew. "Oh, Lily, my darling, don't say I have beguiled you! What could it be else, what could it be? I might have held out by myself and kept away. I might have sworn I would never go near you, for your sweet sake. Would you rather I had done that, Lily? Is it not better to belong to each other, my darling, at any cost, so as to be ready in a moment to take advantage of a bright day when it comes?"

"Of a bright day when it comes?" she said, suddenly taking her hands from her face. A chill as if of the ice outside came upon Lily. She was as white as the snow, and cold, and trembled. "Is that all—is that all that is between you and me, Ronald?" she cried.

"Now, Lily, my dearest, how can you ask such a question? Is that all? Nothing is all! There are no bounds to what is between you and me; but because we have to be parted for a time that was not a reason for always keeping apart, was it, Lily? I thought, my darling, you agreed with me there. We have had a happy honeymoon as ever any pair had, happier, I think, than ever any blessed man but me. And now I must go out to the bleak world to work for my bonnie wife. Oh, it will be a bleak world no longer; it will all be bright with the thought that it is for my bonnie Lily. And you will just wait and keep your heart in a kist of gold, and lock it with a silver key."

"Ah, that was what she says she should have done before—" cried Lily with a sharp ring of pain in her voice. Then she subdued herself and looked up into his face. "I am ready to share whatever you have, Ronald. I want no luxuries, no grand house. I want no time to get ready. I'll be up before you to-morrow and my little things in a bundle and ready to follow you, if it was in a baggage-wagon or at the plough's tail!"

"I almost wish it was that," he said, eager for any diversion. "If I had been a ploughman lad, coming over the hills to Nannie O; with a little cot to take her to as soon as she could be my own!" These were echoes of the songs Lily had sung to him, and he to her, in their hermitage when shut in by the snow.

"But just up under the roof in a high house in the old town, or one of the new ones out to the west of Princes Street—that new row, with a nice clean stair and a door to it to shut it in: to me that would be as good as any little cot upon the ploughed fields." Lily spoke eagerly, turning round to him with hands involuntarily clasped.

"A strange place," he said, "for Sir Robert Ramsay's heir."

"Oh, what am I caring for Sir Robert Ramsay! If he was ill and wanted me, I would be at his call night and day—he is my uncle, whatever happens; but because he is rich and can leave me a fortune! that is nothing, Ronald, to you and me."

He made no immediate reply, but smoothed the little curls of her hair upon her forehead, which was at once an easier and a much more pleasant thing to do.

"Besides," she said, "I have known plenty of kent folk, as good as you or me, who lived, and just liked it very well, up a common stair."

"I would not like my Lily, coming out of George Square, to set up in life like that."

"Would you like your Lily," she cried again, turning upon him with glowing cheeks, "to sit alone and pingle at her seam and eat her heart away, even at George Square, where she might see you whiles, or, worse still, here at Dalrugas," she said, springing from her seat with energy, "to be smoored in the snow?"

He followed her round to the window, and stood holding her in his arm and looking at her admiringly. "You will never be smoored in the snow, my Lily! The fire in you is enough to melt it into rivers all about."

"Rivers that will carry me—where?" she cried in a tone half of laughter, half of despair.

"Listen to me, my darling," he said. "We will be practical: there is always the poetry to fall back upon. For one thing, I've no house, even if it were up a common stair or in the highest house of the old town, to take you to. Houses, as you know as well as me, can only be got at the term. There is no chance now till Whit-Sunday of finding one. We must just be patient, Lily; we can do no more. It is not you, my darling, that will suffer the most. Think of me in all the old places that will mind me of you at every moment, and seeing all the folk that know you, and even hearing your name—"

"Oh," cried Lily, and then suddenly she fell a-crying, leaning on her husband, "I would like to hear your name now and then just to give me heart, and to see the folk that know you, and the old places—"

"My bonnie Lily!" he cried.

Perhaps this outburst did her good. She cried for a long time, and all the evening an occasional sob interrupted her voice, like the lingering passion of a child. But Lily, like a child, had to yield to that voice of the practical, the voice of reason. She said no more at least, but sadly assisted at the packing of the portmanteau, which had been brought across the snow somehow from the cottage in which Ronald had found refuge before the storm and all its privileges began.

"I am not going with him," she said to Robina, when these doleful preparations were over. "You see, there are no preparations made, and you cannot get a house between the terms. You might have minded me of that, Beenie. What is the use of being a person of experience if you cannot tell folk that are apt to forget?"

"I ought to have minded, my bonnie dear," said Beenie with penitence.

"And it's a long time till Whit-Sunday; but we'll need to have patience," Lily said.

"So we will, my darling bairn," Beenie replied.

"You say that very cut and dry. You are not surprised; you look as if you had known it all the time."

"Eh, Miss Lily, my dear, how could I help but ken? Here's a young gentleman that has little siller, and no the mate that Sir Robert would choose."

"I wish," cried Lily, "that Sir Robert was at the bottom of the sea! No, no, I'm wishing him no harm, but, oh, if he only had nothing to do with me!"

"The only thing ye canna do in this world is to change your blood and kin," said Beenie; "but, oh, Miss Lily, ye must just be real reasonable and think. If he were to take you away, it would spoil a'. He has gotten you for his ain, and you have gotten him for your ain, and nothing can come between you two. But he hasna the siller to give ye such a down-sitting as you should have, and nae house at all possible at this time of the year. No, I'm no way surprised. I just knew that was how it had to be, and Katrin too. It would be just flyin' in the face of Providence, she says, to take ye away off to Edinburgh, without a place for the sole of your foot, when ye have a' your uncle's good house at your disposition, and good living and folk about you that tak' a great interest in you. Katrin herself she canna bide the thought of losing her bonnie leddy. 'If Miss Lily goes, I'll just take my fit in my hand and go away after her,' she says. But what for should ye go? It will be far more comfortable here."

"Comfortable!" said Lily in high disdain, "and parted from my husband!" The word was not familiar to her lips, and it brought a flush of color over her face.

"Oh, whisht, my bonnie leddy," Beenie cried.

"Why should I whisht? for it is true. I might not have said it before, but I will say it now, for where he is I ought to be, and whatever he has I ought to share, and what do I care for Dougal's birds and Katrin's fine cooking when my Ronald (that has aye a fine appetite for his dinner," cried Lily in a parenthesis, with a flash of her girlish humor) "is away?" The last words were said in a drooping tone. Her mood changed like the changing skies. Even now she had irruptions of laughter into the midst of her trouble, which was not yet trouble, indeed, so long as he was still not absolutely gone; and who could tell what might happen before morning, the chill morning of the parting day?

Lily was up and astir early on that terrible morning. There had been a hope in her mind that Providence would re-tighten the bonds of the frost and bring the snow blinding and suffocating to stop all possibility of travel; but, alas! that was not the case: bands of faint blue diversified the yellow grayness of the clouds, and the early sun gave a bewildering glint over the moor, making the snow garment shrink a little more and show its rents and crevasses. Every thing was cheerfully astir in the yard, the black pony rearing as Sandy backed him into the shafts of the cart, snorting and shaking his head for joy at thought of the outing, and the sniff of the fresh, exhilarating air into which, as yet, there had come little of the limpness of the thaw. There was an air out of doors partly of pleasure in the excitement of the departure, or at least in the little commotion about something which is an agreeable break in the monotony of all rural solitudes. Dougal looked on and criticised with his hands in his pockets and gave Sandy directions as if this were the first time the boy had ever touched the pony which had been his charge for more than a year; and Katrin, too, stood at the door watching all these preparations, though the air was cold as January air could be. Upstairs there was a very different scene. Lily had tried to insist upon driving to the town to see her husband off, a proposal which was crushed by both Ronald and Robina with horror. "Expose yoursel' to the whole countryside!" Beenie cried.

"Expose myself! and me his wife! Who should see him off if not his wife?" said Lily. And then Ronald came behind her and drew her against his breast once more.

"My bonnie Lily! We need not yet flourish that before the world. You are as safe here as a bird in its nest. Why should we set everybody talking about you and me? Sir Robert will hear soon enough and there is no need to send him word. There's nobody to penetrate our secret and publish it if you will be patient a little till better things can be."

"Our secret!" said Lily, springing from his hold with a great cry.

"A secret that is well shared by those that care for my Lily; but we need not flourish it before the world." Lily's color rose from pale to red, then faded. She stood apart from him, her countenance changing; her pride was deeply wounded that she should be supposed to be desirous of flourishing anything before the world. It was an injury to her and a scorn, though this was no moment to resent it, and the sharp impression only mingled with the anguish of parting a sense of being wronged and misjudged, which was very hard to bear. "I may come down to the door, I suppose," she said, in a voice from which she tried to banish every tone of offence.

"No, my darling," he said, "not even to the door. I could not say farewell to my Lily with strangers looking on. I will like to think when I am gone of every thing round you here, all the old chairs and tables even, where my Lily and I have had our honeymoon." Oh, there was nothing to complain of in the warmth of his farewell. No man could have loved his young wife better, or have held her close to him with deeper feeling. "I will soon be back, I will soon be back!" he cried. His eyes were wet like hers. It was as great a thing for him to tear himself away as it was for her to remain behind and see him go. But then Lily could only stand trembling and weeping at the head of the stairs, that nobody might see, and catch a distorted glimpse through the window over the door of the cart, into which he got with Sandy, while Dougal still murmured that "a stoot gentleman would have done better to walk," and to see him hold out his hand to sulky Dougal, and to Katrin, who had her apron at her eyes, and Beenie, who was sobbing freely! They could stand there and cry, but she might not go down stairs lest she should flourish her story before the world. And why should she not, after all, flourish it before the world? Is a marriage a thing to be hid? When the little cart drove away, the pony, very fresh after his long confinement, executing many gambols, Lily went back to her window, from which she could see them disappear under the high bank, coming out again lower down. The deep road was so filled up with snow that the moment of disappearance was a very short one, and then she could trace for a long time along the road the little dark object growing less and less, till it disappeared altogether. The pony's gambols, which, though he was too far off to be distinctly visible, still showed in the meandering of his progress and sudden changes of pace, the head of one figure showing over the other, the gradual obliteration in the gray of distance, kept all her faculties occupied. It seemed hours, though it was but a very little time, when Lily let her head droop on the arm of the old-fashioned sofa and abandoned herself to the long-gathering, long-restrained torrent and passion of tears.

It was a heavy, dreary day. When you begin life very early in the morning, it ought to be for something good, for some natural festivity or holiday, in the light of which the morning goes brightening on to some climax, be it a happy arrival for which the moments are counted or a birthday party. But to begin with a parting and live the livelong day after it, every hour more mournful and more weary, is a melancholy thing. This used to be very common in the old days, when travelling was slower, and night trains not invented, and night coaches not much thought of. It added a great deal to the miseries of a farewell: in the evening there is but little time before the people who are left behind; they have an excuse for shutting themselves up, going to bed, most likely, if they are young, sleeping before they know, with to-morrow always a new day before them. But Lily had to live it all out, not excused by Beenie or her other faithful retainers a single hour or a single meal. They brought her her dinner just as though he had not shared it with her yesterday, and pressed her to eat, and made a grievance of the small amount she swallowed. "What is the use," Katrin said majestically, "of taking all this trouble when Miss Lily turns her back upon it and will not eat a morsel?" "Oh, try a wee bit, Miss Lily," Beenie cried, adding in her ear, with a coaxing kindness that was insupportable: "Do you think he would relish the cauld snack he'll be getting on the road if he thought his bonnie leddy was not touching bite or sup?"

"Go away, or you will drive me daft!" said Lily. "He will just clear the board of every thing that's on it and never think of me. Why should he, with such a fine appetite as he has? Do I want him to starve for me?" she cried, with a laugh. But the result was another fit of tears. In short, Lily was as silly as any girl could be on the day her lover left her. She was not even as she had been for a moment, and was bound to be again, a young wife astonished and disappointed at being left behind, not knowing how to account for this strange, new authority over her which had it in its power to change the whole current of her life. She had never looked at Ronald in that light or thought of him as a power over her, a judge, a law-giver, whose decisions were to be supreme. She was astonished to find herself subdued before him now, her own convictions put aside; but this was not the channel in which for the moment her thoughts were running. She was weeping for her lover, for the happiness that was over, for him who was away, and dreaming dreams to herself of how the coach might be stopped by the snow, or some accident happen that would still bring him back. She imagined to herself his step on the stair and the shriek of joy with which she would rush to welcome him. This was the subject of her thoughts, broken into occasionally by divergences to other points, by outbursts of astonishment, of disappointment, almost of resentment, but always returning as to the background and foundation of every thing. The other thoughts lay in waiting for her, biding their time. It was the dreadful loss, the blank, the void, the silence, that afflicted her now. Ronald gone, who for this week, which had been as years, as a whole life, her life, the real and true one, to which all the rest was only a preface and preliminary, had been her companion, almost herself! It was of this that her heart was full. Without him, what was Lily now? She had been often a weary, angry, dull, disappointed little girl before, but there were always breaks in which she felt herself, as she said, her own woman and was herself all the Lily there was. But now she had merged into another being; she was Lily no longer, but only a broken-off half of something different, something more important, all throbbing with enlarged and bigger life. This consciousness was enough for the girl to master during that endless, dreary, monotonous day.

CHAPTER XXIII

The next day after anything, whether happiness or disaster, is different from the day on which the event took place. The secondary comes in to complicate and confuse the original question more or less, and the abstract ends under that compulsion. Nothing is exactly as it seems, nor, indeed, as it is; it takes a color from the next morning, however opaque that morning may be. This was especially the case with Lily, whom so many of these secondary thoughts had already visited, and who had now to go back from the dream of that eight days in which every thing had been put to flight by that extraordinary invasion of the new and unrealized which comes to every girl with her marriage, and amid which it is so difficult to keep the footing of ordinary life. She was that morning, however, not any longer the parted lover, the mourning bride, but again, more or less, "her own woman," the creature, full of energy and life, and thoughts and purposes of her own, who had not blindly loved or worshipped, but to whom, at all times, it had been apparent that Ronald's way of loving, though it was to her the only way, was not the way she would have chosen or which she would have adopted herself had she been the man. A very different man Lily would have made, much less prudent, no doubt, but how decisive in the beginning of that youthful career! how determined to have no secrets, but every thing as open as the day! to involve the woman beloved in no devious paths, but to preserve her name and her honor above all dictates of worldly wisdom! Lily would have had her lover vindicate her at once from her uncle's tyranny. She would have had him provide the humble home for which she longed, without even suffering his lady to bear the ignominy of that banishment to the moor. And now! with what a flame of youthful love and hope Lily would have had him carry off his bride, snapping his fingers with a Highland shout at all the powers of evil, who would have had no chance to touch them in their honest love and honorable union. Oh, if she had been the man! Oh, if she could have showed him what to do!

And all these thoughts, intensified and increased, came back to Lily the day after her husband left her. She was not drooping and longing now for her departed lover. Her energies, her clear sense of what should have been, her objection to all that was, came back upon her like a flood. She sat no longer at the window gazing out upon the expanse of snow, which shrank more and more, and showed greater and blacker crevasses in its wide expanse every hour, but walked up and down the room, pausing now and then to poke the fire with energy, though the glowing peats were not adapted to that treatment, and flew in tiny morsels about, requiring Beenie's swift and careful ministrations. Lily felt, however, for one thing, that her position was far better now for expounding her views than it had ever been. A girl cannot press upon her lover the necessity of action. She has to wait for him to take the first step, to urge it upon her, however strongly she may feel the pressure of circumstances, the inexpediency of delay. But now she could plead her own cause, she could make her own claim of right, her statement of what she thought best. She said to herself that she had never yet tried this way. She had been compelled to wait for him to do it, but perhaps it was no wrong thing in him, perhaps it was only exaggerated tenderness for her, desire to save her from privations, or what he thought privations, that had prevented any bolder action, and made him think first of all of saving her from any discomfort. It was possible to think that, and it was very possible to show him now that she cared for no discomfort, that her only desire was to be with him, that it was far, far better for Lily to meet the gaze of the world in her own little house, however small it might be, than hide in the solitude as if there was something about her that should be concealed. This thought made Lily's countenance blaze like the glowing peat. Something about her that should be concealed! a secret hidden away in the heart of the moor, in the midst of the snow, which he, going away from her, would keep silent about, silent as if it were a shame! Lily threw herself into the chair beside her writing-table with impetuosity, feeling that not a moment should be lost in putting this impossible case before him and making her claims. She was no fair Rosamond, but his wife. A thing to be concealed? Oh, no, no! She would rather die.

In any case she would have written him a long letter, seizing the first possible moment of communicating with him, carrying out the first instinct of her heart to continue the long love-interview which had made this week the centre of all her days. But Lily threw even more than this into her letter. She said more, naturally, than she intended to say, and brought forth a hundred arguments, each more eloquent, more urgent than the other, to show cause why she should join him immediately, why she should not be left, nobody knowing anything about her, in this Highland hermitage. The lines poured from her pen; she was herself so moved by her own pleas that she got up once or twice and walked about to dissipate the impulse which she had to set out at once, to walk if it were needful to Edinburgh, to claim her proper place. And it was not till the long, glowing, fervent letter was written that she paused a little and asked herself if Ronald had really only left her behind because it was impossible to get a house between the terms, if his first business was to look out for a house, so as to have it ready for her by the next term, by Whit-Sunday, was it right to argue with him and upbraid him as if he intended the separation to go on forever? Lily threw down her pen which she had dipped in fire—not the fire of anger, but of love just sharpened and pointed with a little indignation—and her countenance fell. No, if that were so, she must not address him in this heroic way. After all it was quite reasonable what he had said: it was extremely difficult to get a house between the terms. And perhaps he would not have been justified in engaging one at Michaelmas, before anything was decided what to do. He could not have done that; and what, then, could he do but wait till Whit-Sunday? and, for a man like him, with his own ways of action, not, unfortunately, though she loved him, like Lily's, it was perhaps natural that there should be no premature disclosure, that as they were parted by circumstances it should remain so, without taking the world into their confidence, or summoning Sir Robert to cast his niece who had deceived him out of the shelter which her husband did not think unbecoming for her now. Lily threw down her pen, making a splash of ink upon the table—not a large one, to spoil it, but a mark, which would always remind her of what she had done or had been about to do.

And then there fell a pause upon her spirit, and tears were the only relief for her. To take the heroic way, to walk to Edinburgh through the snow, or even to think of doing so, to pour forth an eloquent appeal against the cruel fate of her isolation and concealment as if it were to last forever, was an easier method than to wait patiently until Whit-Sunday and make the best of every thing, which would really be the wise thing; for what could Ronald do more than that which he could of course begin to do as soon as he arrived, to look for a house? And how could it have been expected of him when every thing was so vague, and he did not know what might happen, to have provided one, months in advance, on the mere chance that he could persuade her into that strange marriage, and the minister into doing it? It would be strange and embarrassing after that scene to see the minister again, and Lily fell a-wondering how Ronald had persuaded him, what he had said. Mr. Blythe was not a very amiable man, ready to do what was asked of him. He made objections about most things and hated trouble. But Ronald could persuade any body; he could wile a bird from the tree. And what a grand quality that was for an advocate! and how proud she would be hereafter to go to the court and hear him make his grand speeches. Perhaps now he would talk over some man that wanted to get rid of his house, and make him see that it would be better to do it now than to wait for the term. There was, indeed, nothing that Ronald could not persuade a man into if he tried. Lily felt that her own periods were more fiery, those eloquent sentences which her good sense had already condemned, but Ronald's arguments were beyond reply, there was no getting the better of them. You might not be sure that they were always sound, you might feel that there was a flaw somewhere; but to find out what it was, or to get your answer properly formed, or to convict him of error was more than any one, certainly more than Lily, could do.

She had risen up, and was stretching her arms above her head in that natural protest against the languor and solitude which take the form of weariness, when she saw a dark speck approaching on the road, and rushed to the window with the wild hope, which she knew was quite vain, that it might by some possibility be Ronald coming back. But it was only a rural geeg from Kinloch-Rugas or some other hamlet, or one of the farms in the neighborhood, creeping up the road against the wind and the slippery, thawing snow, with a woman in it beside the driver undistinguishable in her wraps. While Lily looked out and wondered if by any chance it might be a visitor, Beenie came in with a look of importance. "Eh, Miss Lily, do you see who that is?" Robina said.

"It is a woman, that is all I know, and keen upon her business to come out on such a day."

"Her business?" said Robina. "It's the Manse geeg, and it's Miss Eelen in it, and as far as I can tell she has nae business, but just to spy out, if she can, the nakedness of the land."

"There is no nakedness in the land, and nothing to spy out!" cried Lily, with a flush. "Have we done anything to be ashamed of that we should be feared of a neighbor's eye?"

"Bless me, no, Miss Lily!" cried Robina; but she added: "Eh, my bonnie bairn, there's many a thing that's no expedient, though it's no wrong. I wouldna just say anything to Miss Eelen if I was you. She's maybe no to be trusted with a story. The minister had sent her out o' the road yon evening in the Manse. Baith me and Katrin remarked it, for she's his right hand and he can do nothing without her in a common way, but yon time she just didna appear."

"Did he think I was not good enough—" Lily began in a flutter, but stopped immediately. "What a silly creature I am! as if there could be anything in that. Do you think I have such a long tongue that I want to go and publish to every-body every thing that happens?"

"Oh, Miss Lily, no me! never such a thought was in my head; but it would be real natural, and you no a person to speak to except Katrin and me, that are servants baith, though we would go through fire and water for you. But you see she wasna there, and if I were you, Miss Lily—"

"You happen not to be me," cried Lily, with eyes blazing, glad of an opportunity to shed upon Beenie something of the vague irritation in her heart, "and since we are speaking of that, what do you mean, both Katrin and you, that were both present, in calling me Miss Lily, Miss Lily, as if I were a small thing in the nursery, when you know I am a married woman?" Lily cried, throwing back her head.

"Oh, Miss Lily!" cried Robina, with a suppressed shriek, running to the door. She looked out with a little alarm, and then came back apologetically. "You never ken who may be about. That Dougal man might have been passing, though he has nothing ado up the stair."

"And what if he had been passing?" Lily said in high disdain.

"Oh, Miss Lily!" cried Robina, again giving the girl a troubled look.

"Do you mean to say that Dougal does not know? Do you mean he thinks—that man that is my servant, that lives in the house— Oh, what can he think?" cried Lily, clasping her hands together in the vehemence of her horror and shame.

"He just thinks nothing at a'. He's no a man to trouble any body with what he thinks. He's keepit very weel in order, and if he daured to fash his head with what he has nae business with! He just guesses you twa are troth-plighted lovers, Miss Lily, and glad he was to get our young maister away."

Lily covered her face with her hands. "Am I a secret, then, a secret!" she cried. "Something that's hidden, just a lie, no true woman! How dared you let me do it, then—you that have been with me all my days? Why did ye not step in and say: 'Lily, Lily, it's all deceiving. It's a secret, something to be hidden!' Would I ever have bound myself to a secret, to be a man's wife and never to say it? Oh, Beenie, I thought you cared, that you were fond of me, and me not a creature to tell me what I was doing! No mother, no friend, nobody but you."

"Miss Lily, Miss Lily, we thought it was for the best. Oh, we thought it was for the best, both Katrin and me! For God's sake dinna make an exhibition before Miss Eelen! Here she is, coming up the stair. For peety's sake, Miss Lily, for a' body's sake, if ye have ainy consideration—"

"Go away from me, you ill woman!" cried Lily, stamping her foot on the ground. She stood in the middle of the room, wild and flushed and indignant, while Beenie disappeared into the bedchamber within. Helen Blythe, coming up a little breathless from the spiral staircase, paused with astonishment to see her friend's excited aspect, and the sounds of tempest in the air.

"Dear me! have I come in at a wrong time?" Helen said.

"Oh, no," cried Lily, with a laugh of fierce emotion, "at the very best time, just to bring me back to myself. I've been having a quarrel with Beenie just for a little diversion. We've been at it hammer and tongs, calling each other all the bonnie names—or perhaps it was me that called her all the names. How do you think we could live out here in the quiet and the snow if we did not have a quarrel sometimes to keep up our hearts?"

"Lily, you are a strange lassie," said Helen, sitting down by the fire and loosening her cloak. "You just say whatever comes into your head. Poor Beenie! how could you have the heart to call her names? She is just given up to ye, my dear, body and soul."

"She is no better than a cheat and a deceiver!" cried Lily. "She makes folk believe that she does what I tell her, and never opposes me, when she just sets herself against her mistress to do every thing I hate and nothing I like, as if she were a black enemy and ill-wisher instead of a friend!"

This speech was delivered with great fervor, and emphasized by the sound of a sob from the inner room.

"Poor Beenie!" cried Helen with mingled amusement and concern, "how is she to take all that from you, Lily? But you do not mean it in your heart?"

"No, I don't mean a word of it," cried Lily, "and it's just an old goose she is if she thinks I do! But for all that she is the most exasperating woman! I never saw any body like her to be faithful as all the twelve apostles, and yet make you dance for rage half the time."

A faint "Oh, Miss Lily!" was heard from the inner room, and then a door was softly opened and shut, and it was evident that Beenie had slipped away.

"I heard ye were down at the Manse one day that I was away. It's seldom, seldom I am from home, and at that hour above all. But I had to see some new folk at the Mill, and it was a good thing I went, for there has not been an open day since then. And I heard ye had a visitor with you, Lily."

Lily's heart seemed to stand still, but she made a great effort and mastered herself. "Yes," she said, "it was Mr. Lumsden [many married persons call their husbands Mr. So-and-So] that had come in quite suddenly with the guisards on the last night of the year."

"I understand," said Helen, with a smile; "he wanted—and I cannot blame him—to be your first foot."

The first person who comes into a house in the New Year is called the first foot in Scotland, and there are rules of good luck and bad dependent upon who that is.

"It might be so," said Lily dreamily, "and I think he was, if that was what he wanted; but the kitchen was full of dancing and singing, the guisards making a great noise, as it was Hogmanay night."

"That was to be expected," said Helen, "and I am glad you had a man, and a young man, and a weel-wisher, or I am sore mistaken, for your first foot. It brings luck to the New Year."

A "weel-wisher" means a lover in Scotland, just as in Italy a girl will say, Mi vuol bene, when she means to say that some one loves her.

"He was here after, twice or thrice, and he wanted to thank the minister for all his kindness, and as I was at the market with Beenie and Katrin, and he had offered to drive the pony, I went too. I thought I would have seen you, but you were not there."

"Oh, how sorry I was, Lily! but a sight of the market would aye be something. It's not like your grand ploys in Edinburgh, but it's diverting too."

"Oh, yes," said Lily, with great gravity, "it is diverting too."

"And you had need of something to divert you. What have you been doing, my bonnie wee lady, all this dreadful storm? I hope at least they have kept you warm. It is a dreadful thing a winter in the country when you are not used to it. But now the snow is over and the roads open: you and me must take a little comfort in each other, Lily. I'm too old for you, and not so cheery as I might be."

Lily, suddenly looking at her visitor, saw that Helen's mild eyes were full of tears, and with one of her sudden impulsive movements, flung herself down on her knees at her friend's feet. "Oh, why are you not cheery, Helen? you that do every thing you should do, and are so good."

"Oh, I'm far, far from good! It's little you know!" said Helen. "My heart just turns from all the good folk, whiles out of a yearning I take for those that are the other way."

"You have some trouble, Helen, some real trouble!" cried Lily with a tone of compassion. "Will you tell me what it is?"

"Maybe another time, maybe another time," said Helen, "for my heart's too full to-day, and I can hear your poor Robina, that you have been so cruel to, coming up the stair, the kind creature, with a cup of tea."

CHAPTER XXIV

Helen stayed till the first shade of the darkening stole over the moor, and till the minister's man had told all the "clash" of the countryside to Katrin and Dougal, and received but a very limited stock of information in return. There was, indeed, much more danger to the secret which now dominated and filled the house of Dalrugas like an actual personage from that chatter in the kitchen than from anything that could have taken place upstairs. For the minister's man was dimly aware that the young lady from Dalrugas had been in the village on that day when something mysterious was believed to have taken place in the Manse parlor; that she had been seen with a gentleman, and that Katrin and Robina had also been visible at the Manse. "Ay, was I," said Katrin; "I just took the minister a dizzen of my eggs. In this awfu' weather nobody has an egg but me. I just warm them up and pepper them up till they've nae idea whether it's summer or winter, and we lay regular a' the year round. I never grudge twa-three new-laid eggs to a delicate person, and the minister, poor gentleman, is no that strong, I'm feared."

"He's just as strong as a horse," said the minister's man, "and takes his dinner as if he followed the ploo, but new-laid eggs are nae doubt aye acceptable. The gentleman was from here that was paying him yon veesit twa days after the New Year?"

"We have nae gentleman here," said Katrin, stolid as her own cleanly scrubbed table, on which she rested her hand. Dougal cocked his bonnet over his right ear, but gave no further sign. "There's been a gentleman, a friend of Sir Robert's, at Tam Robison's and we had to give him a bed a nicht or twa on account of the snaw. Now I think o't, he was a friend o' the minister's too. It's maybe him you're meaning? but he's back in Edinburgh as far as I ken, these twa-three—"

"Weel, it would be him, or some other person," said the minister's man with an affectation of indifference; but he returned to the subject again and again, endeavoring, if he had been strong enough for the rôle, or if he had been confronted by a weak enough adversary, to surprise her into some avowal; but Katrin was too strong for him. It was with difficulty she could be got to understand what he meant. "Oh, it's aye yon same gentleman you're havering about! Eh, what would I ken about a strange gentleman? The minister is no my maister nor yet Dougal's. He might get a visit from Auld Nick himself and it would be naething to him or me."

"It might be much to me," said the minister's man, who was known for a "bletherin' idiot" all over the parish. "It's just a secret, and a secret is aye worth siller."

"Well, I wish ye may get it," Katrin said. During this time she was, to tell the truth, more or less anxious about the demeanor of her husband. It was true that Dougal knew nothing unless what he might have found out for himself, putting two and two together. Katrin had great confidence in the slowness of his intellect and his incapacity to put together two and two. Perhaps her trust was too great in this incapacity, and too little in the dogged loyalty with which Dougal respected his own roof-tree and all that sheltered under it. At least the fact is certain that the authorized gossip of the parish carried very little with him to compensate him for the cold drive and all the miseries of the way.

Lily took out her letter and went over it again when Helen had gone. She found it far too eloquent, too argumentative, too full of a foregone conclusion. Why should she assume that Ronald did not mean to provide a home for her, that there was any reason to believe in an intention on his part of keeping their marriage a secret and their lives apart? All his behavior during the past week had been against this. How could there have been a more devoted lover, a husband more adoring? She asked herself what there was in him to justify such fears, and answered herself: Nothing, nothing! not a shadow upon his love or delight in her presence, the happiness of being with her, for which he had sacrificed every thing else. He might have spent that New Year amid all the mirth and holiday of his kind: in the merry crowd at home, or in Edinburgh, where he need never have spent an hour alone; and he had preferred to be shut up all alone with her on the edge of a snowy wintry moor. Did that look as if he loved her little, as if he made small account of her happiness? Oh, no, no! It was she who was so full of doubts and fears, who had so little trust, who must surely love him less than he loved her, or such suggestions would never have found a place in her heart. If she already felt this in the evening, how much more did she feel it next morning, when the post brought her a little note all full of love, and the sweet sorrow of farewell, which Ronald had slipped into the post in the first halting-place beyond Dalrugas?

It was written in pencil, it was but three lines, but after she received it Lily indignantly snatched her letter from the blotting-book and flung it into the fire, which was too good an end for such a cruel production. Was it possible that she had questioned the love of him who wrote to her like that? Was it possible that she, so adored, so longed for, should doubt in her heart whether he did not mean to conceal her like a guilty thing? Far from her be such unkind, disloyal thoughts. Ronald had gone off into the world, as it is the man's right and privilege and his duty to do, to provide a nest for his mate. If she were left solitary for a moment, that was inevitable: it was but the natural pause till he should have prepared for her, as every husband did. Instead of the indignation, the resentment, the bitter doubt she had felt, nothing but compunction was now in Lily's mind. It was not he but she who was to blame. She was the unfaithful one, the weak and wavering soul who could never hold steadily to her faith, but doubted the absent as soon as his back was turned, and was worthy of nothing except to undergo the fate which her feeble affection feared. She was, perhaps, a little high-flown in the revulsion of her feelings, as in the fervor of these feelings themselves. A little less might have been expected from Ronald, a little charity extended to him in his short-coming; and certainly the vehemence and enthusiasm of her faith in him now was a little excessive. "Yes, it is better you should call me Miss Lily," she said to Robina; "it is best just to keep it to ourselves for a while. Mr. Lumsden thought of all that, though he left it entirely to me, without a word said. There would be so many questions asked, even Dougal and Helen Blythe. I would have had to summer and winter it, and her not very quick at the uptake. It is a long time till Whit-Sunday," said Lily, with a little quiver of her lip. "I will just be Miss Ramsay tlll then."

"Eh, you will aye be Miss Lily to me, whatever!" Beenie cried.

"And I am just Miss Lily," said her mistress, with a little air of dignity which was new to the girl. It was as if a princess had consented to that humiliation, sweetly, with a grace of self-abnegation which made it an honor the more.

It cannot be denied, however, that it was difficult, after all the agitations that had passed, after the supreme excitement of the New Year, and the short, yet wonderful, union of their life together, to fall back upon that solitude, and endeavor, once more, to "take an interest" in the chickens and the ponies, and the humors of Sandy and Dougal, which Lily, in the beginning, had succeeded in occupying herself with to some extent. She did what she could now to rouse her own faculties, to fill her mind with harmless details of the practical life. How comforting it would have been had she but been compelled to plan and contrive like Katrin for all those practical necessities—how to feed her family, how to make the most of her provisions, how to diet her cows and her hens; or like Dougal to care for the comfort of the beasts, and amuse himself with Rory's temper, and the remarks that little snorting critic made upon things in general; or even to look over the "napery" and see if it wanted any fine darning, as Beenie did, and to regulate the buttons and strings of the garments and darning of the stockings. Then Lily might have done something, trying hard to make volunteer work into duty, and consequently into occupation and pleasure. But, Beenie being there, she had no need to do what would have simply thrown Beenie, instead of herself, out of work; and this was still more completely the case with Katrin, who, gladly as she would have contributed to the amusement in any way of her little mistress, would have resented, as well as been much astonished by, any interference with her own occupations. Lily could not do much more than pretend to be busy, whatever she did. She knitted socks for Ronald; beguiled by Beenie, she began with a little enthusiasm the manufacture into household necessaries of a bale of linen found by Katrin among the stores of the establishment, but stopped soon with shame, asking herself what right she had to take Sir Robert's goods for that "plenishing" of abundant linen which is dear to every Scotch housewife's heart. This was a scruple which the women could not share. "Wha should have it if no you?" cried Katrin. "Sir Robert he has just presses overflowing with as nice napery as you would wish to see. There is plenty to set up a hoose already, besides what's wanted, and never be missed, let alone that except yourself, my bonnie Miss Lily, there is nae person to use thae fine sheets. But the auld leddy's web that she had woven at the weaver's and never lived to make it up—wha should have it, I should like to know, but you?"

"Not while my uncle is the master, Katrin."

"I've nothing to say against Sir Robert," cried Katrin—"he's our maister, it's true, and no an ill maister, just gude enough as maisters go—but the auld leddy was just your ain grandmother, Miss Lily, and your plenishing would come out of her hands in the course of nature, and for wha but you would she have given all that yarn (that she span herself, most likely) to be made into a bonnie web o' linen? There is not a word to be said, as Robina will tell ye as weel as me. It's just a law afore a' the laws that a woman has her daughter's plenishing to look to as soon as the bairn is born, and her bairn's bairn with a' the stronger reason, the only one that is left in the auld house."

"Eh, Miss Lily, that's just as sure as death," Beenie said.

But Lily was not to be convinced. She flung the great web of linen, in its glossy and slippery whiteness, at the two anxious figures standing by her, involving them both in its folds. "Take it yourselves, then," she said, with a laugh. "I am an honest lass in one way, if not in another. I will have none of grandmamma's linen that belongs to Sir Robert and not to me."

And then Lily snatched her plaid from the wardrobe and wrapped it round her, and ran out from all their exclamations and struggles for a ramble on the moor. Oh, the moor was cold these February days, the frost was gone and every thing was running wet with moisture, the turf between the ling bushes yielding like bog beneath the foot, the long, withered stalks of the heather flinging off showers of water at every touch, the black cuttings gleaming, the burn running fast and full. Lily began a devious course between the hummocks, leaping from one spot to another, as she had done with Ronald, saturating herself with the chilly freshness, as well as with the actual moisture, of the moor; but this was an amusement which soon palled upon the girl alone. She felt the exercise fatigue her. And the contrast between her solitude and the hand so ready and so eager to help her was more than she could bear. It was because they had to cling to each other so, because the mutual help was so sweet, that they had loved it. Lily was reluctantly obliged to confess that it was no fun alone, and though it was a relief to walk even a little on the road, that was but a faint alleviation of the monotony of life. Sometimes the aspect of the mountains stole her from herself, or a sudden pageant of sunset, or something of a darker drama going on, if she had but any interpretation of it, among those hills. Anything going on, if it were but the gathering of the mist and the scent of the coming storm, was a relief to Lily. It was the long blank, not a passenger on the road, not an event in the day, which she could not bear.

And then even if the walk, by dint of a sunset or some other occurrence, had been enlivening, there was always the shock of coming back, the shutting of her door against every invasion of life, the quiet that might have been comfort to her old grandmother, the old leddy who had spun the yarn for that web of linen, and received it home with triumph—was it for the plenishing of Lily unborn? Lily came to have a little horror of that old leddy. She figured her to herself spinning, spinning, the little whirr of the wheel in its monotony going on for day after day. Lily did not think of the sons away in the world—Robert wherever there was fighting; her own father always in trouble—that filled the old leddy's thoughts, which were spun into that yarn, and might have made many a pattern of mystic meaning in the cold snowy linen which looked so meaningless. She used to sit in the silent room, feeling that from some corner the old leddy's eye was fixed upon her over the whirring wheel, till she could bear it no more.

She went down to Kinloch-Rugas to return Helen's visit, but that was not a happy experience. The old minister, half seen in the gloaming, seated like a large shadow by the fire, gave her always a thrill of alarm. She had hoped that he would not have treated her as a secret, that he would have addressed her by her new name, and set her at once in a true position. But he did not do this. He looked at her not unkindly, and spoke to her with a compassionate tone in his voice. But he too seemed to accept the necessity which had been forced on her by a kind of unspoken command, a dilemma from which she could not escape. In that case the consciousness of being in the presence of a man who knew all, but made no sign, sitting there by the side of innocent Helen, who knew nothing, and who treated herself in all simplicity as the girl-Lily, the same as she had known before, was intolerable; and Lily did not go back again, much as the refuge of some other house to go to was wanted in her desolate state. "You'll come and see me, Helen?" "That will I, my dear. You must not mind my father. He is kind, kind in his heart, and always a soft place for you." "I am not thinking that he is unkind," said Lily. Ah, no, the minister was not unkind! He was sorry for the young abandoned wife; for, as he thought, the young betrayed woman; and Lily, though she was not aware of this last aggravation, yet resented it, feeling the pity in his tone. And why should any one pity her, or venture to be sorry for her, and she, with no secret in her own honest intention, Ronald Lumsden's lawful wife?

As the days lengthened it was possible to be out of doors more, and Lily began to scour the country upon Rory, and to see, though in the doubly cold aspect of this formidable northern spring, many places about in which, in more genial weather, when "the families" were at home, there might be friends to be made. She had come home tired from one of these rides, and the day having been dry, had ventured a little on the moor, holding up her riding-skirt, and looking toward the western hills, where a great sunset was about to be accomplished and all the unseen spectators were hastily putting on garments of gold and rose-color and robes of purple for the ceremony. It was not like a mere bit of limited sky, but a world of color, one hue of glory surging up after another as from some great treasury in the depths below, changing, combining, deepening, melting away in every kind of magical circle. Lily's heart was not very light, but it rose instinctively to that wonderful display of nature. Oh, how beautiful it was! Oh, if there had only been some one to whom to say that it was beautiful! Whether it was the glorious color half blinding her with excessive radiance, or the thought of the unshared spectacle, Lily's eyes filled full of tears. Either cause was enough. At Lily's age, and in such circumstances as hers, the tears are not slow to come.

And then in a moment she felt a touch upon her waist and a voice in her ear. "Was it ever like this before, my Lily, my Lily? or has it all lighted up for you and me, and because I am back again?"

There is one compensation for those who suffer from great anxiety, from the misery of separation, from longing after things that seem unattainable. In a moment, in the twinkling of an eye, a flood of blessedness comes over them in the momentary attainment, the momentary meeting, the instantaneous relief. It was like a warm tide that flooded the heart of Lily, sweeping every fancy and every doubt away. She leaned her head upon his shoulder, and murmured in her rapture: "Oh, Ronald, you've come back!"

"Did you think I could keep away from you?" he said. No, no; how could he have kept away from her? He had come to claim her, as he had always intended to claim her, now, this moment, before the world.

CHAPTER XXV

He had come back; he had come—could there be any doubt on that point?—to take his wife away, to take her home.

Lily, at least in her own mind, would admit of no doubt. She was transported in a moment from the depths to the heights. So much the more as it had been impossible yesterday to see any light, there was now such a flushing of the whole horizon that doubt was out of the question. She came toward the house with him with his arm around her, thinking of no precautions. Why should they conceal anything, this young pair? The man had come to take his wife away. When he withdrew his arm from her waist and drew her hand through it, it did not, however, strike her that there was anything in that. It was more decorous, like old married people, no longer mere lad and lass. She walked proudly by his side, leaning on his arm. Who cared if Sir Robert himself were there to see? Lily had never cared much for Sir Robert, had always been ready to defy him and vindicate her rights over her own life. As it happened there was nobody but Katrin standing at the door, looking out with her hand over her eyes. Katrin was very quick to make believe that she was dazzled by any little bit of light.

And the lonely moor lighted up and became as paradise to Lily. He brought her all kinds of news, besides the best news of all, which was to see him there. He brought back her old world to her—the world where she had been so happy and so full of friends; her new world, where so soon, in a day or two, she was to find her young companions again, and resume the former life more cordial, more kind, more full of friendship and every gentle affection than ever.

While he sat there thawing, expanding, shaking the cold from him, Lily, who a little while ago had been the fastidious little maiden, courted and served, began to move about the room serving him, eager to get every thing for him he wanted, to undo his muffler, to bring him his slippers. Yes, she would have liked to bring him his slippers as she brought him, like a house-maid, on a little silver salver, not a cup of tea, which probably Ronald would not have appreciated, but something stronger, "to keep out the cauld," which Katrin recommended and brought upstairs with her own hands to the drawing-room door.

"You are not going to serve me, my Lily?" Ronald said. "But I am just going to serve you," she cried, with a little stamp of her foot, "and who has a better right? and who should wait on my man but me that am bound to take care of him? and him come to take me away."

Was she afraid to say these words out loud lest they should break the spell? or was he afraid that she might say them and he not be able to ignore them? But between them something was thrown down, a noise was made in which they were inaudible. I do not know if Lily had any little tremor that made her avoid explanation that evening; at all events she had a sort of hunger to be happy, to enjoy it to the utmost. She laid the table with her own hands, shutting the door in the face of the astonished Robina, who hurried up as soon as she came in to have her share. "I can do without you for all so grand as you think yourself," Lily cried; "I am just going to wait upon my own man!"

"Oh, Miss Lily!" cried Beenie, terrified; but she added to herself: "What a good thing there's naebody in the house! Dougal will not be in till it's late, and most likely he'll be fou when he comes—and be nane the wiser. And naething will need to be said." I cannot tell whether Katrin made quite the same explanation to herself; but she had taken her precautions in case that should happen to Dougal which happened in these days to many honest men on a market night without much infringement of their character for sobriety. It would make the explanation much simpler about the gentleman upstairs. In short, it would not be necessary to make any explanation at all.

"Get out the boxes, Beenie," said Lily, at a later hour. "Do not make any fuss or have things lying about, for gentlemen, you know, cannot endure that; but just prepare quietly, without any fuss."

"Oh, Miss Lily! do you think it has come to that?" Beenie cried, clasping her hands with a start of joyful surprise, but with a countenance full of doubt.

"And what else should it come to?" cried Lily, radiant. "Is this what folk are married for, to live one in Edinburgh and one up far in the Hielands? And what should my man come for but to take me home?"

She must have believed it or she would not have said it with such boldness. She gave Beenie a shake and then a kiss, but cried: "Don't make a confusion, don't leave the things lying about, for that is what gentlemen cannot endure," as she ran away to rejoin her husband. Robina stood immovable, looking after her. "Who has learnt her that?" she said to herself; and then she began to shake her head. "They soon, soon learn what a gentleman canna bide; and set him up! that he should not bide anything coming from her!" But Beenie did not bring out any boxes. She concluded that at all events it would be time enough for that to-morrow.

Ronald remained for three or four days, during which time Dougal, who had carried out the judicious previsions of the women, and had required no explanations of any kind on the market night, maintained a very sullen countenance and did not welcome the visitor, of whom he was suspicious without well knowing why. During this time there was scarcely any pretence kept up of sending Ronald off to the cottage of Tam Robison or in any way making a stranger of him. He was "the young leddy's freend." "Young leddies had nae sic freends in my time," said Dougal. "They have aye had them in my time," said Katrin, "and that cannot be far different." He did not know what to say; but he was very glum, and open to no blandishments on the part of the stranger. And those were days of anxious happiness for Lily. Ronald said nothing upon that one sole subject which she longed to know of. He sounded no note of freedom amid all the litanies he sang to her about her own sweetness, her beauty, her kindness. Lily grew sick of hearing her own praises. "Oh, if he would but say I was an ugly, troublesome thing! and then say: 'You must be ready, Lily, for we're going home to-morrow!'" But Lily was very sweet to her husband; this short visit was full of delight to him; he loved to look at her, to take her in his arms, to know she was his. Going away from her was hard to bear. He would have bemoaned his very hard case if he had not feared that she would beseech him to put an end to it, to take her away with him, and that it need be hard no longer. That was not what he wanted. He preferred the moments of rapture and the separations between. At least he preferred them to the loss of many other things which would be otherwise involved.

One day they went down to the Manse, Lily riding upon Rory, and her husband walking by her side. "You can say I have just come over for the day," he said. "The minister of course knows very well, but your friend Miss Helen—"

"Why should we tell lies about it, Ronald? Isn't it very easy, very easy to understand?"

"Oh, yes," he said, "in any case it's easy to understand; but we might as well avoid gossip if we could."

"There would be no gossip," cried Lily, "about a man coming to see his wife! The only thing would be that folk would wonder why he did not take her home."

"Folk would wonder about something, you may be sure; but I've noticed that ladies think less of that than men. You think it is natural that people's minds should be occupied with you, my bonnie Lily. And so it is; but not with a common man. Maybe it is the jealousy that's in human nature. I hate the chance of it, you see!"

He spoke with a little vehemence, and Lily's eyes filled with tears. It was almost approaching the border of a first quarrel. "You and me," she said plaintively, "though I would not have believed it, Ronald, do not always think the same."

"Did we ever think the same? No, Lily. But so long as we feel the same—and it's best to be on the safe side. I'll say I have come over for the day from—what do you call that place?—Ardenlennie, on the other side, where I had to see Sir John's man of business—which is true. And I found you coming out to pay your visit and came with you. Will that do?"

"Oh, it will do as well as any other—false story," said Lily, "if we are to go on telling lies all our days!"

"Not all our days, I hope," he said gently. He was very good to her. No lover could have been more devoted to her service, with no eyes or ears but for her. That ride, though Lily was not happy in the depths of her heart, though she was fretted almost beyond endurance, was yet sweet to her in spite of herself. "Do you mind how we careered along that other day, me riding, you running," he said, "pushing at Rory behind, and pulling him before, and the poor little beast astonished with the weight on him of a long-legged chield instead of a bonnie lady? My Lily, what you did for me that day! What should I have done without you—at that or any other time?"

"You have to do without me—not that I think I am much good—when you go away."

"Come," he said, "you must not harp forever on this going away. Holloa!" he added immediately, retiring from her side with a sudden impulse as if some hand had pushed him away, "there is a man I know."

"A man you know!" she cried, startled, not so much by this intimation as by the start it produced in him.

"Not a very creditable acquaintance," he went on, with a short laugh, dropping Rory's bridle and keeping, as Lily remarked with a pang, quite apart from her. "I thought he had been at the other end of the world. He is Alick Duff, one of the Duffs of Blackscaur. They were once the great people up here; but the present laird, I believe, is never at home. You might ride on while I say a word to him. He's not an acquaintance for you."

Rory, however, at this moment did not show any inclination to quicken his pace, and Lily heard the greeting between the two men. "Holloa, Lumsden, is that you?" and "Duff! I thought you were at the other end of the world!"

"Well, no, here I am—no in such clover as you," said the new-comer, with a rough laugh. "Present me to the lady, Ronnie—Miss Ramsay, I'm sure."

"This is Mr. Alick Duff—Miss Ramsay," Lumsden said with a dark color on his face. "We are going the same way."

"And I'm going the contrary road—I'm sorry," said the stranger, who was a heavy man, older and far less well looking than Ronald. "I'm going to have a look at the old place and see if they'll have anything to say to me there. Then I'm off again to the ends of the world, as you say; and the further the better," he added, again with a harsh laugh. Rory by this time had moved on, and Lily, though she heard the men's voices almost loud on the still air, did not make out what they said. In a few moments Ronald rejoined her almost out of breath.

"That's the black sheep of the family," he said; "not likely he'll get much of a reception at home, even if there's any body there. The only thing that could be wished, for all belonging to him, is that he should never be heard of more."

"He is a dreadful-looking man," said Lily, with a shudder, "and seems to laugh at every thing, and looks as if he might do any terrible thing."

"You should ask Helen Blythe about that," Ronald said. He was still keeping at a certain distance, the other wayfarer being still in sight. Ronald did not know that, when at the sudden turn of the next corner he resumed his place at Rory's bridle, it was almost in the heart of his wife to have pushed him back with her hands. This incident stopped the question about Helen Blythe which was trembling on Lily's lips. What could he know about Helen Blythe, and what could she have to do with this dreadful man?

The minister sat in his big chair as usual, immovable, by the fire, with a keen glance at Ronald and another at Lily as they came in. Lily was a little flushed with the fresh air and exercise, and with the associations of the place, and the sense that to one person here at least her secret was known. She would not take upon herself a syllable of the explanation which Ronald hastened to give fluently over her shoulder. "I am up at Ardenlennie, on business with Sir John's factor," he said, "and I was so fortunate as to find Miss Ramsay just setting out on a visit to you, so I thought I might come too."

"You're welcome," said the minister curtly. "Come in to the fire, my dear young lady, and take a seat here."

"Eh, Lily, my dear," cried Helen, "I am feared you are not well, for you've turned white in a moment after that bonnie color you had!" Helen herself was not looking well. There was a little redness in her eyes, as if she had been crying, and her cheeks were still paler than Lily's. She was interrupted by her father's peremptory voice:

"If you would but let your friends be! Sit down here and rest. No doubt ye're both tired and cold. And, Eelen, if you had any sense, you would get the tea."

"That's one word for you, Lily, and two for himself," said Helen, with a smile. "He's as fond of his tea as if he were an old woman. I will just tell Marget and come back in a moment." Perhaps she was glad to be out of sight, even for that moment; but poor Lily, wholly occupied with her own concerns, and wondering whether Helen knew anything, or how much she knew, or what she would think of this dreadful deception, had no leisure in her mind to think of any possible troubles of Helen's own.

"Did you meet any—waif characters on the road?" the minister said, with a bitter pause before the last words to give emphasis. It was said loud enough for Helen to hear.

"We met—Alick Duff; I thought he was in Australia or America. He is not precisely what one would call a—fine character," Lumsden said.

"There are not very many of them about," said the old man; "some take one turn and some another; but them that stick to the straight road are few, as was said on a—more important occasion. And how will you be liking your stay in Dalrugas, Miss Lily, after all the daffing of the New Year is over? A visitor for a day or so maybe makes it bearable; but it's lonely for the like of you."

"Oh," cried Lily, involuntarily putting her hands together, "I get very tired of it! But I think," she added, with a confidence she was far from feeling, "that I shall not be very long there now."

"Oh! ye think ye will not be very long there?" he repeated after her. There was not very great assurance or encouragement in his voice.

"Well," said Helen, who had come back, "I understand it's dull for you; but here is one person that will be very sorry, Lily. It will, maybe, be better for you, but the whole countryside will miss you; for many a one takes pleasure to see you pass—you and the powny—that never has said a word to you. She is just a public benefit," said the minister's daughter, "with her bonnie face."

A silence ensued, nobody said a word, and it became visible that Helen's cheeks were a little glazed, as if by sudden application of cold water to wash away certain stains from her eyes. She had seated herself for a moment where all the light from the window fell on her, but restlessly jumped up again and began to remove her work and some books from the table in preparation for tea. "And when are you leaving this neighborhood, Mr. Lumsden? I hope you have some time to stay."

"Alas! I am going to-morrow. A man who has his work to do has little leisure," said Ronald. "We must keep our noses to the grindstone whatever happens. Ladies are better off."

"Do you think we are better off," said Helen, with a sigh, "to bide at home whatever happens, and wait for news that maybe never comes? to see the others go away, and never be able to follow them, except with the longings of our hearts? I have had two brothers—" she said, with a sudden little catch in her throat.

"Eelen," said the minister, "I never knew you for a hypocrite, whatever you were. It is none of your brothers—"

"Oh, father, how can you ken? Do I wear my heart on my sleeve that you can tell what's in it? You never thought much about them yourself, and how could you know what was in another's heart? But it's not for me to speak. I have aye my duty. It's just Mr. Lumsden's notion that it's a fine thing for us to sit quiet at home and endure all things and never hear."

"Well, here is your tea at all events," said Mr. Blythe, "and I see James Douglas passing the window to get a cup. When there's nothing to do in an afternoon and every thing low, as it is at that period in the day, there is a great diversion in tea. In fact," he added, "the best of meals is just the diversion they make. You are shaken out of yourself. Ye say your grace and ye carve your chuckie, or even a sheep's head on occasion, and your thoughts are taken clean away from the channel, maybe a troublesome one, that they are in. Still better is a cup of tea. Come ben, come ben, Mr. Douglas; there's plenty of room for you. We were just thinking, Eelen and me, that it is a long time since you have been here."

A pleasant light shone in the young minister's face. "If I thought I could make myself missed, I would have the heart to stay away longer still," he said, "but then I think that out of sight is often out of mind."

It was pathetic to observe how he sought the eyes of Helen, and how he contrived to put his chair next hers at the table, round which they all sat. Helen took but little notice of the gentle young man; she set down his cup before him with a precipitation that was almost rude, and turned away to Lily, with whom she talked in an undertone. What about? Neither one nor the other knew. Yet neither one nor the other had any perception of what was in her neighbor's bosom. Helen's trouble to her filled all the world. It was greater than anything else she knew; the air tingled with it; the very horizon could scarcely contain it. Lily, a child, with all the world smiling upon her!—what could there be in her lot to approach the greatness of the pain which Helen had to bear? She was half angry with the girl for making a fuss about being dull, as if that mattered; or seeing her sweetheart only by intervals, which was all, she thought, that Lily had to complain of. The little spoiled child! but what a real heartbreak was, Helen knew.

CHAPTER XXVI

"Did you mean that, Ronald—that you are really going away to-morrow?"

"Indeed and alas, I meant it, Lily. It is the middle of the session. How could I stay longer? It was, as I said to the minister—though you never more than half believe what I say—a real piece of business with Sir John's factor at Ardenlennie that gave me the occasion of spending a few days with my Lily, which I seized upon without giving you any warning, as you know."

"And me that thought you could not do without me one day longer, and were coming hurrying to bring your wife home!"

"My darling!" said Ronald, with no lack of ardor on his part. "But then my bonnie Lily has always sense to know that the longing of the heart changes nothing, and that it is no more the term in March than it is in January. Where could I find a place to put you now, or till Whit-Sunday comes?"

Was it true? Oh, yes; it was true. In Scotland you do not find an empty house and go into it whenever you want to—especially not in the Scotland of those days. You have to wait for the term, which is the legitimate time. Nevertheless Lily was very sure that, if she were now in Edinburgh looking for a place to establish her nest in, she would find it; but perhaps a man has not the time, perhaps he cannot take the trouble, going upstairs and down stairs looking at all kinds of unlikely places. This, Lily felt sure, was another of the things that gentlemen could not abide.

"We must make the best of you, then, while we have you," she said, drawing her chair to the side of the fire after their dinner together. It was cold at night, though the hardy folk of the North were content to believe that spring was coming, and that there was a different "feel" in the air. The wind was sweeping over the moor as keen as a knife, bending the gray bushes of the ling and spare rowan-trees that cowered before it like human travellers caught in the cutting breeze. There was a cold moon shining fitfully, with frightened, swift-flying glimpses from among the clouds which flew over her face. Colder than the depth of winter outside, but within, with the firelight and lamplight, and Lily making the best of her husband's flying visit, very bright and very warm.

"I will just look for the next term, Ronald, and pack up all my things and be ready, so that if you came suddenly, as you did the other day—"

"Do you bid me, then," he said, "not to come till Whit-Sunday? which is a long time to be without a sight of my Lily. If I should have another chance like this of getting a day or two—which is better than nothing—"

"Oh, no, do not miss the day or two," cried Lily; "how could you think I meant that? But I'll look for the term-time, like the maids when they're changing their places. It's more than that to me, for it will be the first home I have ever had. Uncle Robert's house was never a home—there was no woman in it."

"Nor will there be any woman, Lily—"

"I will be the woman," she cried, with a playful blow on his shoulder; "it is me that will make it home. And you will be the man. And if any stranger comes into it—not to say a poor, motherless bairn like what I was—their hearts will sing for pleasure; for there will be one for kindness and warmness, and one for protecting and caring, and that will make it home. Uncle Robert was but one, and not one that was caring. If you were there, he just let you be. 'Oh,' he would say, 'you are here!' as if it was a surprise. Do you wonder that I hunger and thirst for my own home, Ronald, when I never had in my life anything but that?"

"It will come in its time, my Lily," he said, holding her close to him, with her hands in his.

"Ay, but you mind what Shakespeare says: 'While the grass grows—'"

"If the proverb was musty then," said Ronald, with a laugh, "it's mustier now."

"So it is; but as true as ever. And I weary for it, I weary for it!" cried the girl. "However, sit you there, and me here; and we'll think it is our own house—that you will have come in, and you will have had your dinner, and you will be telling me every thing that has passed in the day."

"What, all the pleas before the Fifteen, and old Watty's speeches, and the jokes of Johnny Law, and the wiles of—"

"Every one of them! When you are in a profession, you should know every thing about it. If you were a—tailor, say, who would make your fine buttonholes, and the braiding of the grand waistcoats, but your wife? Or a—school-master it would be me to look after the exercises; and wherefore not an advocate's wife to know all about the Parliament House, and how to conduct a case if there should be occasion?"

"So that you might go down to the court instead of me, and plead for me if I had a headache," said Ronald, laughing. "It would be grand for my clients, Lily, for I'll answer for it, with Symington on the bench, and Hoodiecraw and the two Elders, you would gain every plea."

"That's while I am young and—" said Lily, with a little toss of her head. She was saucy and gay and full of malice, as he had never seen her, for this was not much Lily's way. "I did not say I would plead; but I would have to know. Every thing you would have to tell me, as well as the jokes of the old lords."

"Well," said Ronald, "I might do that, and you would take no harm, for you would not understand them, my Lily. But they all like a bonnie lass, and you would win every plea. I'll tell you all the stories, Lily, and there are plenty of them. The plainstanes of the Parliament House know more human trouble and vice than any other place in Edinburgh. I'll tell you—"

"Oh, not the wicked things!" cried Lily, clasping her hands, "for how could we help those that suffer by them? or what could that have to do with you and me?"

"If you leave out the wicked things, there would be little to do," said Ronald, "for the courts of law."

"But we will leave them out!" cried Lily. "All our cases shall be about mistakes, or something that comes from not understanding; so that as soon as you put it to them very clear they will see the right and own it and go back to the just way. For there is nobody that would not rather be in the right than in the wrong if they knew, and that is my principle; things are so twisted in and out it's hard to understand; and bad advice and thinking too much of himself make a man do a sudden thing without thinking, till he finds that it is wrong. And then when he sees, he is sorry and puts it back."

"If it were so easy as all that, Lily, it would be new heavens and a new earth."

"Well, we'll try," said Lily gayly. She was so gay, she was so full of quips and cranks, so ready with amusing turns of speech and audacious propositions, that Ronald found her a new Lily, full of brightness and fun and novel, ridiculous suggestions and high-flown notions, which she was ready herself to laugh at as high-flown, yet taking his sober thoughts to pieces and turning them upside down. What would it be, indeed, to carry her away with him, to have her always there, turning every little misfortune into fun and laughter, making every misadventure a source of amusement instead of trouble! A gleam of light rose in his eyes, and then he shook his head slightly to himself and sighed. The shake of the head and the sigh were when Lily's back was turned. He dared not let her see them, divine them, answer them with a hundred quick-flashing arguments. She had an answer for every thing, he knew. She cared nothing for the things that were, after all, the chief things to care for—money, progress in the world, that sound foundation in life without which no man could make sure of rising to the head of his profession. Some did it without doubt. There was Lord Pleasaunce, that had fought his way to the bench, marrying a wife and beginning in a garret, as Lily wished; now he thought of it, she was something like Lily, the judge's wife, though fat now and roundabout. They had even been Lord Advocate in their time, and gone to London (with such a couple, even Ronald felt instinctively, you don't say he, but they) and struggled through somehow; but always poor, always poor! They did not seem to mind; but then Ronald knew that he would always mind. They had no fortunes for their daughters nor to put out their sons well in the world. He shook his head again as he rejected once more that possibility which for a moment, only for a moment, had caught and almost beguiled him. Lily had gone out of the room, but, coming back, caught that last shake of his head.

"And what is that for?" she said. "You will have been thinking that Lily is good for very little, that she could not keep the house and make the meat as she thinks, but would look to be served herself, hand and foot, as she is here."

"Not that—but still my Lily has always been served hand and foot. There is Beenie, without whom we cannot budge a step—"

"No," said Lily gravely, "without Beenie I could not budge a step—not because Beenie is my maid, and I need her to serve me, but because it would break her heart."

"My love, poor folk as we shall be cannot afford to think of breaking hearts."

"I will break yours rather!" cried Lily, with a little stamp of her foot. "I will give ye ill dinners and a house that is never redd up, and keep Beenie like a lady in the best room and give her all the good things."

"That is just what I say," said Ronald; "we will have a train—all the old servants that cannot endure their lives without Miss Lily, perhaps Katrin and Dougal, too."

Lily stood looking at him for a moment, with her eyes enlarged and her face pale. "Is it in fun, or in earnest?" she said, with a little gasp.

"Oh, in fun, in fun," he said hastily, "though considering how they have fulfilled their duty to Sir Robert, it would not be strange if he turned them out of his doors—and whom, then, could they turn to but you and me?"

"It is not for you and me to blame them," said Lily, still under the impression of what he had said, "and this is not the kind of fun that is good fun. But it is true, after all, though I never thought of that before. Katrin is kind, but she has, perhaps, not been quite as true to Uncle Robert as to me; but Dougal, he knows nothing. Dougal has never known anything; he has never meant to desert Uncle Robert. Ronald," cried Lily, with sudden affright, "we have all been cheating Uncle Robert! This is what we have done, and nothing else, since you first came here."

"I am well aware of it, Lily," said Ronald, with a laugh, "and for my part I am quite agreed to go on cheating Uncle Robert for as long as you please."

"It does not please me!" she said; "I would like to cheat nobody. It is a new thing to me—I did not think of that. Oh, Ronald, take me away! I laugh and I chatter, but my heart's breaking. We are cheating every body—not Uncle Robert only, but Helen Blythe and every creature that knows me. What do I care how poor we are, or if I have to work for my living? I will work, oh, with a good heart! but take me away, take me away!"

Ronald held her hands in his and steadied her against her will. He had foreseen such an outburst, as well as the other manifestations of her agitated and disturbed life. He was ready to allow even that it was no wonder she became excited by times, that she had been more patient than he could have hoped. He was himself very cool, and could afford to be moderate and humor her. He held her hands in his, and restrained the violence of her feelings by that steady clasp. "My Lily, my Lily!" he said. The girl yielded to that restraining influence in spite of herself. She could almost have struck him in the vehemence of her passion and in the intolerable sensation of this sharp light upon the situation altogether; but the cool touch of his hands, his firm hold, his soothing voice, subdued her. The question between two people at such a crisis is almost entirely the question which is stronger, and on this occasion Ronald was certainly the stronger. When Lily's passion ended in the natural flood of tears, she shed them on his shoulder, encircled by his arm, all her resistance quenched. And he was very kind to her; no one could have consoled her more lovingly, or more tenderly soothed the nervous and excited feelings which had got beyond her control. He was master of the situation, and felt it, but used his power in the most gentle way. And Lily said not a word more—what was there to be said? She had put herself in the wrong by her passion and by her tears. This was not the calm reason with which a woman ought to discuss the beginning of her life—with which, she said to herself, a man expected his wife to consider and discuss these affairs. She had neither been calm nor reasonable. She had been passionate, excited, perhaps hysterical. Lily was deeply ashamed of herself. She was humble toward him who must, she thought, be disappointed in her, and find her like the women in books, all folly and excitement, instead of a creature able to take all the circumstances into consideration. Nothing could have subdued her spirits like that sense of being in the wrong.

Later in the evening she endeavored to make up for her foolishness by returning to the mood of gayety with which she began the evening. She gave Ronald a little sketch of the humors of Rory, and the respect in which Dougal held that small and fiery personage. She told him about Katrin's cows and her chickens, and the amusement which these living creatures had given during the long winter days to the little family at Dalrugas.

"But spring is coming," he said.

"Oh, yes; spring is coming; the moor will soon be dry enough for walking, and many a ramble I will have. I am beginning," said Lily, "to grow very fond of the moor. You see, it is all we have. It's cross and market and college and court and all together to me. In the morning the bees will be busy among the whins— there is always a bud somewhere on a whin bush—and full of honey as they can hold; and then in the evening there is the sunset, and the hills all standing out against the west, with their old purple cloaks around them. What with the barnyard and what with the moor, there's no want of diversion here."

"My bonnie Lily," he cried in sudden compunction, "not much diversion for the like of you!"

"What do you call the like of me? I am very well off. I have neighbors and all. There is Helen Blythe, poor thing, she is not so well off. The minister is a handful; he holds her night and day. And who was yon glum man, Ronald, and what had he to do with her? Her eyes were red, and she had been crying; and I am sure it was something about that man."

"Alick Duff? Nonsense, Lily! He is a black sheep, if ever there was one. That was all a foolish story, we'll suppose. A good little thing like the minister's daughter should never be thrown away on him."

"Perhaps she is a good little thing. We are all good little things till we show ourselves different. But her eyes were red and her cheeks were pale. I must see if I can comfort her," said Lily half to herself. "And now, sir, if you are going away to-morrow, you should go to your bed, for you'll have a weary day."

"Yes, I shall have a weary day; but I could bear that and more to see my Lily," Ronald said.

"Well, if you care for her at all, you would need to do that, for she must either be there or here," Lily said. "It's a pity I'm solid, that I cannot fly away like the birds, and tap at your window as the lady does in the ballad. What ballad? I don't remember. Perhaps it was after she was dead. And does Mrs. Buchanan always make you comfortable and cook as well as Katrin? Oh, Katrin is very good for some things, though you think her an ill housekeeper for Uncle Robert. But never mind that. Tell me about Luckie Buchanan. I will wager you a silver bawbee, as Beenie says, that she does not send you up your bird as good as we do here."

"Nothing is so good as it is here. You take me up too quick, Lily."

"Me take you up quick? I do nothing but try to please you. But I know how it is, Ronald. You think shame of Luckie Buchanan. She burns your bird, and she does your chop in the frying-pan, and her kettle is not half boiled. Young men are very badly treated in their lodgings. I know very well. Uncle Robert's men that came to see him were always complaining, and they were old men that could make their curries themselves and drive womenfolk desperate, whereas you're only young and would think shame to look as if you cared. I wonder if she brushes your clothes right, and gives you nice burnished boots, as you like them to be," said Lily, with a critical look at the sleeve of his coat, which she was smoothing down with her hand.

"You will make me think myself a terrible being, taken up with my own wants," he said in a vexed tone.

"It is me that am taken up with your wants," she said, "and what more right than that—a man's wife! What is the good of her but to look after her man! And when I cannot do it for failure of circumstances, not good will, then I must just ask and plague you till you tell me there's nothing more for me to do—till the term comes, and I go home to my place," cried Lily, with a laugh, but with two tears, which she turned away her head that he might not see. "It's my first place!" she cried. "You cannot wonder I am excited about it, Ronald; and I hope I will give you satisfaction—Beenie and me!"

Next morning Lily got up without, as appeared, any cloud on her face, and gave him his breakfast, and saw to the packing of his bag, and that his big coat was well strapped on to Sandy's shoulders, who was to walk into the town with him and carry his small belongings. "You will not want it walking, but you will want it in the coach," she said, "and be sure you keep yourself warm, for, though it's March, the wind is terrible cold over the moor; and here is a scarf to put round your neck for the night journey. It will keep you warm, and it will mind you of me."

"Do I want that to mind me of my Lily?" he said reproachfully.

"No, after I have been giving you such a taste of my humors, and you know I am not just the good thing you thought. But you might be more grateful for my bonnie scarf that I took out of the lavender to give you to wrap round your throat at night! And it is a very bonnie scarf," said Lily; "look at the flowers worked upon it, the same on both sides, and as soft as a dove's feathers that are of silver. You will put it round your neck and say Lily gave me this; and then at Whit-Sunday, when I take up my place, I will find it again, laid away in some drawer, and I will take it back, and it will belong then both to you and me."

"That is a bargain," he said, more moved by the parting than he had ever been; but Lily went with him to the head of the stairs, and there stood looking after him from the staircase window, to keep up some sort of transparent fiction for Dougal's sake, with her eyes shining and a smile upon her mouth. She was resolved that this was how he should see her when he went away. There should be no more breakings down. She would importune him no more. She would not shed a tear. When he turned round to wave his hand before he disappeared under the bank, she was still smiling and calm. It was, perhaps, a little startling to Ronald, who had never seen her so reasonable before—and reasonableness, though so desirable, is sometimes a little alarming too.

CHAPTER XXVII

When she was sure that the travellers were out of sight, Lily flew down the spiral stairs, snatched her plaid from where it hung as she passed, and rushed out to the only shelter and refuge she had—the loneliness and silence of the moor. She had to push through between the two women, who would so fain have stopped her to administer their consolation and caresses, but whom, in her impatience, she could not tolerate, shaking her head as they called after her to put on her plaid and that she would get her death of cold. It was March and a beautiful morning, the air almost soft in the broad beaming of the sun, and the moisture, which lay heavy on the moss-green turf and ran and sparkled in little pools and currents everywhere; but the breeze was keen and cold, and blew upon her with a sharp and salutary chill, cooling her heated cheeks. Lily sprang over the great bushes of the ling, which, bowed for a moment by her passage, flung back upon her a shower of dew-drops as they recovered their straightness, and the whins caught at the plaid on her arm as she brushed past; but she took no notice of these impediments, nor of the wetness under her feet, nor the chill of the air upon her uncovered head, and shoulders clothed only in her indoor dress. She paused upon a little green hillock slightly rising over the long level, which was a favorite point of vision, and from which, as she had often found, the furthest view was possible of anything within the horizon of this little world. But it was not to see that little speck on the road, which was Ronald, that Lily had made this rush into the heart of the moor. It was for the utter solitude, the silence which enclosed and surrounded her, the separation from every thing that could intrude upon that little speck of herself, so insignificant in the great fresh shining world, yet so much more living in her trouble than all the mountains and the moors. Lily sank down on the mossy green and covered her face with her hands. She had shed passionate tears on her husband's shoulder last night, but these were different which forced their way now without anything to restrain them. They were not mere tears of a parting, which, after all, was no wonderful thing. He would come again. Lily had no fear that he would come again. She had no doubt of his love, no thought that he might grow cold to her. Of the two it was Ronald who was the warmer lover, holding her in perfect admiration as well as in all the fondness of a young husband, which was not exactly what could be said on her side. But his love was of a different kind, as perhaps a man's always is. He did not want all that she did in their marriage. A little house of their own, wherever it was—a home, a known and certain place: was it the woman who thought of this rather than the man? It gave her a pang even to think that it might perhaps be so, or at least that Ronald did not care for what she might suffer in this respect. He might be content with casual visits, but what she wanted was her garret, her honest name, and honor and truth.

And then Whit-Sunday, Whit-Sunday, the term when people did their flitting, and the maids went to their new places! Oh, happy, honest prose that had nothing to do, Lily thought, with romance or poetry. Would it come—in two months, not much more—and make an end of all this? or would it never come? Poor Lily's heart was so wrung out of its right place that she lost her confidence even in the term; she could scarcely think of anything in earth or heaven, she who had once been so confident, of which she could now think that there was no fear.

By this time the cold had begun to creep to Lily's heart, her fever of excitement having found vent, and she was glad to wrap herself closely in her plaid, putting it over her head and gathering the soft folds round her throat. She put back the hair which the cold breeze and the disorder of her weeping had brought about her face, smoothing it back under the tartan screen, the soft warm folds that gave a little color to her pale face. Oh, if she could have had a plaid, but that of Ronald's tartan, to wrap about her heart, the chilled spirit and soul that had no warmth of covering! But that must not be thought of now, when Lily's business was to go back to her dreary home, to meet the eyes that would be fixed upon her, to bear her burden worthily, and to betray to no one, even her most confidential companion, the doubts and terrors that were in her own heart.

As she came out upon the road, having made a long round of the moor to give herself more time, Lily perceived two figures in front of her, whom she did not at once recognize; but after a moment or two her attention was attracted by the voice of the man, who spoke loudly, and by something in the attitude of the little figure walking by his side, and replying sometimes in an inaudible monosyllable, sometimes by a deprecating gesture only, to his vehement words. Was it Helen Blythe who was here so far from home by the side of a man who spoke to her almost roughly, certainly not as so gentle a creature ought ever to have been spoken to? It was some time before Lily's faculties were sufficiently roused to hear what he was saying, or at least to discover that she could hear if she gave her attention; when, however, a sudden "If you had ever loved me, Helen!" caught her ear, Lily cried out in alarm: "Oh, whisht, whisht! Whoever you are, I am coming behind you and I can hear what you say."

The man turned round almost with rage, showing her the dark and clouded face of the stranger whom she had met the day before with Ronald, and who was the cause, as she had divined, of Helen's sad eyes. "Confound you!" he cried in his passion, "can ye not pass on, and leave the road free to folk going about their own business?" These words came out with a rush, and then he paused and reddened, and took off his hat. "Miss Ramsay!" he said, "I beg your pardon," placing himself hastily between her and his companion.

"I neither want to see nor hear," cried Lily. "Let me pass; you need have no fear of me."

At the voice Helen came quietly out of his shadow. "You need not hide me from Lily," she said, "for Lily is my dear friend. I've walked far, far from home, Lily, with one that—one that—I may never see again," she said, turning a pathetic look upon the man by her side. "He blames me now, and perhaps I am to be blamed. But to think it is, maybe, the last time, as he is telling me, breaks my heart. Lily, will you take us in, if it was only for half-an-hour? I feel as if I could not go on another step, for my heart fails me as well as my feet."

"You never told me you were wearied, Helen!" he cried in a tone of fierce penitence. "How was I to know? I could have carried you like a feather."

She shook her head. "You could carry more weight than me, Alick, but as soon Schiehallion as me. And I was not wearied till I saw rest at hand."

"Miss Ramsay," he said, "you know what she and I are to each other."

"I know nothing," cried Lily, "and you need not tell me, for what Helen does is always right; but come in and welcome, and have your talk out in peace. Never mind to explain to me—I scarcely know your name."

"It is, alas, no credit, or rather I am no credit to a good name that has been well kept on this countryside; but we are old, old friends, Helen Blythe and me. She should have been my wife, Miss Ramsay, though you might not think it, nearly ten long years ago. If she had kept her promise, they would never have called me wild Alick Duff, and the black sheep of the family, as they do now. This is the third time I've come back to bid her keep her word; for I have her word, rough and careless as you may think me. Each time I'm less worth taking than I was the time before, and I'm not going to risk it any more. When she drops me this time, I will just go to the devil, which is the easiest way, and trouble nobody more about me."

"And why should you go to the devil?" said Lily, "for that is what nobody except your own self can make you do."

"Oh, do not hearken to him, Lily; let us come in for half-an-hour, for neither will my feet carry me nor will my heart hold me up if there is more."

Lily made her guests enter before her when they reached the door of Dalrugas; but lingering behind as Helen made her way slowly with her tired steps up the spiral stairs, caught Duff by the sleeve and spoke in his ear: "Do you not think shame of yourself to break her heart, a little thing like that, with putting the weight of your ill deeds upon her, and you a big strong man?"

"Me—think shame!" he said, with a low laugh.

"I would think shame," cried Lily vehemently, all her hot blood surging up in her veins, "to lay the burden of a finger's weight upon her, and her not a half or a quarter so big as me!"

This sharp, indignant whisper Helen heard as a murmur behind her while she went up the stairs. She turned round when she reached the drawing-room, meeting the others as they appeared after her. "And what were you two saying to each other?" she asked, with a tremulous smile.

"I am going," said Lily, "to leave you to yourselves; and when you have had your talk out, you will come down to me to have something to eat; and then we will think, Helen, how we are to get you home."

"You are coming in here, Lily. Him and me we have said all there is to be said. And he has told you what there is between us, as perhaps I would never have had the courage to do. Come and tell him over again, Lily, you that are a young lass and have known no trouble—tell him what a woman can do and cannot do, for he will not believe me."

"How can I tell? that have known no trouble, as you say," cried Lily. But Helen knew nothing to explain the keen tone of irony that was in the words, and looked at the girl with an appeal in her patient eyes, too full of her own sorrow to remember that, perhaps, this younger creature might have sorrows too. "How should I know," said Lily, "what a woman cannot do? If it is to keep a man from wrong-doing, is that a woman's business, Helen? How do I know? They say in books that it's the women that drive them to it. Are you to take him on your shoulders and carry him away from the gates of — Or what are you expected to do?"

"If she had married me when I asked her," cried Duff, "she would have done that. Ay, that she would! From the gates of hell, that a little thing like you daren't name. I would never have known the way they lay if she had put her hand in mine and come with me. And that I have told you, Helen, a hundred times, and a hundred more."

"Oh, Alick, Alick!" was all that Helen said.

"And you never would have thought shame," cried Lily, "to ride by on her shoulders, instead of walking on your own feet? I would have set my face like a flint and passed them by, and scorned them that wiled me there! I would have laid it upon nobody but myself if I had not heart enough to save my own head!"

"Oh, Lily, Lily!" cried Helen, turning upon her champion, "my bonnie dear! it's you that are too young to understand. Maybe he's wrong, but he's a kind of right, too. I am not blaming him for that. Many a woman keeps a man on the straight road almost without knowing, and him no worse of it nor her either. I could tell you things! And, Alick, I will not deceive you; if I had not been so young that time—if I had only had the courage—for there was no reason then, but just that I was a young lass, and frightened, and did not know— There was no reason—then—"

"Except that I was wild Alick Duff, that they said would settle to nothing, and not a man that would ever make salt to his kale."

Helen made no answer, but shook her head with a sigh.

"How can I stand between you and him?" said Lily. "You take away my breath. I cannot understand the tongue you are speaking. It's not good English nor Scots either, but another language. Are we angels, to make men good? and is it no matter what evil thing a woman takes into her heart if she can but make her man look like a whited sepulchre, and keep him, as you say, on the straight road? Is that what we were made for?" she cried in all the indignation of her youth.

Duff, a little surprised, a little confused by this unexpected controversy, too much occupied with his own purpose not to be impatient with any digression, yet uncertain whether this strange digression might not serve his cause in the end, made answer, first fixing his eyes upon Lily, the little girl who knew no trouble: "I'm thinking that was a good part of it," he said. "You had the most to do with bringing ill into the world; you should have the most to do with driving it out. But what do I care about women?" he cried. "It's Helen I'm thinking of. There might never be such another, but there she is that could have done it, and would not lift her little finger. And now she will smile and send me away."

"He speaks," cried Lily, "as if it were your responsibility and not his—as if you would be answerable!"

"Oh," said Helen in a hurried undertone, "and that is what I lie and think upon in the watches of the night. Will the Lord demand an account at my hands? Will he say: 'Helen, where is thy brother?' I that was maybe appointed for him to be his keeper, to take care of him, with all his hot blood and all his fancies that nobody understood but me!"

Duff was walking impatiently about the room, not listening to what the two women spoke between themselves, and Lily was too much bewildered by this new view to make any answer, except by a brief exclamation: "It is like a coward to put the blame upon you!"

"I would not shrink from it if I might bear it," said Helen. "It's not that. But to think it might be a man's ruin that a poor frightened creature of a woman—no, a lassie, twenty years old, no more—could not see her duty. For there was no reason then. My mother was living, my father was a strong man. The boys had been unlucky, but me, I was free. And I let him go away. Oh, lay the wyte on me!" she said, clasping her hands. "Oh, lay the wyte on me!"

Duff came suddenly to a stand-still before her, catching up something of what she said. "I'll forgive you all that's come and gone, and all that might have been, and the vows I've broken, and the little good I've ever done"—a tender light came over his dark face—"Helen, I'll forgive you all my ruin, and we'll gather up the fragments that are left, if you will but come with me now."

"Forgive her!" cried Lily, indignant.

"Ah, forgive her! you that know nothing of the heart of man. Can she ever give it back? She says herself the Lord will seek my blood at her hands: how much more me, that knows what might have been and never has been because she was not there? But, Helen, let it be now! It may be but the hinder end of life that's left, but better that than nothing at all. We are not so old yet, neither you nor me. And there's the fragments that remain—the fragments that remain." He held out his hands toward her, the face that Lily had thought so dark and forbidding melting in every line, the lowering brows lifted, the fierce eyes softened with moisture. And Helen looked up at him with her own overflowing, and a light as of martyrdom on her face.

"Oh, Alick, my father, my father! I cannot leave my father now."

He kicked away a footstool on the carpet with a sudden movement which, to Lily, at first appeared as if he were offering violence to Helen herself. "Your father!" he cried, "the minister that will have no broken man for his daughter nor ill name for his house, that wants the siller of them that come to woo, that would sell you away to that white-faced lad because he has something to the fore and a respectable name! Oh, don't speak to me of your father, Helen Blythe, him that should be all spirit and that's all flesh! Confound him and you and all your sleekit ways! In what way is he better than me?"

"Man! you will kill her!" cried Lily, springing forward and putting herself between them. "How dare you swear at her, that is far, far too good for you!"

But Helen was not horrified, like Lily. She looked at him still, bending her head to the other side. "My father," she said, "has his faults, like us all. He is a mixture, as you are yourself. I am not angry at what you say. He likes his pleasure as you do, Alick. He is more moderate: he is a minister. He has not, maybe, been tempted like you, but I allow that it is not far different. Perhaps in the sight of God—" But here her voice failed her, suddenly interrupted by something deeper than tears.

"He likes his pleasure," said Duff, with a short laugh; "he likes a good glass of wine, not to say whiskey, and a good dinner, and tells his stories, and is no more particular when he's with his cronies than me. Only I'll tell you what he does, Helen, that me I cannot do. Would he have had it in him if he had not been a minister, nor had a wife, nor been kept from temptation? That is what none of us can tell. He knows when to stop; he likes himself better than his pleasures. He keeps the string about his neck and stops himself when he's gone far enough. I do not esteem that quality," cried the big man, striding about the room, making the boards groan and creak. "I am not fond of calculation. Alick Duff has cost me many a sore head and many a sore heart. I scorn him," he cried, with a strong churning out of the fierce letters that make up that word, "both for what he's done and what he hasn't done. But it's no for him I would draw bridle if I were away in full career. But I would for you!" he said, suddenly sinking his voice, and throwing himself in a chair that swung and rocked under him by Helen's side. "Helen, I would for you!"

CHAPTER XXVIII

Lily had an agitating and troubled day between this strange pair, which had the good effect upon her, however, of turning her thoughts entirely away from her own affairs, the struggle and trouble of which seemed of so little importance beside this conflict which had the air of being for life or death. She did not understand either of the combatants: the man who so fearlessly owned his weaknesses, and put the weight of his soul upon the woman who ought to have saved him; or the woman who did not deny that responsibility, nor claim independence or a right irrespective of him to follow her own way. Helen Blythe had ideas of life, it was evident, very different from those that had ever come into Lily's mind. In those days there were no discussions of women's rights; but in those days, alas! as in all other periods, the heart of a high-spirited young woman here and there swelled high with imagination, wrath, and indignation at the thought of those indignities which all women had to suffer. That it should be taken as a simple thing that any man, after he had gone through all the soils and degradations of a reckless life, should have a spotless girl given to him to make him a new existence, was one of those bitter thoughts that rankled in the minds of many women, though nothing was said on the subject in public, and very little even among themselves. For those were subjects which girls shrank from and blushed to hear of. The knowledge was horrible, and made them feel, when any chance fact came their way, as if their very souls were soiled by the hearing. Not that the elder women, especially those inconceivably experienced and impartial old ladies of society, who see every thing with the sharpest eyesight, and discuss every thing with words that cut and glance like steel, and who have surmounted all that belongs to sex, except a keen dramatic interest in its problems, did not talk of these matters after their kind, as in all the ages. But the girls were not told, they did not know, they shrank from information which they would not have understood had it been conveyed to them, except, indeed, a few principles that were broad and general: that to marry a girl to an old man or a wicked man was a hideous thing, and that the old doctrine of a reformed rake, which had been preached to their mothers, was a scorn to womankind, and no longer to be suggested to them. For the magic of the Pamelas was over, and Sir Walter had arisen in the sky, which cleared before him, all noisome things flying where he made his honest, noble way. Not much these heroes of his, people say, not worth a Tom Jones with his stress and storm of life; but bringing in a new era, the young and pure with the young and true, and not a whitewashed Lovelace in the whole collection. Lily was of Scott's age; and when she saw this wolf approaching the lamb, or rather this black sheep, as every-body called him, demanding a maiden sacrifice to clean him from his guilt, her heart burned with indignation and the rage of innocence. She could not understand Helen's strange acquiescence, nor her sense of possible guilt in not having accepted that part which was offered to her. The very atmosphere which surrounded Duff was obnoxious to Lily: the roughness of his tones and his clothes, his large, noisy movements and vehemence and gestures. He had lost, she thought, that air of a gentleman which is the last thing a man loses who is born to it, and never, as she believed, loses innocently.

She was glad beyond description when, after much more conversation, and a meal to which his excitement and passion did not prevent him from doing a certain justice, Duff was got out of the house, leaving Helen behind, for whom the cart with the black pony had to be brought out once more. Helen was greatly exhausted by all the agitations of the day. He had left her without bringing her to any change of mind, yet vowing he would see her once again and make her come with him still, that he would not yet abandon all hope, while she sat tired out, shaking her head softly, with a melancholy smile on her face—a smile more pitiful than many complaints. She did not rise from her chair to see him go away, but followed him with wistful eyes to the door—eyes that were full of a dew of pain that flooded them, but did not fall. She did not say anything for a long time after he had gone. Was she listening to his steps as he went away, leaving on the air a lingering sound, measured and heavy? Helen had thought that footstep like music. She had watched for it many a day, and heard it, as she thought, miles off, in the stillness of the long country roads, and again, in imagination, many and many a day when he was far out of hearing. She heard it now, long after it had been lost by every ear but her own. Her face had a strained look, as if that sound drew her after him, yet stronger resolution kept her behind.

"You did not mean that, Helen—oh, not that!" Lily said, encircling her friend with her arm.

"My bonnie Lily! but that I did, with all my heart!"

"That you, a good woman, would go away out into the world with an ill man, knowing he was an ill man, and thinking that you could turn him and mend him! Oh, Helen, Helen! take him to your heart, that is pure as snow, knowing he was an ill man?"

"Lily, you are very young—you are little more than a bairn. What are our small degrees of good and ill—or rather of ill and worse—before our Maker? Do you think he judges as we judge? They say my poor Alick is wild, and well I wot he is wild, and has taken many, many a wrong step on the road. Oh, if you think it presumptuous of me to believe I could have held him fast so that he should not fall, that would be more true! But, Lily, if ye were long in this countryside, you would see it with your own e'en. The women long ago were not so feared as we were. They just married the lad they liked, and if he were wild, forgave him; and I've known goodwives that have just pushed them through—oh, just pushed them through!—till they came to old age with honor on their heads and a fine family about them, that would have sunk into the miry pit and the horrible clay if the woman had not had the heart to do it. I am not saying I had not the heart," said Helen, with a melancholy shake of her head, "but I was young and knew nothing, and the moment passed away."

"It can never be right," cried Lily, "to run such a dreadful risk! Oh, if they cannot guide themselves, who are we that we should guide them? I am not like you, Helen. I know for myself I could guide no man."

No! well she knew that! Not so much as for the taking of a little house—not so much as the simplest duty as ever lay in a man's road. Helen was not so clever as Lily, she had no such pretensions in any way; every thing—blood and breeding, and the habit of carrying out her own projects and holding her head high—was in the favor of the younger. But Lily had no such confidence as Helen. She did not believe in any influence she could exert. Her opinion, her entreaties, were of no use. They did not move Ronald. He dismissed them with a kiss and a smile. "I could guide no man," she repeated with a bitter conviction in her heart.

"It would, maybe, not be a perfect life," said Helen; "far from that; there would be many an ill moment. The goodwife has her cross to carry, and it's not light; but, oh, Lily, better that than ruin to the man, and a lonely life, with little use in it, to her; and there is aye the hope of the bairns that will do better another day."

"The bairns," said Lily, "that would be the worst of all. An ill man's bairns—to carry on the poison in the blood."

"You are a hard judge," said Helen, pausing to look at her, "for one so young; but it's because you are so young, my bonnie dear. We are all ill men and women, too. There's a line of poetry that comes into my head, though it's a light thing for such a heavy subject, and I cannot mind it exact to a word. It says we were all forfeit once, but he that might have best took the advantage found out the remedy. It is bonnier than that, and it is just the truth. The Lord said: 'Neither do I condemn thee.' Ye will mind that at least, Lily."

"I mind them both," cried Lily, piqued to have her knowledge doubted, "but yet—"

"And you must not speak of my poor Alick as an ill man. Oh, if I could but let you see how little he is an ill man! His heart is just as innocent as a bairn's in some things, I'm not saying in all things. He is wild, poor lad, the Lord forgive him! He does a foolish thing, and then he thinks after that he shouldn't have done it. If I were there, I would make him think first, I would think for him; and then, if the thing was done, there would be me to try to mend it and him, too. But why should I speak as if that was in my power?" cried Helen, with a sudden soft momentary rush of tears, "for I cannot, I cannot, go with Alick and leave my father! I will have to stand by and see my poor lad go out again without a friend by his side into the terrible, terrible world."

Lily put her arm round her friend, kneeling beside her, giving a warm clasp of sympathy if nothing more. Helen's heart was beating sadly, with a suppressed passion, but Lily felt as if her slim young frame was all one desperate pulse, clanging in her ears and tingling to her fingers' ends. Was it her fault that in all her veins there burned this sense of impotence, this dreadful miserable consciousness that she could do nothing, move no one, and was powerless to shape her own fate? Helen was powerless too, but in how different a way! sure that she would have been able to fulfil that highest purpose if only her steps had been free, whereas Lily was humiliated by the certainty that there was no power at all in her, that to everybody with whom she was connected she was a creature without individual potency, whose fate was to be decided for her by the will of others. The contrast of Helen's feeling, which was so different, gave a bitterness to her pain.

"It was all very simple," said Helen. "My father—you have never seen him at his best, Lily; there is not a cleverer man, nor a better learned, in all this countryside—was tutor to Mr. Duff when they were both young, and the boys, as they grew up, used to come to him for lessons. Alick was the youngest, just two years older than me, that am the last of all. They were great friends with our own boys, who are both out in the world, and, oh, alack! not doing so very well that we should cast a stone at other folk. Eh but he was a bonnie boy! dark, always dark, like his mother, but the flower of the flock, and courted and petted wherever he went. He was a wild boy, and wild he was, I will not deny it, in his youth, and began by giving me a very sore heart; for, from the first that I can mind of, I have never thought of any man but him. And then he was sent away abroad—oh, not for punishment—to do better and make up the lost way. He came to my father and he said: 'Let Helen go with me and I'll do well.' I was but nineteen, Lily, and him twenty-one. They just laughed him to scorn. 'It would be the Babes in the Wood over again,' they said, and what was I, a little lass at home, that I could be of any help to a man? Lily!" cried Helen, her mild eyes shining, her cheeks aglow, "I knew better myself, though I dared not say it, and he, poor laddie, he knew best of all. I should have gone with him then! that very moment! if I had but seen it; and, oh, I did see, but I was so young, and no boldness in my heart. My father said: 'Work you your best for five years and wipe out all the old scores, and come back and ye shall have her, whether it pleases your father or no.' For the family would not have it. I was not good enough for them. But little was my father minding for that. He never thought upon the old laird but as a boy he had given palmies to, and kept in for not knowing his lessons. He did not care a snap of his fingers for the old laird."

"At nineteen, and him twenty-one!" Lily said.

"Oh, yes—they all said it was folly, and maybe I would say so, too, if I saw another pair. But for all that it was not folly, Lily. He wanted me to run away with him and say no word. And, oh, but I was in a terrible swither what to do. It's peetiful to be so young: you have no experience; you cannot answer a word when they preach you down with their old saws. I thought upon my mother that was weakly, and Tom and Jamie giving a good deal of trouble. And at the last I would not. It was my moment," she said softly, with a sigh, "and I had a perception of it; but I was frightened, Lily, and, oh, so silly and young!"

"Helen, you could not, you should not, have done it. It would have been impossible! It would have been wrong!"

Helen only shook her head with a melancholy smile. "And then he came back," she said, "at the end of the five years. Never, never, Lily, may you have the feeling I had when I saw Alick Duff again. Something said in me: 'Eelen, Eelen, that is your work!' The light had gone from his eyes, and the open look; his bonnie brow was all lined. He had grown to be the man you saw to-day. But what would that have mattered to me? He had but the more need of me. Alas, alas! my mother was dead, the boys all adrift, and my father taken with his illness, and what could I do then? He pleaded sore and my heart went with him. Oh, I fear he had been wild, wild! He came back without a shilling in his pocket or a prospect before him. The old laird was still living and went about with a brow like thunder. He looked as if he hated every man that named Alick's name; but them that knew best said he was the favorite still of all the sons. And Mrs. Duff, that had been so proud, that would not have the minister's daughter for her bonnie boy, she came to me herself, Lily. You see, it was not me only that thought it. She said: 'Eelen, if you will marry him, you will save my bonnie lad yet.' But I could not, I could not, Lily. How could I leave my own house, that had trouble in it, and nobody to make a stand but me?"

"They were selfish and cruel!" cried Lily; "they would have sacrificed you for the hope of saving an ill man!"

"Oh, whisht, whisht," cried Helen again. "And now he has come back. And every thing is changed. The old laird is dead and gone, and John Duff, that was never very kind, is laird in his stead, and there's no home for him there in his father's house. And he's a far older man—eight years it was this time that he was away. And you will wonder to hear me say a bonnie lad when you look at that black-browed man. But I see my bonnie lad in him still, Lily; he is aye the same to me. And, oh, if you knew how it drags my heart out of my bosom when he bids me come with him and I cannot! He says we might save the fragments that remain—but there's more than that, more than that! He has wasted his youth, but he has not yet lived half his life. And there's that to save, Lily; and him and me together we could stand. Oh, Lily, there's neither man nor devil that I would fear for Alick's sake, and at Alick's side, to save him—before it is too late!"

"Helen," cried Lily, "what do I know? I dare not speak; but what if after all you could not save him? If he cannot stand by himself, how could you make him? You are but a little delicate woman; you are not fit to fight. Oh, Helen, Helen, what if you could not save him when all is done!"

"I am not feared," Helen said with a serene countenance. And then there suddenly came a cloud over her, and tears came to her eyes. "What is the use of speaking," she said, throwing up her hands with an impatience unlike her usual calm, "when I can do nothing? when he must just go away again without hope, my poor Alick! and come back no more? And that will be the end both of him and me," she went on, "two folk that might have made a home, and served God in our generation, and brought up children and received strangers and held our warm place in the cold world. One of us will perish away yonder, among wild beasts and ill men, and one of us will just fade away on the roadside like a flower thrown away when its sweetness is gone—and it will be no better for any mortal, but maybe worse, that Alick Duff and Helen Blythe were born into this weary world."

"Oh, Helen, Helen!" cried Lily, "I think Alick Duff must have been the cloud that has come over your life and turned its brightness to dark. If you had not always been thinking of him, you would have had another home and a brighter life. And even now—can I not see myself?—don't you know very well there is a good man—"

"Oh," cried Helen, rising up with sudden animation, almost pushing Lily's kneeling figure from her, "go away from me with your good man! It is enough to make a person unjust, to make ye hate the name of good! How do you know whether they are good or no, one of them? Were they ever tempted like him? Had they ever the fire of hot thoughts in their head, or the struggle in their hearts? Was nature ever in them running free and wild like a great river, carrying the brigs and the dams away? or just a drumlie quiet stream, aye content in its banks, and asking no more? Oh, dinna speak to me of your good man! It's blasphemy, it's sacrilege, it's the sin that will never be pardoned! There is but one man, be he good or bad, and one woman that is bound to do her best for him; and ill be her lot if she fails to do it, for it is not herself she will ruin,—that would matter little—the feckless creature, no worth her salt,—but him, too, but him, too!"

She sat down again after this little outburst and dried her eyes. Lily, who had risen hurriedly to her feet, too, startled and almost angry, stood irresolute, not knowing how to reply, when Helen put out to her a trembling hand. "You are not to be troubled about me," she said; "you are not to be angry at what I say. It is a comfort to speak out my mind. Who can I speak to, Lily? Not to my father, who stands between me and my life; not to him, that rages at me as you have heard because I cannot arise and follow him, as I would do if I could, to the end of the world. Oh, Lily, it is good for the heart, when it is full like mine, to speak. It takes away a little of the burden. 'I leant my back until an aik'—do you mind the old song? You are not an oak, you're only a lily-plant, but, oh! the comfort to lean on you, Lily, just for a moment, just till I get my breath."

"Say to me whatever you like, Helen; say anything. I may not agree—"

"I am not asking you to agree—how should you agree, you that know nothing? Oh, Lily, my bonnie Lily," cried Helen, suddenly looking in her face, "am I speaking blasphemy, too? You may know more than I think; there is that in your face that was not there six months ago."

The color changed in Lily's cheek, but she did not flinch. "If I know anything," she said, "it is not in your way, Helen. I am not the kind of woman that can change a man's thoughts or his life. I am one that has no power. If I tried your way, I would fail. No one has changed a thought or a purpose in all my life for me. I am useless, useless. I have to do what other folk tell me, and wait other folk's pleasure, and blow here and blow there like a straw in the wind. And I love it not, I love it not!" she cried. "It is as bad for me as for you."

Helen thought she knew what the girl meant. She was here in durance, bound by her uncle's hard will; prevented, too, from carrying out the choice of her heart. It had not yet dawned upon the elder woman that Lily's experience had gone further than this. And it is possible that the gentle Helen, used all her life to an influence over others far stronger than seemed natural to her character, and believing fully and strongly in that power, could not have understood the higher trial of the far more vivacious and vigorous nature beside her, which flung itself in vain against the rock of another mind inaccessible to any power it possessed, and, clear-sighted and strong-willed, had yet to submit and do nothing but submit.

CHAPTER XXIX

Alick Duff went away from the valley of the Rugas, calling on heaven and earth to witness that he would never be seen there more, and that from henceforward he was to be considered as an altogether shipwrecked and ruined man. "There is nobody that will contradict you there," the minister said sternly, "and nothing but the grace of God, my man, for all you threep and swear to make my poor Eelen meeserable, that would ever have made any difference." "And who will say," cried Duff, "that it was not just her that would have been the grace o' God?" The minister shook his head, yet was a little startled by the argument. As for Helen, she said little more to her strange lover. "It is no use speaking now. There is nothing more to say. I cannot leave my father." Lily, to whom this story had come like a revelation in the midst of the quiet country life which seems, especially in Scotland, never to be ruffled by emotion, much less passion, and on whom it acted powerfully, restoring her mental balance and withdrawing at least a portion of her thoughts from herself, was a great deal at the Manse during this agitating period, which was all the more curious that nothing was ever said about it on the surface of the life which flowed on in an absolutely unbroken routine, as if there was no impassioned despairing man outside in the darkness waiting the moment to fling himself and his terrible needs and wishes at Helen's feet, and no terrible question tearing her heart asunder. That it was there underneath all the time was plain enough to those who were in the secret. The minister had an anxious look, even when he laughed and told his stories; and Helen, though her serenity was extraordinary, grew pale and red with an unconscious listening for every sound which Lily divined. He might burst in at any moment and make a scene in the quiet Manse parlor, destroying all the pretence of composure with which they had covered their life, or, worse still, he might do something desperate—he might disappear in the river or end his existence with a shot, leaving an indelible shame on his memory, and upon those who belonged to him, and upon her who, as the country folk would say, "had driven him to it." If she had married Alick Duff and gone away with him, there would have been an unanimous cry over her folly; but if in his despair he had cut the thread in any such conclusive way, Helen never would have been mentioned afterward but as the woman who drove poor Alick Duff to his death. There was a thrill of this possibility even in the air of the little town, where he was seen from time to time wandering about the precincts of the Manse, and where every-body knew him and his story. But the most exciting thing of all to Lily was to see the face and watch the ways of the excellent young minister, Mr. Blythe's assistant and successor, who went and came through these troubled days, talking of the affairs of the parish, sedulously restraining himself that he might not appear to think of, or be conscious of, anything else, but with a countenance which reflected Helen's, which followed every change of hers, yet when her attention was attracted toward him, closed up in a moment, with the most extraordinary effort dismissing all meaning from his countenance. Lily became fascinated by Mr. Douglas, through whom she could read, as in a mirror, every thing that was happening. He said not a word on this subject, which, indeed, nobody spoke of, nor did he betray any consciousness of the other man's presence, about which even the maid in the kitchen and the minister's man, who never had been so assiduous in the discharge of his duties as now, were so perfectly informed; but yet she felt sure that something in him tingled to the neighborhood of his rival like an elastic chord. He would come in sometimes pale, with a stern look in his closely drawn mouth, and then Lily would feel sure that he had seen Alick Duff in the way, waiting till Helen should appear. And sometimes the lines of his countenance would relax, so that she felt sure he had heard good news and believed that haunting figure to have gone away; and then at a sound which was no sound outside, at the most trifling change in Helen's face, the veil, the cloud, would shut again over his face.

The manner in which Lily attained the possibility of making these studies was that by the minister's invitation, seconded, but not with very much warmth, by Helen, she had come to the Manse on a visit of a few days. Whatever prejudice Mr. Blythe had against her—and she was sure he had a prejudice, though she could not imagine any cause for it—had disappeared under the pressure of his own sore need. He himself was helpless either to watch over or to protect his daughter, and in despair he had thought of the other girl, herself caught in a tangle of the bitter web of life, and full of secret knowledge of its difficulties, who, though she was so much younger, had learned to some degree the lesson which Helen was so slow to learn. "She's but a girl, but I'll warrant she could give Eelen a fine lesson what it is to lippen to a man," the minister said to himself. He had no high view of human nature, for his part. To lippen to a man seemed to him, though he had been in that respect severely virtuous himself, the last thing that a woman should do. For his own part he lippened to, that is, trusted, nobody very much, and thought he was wise in so doing. To have Lily there, seeing every thing with those young eyes, no doubt throwing her weight on the other side, allowing it at least to be seen that a man was not so easily turned round a woman's little finger as poor Helen thought, would be something gained in the absence of all other help. Mr. Blythe had a tacit conviction that Lily's influence would be on the opposite side, though his chief reason for thinking so was one that was fictitious.

This was how Lily came to be acquainted with all that was going on. They all appealed to her behind backs, each hoping he or she was alone in calling for her sympathy. "You will tell her better than I can; they all distrust an old man. They think the blood's dry in his veins and he has forgotten he was once like the rest. And she will listen to him at the last. The thought that he's going away, to fall deeper and deeper, and that strong delusion she has got that she can save him, will overcome her, and I'll be left in the corner of the auld Manse sitting alone."

"Oh, no, Mr. Blythe, never think that; Helen will not leave you."

"I would not trust her, nor one of them," he cried, and there in the dark, sitting almost unseen beside the fire, his voice came forth toneless, like that of a dead man. "I have never been thought to make much work about my bairns: one has gone and another has gone, and it has been said that the minister never minded. But there was once an auld man that said: 'When I am bereaved of my children, I am bereaved.'"

Lily put her hand upon the large, soft, limp hand of the old minister in quick sympathy. "She will never leave you," she repeated: "you need fear nothing for that—she will never go away."

He shook his head and put his other hand for a moment over hers. "You may have been led astray," he said, "poor little thing! but your heart is in the right place."

Lily did not think or ask herself what he meant about being led astray. She was too much occupied with Helen, who came in at the moment with the thrill and quiver in her which was the sign that she had seen her lover. The waning sunset light from the window which had seen so many strange sights indicated this movement too, the tremor that affected her head and slight shoulders like a chill of colder air from without. She said softly as she passed Lily: "There is one at the door would fain speak a word to you." It was not a call which Lily was very ready to obey. She had kept as far as possible out of the reach of Duff, and she had not the same sympathy for him as for the others involved; indeed, it must be allowed that, notwithstanding the charm of the romance, Lily's feelings were far more strongly enlisted on the side of the gentle and patient young minister than on any other. She lingered, putting away some scraps of work which had been on the table, until she could no longer resist Helen's piteous looks. "Oh, go, go!" she whispered close to Lily's ear. It was a blustering March night, the wind and the dust blowing in along the passage when the Manse door was opened, and Lily obeyed, very reluctantly, the gesture of the dark figure outside, which moved before her to a corner sheltered by the lilac bushes, which evidently was a spot very familiar. She felt that she could almost trace the steps of Helen on the faint line which was not distinct enough to be a path, and that opening among the branches—was it not the spot where she had leaned for support through many a trying interview? Duff tacitly ceded that place to Lily, and then turned upon her with his eyes blazing through the faint twilight. "You are with them all day, you hear all they're saying. They're all in a conspiracy to keep me hanging on, and no satisfaction. Tell me: am I to be cast off again like an old clout, or is there any hope that she'll come at the last?"

"There is no hope that she'll come; how could she?" cried Lily. "Her father is old and infirm, Mr. Duff, she has told you. It is cruel to keep her like this, always in agitation. She cannot; how could she? Her father—"

"Confound her father!" he cried, swinging his fist through the air. "What's her father to her own life and mine? You think one person should swamp themselves for another, Lily Ramsay. You've not been so happy in doing that yourself, if all tales be true."

"What tales?" cried Lily, breathless with sudden excitement; and then she paused and said proudly: "Take notice, Mr. Duff, that I am not Lily Ramsay to you!"

"What are you, then?" he cried, with a laugh of scorn. "If you've kept your father's name, you are just Lily Ramsay to Alick Duff, and nothing else. Our forefathers have known each other for hundreds of years. There was even a kind of a cousinship, a grandmother of mine that was a Ramsay, or yours that was a Duff, I cannot remember; but if you expect me, that knew you before you were born, to stand on ceremony—and Lumsden too," he added, in a lower tone, "whatever you may be to him."

"If it was my concerns you asked me out here to discuss, I think I will go in," said Lily, "for it is cold out of doors, and I have nothing to say to you."

"You know well whose concerns it was. Is she coming? Does she understand that it's for the last time? I know what she thinks. I've been such a fool hitherto she thinks I will be as great a fool as ever, and come hankering after her to the stroke of doom. If she thinks that, let her think it no more. This time I will never come back. I will just let myself go. Oh, it's easier, far easier, than to hold yourself in, even a little bit, as I've done. I've always had the fear of her before my eyes. I've always said to myself: 'Not that! not that! or she will never speak to me again;' but now—" He swung his fist once more with a menacing gesture through the dim air. It seemed to Lily as if he were shaking it in the face of Heaven.

"And you don't think shame to say so!" cried Lily, tremulous with cold and agitation, and finding no argument but this, which she had used before.

"Why should I think shame? There are things a woman like Eelen Blythe can look over, but there are some you would not let her hear of, not to save your soul. It's a matter of saving a man's soul, Lily Ramsay, whatever ye may think. The worst is she knows every word I have to say: there's nothing new to tell her—except just this," he said with vehement emphasis: "that this time I will never come back!"

"And that is not new either. I have heard you tell her so fifty times. Oh, man," cried Lily, "cannot you go and leave her at peace? She will never forget you, but she will accept what cannot be helped. Me, I fight against it, but I have to submit too. And Helen will not fight. She will just live quiet and say her prayers for you night and day."

"Her prayers! I want herself to stand by my side and keep my heart."

"You would be better with her prayers than with many a woman's company. Your heart! Can you not pluck up a spirit and stand for God and what is right without Helen? How will you do it with her, then? You would mind her at first—oh, I do not doubt every word she said—but then you would get impatient, and cry: 'Hold your tongue, woman!'"

"Is that," he cried quickly, "what he says to you? He is just a sneaking coward, and that I would tell him to his face!"

"You are a coward to call any man so that is not here to defend himself!" cried Lily, wild with rage and pain, "though who you mean I know not, and what you mean I care not. Never man spoke such words to me, but you would do it, you are of the kind to do it. You have thought and thought that she could save you, and then when you found it was not so, you would be fiercer at her and bitterer at her than you have been at your own self. Oh, let Helen be! She will never forget you, but she will never go with you so long as her old father sits there and cannot move in his big chair."

"If I thought that—" he said, then paused. "If that's what's to come of it all after more than a dozen years! Would I have been a vagabond on the face of the earth if she had taken me then? I trow no. You will think I am not the kind good men are made of? Maybe no; but there's more kinds than one, even of decent men. I would not drag what was her name in the dust."

"You think not," said Lily, "but if you have dragged your father's—"

"You little devil," he cried, "to mind me of that!" and then he took off his hat stiffly, and with ceremony, and said: "I beg your pardon, Miss Ramsay, or whatever your name may be."

"You are very insulting to me!" said Lily. "Why should I stand out here and let you abuse me? What are you to me that I should bear it?" But presently she added, softening: "I'm very sorry for you, all the same."

She was hurrying away when he seized her by the arm and held her back. "Do you see that? Am I to stand still and see that, and hold my peace forever?"

The corner among the lilacs had this advantage, carefully calculated, who could doubt, years ago? that those who stood there, though unseen themselves, could see any one who approached the door of the Manse. The young minister, Mr. Douglas, had come quietly in while they were speaking: his footstep was not one that made the gravel fly. He stood, an image of quietness and good order, on the step, awaiting admittance. Scotch ministers of that date were not always so careful in their dress, so regardful of their appearance, as this young Levite. He had his coat buttoned, his umbrella neatly folded. He was not impatient, as Duff would have been in his place, but stood immovable, waiting till Marget in the kitchen had snatched her clean apron from where it lay, and tied it on to make herself look respectable before she answered the bell. Duff gripped Lily's arm, not letting her go, and shaking with fierce internal laughter, which burst forth in an angry shout when the door was closed again and the assistant and successor admitted. "Call that a man!" he said, "with milk in his veins for blood; and you're all in a plot to take her from me, and give her to cauld parritch like that!"

"He would keep her like the apple of his eye. There would no wind blow rough upon her if he could help it!" cried Lily, shaking herself free.

"And you think that a grand thing for a woman?" he cried scornfully, "like a petted bairn, instead of the guardian of a man's life."

"Oh, Alick Duff!" cried Lily, half exasperated, half overcome, "come back, come back an honest man, for her father will not live forever."

"What would I want with her then if I was all I wanted without her?" he said, with another harsh laugh, and then turned on his heel, grinding the gravel under his foot, and without another word stalked away.

How strange it was to go in with fiery words ringing in her ears and the excitement of such a meeting in her veins, and find these people apparently so calm, sitting in the little dimly lighted parlor, where two candles on the table and a small lamp by Mr. Blythe's head on the mantel-piece were all that was thought necessary! Lily was too much moved herself to remark how they all looked up at her with a certain expectation: Helen wistful and anxious, the old minister closing his open book over his hand, the young one rising to greet her, with almost an appealing glance. They seemed all, to Lily's eyes, so harmonious, the same caste, the same character, fated to spend their lives side by side. And what had that violent spirit, that uncontrollable and impassioned man, with his futile ideal, to do in such a place? Mr. Douglas belonged to it and fell into all its traditions, but the other could never have had any fit place within the little circle of those two candles on the table. When the pause caused by her entrance—a pause of marked expectation, though none of the party anticipated that she would say a word—was over, the usual talk was resumed, the conversation about the parish folk who were ill, and those who were in trouble, and those to whom any special event had happened. John Logan and the death of his cows, poor things, who were the sustenance of the bairns; and the reluctance of poor Widow Blair to part with her son, who was a "natural," and had just an extraordinary chance of being received into one of those new institutions where they are said to do such wonderful things for that kind of poor imbecile creature: this was what Helen and her friend were talking of. The minister himself had a more mundane mind. He held his Scotsman fiercely, and read now and then out loud a little paragraph; and then he looked fixedly at Lily behind the cover of the newspaper, till his steady gaze drew her eyes to him. Then he put a question to her with his lips and eyes, without uttering any sound, and finding that unsuccessful, called her to him. "See you here, Miss Lily: there's something here in very small print ye must read to me with your young eyes."

"Can I do it, father?" said Helen.

"Just let me and Miss Lily be. She will do it fine, and not grudge the trouble. Is that man hovering about this house? Is he always there? I will have to send for the constable if he will not go away."

"I hope he is gone for to-night, Mr. Blythe."

"For to-night—to be back to-morrow like a shadow hanging round the place. You're a young woman and a bonnie one, and that carries every thing with a man like him. Get him away! I cannot endure it longer. Get him away!"

"Mr. Blythe—"

"I am saying to you get him away!" said the minister in incisive, sharp notes. And then he added: "After all, the old eyes are not so much worse than the young ones. Many thanks to you all the same."

CHAPTER XXX

This agitating episode in Lily's life was a relief to her from her own prevailing troubles. They all apologized to her for bringing her into the midst of their annoyances, but it was, in fact, nothing but an advantage. To contrast what she had herself to bear with the lot of Helen even was good for Lily. If she had but known a little sooner how long and sweetly that patient creature had waited, how many years had passed over her head, while she did her duty quietly, and neither upbraided God nor man, Lily thought it would have shamed herself into quiet, too, and prevented, perhaps, that crowning outcome of impatience which had taken place in the Manse parlor on that January night. Did she regret that January night with all its mystery, its hurry, and tumult of feeling? Oh, no! she said to herself, it would be false to Ronald to entertain such a thought; but yet how could she help feeling with a sort of yearning the comparative freedom of her position then, the absence of all complication? Lily had believed, as Ronald told her, that all complications would be swept away by this step. She would be freed, she thought, at once from her uncle's sway, and ready to follow her husband wherever their lot might lie. Every thing would be clear before her when she was Ronald's wife. She had thought so with certain and unfeigned faith. She might perhaps have been in that condition still, always believing, feeling that nothing was wanted but the bond that made them one, if that bond had not been woven yet. Poor Lily! She would not permit herself to say that she regretted it. Oh, no! how could she regret it? Every thing was against them for the moment, but yet she was Ronald's, and Ronald hers, forever and ever. No man could put them asunder. At any time, in any circumstances, if the yoke became too hard for her to bear, she could go unabashed to her husband for succor. How, then, could she regret it? But Helen had waited through years and years, while Lily had grown impatient before the end of one; or perhaps it was not

Lily, but Ronald, that had grown impatient. No, she could not shelter herself with that. Lily had been as little able to brave the solitude, the separation, the banishment, as he. And here stood Helen, patient, not saying a word, always bearing a brave face to the world, enduring separation, with a hundred pangs added to it, terrors for the man she loved, self-reproach, and all the exactions of life beside, which she had to meet with a cheerful countenance. How much better was this quiet, gentle woman, pretending to nothing, than Lily, who beat her wings against the cage, and would not be satisfied? Even now what would not Helen give if she could see her lover from time to time as Lily saw her husband, if she knew that he was satisfied, and, greatest of all, that he was unimpeachable, above all reproach? For that certainty Helen would be content to die, or to live alone forever, or to endure anything that could be given her to bear. And Lily was not content, oh! not at all content! Her heart was torn by a sense of wrong that was not in Helen's mind. Was it that she was the most selfish, the most exacting, the least generous of all? Even Ronald was happy—a man, who always wanted more than a woman—in having Lily, in the fact that she belonged to him; while she wanted a great deal more than that—so much more that there was really no safe ground between them, but as much disagreement as if they were a disunited couple, who quarrelled and made scenes between themselves, which was a suggestion at which Lily half laughed, half shuddered. If it went on long like this, they might turn to be—who could tell?—a couple who quarrelled, between whom there was more opposition and anger than love. Lily laughed at the thought, which was ridiculous; but there was certainly a shiver in it, too.

Duff had gone away before her short visit to the Manse came to an end. He disappeared after a last long interview with Helen under the bare lilac bushes, of which the little party in the parlor was very well aware, though no one said a word. The minister shifted uneasily on his chair, and held his paper with much fierce rustling up in his hands toward the lamp, as if it had been light he wanted. But what he wanted was to shield himself from the observation of the others, who sat breathless, exchanging, at long intervals, a troubled syllable or two. Mr. Douglas had, perhaps, strictly speaking, no right to be there, spying, as the old minister thought, upon the troubles of the family, and, as he himself was painfully conscious, intrusively present in the midst of an episode with which he had nothing to do. But he could not go away, which would make every thing worse, for he would then probably find himself in face of Helen tremblingly coming back, or of the desperate lover going away. A consciousness that it was the last was in all their minds, though nobody could have told why. Lily sat trembling, with her head down over her work, sometimes saying a little prayer for Helen, broken off in the middle by some keen edge of an intrusive thought, sometimes listening breathless for the sound of her step or voice. At last, to the instant consciousness of all, which made the faintest sound audible, the Manse door was opened and closed so cautiously that nothing but the ghost of a movement could be divined in the quiet. No one of the three changed a hair-breadth in position, and yet the sensation in the room was as if every one had turned to the door. Was she coming in here fresh from that farewell? Would she stand at the door, and look at them all, and say: "I can resist no longer. I am going with him." This was what the old minister, with a deep distrust in human nature, which did not except Helen, feared and would always fear. Or would she come as if nothing had happened, with the dew of the night on her hair, and Alick Duff's desperate words in her ears, and sit down and take up her seam, which Lily, feeling that in such a case the stress of emotion would be more than she could bear, almost expected? Helen did none of these things. She was heard, or rather felt, to go upstairs, and then there was an interval of utter silence, which only the rustling of the minister's paper, and a subdued sob, which she could not disguise altogether, from Lily, broke. And presently Helen came into the room, paler than her wont, but otherwise unchanged. "It is nine o'clock, father," she said; "I will put out the Books." The "Books" meant, and still mean, in many an old-fashioned Scotch house, the family worship, which is the concluding event of the day. She laid the large old family Bible on the little table by his side, and took from him the newspaper, which he handed to her without saying a word. And Marget came in from the kitchen, and took her place near the door.

Thus Helen's tragedy worked itself out. There is always, or so most people find when their souls are troubled, something in the lesson for the day, or in "the chapter," as we say in Scotland, when it comes to be read in its natural course, which goes direct to the heart. Very, very seldom, indeed, are the instances in which this curious unintentional sortes fails. As it happened, that evening the chapter which Mr. Blythe read in his big and sometimes gruff voice was that which contained the parable of the prodigal son. He began the story, as we so often do, with the indifferent tones of custom, reverential as his profession and the fashion of his day exacted, but not otherwise moved. But perhaps some glance at his daughter's head, bent over the Bible, in which she devoutly followed, after the prevailing Scotch fashion, the words that were read, perhaps the wonderful narrative itself, touched even the old minister's heavy spirit. His voice took a different tone. It softened, it swelled, it rose and fell, as does that most potent of all instruments when it is tuned by the influence of profound human feeling. The man was a man of coarse fibre, not capable of the finer touches of emotion; but he had sons of his own out in the darkness of the world, and the very fear of losing the last comfort of his heart made him more susceptible to the passion of parental anguish, loss, and love. Lower and lower bowed Helen's head as her father read; all the little involuntary sounds of humanity, stirrings and breathings, which occur when two or three are gathered together, were hushed; even Marget sat against the wall motionless; and when finally, like the very climax of the silence, another faint, uncontrollable sob came from Lily, the sensation in the room was as of something almost too much for flesh and blood. Mr. Blythe shut the book with a sound in his throat almost like a sob. He waved his hand toward the younger man at the table. "You will give the prayer," he said in what sounded a peremptory tone, and leaned back in the chair, from which he was incapable of moving, covering his face with his hands.

It was hard upon the poor, young, inexperienced assistant and successor to be called upon to "give" that prayer. It was not that he was untouched by the general emotion, but to ask him to follow the departure of that prodigal whose feet they had all heard grind the gravel, the garden gate swinging behind the vehemence of his going—the prodigal who yet had been all but pointed out as the object of the father's special love, and for whom Helen Blythe's life had been, and would yet be, one long embodied prayer— was almost more than Helen Blythe's lover, waiting, if perhaps the absence of the other might turn her heart to him, could endure. None of them, fortunately, was calm enough to be conscious how he acquitted himself of this duty, except, perhaps, Mr. Blythe himself, who was not disinclined to contemplate the son-in-law whom he would have preferred as "cauld parritch," Duff's contemptuous description of him. "No heart in that," the old minister said to himself as he uncovered his face and the others rose from their knees. The mediocrity of the prayer, with its tremulous petitions, to which the speaker's perplexed and troubled soul gave little fervor, restored Mr. Blythe to the composure of ordinary life.

Helen said little on that occasion or any other. "He will be far away before the end of the week," she said next morning. "It's best so, Lily. Why should he bide here, tearing the heart out of my breast, and his own, too? if it was not for that wonderful Scripture last night! He's away, and I'm content. And all the rest is just in the Lord's hands." The minister, too, had his own comment to make. "She'll be building a great deal on that chapter," he said to Lily, "as if there was some kind of a spell in it. Do not you encourage her in that. It was a strange coincidence, I am not denying it; but it's just the kind of thing that happens when the spirits are high strung. I was not unmoved myself. But that lad's milk and water," he added, with a gruff laugh, "he let us easy down." The poor "lad," time-honored description of a not fully fledged minister, whose prayer was milk and water, and his person "cauld parritch" to the two rougher and stronger men, accompanied Lily part of the way on foot as she rode home, Rory having come to fetch her, while the black powny carried her baggage. He was very desirous to unbosom his soul to Lily, too.

"Miss Ramsay, do you think she will waste all her heart and her life upon that vagabond?" he said. "It's just an infatuation, and her friends should speak more strongly than they do. Do you know what he is? Just one of those wild gamblers, miners, drinkers—it may be worse for anything I know, but my wish is not to say a word too much—that we hear of in America, and such places, in the backwoods, as they call it—men without a spark of principle, without house or home. I believe that's what this man Duff has come to be. I wish him no harm, but to think of such a woman as Helen Blythe descending into that wretchedness! It should not be suffered, it should not be suffered! taking nobody else into consideration at all, but just her own self alone."

"I think so, too, Mr. Douglas," said Lily, restraining the paces of Rory, "but then what can any one say if Helen herself—"

"Helen herself!" he said almost passionately; "what does she know? She is young; she is without experience. She is very young," he added, with a flush that made it apparent for the first time to Lily that he was younger than Helen, "because she is so inexperienced. She has never been out of this village. Men, however little they may have seen of themselves, get to know things; but a woman, a young lady—how can she understand? Oh, you should tell her, her friends should tell her!" he cried with vehemence. "It is a wicked thing to let a creature like that go so far astray."

"I agree with you, Mr. Douglas," said Lily again, "but if Helen in her own heart says 'Yes,' where is there a friend of hers that durst say 'No'? Her father: that is true. But he will never be asked to give his consent, for while he lives she will never leave him."

"You are sure of that?" the young minister asked.

"If it had not been so, would she have let him go now? She will never leave her father, but beyond that I don't think Helen will ever change, Mr. Douglas. If he never comes back again, she will just sit and wait for him till she dies."

"Miss Ramsay, I have no right to trouble you. What foolish things I may have cherished in my mind it is not worth the while to say. I thought, when the old man is away, what need to leave the house she was fond of, the house where she was born, when there was me ready to step in and give her the full right. It's been in my thoughts ever since I was named to the parish after him. It's nothing very grand, but it's a decent down-sitting, what her mother had before her, and no need for any disagreeable change, or questions about repairs, or any unpleasant thing. Just her and me, instead of her and him. I would not shorten his days, not by an hour—the Lord forbid! but just I would be always ready at her hand."

"Oh, Mr. Douglas," cried Lily, "her father would like it—and me, I would like it."

"Would you do that?" cried the young minister, laying his hand for a moment on Lily's arm. The water stood in his eyes, his face was full of tender gratitude and hope. But either the young man had pulled Rory's bridle unawares, or Rory thought he had done so, or resented the too close approach. He tossed his shaggy head and swerved from the side of the path to the middle of the road, when, after an ineffectual effort to free himself of Lily, he bolted with her, rattling his little hoofs with triumph against the frosty way. It was perhaps as well that the interview should terminate thus. It gave a little turn to Lily's thoughts, which had been very serious. And Rory flew along till he had reached that spot full of associations to Lily, where the broken brig and the Fairy Glen reminded her of her own little romance that was over. Over! Oh, no, that was far from over; that had but begun that wonderful day when Ronald and she picnicked by the little stream and the accident happened, without which, perhaps, her own story would have gone no further, and Helen's would never have been known to her. Rory stopped there, and helped himself to a mouthful or two of fresh grass, as if to call her attention pointedly to the spot, and then proceeded on his way leisurely, having given her the opportunity of picking up those recollections which, though so little distant, were already far off in the hurry of events which had taken place since then. Had it been possible to go back to that day, had there been no ascent of that treacherous ruin, no accident, none of all the chains of events that had brought them so much closer to each other and wound them in one web of fate, if every thing had remained as it was before the fated New Year, would Lily have been glad? That the thought should have gained entrance into her mind at all gave a heavy aspect to the scene and threw a cloud over every thing. She did not regret it: oh, no, no! how could she regret that which was her life? But something intolerable seemed to have come into the atmosphere, something stifling, as if she could not breathe. She forced the pony on, using her little switch in a manner with which Rory was quite unacquainted. Let it not be thought of, let it not be dwelt upon, above all, let it not be questioned, the certainty of all that had happened, the inevitableness of the past!

CHAPTER XXXI

The spring advanced with many a break and interval of evil weather. The east winds blew fiercely over the moor, and the sudden showers of April added again a little to the deceitful green that covered bits of the bog. But May was sweet that year; in these high-lying regions the whins, which never give up altogether, lighted a blaze of color here and there among the green knowes and hollows where there was solid standing-ground, and where one who did not mind an occasional dash from the long heads of the ling which began to thrill with sap, or an occasional sinking of a foot on a watery edge, might now venture again to trace the devious way upon the most delicious turf in the world here and there across the moor. The advancing season brought many a thrill of rising life to Lily. It seemed impossible to dwell upon the darker side of any prospect while the sunshine so lavished itself upon the gold of the whins and the green of the turf, and visibly moved the heather and the rowan-trees to all the effort and the joyous strain of life. I do not pretend that the sun always shone, for the history of the north of Scotland would, I fear, contradict that; but the number of heavenly mornings there were—mornings which lighted a spark in every glistening mountain burn and wet flashing rock over which it poured, and opened up innumerable novelties of height and hollow, projecting points and deep withdrawing valleys, in a hillside which seemed nothing but a lump of rock and moss on duller occasions—were beyond what any one would believe. They are soon over: the glory of the day is often eclipsed by noon; but Lily, whose heart, being restless, woke her early, had the advantage of them all. And many a tiny flower began to peep by the edges of the moor—little red pimpernels, little yellow celandines, smaller things still that have no names. And the hills stood round serenely waiting for summer, as with a smile to each other under the hoods which so often came down upon their brows even while the sun was shining. What did it matter, a storm or two, the wholesome course of nature? Summer was coming with robes of purple to clothe them, and revelations of a thousand mysteries in the hearts of the silent hills.

Amid such auguries and meditative expectations it was not possible that Lily could remain unmoved. And thus her expectation, if not so sublime as that of nature, was at least as exact and as well defined. Alas, the difference was that nature was quite sure of her facts, while an unfortunate human creature never is so. The course of the sun does not fail, however he may delay that coming forth from his chamber, like a bridegroom, which is the law of the universe. But for the heart of man no one can answer. It was such a little thing to do, such an easy thing—no trouble, no trouble! Lily said to herself. To find the little house they wanted, oh, how easily she could do it if she could but go and see herself to this, which was really a woman's part of the business. Lily imagined herself again and again engaged in that delightful quest. She saw herself running lightly up and down the long stairs. Why take Ronald from his work when she could do it so easily, so gladly, so pleasantly, with so much enjoyment to herself? And though she had been banished for so long, there was still many a house in Edinburgh which would take her in with kindly welcome, and rejoice over her marriage, and help and applaud the young couple in their start. Oh, how easy it all was were but the first step sure. She had thought, in her childishness, that the mere fact of marriage would be enough; that it would bring all freedom, all independence, with it; that the moment she stood by Ronald's side as his wife the path of their life lay full in the sunshine and light of perfect day. Alas, that had not proved so!

He came again another time between March and May. It was wonderful the journeys he took, thinking nothing of a long night in the coach coming and going, to see his love, for the sake of only a couple of days in her society. The women at Dalrugas were very much impressed, too, by the money it must cost him to make these frequent visits. "Bless me," Katrin said, "he is just throwing away his siller with baith hands; and what are they to do for their furnishing and to set up their house? I am not wanting you to go, Beenie—far, far from that. It will be like the sun gone out of the sky when we're left to oursel's in the house, nothing but Dougal and me. But, oh! only to think of the siller that lad is wastin' with a' his life before him. They would live more thrifty in their own house than him there and her here, and thae constant traiks from one place to another, even though her and you at present cost him naething—but what, after a', is a woman's meat?"

"I wot weel it would be more thrift, and less expense, not to say better in every way; but if the man does not see it, Katrin, what can the wife do?"

"I ken very weel what I would do," said Katrin, with a toss of her head. These were the comments below stairs. But when May came and went, and it was not till early June that Lily received her husband, the fever of expectation and anxiety which consumed her was beyond expression. She met him at the head of the spiral stair as usual, but speechless, without a word to say to him. Her cheeks flamed with the heat of her hopes, her terrors, her wild uncertainty. She held out her hands in welcome with something interrogative, enquiring, in them. She did not wish to be taken to his heart, to be kept by any caress from seeing his face and reading what was in it. Was it possible that it was not Ronald at all she was thinking of, but something else—not her husband's visit, his presence, his love, and the delight of seeing him? And how common, how trivial, how paltry a thing it was which Lily was thinking of first, before even Ronald! Had he found the little house? Had he got it, that hope of her life? was it some business connected with that that had detained him? Had he got the key of it, something resembling the key of it, to lay at her feet, to place in her hand, the charter of her rights and her freedom? But he did not say a word. Was it natural he should when he had just arrived, barely arrived, and was thinking of nothing but his Lily? It was his love that was in his mind, not any secondary thing such as filled hers. He led her in, with his arms around her and joy on his lips. His bonnie Lily! if she but knew how he had been longing for a sight of her, how he had been stopped when he was on the road, how every exasperating thing had happened to hold him back! Ah, she said to herself, it would be the landlord worrying for more money, or some other wicked thing. "But now," cried Ronald, "the first look of my Lily pays for all!" That was how it was natural he should speak. She supported it all, though her bosom was like to burst. She would not forestall him in his story of how he had secured it, nor yet chill him by showing him that while the first thought in his mind was love, the first in hers was the little house. Oh, no, she would respond, as, indeed, her heart did; but she was choked in her utterance, and could speak few words. If he would only say a word of that, only once: "I have got it, I have got it!" then the floodgates would have been opened, and Lily's soul would have been free.

Ronald spoke no such word; he said nothing, nothing at all upon that subject, or anything that could lead to it. He was delighted to see her again, to hold her in his arms. Half the evening, until Beenie brought the dinner, he was occupied in telling her that every time he saw her she was more beautiful, more delightful, in his eyes. And Lily gasped, but made no sign. She would wait, she would wait! She would not be impatient; after all, that was just business, and this was love. She would have liked the business best, but perhaps that was because she was common, just common, not great in mind and heart like—other folk, a kind of a housewife, a poor creature thinking first of the poorest elements. He should follow his own way, he that was a better lover, a finer being, than she; and in his own time he would tell her—what, after all, was no fundamental thing, only a detail.

The dinner passed, the evening passed, and Ronald said not a word, nor Lily either. She had begun to get bewildered in her mind. Whit-Sunday! Whit-Sunday! Was it not Whit-Sunday that was the term, when houses were to be hired in Edinburgh, and the maids went to their new places? And it was now past, and had nothing been done for her? Was nothing going to be done? Lily began to be afraid now that he would speak; that he would say some word that would take away all hope from her heart. Rather that he should be silent than that! There was a momentary flagging in the conversation when the dinner was ended, and in the new horror that had taken possession of her soul Lily, to prevent this, rushed into a new subject. She told Ronald about Alick Duff and Helen Blythe, and how she had received them at Dalrugas, and had passed some days at the Manse seeing the end of it. Ronald, with the air of a benevolent lord and master, shook his head at the first, but sanctioned the latter proceeding with a nod of his head. "Keep always friends with the Manse people," he said; "they are a tower of strength whatever happens; but I would not have liked to see my Lily receiving a black sheep like Alick Duff here."

What had he to do with the house of Dalrugas, or those who were received there? What right had he to be here himself that he should give an authoritative opinion? Oh, do not believe that Lily thought this, but it flashed through her mind in spite of herself, as ill thoughts will do. She said quickly: "And the worst is I took his part. I would have taken his part with all my heart and soul."

Ronald did nothing but laugh at this protestation. And he laughed contemptuously at the thought that Helen could have saved the man who loved her. "That's how he thinks to come over the women. He would not dare say that to a man," he cried. "Helen Blythe, poor little thing!" He laughed again, and Lily felt that she could have struck him in the sudden blaze out of exasperation which somewhat relieved her troubled mind.

"When you laugh like that, I think I could kill you, Ronald!"

"Lily!" he cried, sitting up in his chair with an astonished face, "why, what is the matter with you, my darling?"

"Nothing is the matter with me! except to hear you laugh at what was sorrow and pain to them, and deadly earnest, as any person might see."

"Havers!" cried Ronald; "he had his tongue in his cheek all the time, yon fellow. He thought, no doubt, her father must have money, and it would be worth his while—"

"If you believe that every-body thinks first of money—" Lily said, her hand, which was on the table, quivering to every finger's end.

"Most of us do," he said quietly; "but what does it mean that my Lily should be so disturbed about Alick Duff, the ne'er-do-well, and Helen Blythe?"

"I can't tell you," cried Lily, struggling with that dreadful, inevitable inclination to tears which is so hard upon women. "I am—much alone in this place," she said, with a quiver of her mouth, "and you away."

"My bonnie Lily!" he cried once more, hastening to her, soothing her in his arms, as he had done so often before. That was all, that was all he could say or do to comfort her; and that does not always answer—not, at least, as it did the first or even the second or third time. To call her "My bonnie Lily!" to lean her head upon his breast that she might cry it all out there and be comforted, was no reply to the demand in her heart. And the hysteria passion did not come to tears in this case. She choked them down by a violent effort. She subdued herself, and withdrew from his supporting arm, not angrily, but with something new in her seriousness which startled Ronald, he could not tell why. "We will go upstairs," she said, "or, if you would like it, out on the moor. It is bonnie on the moor these long, long days, when it is night, and the day never ends. And then you can tell me the rest of your Edinburgh news," she said, suddenly looking into his face.

Oh, he understood her now! His face was not delicate like Lily's to show every tinge of changing color, but it reddened through the red and the brown with a color that showed more darkly and quite as plainly as the blush on any girl's face. He understood what was the Edinburgh news she wanted. Was it that he had none to give?

"Let us go out on the moor," he said. "Where is your plaid to wrap you round? It may be as beautiful as you like, but it's always cold on a north country moor."

"Not in June," she cried, throwing the plaid upon his shoulder. It was nine o'clock of the long evening, but as light still as day, a day perfected, but subdued, without sun, without shadow, like, if anything human can be like, the country where there is neither sun nor moon, but the Lamb is the light thereof. The moor lay under the soft radiance in a perfect repose, no corner in it that was not visible, yet all mystery, spellbound in that light that never was on sea or shore. At noon, with all the human accidents of sun and shade, they could scarcely have seen their own faces, or the long distance of the broken land stretched out beyond, or the hills dreaming around in a subdued companionship, as clearly as now, yet all in a magical strangeness that overawed and hushed the heart. Even Lily's cares—that one care, rather, which was so little, yet so great, almost vulgar to speak of, yet meaning to her every thing that was best on earth—were hushed. The stillness of the shining night, which was day; the silence of the great moor, with all its wild fresh scents and murmurs of sound subdued; the vast round of cloudless sky, still with traces on it of the sunset, but even those forming but an undertone to the prevailing softness of the blue—were beyond all reach of human frettings and struggles. They were on the eve of discovering that the earth had been rent between them, closely though they stood together, but in a moment the edges of the chasm had disappeared, the green turf and the heather, with its buds forming on every bush, spread over every horrible division. Lily put her arm within her husband's with a long, tremulous sigh. What did any uneasy wish matter, any desire even if desperate, compared with this peace of God that was upon the hills and the moor and the sky?

I doubt, however, whether all of this made it easier for Ronald to clear himself at last of the burden of the unfulfilled trust. When she said next morning, with a catch in her breath, but as perfect an aspect of calm as she could put on: "You have told me nothing about our house," his color and his breath also owned for a moment an embarrassment which it was difficult to face. She had said it while he stood at the window looking out, with his back toward her. She had not wished to confront him, to fix him with her eyes, to have the air of bringing him to an account.

Ronald turned round from the window after a momentary pause. He came up to her and took both her hands in his. "My bonnie Lily!" he said.

"Oh," she cried with sudden impatience, drawing her hands from him, "call me by my simple name! I am your wife; I am not your sweetheart. Do I want to be always petted like a bairn?"

"Lily!" he said, startled, and a little disapproving, "there is something wrong with you. I never thought you were one to be affected with nerves and such things."

"Did you ever think I was one to live all alone upon the moor? to belong to nobody, to see nobody, to be married in a secret, and get a visit from my man now and then in a secret, too? and none to acknowledge or stand by me in the whole world?"

"Lily! Lily!" he cried, "how far is that from the fact? Am I not here whenever I can find a moment to spare, and ready to come at any time for any need if you but hold up your little finger? Why is it you are not acknowledged and set by my side as I would be proud to do? Can you ever doubt I would be proud to do it? But many a couple have kept their marriage quiet till circumstances were better. You and I are not the first—I could tell you of a score—that would not keep apart half their days and lose the good of their life, but just kept the fact to themselves till better times should come."

"You said nothing to me about better times coming," said Lily; "you spoke of the term, and that you could not get a house to live in till the term."

"And I said quite true," said Ronald. As soon as he got her to discuss the matter he felt sure of his own triumph. "You knew that as well as I did. And now here is just the truth, Lily: I am not very well off, and it does not mend my practice that I've been so often here in the North. Don't tell me I need not come unless I like; that's a silly woman's saying, it is not like my Lily. I am not very well off, and you have nothing if there is a public breach with Sir Robert. And for a little while I have been beginning to think—"

He paused, hoping she would say something, but Lily said nothing. She had covered her face with her hands.

"I have been beginning to think," he continued slowly, "that this is a bad time for beginning life in Edinburgh. You are not ignorant of Edinburgh life, Lily; you know that in the vacations, when the courts are up, nobody is there. If we had twenty houses, we could not stay in them in August and September, when every-body is away. As this is a bad time for beginning in Edinburgh, I was thinking that to take the expense of a house upon me now would be a foolish thing. Think of a garret in the old town from this to autumn, with all the smoke and the bad air instead of the bonnie moor! And in six weeks or a little more, Lily, I would be able to get some shooting hereabouts, which will be a grand excuse, and we could be together without a word said, with nobody to make any criticisms."

She cried out, stamping her foot: "Will you never understand? It is the grand excuse and the nobody to criticise that is insufferable to me. Why should there be any excuse? Why should there be a word said? I am your wife, Ronald Lumsden!"

"My dear, you are ill to please," he said. "But nobody can see reason better than you if you will but open your eyes to it. See here, Lily: two months and more are coming when our house, if we had it, would be useless to us, and in the meantime you are very well off here."

She gave him a sudden glance, and would have said something, but arrested herself in time.

"You are very well here," he repeated, "far better than even going upon visits, or at some other little country place, where we might take lodgings, and be very uncomfortable. Your moor is a little estate to you, Lily; it's company and every thing. And if I had a little shooting which I could manage—a man with a gun is not hard to place in Scotland, and up in the north country there is many an opportunity; and there is always Tom Robison's cottage to fall back on, where you are very well off as long as you neither need to eat there nor to sleep there. Your servants here are used to me. Whatever explanations Dougal has made to himself, he has made them long ago. I have no fears for him. Where would you be so well, my Lily, as in your home?"

"And where would you be so ill, Ronald," she cried, "as in—as in—" But Lily could not finish the sentence. How could it be that he did not say that to himself, that he left it to her to say—to her, who was incapable, after all, of saying to the man she loved such hard words? Her own home, her uncle's house, who had sent her here to separate her once for all from Ronald Lumsden, while Ronald arranged so easily to establish himself under his enemy's roof.

"Where would I be so ill as in Sir Robert's house?" he said, with a laugh. "On the contrary, Lily, I am very happy here. I have been happier here than in any other house in the world, and why should I set up scruples, my dear, when I have none? If Sir Robert had been a wise man he never would have tried to separate you and me; and now that we have turned his evil to good, and made his prison a palace, why should we banish ourselves when all is done to do him a very doubtful pleasure? He will never hear a word of it in my belief, and if he does, he will hear far more than that I have come to share your castle for another vacation. It was the first step that was the worst: yon snow-storm, perhaps, at the New Year; but that was the power of circumstances, and no Scots householder would ever have turned a man out into the snow. When we did that, we did the worst. A few weeks, more or less, after that— what can it matter? And, short time or long time, it is my belief, Lily, that he will never be a pin the wiser. Then why should we trouble ourselves?" Ronald said.

As for Lily, this time she answered not a word.

CHAPTER XXXII

It may be imagined that after this there was very little said of the house in Edinburgh, which now, indeed, it was impossible to do anything about till the term at Martinmas. But Lily, I think, never alluded to the Martinmas term. Her heart sank so that it recovered itself again with great difficulty, and the very suggestion of the thing she had so longed for, and fixed all her wishes upon, now brought over her a sickness and faintness both of body and soul. When some one talked by chance of the maids going to their new places at the term, the color forsook her face, and Helen Blythe was much alarmed on one such occasion, believing her friend was going to faint. Lily did not faint. What good would that do? she said to herself with a sort of cynicism which began to appear in her. She dug metaphorically her heels into the soil, and stood fast, resisting all such sudden weaknesses. Perhaps Ronald was surprised, perhaps he was not quite so glad as he expected to be, when she ceased speaking on that subject; but, on the whole, he concluded that it was something gained. If he could but get her to take things quietly, to wait until he was quite ready to set up such an establishment as he thought suitable, or, better still, till Sir Robert died and rewarded her supposed obedience by leaving her his fortune, which was her right, how fortunate that would be! But Lily was taking things too quietly, he thought, with a little tremor. It was not natural for her to give in so completely. He watched her with a little alarm during that short stay of his. Not a word of the cherished object which had always been coming up in their talk came from Lily's lips again. She made no further allusion to their possible home or life together; her jests about cooking his dinner for him, about the Scotch collops and the howtowdie, were over. Indeed, for that time all her jests were over; she was serious as the gravest woman, no longer his laughing girl, running over with high spirits and nonsense. This change made Ronald very uncomfortable, but he consoled himself with thinking that in a light heart like Lily's no such thing could last, and that she would soon recover her better mood again.

He did not know, indeed, nor could it have entered into his heart to conceive—for even a clever man, as Ronald was, cannot follow further than it is in himself to understand the movements of another mind— the effect that all this had produced upon Lily, the sudden horrible pulling up in the progress of her thoughts, the shutting down as of a black wall before her, the throwing back of herself upon herself. These words could not have had any meaning to Ronald. Why a blank wall? Why a dead stop? He had said nothing that was not profoundly reasonable. All that about the vacation was quite true. Edinburgh is empty as a desert when the courts are up and the schools closed. The emptiness of London after the season, which is such perfect fiction and such absolute truth, is nothing to the desolation of Edinburgh in the time of its holiday. To live, as he said, in a garret in the old town, or even in the top story of one of the newer, more convenient houses in the modern quarter, while every-body was away, instead of here on the edge of the glorious heather, among the summer delights of the moor, was folly itself to think of. It was impossible but that Lily must perceive that, the moment she permitted herself to think. Dalrugas might be dreary for the winter, especially in the circumstances of their separation, he was ready to allow; but in August, with the birds strong on the wing, and the heather rustling under your stride, and no separation at all but the punctual return of the husband to dinner and the evening fire—what was there, what could there be, to complain of? Sir Robert's house an ill place for him! he said to himself, with a laugh. Luckily he was not so squeamish. Such delicate troubles did not affect his mind. He could see what she meant, of course, and he was not very sure that he liked Lily to remind him of it; but he was of a robust constitution. He was not likely to be overwhelmed by a fantastic idea like that.

And the autumnal holiday was, as he anticipated, actually a happy moment in their lives. Before it came Lily had time to go through many fits of despair, and many storms of impatience and indignation. To have one great struggle in life and then to be forever done, and fall into a steady unhappiness in one portion of existence as you have been persistently happy in another, is a thing which seems natural enough when the first break comes in one's career. But Lily soon learned the great difference here between imagination and reality. There was not a day in which she did not go through that struggle again, and sank into despair and flamed with anger, and then felt herself quieted into the moderation of exhaustion, and then beguiled again by springing hopes and insinuating visions of happiness. Thus notwithstanding all the bitterness of Lily's feelings on various points, or rather, perhaps, in consequence of the evident certainty that nothing would make Ronald see as she did, or even perceive what it was that she wanted and did not want—the eagerness of her passion for the house, which meant honor and truth to her, but to him only a rash risking of their chances, and foolish impatience on her part to have her way, as is the worst of women—and her bitter sense of the impossibility of his calm establishment here in her uncle's house, a thing which he regarded as the simplest matter in the world, with a chuckle over the discomfiture of the old uncle—all these things, by dint of being too much to grapple with, fell from despair into the ordinary of life. And Lily agreed with herself to push them away, not to think when she could help it, to accept what she could—the modified happiness, the love and sweetness which are, alas! of themselves not enough to nourish a wholesome existence. She was happy, more or less, when he came in with his gun over his shoulder, and a bag at which Dougal looked with critical but unapproving eyes. Dougal himself took, or had permission, to shoot over Sir Robert's estate, which was not of great extent. These were not yet the days when even a little bit of Highland shooting is worth a better rent than a farm, and the birds had grown wild about Dalrugas with only Dougal's efforts at "keeping them down." What the country thought of Ronald's position it would be hard to say. He gave himself out as living at Tam Robison's, the shepherd's, and being favored by Sir Robert Ramsay's grieve in the matter of the shooting, which there was nobody to enjoy. No doubt it was well enough known that he was constantly at Dalrugas, but a country neighborhood is sometimes as opaque to perceive anything doubtful as it is lynx-eyed in other cases. And as few people visited at Dalrugas, there was no scandal so far as any one knew.

And with the winter there came something else to occupy Lily's thoughts and comfort her heart. It made her position ten times more difficult had she thought of that, but it requires something very terrible indeed to take away from a young wife that great secret joy and preoccupation which arise with the first expectation of motherhood. Besides, it must be remembered that there was in Lily's mind no terror of discovery. Perhaps it was this fact which kept her story from awakening the suspicious and the scandal mongers of the neighborhood. There was no moment at which she would not have been profoundly relieved and happy to be found out. She desired nothing so much as that her secret should be betrayed. This changes very much the position of those who have unhappily something to conceal, or rather who are forced to conceal something. If you fear discovery, it dodges you at every step, it is always in your way. But if you desire it, by natural perversity the danger is lessened, and nobody suspects what you would wish found out. So that even this element added something to Lily's happiness in her new prospects. That hope in the mind of most women needs nothing to enhance it; the great mystery, the silent joy of anticipation, the overwhelming thought of what is, by ways unknown, by long patience, by suffering, by rapture, about to be, fills every faculty of being. I am told that these sentiments are old-fashioned, and that it is not so that the young women of this concluding century regard these matters. I do not believe it: nature is stronger than fashion, though fashion is strong, and can momentarily affect the very springs of life. But when it did come into Lily's mind as she sat in a silent absorption of happiness, not thinking much, working at her "seam," which had come to be the most delightful thing in heaven or earth, that the new event that was coming would demand new provisions and create new necessities which it seemed impossible could be provided for at Dalrugas, the thought gave an additional impetus to the secret joy that was in her. Such things, she said to herself, could not be hid. It would be impossible to continue the life of secrecy in which she had been kept against her will so long. Whatever happened, this must lead to a disclosure, to a home of her own where in all honor her child should see the light of day.

For a long time Lily had no doubt on this point. She began to speak again about the term and the upper story in the old town. "But I would like the other better now," she said; "it would be better air for—, and more easy to get out to country walks and all that is needed for health and thriving." It had been an uncomfortable sensation to Ronald when she had renounced all the talk and anticipation of the house to be taken at the term. But now that he was accustomed to exemption from troublesome enquiries on that point he felt angry to have it taken up again. He was disposed to think that she did it only to annoy him, at a time, too, when he was setting his brain to work to think and to plan how the difficulties could be got over, and how in the most satisfactory way, and with the least trouble to her, every thing could be arranged for Lily's comfort. But he did not betray himself; he took great pains even to calm all inquietudes, and not to irritate her or excite her nerves (as he said) by opposition. He tried, indeed, to represent mildly that of all country walks and good air nothing could be so good as the breeze over the moors and the quiet ways about, where every thing delicate and feeble must drink in life. But Lily had confronted him with a blaze in her eyes, declaring that such a thing was not possible, not possible! in a tone which she had never taken before. He said nothing more at that time. He made believe even, when Whit-Sunday returned, that he had seen a house, which he described in detail, but did not commit himself to say he had secured it. Into this trap Lily fell very easily. She had all the rooms, the views from the windows, the arrangement of the apartment described to her over and over again, and for the great part of that second summer of her married life there was no drawback to the blessedness of her life. She spent it in a delightful dream, taking her little sober walks like a woman of advanced experience, no longer springing from hummock to hummock like a silly girl about the moor, taking in, in exquisite calm, all its sounds and scents and pictures to her very heart. In the height of the summer days, when the air was full of the hum of the bees, Lily would sit under the thin shade of a rowan-tree, thinking about nothing, the air and the murmur which was one with the air filling her every consciousness. Why should she have sought a deeper shadow. She wanted no shadow, but basked in the warm shining of the sun, and breathed that dreamy hum of life, and watched, without knowing it, the drama among the clouds, shadows flitting like breath as swift and sudden, coming and going upon the hills. All was life all through, constant movement, constant sound, alternation and change, no need of thinking, foreseeing, fore-arranging, but the great universe swaying softly in the infinite realm of space, and God holding all—the bees, the flickering rowan-leaves, the shadows and the mountains and Lily brooding over her secret—in the hollow of his hand.

As the summer advanced, however, troubles began to steal in. She was anxious, very anxious, to be taken to the house, which he allowed her to believe was ready for her. It must be said that Ronald was very assiduous in his visits, very anxious to please her in every way, full of tenderness and care, though always avoiding or evading the direct question. It went to his heart to disappoint her, as he had to do again and again. The house was not ready; there were things to be done which had been begun, which could not be interrupted without leaving it worse than at first. And then was it not of the greatest importance for her own health that she should remain as long as possible in the delicious air of the North—the air which was, if not her own native air, at least that of her family? Lily had been deeply disappointed, disturbed in her beautiful calm, and a little excited, perhaps, in the nerves, which she had never been conscious of before, but which Ronald assured her now made her "ill to please"—by his unreasonable resistance to her desire to take refuge in the house which she believed to be awaiting her—when a curious incident occurred. Beenie appeared one morning with a very confused countenance to ask whether her mistress would permit her to receive the visit of a cousin of hers, "a real knowledgable woman," who was out of a place and in want of a shelter. "You had better ask Katrin than me, Beenie," cried Lily; "I've filled the house too much and too long already. It is not for me to take in strangers." "Eh, mem," cried Katrin, her head appearing behind that of Beenie in the doorway, "it will be naething but a pleasure to me to have her." Katrin's countenance was anxious, but Beenie's was confused. She could not look her mistress in the face, but stood before her in miserable embarrassment, laying hems upon her apron. "Speak up, woman, canna ye?" cried Katrin, "for your ain relation. Mem [Katrin never said Miss Lily now], I ken her as weel as Beenie does. She's a decent woman and no one that meddles nor gies her opinion. I'll be real glad to have her if you'll give your consent." "Oh, I give my consent," Lily cried lightly. And in this easy way was introduced into Dalrugas a very serious, middle-aged woman, not in the least like Beenie, of superior education, it appeared, and a quietly authoritative manner, whose appearance impressed the whole household with a certain awe. It was a few days after the termination of one of Ronald's visits that this incident occurred, and Lily could not resist a certain instinctive alarm at the appearance of this new figure in the little circle round her. "You are sure she is your cousin, Beenie? She is not like you at all." "And you're no like Sir Robert, Miss Lily, that is nearer to ye than a cousin," said Beenie promptly. She added hurriedly: "It's her father's side she takes after, and she's had a grand education. I've heard say that she kent as much as the doctors themselves. Education makes an awfu' difference," said Beenie with humility. I am not sure that Lily was more attached to this new inmate on account of her grand education. But that was, after all, a matter of very secondary importance; and so the days and the weeks went on.

There occurred at this time an interval longer than usual between Ronald's visits, and Lily lost all her happy tranquillity. She became restless, unhappy, full of trouble. "What is to become of me, what is to become of me?" she would cry, wringing her hands. Was she to be left here at the crisis of her fate in a solitude where there was no help, no one to stand by her? She felt in herself a reflection, too, of the visible anxiety of the two women, Beenie and Katrin, who never would let her out of their sight, who seemed to tremble for her night and day. The sight of their anxious faces angered her, and roused her occasionally to send them off with a sharp word, half jest, half wrath. But when she was freed from these tender yet exasperating watchers, Lily would cover her face with her hands and cry bitterly, with a helplessness that was more terrible than any other pain. For what could she do? She could not set out, inexperienced, alone, without money, without knowing where to go. She had, indeed, Ronald's address; but had he not changed into the new house, if new house there was? Lily began to doubt every thing in this dreadful crisis of her affairs. She had no money, and to travel cheaply in these days was impossible. And how could she get even to Kinloch-Rugas, she who had avoided being seen even by Helen Blythe? She wept like a child in the helplessness of her distress. She did not hear any knock at the door or permission asked to come in, but started to find some one bending over her, and to see that it was the strange woman Marg'ret, Beenie's supposed cousin. Lily made this discovery with resentment, and bid her hastily go away.

"Mem, Mrs. Lumsden," Marg'ret said.

Lily quickly uncovered her face. "You know!" she cried with a mixture, which she could not explain to herself, of increased suspicion, yet almost pleasure; for nobody had as called yet her by that name.

"I would be a stupid person indeed if I didna know. Oh, madam, I've made bold to come in, for I know more things than that. Beenie would tell you I've had an education. I've come to beg you, on my bended knees, to give up all thoughts of moving—it's too late, my dear young leddy—and just make yourself as content as you can here."

"Here!" cried Lily, with a scream of distress. "No, no, no, I must be in my own house. Woman, whoever you are, do you know I'm Miss Ramsay here? It's not known who I am, and what will they think if anything—anything—should happen?"

"Are you wanting to conceal it, Mrs. Lumsden?"

"No, no, no! Anything but that! If you will go to the cross of Kinloch-Rugas and say Lily Ramsay has been Ronald Lumsden's wife for more than a year, I will—I will kiss you," cried Lily, as if that was the greatest sacrifice she could make.

"Then why should you not bide still? If it's found out, it's found out, and you're pleased. And if it's not found out, maybe the gentleman's pleased. Mrs. Lumsden, I'm a real, well-qualified nurse. I will tell you the truth: they were frightened, thae women. I said, when Beenie told me, I would come and just be here if there was any occasion. Mistress Lumsden, I will show you my certificates. I am just all I say, and maybe a little more. Will you trust yourself to me?"

And what could Lily do? She was in no condition to enquire into it, to satisfy herself if it was a plot of Ronald's making, or only, as this woman said, a scheme of the women. To think over such subjects was no exercise for her at that moment. She yielded, for she could do nothing else. And a very short time after there was an agitated night in the old tower. It was the night of the market, and Dougal had come in, in the muzzy condition which was usual to him on such occasions, and consequently slept like a log and was conscious of nothing that was going on. Ronald had arrived the day before. And when the morning came, there was another little new creature added to the population of the world.

It was more like a dream than ever to Lily—a dream of rapture and completion, of every trouble calmed, and every pang over, and every promise fulfilled. She was surrounded by love and the most sedulous watching. She seemed to have no longer any wishes, only thanks in her heart. She even saw her husband go away without trouble. "Come back soon and fetch us. Come back and fetch us," she said, smiling at him through half-closed eyes.

It was not, however, much more than a week after when Ronald, without warning or announcement, rushed into her room, pale with fatigue, and dusty from his journey. "I have come here post-haste!" he cried. "Lily, your Uncle Robert is in Edinburgh. He is coming on here for the shooting, and other men with him. If I'm a day in advance, that is all. I have thought of the only thing that is to be done if you will but consent."

"The only thing to be done," said Lily, raising herself in her bed, with sparkling eyes, "is what I have always wished: to tell him all that's happened, and, oh! what a light conscience I will have, and what a happy heart!"

"He would turn you out of his doors!" cried Ronald in dismay.

"Well!" cried Lily, who felt capable of every thing, "I may not be a great walker yet, but I'll hirple on till a cart passes or something, and they'll take me in at the Manse."

"Oh, my darling, don't think of such a risk!" he cried. "For God's sake, keep quiet! Say nothing and do nothing till you hear from me again. I have thought of a plan. Will you promise to do nothing, to make no confession, till I'm at your side, or till you hear from me?"

"Are you not going to stay with me, to meet him?"

"I cannot, I cannot! I've come now at the greatest risk. Lily, you will promise?"

"I am going to dress the baby for the night," said the nurse, interposing. "Will ye give him a kiss, mem, before I take him away?"

Lily's lips settled softly on the infant's cheeks like a bee on a flower. "He's sweeter and sweeter every day. Ronald, you must not ask me too much. But I will try, so long as all is well and safe with him."

"I will see that all is safe with him," Ronald cried. He lingered a little with the young mother, half jealous of the looks she cast at the door for the return of the child in Margaret's arms.

"You have told her not to bring him back," she said with smiling reproach, "but I'll have him all to myself after." She was not afraid of his news, she was not shaken by his excitement. The approach of this tremendous crisis seemed only to exhilarate Lily. She was so glad, so glad, to be found out. It was the only thing that was wanting to her perfect happiness.

Ronald's gig had been waiting all the time while he lingered. He had to rush away at last in order to catch the night coach from Kinloch-Rugas, he said; and Lily waited, with smiles shining through the tears in her eyes, to hear the sound of the wheels carrying him away. And then she cried impatiently: "Marg'ret, Marg'ret, bring me my baby!"

But Marg'ret, it seemed, did not hear.

CHAPTER XXXIII

Sir Robert arrived, as they had been warned, next day. An express came in the morning, preceding him, to order rooms to be prepared for three guests—to the great indignation of Katrin, who demanded where she was expected to get provender for four men, and maybe men-servants into the bargain, that were worse than their masters, at a moment's notice. "As if there was naething to do but put linen on the beds," she cried. "The auld man must have gaun gyte. Ye canna make a dinner for Sir Robert and his gentlemen out of a chuckie and a brace o' birds frae the moor. If I had but a hare to make soup o', or a wheen trout, or a single blessed thing. You'll just put the black powny in the cart, Dougal, and ye'll gang down yoursel' to the toun. Sandy! What does Sandy ken? How could I trust that callant to look after Sir Robert's denner? You're nane so clever yoursel'—but it's you that shall go, and no another. Man, have ye no thought of your auld maister and his first dinner when the auld man comes home?"

"I think of him maybe mair than some folk that have keepit grand goings on in his auld hoose."

"What were ye saying?" cried Katrin, fixing him with a commanding eye. She pronounced this, as I have gently insinuated before, "F'what," which gave great force to the sound. "I might have kent," she cried, with a toss of her head, "there wasna a man breathing that could hold his tongue when he thought he had a story to tell!"

"Me—tell a story!" said Dougal in instinctive self-defence. Then he added: "It a' depends—on what a man has to tell."

"Ye're born traitors, a' the race o' ye, from Adam doun!" cried Katrin in her wrath, "and aye the women to bear the wyte, accordin' to you. Tell till ye burst!" she exclaimed with concentrated fury, "and it's no me 'll say a word; but put the powny in the cart and gang doun to the town, and try what ye can get for my denner. I'll no have the auld man starved, no, nor yet shamed afore his freends, nor served with an ill denner the first night—him that hasna been in his ain auld hoose for years."

"Ye're awfu' particular about his denner, considering every thing that's come and gone, and the care you've ta'en of him and his."

"Yes!" cried Katrin, "I'm awfu' particular about his denner. Are you going? or will I have to leave the rooms to settle themselves and go mysel'?"

Dougal at last obeyed this strong impulse; but the black powny and the cart were not for so important a person as Sir Robert's factotum the day his master came home. He put Rory into the geeg, and drove down in such state as was procured by these means, with his countenance full of unutterable things. He was, indeed, when the little quarrel with Katrin was over, a man laden with much thought. Dougal had observed not very clearly, but yet more than he was believed to have observed. His stolid understanding had been played upon unmercifully by the women, and he had been taken in many times in respect to Ronald's presence or absence in the house. Often it had occurred that he "could have sworn" the visitor was there when he was not there, and still oftener he could have sworn the reverse; but at the end of all the tricks and deceptions he was tolerably clear as to the position of affairs, if he had possessed the faculty of speech, and sufficient indifference to other motives to have used it. But Dougal, who was a very simple soul, was held in the grasp of as great a complication of influences as if he had been the most subtle and the most self-analyzing. Should he tell Sir Robert what he had seen and guessed? Sir Robert was his master, and it was Dougal's duty, as guardian of the house, to report what had occurred in it. Ay! but would he shame the house by raising a story that maybe never would be got at by the right end? For what could he say? That a gentleman from Edinburgh had been about the place, coming and going by night and by day; that a person could never tell when he was there and when he wasna there; and, finally, that it was clear as daylight him and Miss Lily were "great freends." Ah, Miss Lily! That brought up again another series of motives. She was his, Dougal's, young leddy, by every lawful tie, the only bairn of the house, the real heir. If Sir Robert, as he was perfectly capable, were to leave Dalrugas away from her the morn, she would not a whit the less be the only Ramsay left of the old family, Mr. James's daughter, who had been Dougal's adoration in his youth. Was he to raise a scandal on Miss Lily—he, her own father's man? Dougal's heart revolted at the thought. And Katrin, that spoiled the lassie, that could see nothing that was not perfect in her—Katrin would never have a good word for her man again. She would call him a traitor—that word that burns and never ceases to wound—like black Monteith that betrayed the Wallace wight, like— But Dougal's courage was not equal to that anticipation; rather any thing than that, rather flee the country than that—to betray a bit creature that trusted him, Mr. James's daughter, the last Ramsay, a little lass that could not fight for herself. "No me!" cried Dougal to all the winds that blew. "No me!" he said, confronting old Schiehallion, as if that tranquil mountain had tempted him. He shook his fist at the hills and at the world. "No me, no me!" he said.

I do not believe that Katrin ever was in the least afraid in respect to Dougal, but a very troubled woman was Katrin that day. She had been in Ronald Lumsden's confidence all along, more than his wife knew, and in her way had abetted him and helped him, though often against her conscience. Beenie had done the same, but she had not Katrin's head, and meekly followed where the other led. They had both been partially guilty in respect to Marg'ret, a woman introduced into the house by the clumsiest means, which Lily could have seen through in a moment had she tried, but whose presence was so great a comfort and relief to the other two that their eagerness to accede to the artifice by which she was brought as a guest to Dalrugas was very excusable. "What would you and me do, Beenie?" Katrin had said, for once acknowledging a situation with which she was not able to cope. They had been able "to sleep at night," as they both said, since that woman was there, and there was nothing to be said against the woman. She was not troublesome, she was kind, she knew what she was about. That she was Ronald's emissary was nothing against her. She was, on the contrary, an evidence of the husband's tender care for his wife; his anxiety that she should have the best and most costly attention. "And a bonnie penny she will cost him," the two women said to themselves. But the events of the last twenty-four hours had altogether overwhelmed Katrin, and she had not the comfort even of speaking to any one on the subject, of expressing her horror, her amazement and dismay, for Beenie was shut up with Lily, whose state was such that she could not be left alone for a moment. It was well for the housekeeper that her head was filled with Sir Robert's dinner and the airing of the mattresses. It gave her a relief from her heavy thoughts to drag down the feather beds and turn them over and over before a blazing fire, though it was August, and the sun blazing hot out of doors. She worked—as a Highland housekeeper works the day the gentlemen are to arrive—for the credit of the house and her own. "Would I let strangers find a word to say, or a thing forgotten, and me the woman in charge of Dalrugas this mony and mony a year?" she said to herself. And it did Katrin a great deal of good, as she did not hesitate to acknowledge. It took off her thoughts.

Sir Robert arrived in the evening with two elderly friends and one young one, with all their guns and paraphernalia, Sir Robert's own man directing every thing, and at least one other man-servant, bringing dismay to Katrin's heart. "You will not have more than two or three good days on my little bit of moor," the old gentleman had said with proud humility, "but the neighbors are very friendly, and no doubt my niece has got a lot of cheerful Highland lassies about her that will enliven the time for you, my young friend." The friends, young and old, had protested their perfect prospective satisfaction with the entertainment Sir Robert had to offer, none of them believing, as, indeed, he did not believe himself, his own disparaging account of the moor. They arrived very dusty in their post-chaise, but in high spirits, the old gentleman with an excited pleasure in returning to the old house of his fathers, which he had not seen for years. Perhaps it looked to him small and gray and chill, as is the wont of old paternal houses when a long-absent master comes back. He called out almost as soon as he came in sight of the door, where Dougal was waiting with his bonnet poised on the extreme edge of his head, on one hair, and Sandy behind him, ready with awe to follow the directions of the gentlemen's gentlemen, and carry the luggage upstairs. "Where is Miss Lily? Where is my niece?" Sir Robert cried. "Does she not think it worth her trouble to come and meet her old uncle at the door?"

Katrin came forward from the threshold, within which she had been lurking, and courtesied to the best of her ability. "You're welcome, Sir Robert; you're awfu' welcome," she said; "but Miss Lily, I'm sorry to say, is just very ill in her bed."

"Ill in her bed!" cried Sir Robert. "Nonsense! Nonsense! I know that kind of illness. She is vexed at me for sending her here, and she's made up her mind to sulk a little that I may flatter her and plead with her. You may tell her it won't do. I'm not that kind of man. I'll pardon, maybe, a bonnie lass in all her braws and showing her pleasure in them, but a sulky, sour young woman— Eh, Evandale, what were you saying—an old house? It's old enough if ye think that to its credit, and bare enough. Katrin, I hope you'll be able to make these gentlemen comfortable in the old barrack, such as it is."

"I hope so, Sir Robert," said Katrin. She was relieved that his animadversions on Lily should be cut short.

And then they mounted the spiral staircase with the worn steps, which in one or two places were almost dangerous, and which the elder men mounted very cautiously, one after the other, the loud footsteps of the men echoing through the place, their deeper voices filling the air.

"Lord bless us all!" Katrin cried within herself, "if they had arrived ten days ago!" It was a comfort, in the midst of all the trouble, that Lily was safe in her bed, and, whatever happened, could not be disturbed.

Sir Robert's enquiries again next morning after his niece were made late and after long delay. It was the 12th of August, and unnecessary to say that Dalrugas was full of sound and hurry from an early hour; the manufacture and consumption of an enormous breakfast, and the preparations for the first great day with the grouse, occupying every-body, so that Katrin herself, though very anxious, had not found a moment to visit Lily's room, or even to snatch a moment's talk with Beenie over her mistress's state. "Just the same, and that's very bad," Beenie said, through the half-open door, "and just half out of her wits with the noise, and no able to understand what it means." "Oh, it's a' thae men!" cried Katrin. "The gentlemen and their grouse, and the others with the guns and the douges and a' the rest o't. Pity me that have not a moment, that must gang and toil for them and their breakfasts!" When every thing was ready at last, and the party set out, Sir Robert, whose shooting days were over, accompanied them to a certain favorite corner upon Rory, who, though the old gentleman was not a heavy weight, objected to the unusual length of his limbs and decision of his proceedings; but he returned to the house shortly after, musing, with a sigh or two. Perhaps it was a rash experiment to come back after so many years; his doctor had advised it strongly, giving him much hope from his native air, the air of the moors and hills, and from the quiet and regular hours and rule of measured living which he would have no temptation to transgress. "We must remember we are not so young as we once were—any of us," the physician had said, notwithstanding that he himself was but forty. When a man is old and ailing, and lives too perilously well, and sees and does too much in the gayer regions of the land, and is known at the same time to have a castle in the North, an old patrimony in the Highlands, delightful in August at least, and probably the best place in the world for him at all times of the year, such a prescription is easy. "Your native air, Sir Robert, and a quiet country life." The 12th of August, a fine day, and already the sharp, clear report of the guns in the brilliant air, and a sense of company and enjoyment about, and the moor a great magnificent garden, purple with heather, is about as cheerful a moment as could be chosen to make a beginning of such a life. But old Sir Robert, returning from the beginning of the sport which he was not able to share to his old house, his Highland castle, which, as he turned toward it in the glorious sunshine of the morning, looked so gray and pinched and penurious, with the tower, that was only a high outstanding gable, and the farm buildings, which had for so long a time been the chief and most important points of the cluster of buildings to its humble occupants, had little to make him cheerful. A sharp sensation almost of shame stung the old man as he realized what his friends must have thought of his Highland castle. Taymouth and Inverary are castles, and so are the brand-new houses down the Clyde in which the Glasgow merchants establish themselves with all the luxuries which money can buy. But where did old Dalrugas come in, so spare and poor, rising straight out of the moor without garden or plaisance, not to speak of parks or woods? He smiled to himself a little sadly at the misnomer. He was wounded in the pride with which he had regarded that shrunken, impoverished little place—a pride which he felt now was half ludicrous and yet half pathetic. How was it that he had not thought so when last he was here, then a mature man and having passed all the glamour of youth? He shook his head at the pinched, tall gable, the corbie steps cut so clearly against the blue sky, the gray line of the bare, blank wall. After all, it was but a poor house for a family with such pretensions as the Ramsays of Dalrugas—a poor thing to brag to his Southern friends about. And it was not very gay. He, who had been a man who loved to enjoy himself, and who had done so wherever he had been, to come back here in the end of his days to settle down to the dreariness of the solitary moor and the silence of a country life—was it not a discipline more than he could bear that "those doctors" had put him under? Was a year or two more of vegetation here worth the giving up of all his old gratifications and amusements? It is hard even upon a man who knows he is old, but does not care to acknowledge it, to accompany on a pony for a little way his friends, who are keen for their sport, to set them off on the 12th without being able to go a step or fire a shot with them. Those doctors—what did they know? They had probably sent him off, not knowing what more to do for him, that they might not be troubled with the sight of him dying before their eyes.

Then, however, there came before Sir Robert, by some more kindly touch of memory, certain scenes from the old life, when Dalrugas was the warmest and happiest home in the world, always overflowing with kindly neighbors and friends of youth. Their names came back to him one by one—Duffs, Gordons, Sinclairs. Where were they all now? There would be at least their representatives in all the old places— sons, nay, perhaps grandsons, of his contemporaries, young asses that would turn up their noses at a vieille moustache; yet perhaps some of the old folk too. Lily would know; no doubt but Lily would know every one of them. She would have her partners among the boys and her cronies among the girls. He felt glad that Lily was here to renew the alliances of the old place. What had he sent her here for, by-the-bye? Something about a silly sweetheart that she would not give up, the silly thing. Probably she would have forgotten his very name by this time, as Sir Robert did; and there would be another now waiting his sanction. Well, no harm if it was a fit match for the last Ramsay. He would insist upon that. Somebody that had gear enough, and good blood, and a proper place in the world. No other should poor James's daughter marry; that was one thing sure.

And then he began to think what had become of Lily that she had neither come to meet him last night nor appeared this morning. Was she bearing malice? or sulking at her old uncle? He would soon see there was an end to that. If she was ill, she must have the doctor. If it was but some silly cold or other, or the headache that a woman sets up at a moment's notice, she must get up out of her bed, she must come down stairs. Self-indulgence was good for nobody, especially at Lily's age. He would see her woman, Beenie, who was her shadow, and whom Sir Robert began to recollect he had not seen any more than Lily herself. And then the alternative should be given her—the doctor, who would stand no nonsense, or to get up and put a shawl about her, and nurse her cold by the fireside, where she could talk to him, and be much better than if she were in bed. Sir Robert quickened Rory's paces, and, indeed, as the pony was nothing loath to reach his stable, appeared at the house with almost undignified haste to put in immediate operation this plan.

CHAPTER XXXIV

"No better this morning! What is the matter with her? I never heard Lily was unhealthy or delicate!"

"She is neither the one nor the other," said Katrin, indignant, "but she's not well to-day. The best of us, Sir Robert, we're subjeck to that."

"Ye think so!" he said rather fiercely, as if it were a dogma to question. And then he added: "There's that big Beenie creature, that is, I suppose, as much with her as ever—send her to me."

"Eh, Sir Robert, how is she to leave Miss Lily, that is just not well at all this morning?"

"Send her to me at once!" the old gentleman said imperatively. He went into the dining-room, which was on the lower floor and the room he liked best, the most comfortable in the house. There were no signs of a woman's presence in that room. A vague wonder crossed his mind if, after all, Lily had been here at all. He forgot that he had been much incommoded the evening before by the books and the work-baskets, the cushions and the footstools, which had demonstrated the some time presence of a woman upstairs. He kept walking up and down the room stiffly, feeling his foot a little, as he owned to himself. Sir Robert truly felt that he would not be sorry if the prescription of his native air failed manifestly at once.

"Well," he said, turning round hastily at a timid opening of the door. "How's your mistress—how's my niece? What does she mean by taking shelter in her bed, and never appearing to bid me welcome?"

"Oh, Sir Robert, Miss Lily—" said Beenie. She held the door open and stood leaning against the edge, as if ready to fly at a call from without or a thrust from within. Beenie's hair, which it was difficult to keep tidy at the best of times, hung over her pale countenance like a cloud, a short lock standing out from her forehead. We are accustomed now to every vagary of which hair is capable, and are not disturbed by loose locks; but in those days strict tidiness was the rule; and Beenie, very white as to her cheeks and red round the eyes, partly with tears, partly with watching, was, to Sir Robert, a being unworthy of any confidence.

"Woman!" he cried, "you look as if you had been up all night—and not a fit person to be a lady's body-servant, and with her night and day!"

"Fit or no," said Beenie, with a sob, "I'm the one Miss Lily's aye had, and her and me will never be parted either with her will or mine."

"We'll see about that," said Sir Robert. But he was wise man enough to know that a favorite servant was a difficult thing to attack. He asked peremptorily: "What is the matter with her?" placing himself, like a judge, in the great chair.

"Eh, Sir Robert, if Marg'ret, my cousin, had been here, that is half a doctor herself! but me I know nothing," cried Beenie, wringing her hands.

"Is it a cold?"

"It was, maybe, a cold to begin with," said Beenie cautiously, but then she melted into tears and cried: "She's awfu' fevered, she's the color o' fire, and kens nothing," in a lamentable voice.

"Bless me," cried Sir Robert, "is there any fever about?"

"There's nae fever about that I ken of—there's nae folk hereby to get a fever," Beenie said.

"Then I'll go and see her myself!" cried Sir Robert, rising from his chair.

"Eh, Sir Robert!" cried Katrin, from behind the door, "you a gentleman that could do the puir thing no good! It's better to leave her to us women folk."

"There is truth in that, too," Sir Robert said. He took a turn about the room and then sat down again in his chair, his forehead contracted with a line of annoyance and perplexity which might have been called anxiety by a charitable onlooker. Beenie had seized the opportunity of Katrin's appearance to hurry away, and he found himself face to face with his housekeeper. He gave a long breath of relief. "It's you, Katrin," he said; "you're a sensible person according to your lights. There's fever with all things—a wound (but that's of course impossible for her), or a cold, or any accident. What's your opinion? Is it a thing that will pass away?"

"Leave her with Beenie and me for another day, Sir Robert, and the morn, if she's no better, I'll be the first to ask for a doctor; and eh, I hope it's safe no to have him the day." The latter part of this speech Katrin said to herself under cover of the door.

"She'll have got cold coming home late from one of her parties," said the old gentleman, regaining his composure.

"Her pairties, Sir Robert!" said Katrin, almost with a shriek. "And where, poor thing, would she get pairties here?"

"She has friends, I suppose?" he said with a little impatience, "companions of her own age. Where will young creatures like that not find parties? is what I would ask."

"Eh, Sir Robert! but I'm doubting you've forgotten our countryside. There's Miss Eelen at the Manse that is her one great friend; and John Jameson's lass at the muckle farm, that has been at the school in Edinburgh, and would fain, fain think herself a lady, poor bit thing, would have given her little finger to be friends with Miss Lily. But you would not have had her go to pairties in the farmhouse; and at the Manse they give nane, the minister being such a lameter. Pairties! the Lord bless us! Wha would ask her to pairties on this side of the moor?"

"There are plenty of people," said Sir Robert almost indignantly, "that should have shown attention to my brother James's daughter, both for my sake and his. What do you call the Duffs, woman? and the Gordons of the Muckle moor, and Sir John Sinclair's family at the Lews? Many a merry night have we passed among us when we were all young. The Duffs' is not more than a walk, even if Lily were setting up for a fine lady, which, to do her justice, was not her way."

"Eh, hear till him!" breathed Katrin under her breath. She said aloud: "Times are awfu' changed, Sir Robert, since your days. The present Mr. Duff he's married on an English lady, and they say she cannot bide the air of the Highlands, though it is well kent for the finest air in a' the world. He comes here whiles with a wheen gentlemen for the first of the shooting—but her never, and there's little to be said for a house when the mistress is never in it. Of the Gordons there's nane left but one auld leddy, the last of them, I hear, except distant connections. And as for Sir John at the Lews, poor man, poor man, he just died broken-hearted, one of his bonnie boys going to destruction after the other. They say the things are to be roupit and the auld mansion-house to be left desolate, for of the twa that remain the one's a ne'er-do-well and the other a puir avaricious creature, feared to spend a shilling, and I canna tell which is the worst."

"Bless me, bless me!" Sir Robert had gone on saying, shaking his head. He was receiving a rude awakening. He saw in his mind's eye the old house running over with lively figures, with fun and laughter—and now desolate. It gave him a great shock, partly from the simple fact, which by itself was overwhelming, partly because of a sudden pity which sprang up in his mind for Lily, and, most of all, for himself. What, nobody to come and see him, to tell the news and hear what was in the London papers; no cheerful house to form an object for his walk, no men to talk to, no ladies to whom to pay his old-fashioned compliments! This discovery went very much to his heart. After a long time he said: "It would be better to let the houses than to leave them to go to rack and ruin, or shut up, as you say—the best houses in the countryside."

"Let them!" cried Katrin. "Gentlemen's ain houses! We're maybe fallen low, Sir Robert, but we're no just fallen to that."

"You silly woman! the grandest folk do it," cried Sir Robert. Then he added in a lower tone: "Lily, I am afraid, may not have had a very lively life."

"You may well say that!" cried Katrin. "Poor bonnie lassie, if she had bidden ony gangrel body on the road, or any person travelling that passed this way, to come in and bear her company, I would not have been surprised for my part."

Katrin spoke very deliberately, avec intention. It seemed well to prepare an argument, in case it might be used with effect another time. And Sir Robert was much subdued. He had not meant to inflict such a punishment upon his niece. He had believed, indeed, that her life at Dalrugas would be even more gay than her life in Edinburgh. There the parties might occasionally be formal, or the convives bores, according to his own experience at least; but here there was nothing but the good, warm, simple intimacy of the country, the life almost in common, the hospitable doors always open. If a compunctious recollection of Lily ever crossed his mind in the midst of his own elderly amusements, this was what he had been in the habit of saying to himself: "There will be lads enough to make a little queen of her, and lasses enough to keep her company, for she's a bonnie bit thing when all is said." He had always been a little proud of her, though she had been a great trouble to him; and he thought he knew that in his old home Lily would be fully appreciated. That he had sent her out into the wilderness had never entered his thoughts. He dismissed Katrin with an uneasy mind, imploring her, almost with humility, to do every thing she could think of for his poor Lily, and if she was not better in the morning, to send at once for the best doctor in the neighborhood. Who was the best doctor in the neighborhood? Indeed, there was but little choice—the doctor at Kinloch-Rugas, who was not so young as he once was, and had, alas, a sore weakness for his glass, and the one at Ardenlennie on the other side, who was well spoken of. "Let it be the one at Ardenlennie," Sir Robert said. He spent rather a wretched day afterward, taking two or three short constitutionals, up and down the high-road, three-quarters of an hour at a time, to while away the lonely day until his friends returned from the moor. It was far too painful an ordeal, to spend the 12th of August alone in this place where, in his recollection, the 12th of August had always been ecstasy. He should have chosen another moment. He had not imagined that he would have felt so much his own disabilities of old age. He had been wont to boast that he did not feel them at all, one kind of enjoyment having been replaced by another, and his desire for athletic pleasures having died a natural death in the perfection of his matured spirit and changed tastes, which were equal to better things. But he had certainly subjected himself to too great a trial now. That the 12th should be his first day at home, and that all his sport should consist of a convoy given to the sportsmen on the back of Rory, but not a gun for his own shoulder, not a step on the heather for his foot! It was too much. He had been a fool. And then this silly misadventure of Lily and her illness to make every thing worse.

A moment of comparative comfort occurred in the middle of the day when he had his luncheon. "Really that woman's not bad as a cook," he said to himself. She was but a woman, and a Scotch, uncultivated creature, but she had her qualities—and there was taste in what she sent him, that priceless gift, especially for an old man. He took a little nap after his luncheon, and then he took another walk, and so got through the day till the sportsmen came back. They came in noisy and triumphant, with their bags, and their stories of what happened at this and that corner, of the cheepers that had been missed and the old birds that were full of guile. Had they been Sir Robert's sons it is possible that he might have listened benignly, and felt more or less the pleasure by proxy which some gentle spirits taste. But they were strangers, mere "friends" in the jargon of the world, meaning acquaintances more or less intimate. Of the three he bore best the laughter and delight and brags and eagerness to show his own prowess of the young man. The others awakened a sharper pang of contrast. "Almost my own age!" Alas! the difference between fifty and seventy is the unkindest of comparisons. They were not even good companions for him in the evening. When they had talked over every step of their progress, and every bird that had fallen before them, and eaten of Katrin's good dishes an enormous dinner, the strong air of the moor, and the hot fire of the peats, and the fatigue of the first day's exercise and excitement, overpowered them one after another with sleep. This would not have been the case had Lily been afoot to sing a song or two and keep them to their manners. Sir Robert was driven to the expedient of sending for Dougal when they had all, with many excuses, gone to bed. Dougal was sleepy, too, and tired, though not so much as "the gentlemen," to whom the grouse and the moor were, more or less, novelties. He gave his wife a curious look when Sir Robert's man called him to his master, and Katrin responded with one that partly entreated and partly threatened. She said: "You can tell him Miss Lily is very bad, and I'll get the doctor the first thing the morn."

Dougal uttered no word. He could not wear his bonnet when he went up to see the laird, but he took it in his hands, which was some small consolation. He was in a dreadful confusion of mind, not knowing what was to be said to him, what was to be demanded of him. He might be about to be put through his "questions," and want all his strength to defend himself; or it might be nothing at all—some nonsense about the guns or the birds. His heavy shock of hair stood up from his forehead, giving something of an ox-like breadth and heaviness of brow. He held his head somewhat down, with a trace of defiance. Katrin might gloom; it was little he cared for Katrin when his blood was up; but there was not a bit of the traitor in Dougal. No blood of a black Monteith in him, if they were to put the thumbscrews on him or matches atween his fingers. That poor bonnie creature, whatever was her wyte—they should get nothing to trouble her out of him.

"Well, Dougal," said Sir Robert, dangerously genial, "you see I'm left all alone. My friends they have gone to their beds, as if they were callants home from the school."

"The gentlemen would be geyan tired," said Dougal; "they're English, and no accustomed to our moors, and some of them no so young either. You never kent that, Sir Robert, you that were to the manner born."

"But too auld for that sort of thing, Dougal, now."

"Maybe, and maybe not," said Dougal. "There's naething like the auld blood and the habit o't. I'd sooner see you cock a rifle, Sir Robert, though I say it as shouldna, than the whole three of them."

"No, no, Dougal," said Sir Robert, "that's flattery. They're not very good shots, then," he said, with a smile. He was not indisposed to hear this of them, though they were his friends.

"Well, Sir Robert, I wouldna say, on their ain kind o' ground, among the stubble and that kind o' low-country shooting, which, I'm tauld, is the common thing there; but no on our moors. When you're used to the heather, it's a different thing."

"No doubt there is something in that," Sir Robert allowed with discreet satisfaction. And then he added: "What's this I hear from your wife about all the old neighbors, and that there's scarcely a house open I knew in my young days?"

"What is that, Sir Robert?" said Dougal cautiously.

"The neighbors, ye dunce, my old friends that were all about the countryside when I was young, and that I thought would be friends for my poor little Lily when she came here. I'm told there's not one of them left."

Dougal did not readily take up what was meant, but he held his own firmly. "There's been nae gentleman's house," he said, "what you would call open and receiving visitors round about Dalrugas as long as I mind—no more than Dalrugas itsel'."

"Ah, Dalrugas itself," said Sir Robert, a little abashed. It was true—if the others had closed their doors, so had Dalrugas; if they were left to silence and decay, so had his own house been. Other reasons had operated in his case, but the result was the same. "I'm afraid, Dougal," he said, "that my poor little Lily has had an ill time of it, which I never intended. Give me your opinion on the subject. Your wife's a very decent woman—and an excellent cook, I will say that for her—but she's like them all, she stands up for her own side. She would have me think that my niece has been very solitary among the moors. Now that was never what I intended. Tell me true: has Miss Lily been a kind of prisoner, and seen nobody, as Katrin says?"

Dougal pushed his mass of hair to one side as if it had been a wig. "The young leddy," he said, "had none o' the looks of a prisoner, Sir Robert. I've seen her when you would have thought it was the very sun itsel' shining on the moor."

"You're very poetical, Dougal," said Sir Robert, with a laugh.

"And she would whiles sing as canty as the birds, and off upon Rory as light as a feather down to the market to see all the ferlies o' the toun, and into the Manse for her tea."

"That sounds cheerful enough," said the old gentleman, "though the ferlies of the town were not very exciting, I suppose. And old Blythe's still at the Manse? He's one of the old set left at least."

"He's an altered man noo, Sir Robert; never a step can he make out o' his muckle chair; they say he's put into his bed at nicht, but it's a mystery to me and many more how it's done, for he's a muckle heavy man. But year's end to year's end he's just living on in his muckle chair."

"Lord bless us!" Sir Robert said. He looked down on his own still shapely and not inactive limbs with an involuntary shiver of comparison, and then he added, with a half laugh: "A man that liked his good dinner, and a good bottle of wine, and a good crack, with any of us."

"That did he, Sir Robert!" Dougal said.

"Poor old Blythe! I must go and see him," said the happier veteran, with an unconscious stretch of his capable legs, and throwing out of his chest. It was not any pleasure in the misfortune of his neighbor which gave him this glow of almost satisfaction. It was the sense of his own superiority in well-being, the comparison which was so much in his own favor. The comparison this morning had not been in his own favor and he had not liked it. He felt now, let us hope with a sensation of thankfulness, how much better off he was than Mr. Blythe.

"Well, well, the Manse was always something, Dougal," he said. "Manses are cheerful places; there's always a great coming and going. I hope there was nobody much out of her own sphere that Miss Lily met there—no young ministers coming up here after her, eh? They have a terrible flair for lasses with tochers, these young ministers, Dougal?"

"Ay, Sir Robert, that have they," said Dougal, "but I've seen no minister here."

"That was good luck for Lily—or we that are responsible for her," said the old gentleman. "Well, Dougal, my man, you'll be tired yourself and ready for your bed, and to make an early start to-morrow with the gentlemen."

"Ay, Sir Robert," said Dougal. He was very glad to accept his dismissal, and to feel that without so much as a fib he had kept his own counsel and betrayed nothing. But when he had reached the door, he turned round again, crushing his bonnet in his hands. "I was to tell you Miss Lily was no better, poor thing, and that the women thought the doctor would have to be sent for the morn."

Sir Robert's countenance clouded over. "Tchick, tchick!" he said, with an air of perplexity. "You'll see that the best man in the neighborhood is the one that's sent for," he cried.

CHAPTER XXXV

There had been a pause after Lily called to Marg'ret to bring the baby on the night when Ronald left her. Marg'ret, though very kind, was a person who liked her own way. If the child's toilet was not complete, according to her own elaborate rule, she did not obey in a moment even the eager call of the young mother. There were allowances made for her, as there always are for those who insist upon having their own way.

Accordingly there was a pause. Lily lay and listened to the wheels of the geeg which carried Ronald away. They did not bring the same chill to her heart as usual, and yet a chill began to steal into the room. The night was warm and soft—the early August, which in the North is the height of summer—and there was no chill at all in the atmosphere. It seemed to Lily's keen ears as she lay listening that the geeg paused as if something had been forgotten, but then went on at double speed, galloping up the brae, till the sound of the wheels was extinguished in the night and distance. Then she called again sharply: "Marg'ret, Marg'ret! bring in my baby!" But still there was no reply.

"She's just a most fastidious woman, with all her dressings and her undressings. She'll no have finished him just to the last string tying," said Robina.

"Bid her come at once, at once!" cried Lily. "I want my little man."

And Beenie dived into the next room, which was muffled in curtains, great precautions having been taken lest the cry of the child should be heard down stairs. There was another room still within that, into which the nurse occasionally retired; but there was no one in either place, nor were there any traces of the little garments lying about which betray a baby's presence—every thing appeared to have been swept away. Beenie, who had come for the child with her rosy countenance beaming, stood still in consternation, her mouth open, her terrified eyes taking in every thing with speechless dismay; for Marg'ret had never ventured down stairs as yet, nor had, they flattered themselves, a sound of the infant been heard, to awaken any question there. Beenie stood silent and terrified for a moment, and then, instead of returning to her mistress, she flew down stairs. Katrin was alone, doing some of her delicate cooking carefully over the fire; all was still, as if nothing but the most commonplace and tranquil events had ever happened there. Beenie, who had burst into the place like a whirlwind, again paused, confounded by this every-day tranquillity. "Katrin, Katrin, where is Marg'ret?" she cried, adding in a lower tone, "and the bairn?"

"What a question to ask me!" said Katrin. "She's with your mistress without a doubt. Have you ta'en leave of your senses," she murmured in a hurried undertone, "to roar out like that about a bairn? What bairn?"

Here Beenie found herself at the end of all her resources. She burst out into loud weeping. "She's no up the stair and she's no down the stair," cried Beenie, "and my bonnie leddy is crying out for her, and will not be satisfied! And she's no place that I can find her—neither her nor yet the bairn."

Katrin thrust her saucepan from her as if it had been the offending thing; she wiped her hands with her apron. She looked at Beenie, both of them pale with horror. "Oh, the ill man!" she cried. "Oh, the monster! Oh, sic a man for our bonnie dear! I have been misdoubting about the bairn—but wha could have expectit that a young man no hardened in iniquity would have thought of a contrivance like that?"

Beenie had no thought or time to spare even on such an enormity. "How am I to face her—and tell her?" she said.

And at this moment they heard Lily's voice calling from above, at first softly, then shouting, screaming all their names. "Marg'ret! Beenie! Katrin! Marg'ret! Marg'ret! Beenie! Katrin! Where is my bairn? where is my bairn?"

The two women flew up the stairs, at the head of which they found Lily in her white night-dress, with her feet bare, her hair waving wildly about her head, her face convulsed and drawn. "My bairn!" she cried, "my bairn! my little bairn! Where is Marg'ret? Where is my baby? Marg'ret! Marg'ret! Beenie! Katrin! bring me my baby—my baby!" She seized Beenie wildly with her trembling hands.

"Oh, my daurlin'!" Beenie cried. "Oh, my bairn—oh, my bonnie Miss Lily!"

Lily flung the large weeping woman from her with a passion of impatience. "Katrin!" she said breathlessly, "you have sense; where is my baby? bring me my baby! My little bairn! Did ye ever hear that an infant like that should be kept from his mother? Marg'ret! Marg'ret! Where has she taken my baby—my baby—my—"

Lily's voice rose to a kind of scream. She ceased to have command of her words, and went on calling, calling, for Marg'ret and for her child in an endless cry, not knowing what she said.

"You will come back to your bed first and then I will tell you," said Katrin. There was no one in the house but themselves, and they were isolated in this sudden tragedy from all the world by the distance and the silence of night and the moor. The door stood open at the foot of the stairs, and a cold air blew up through the long, many-cornered passage, chill and searching notwithstanding the warmth of the night. Lily was glad to lean shivering upon the warm support of the kind woman who encircled her with her arm. "You will tell me—you will tell me," she murmured, permitting herself to be drawn back to her room. The blind had been raised from one of the windows, and the moonlight streamed in, crossing the dimly lighted chamber with one white line of light. The bed, with the little table by it, and the candle burning calmly, seemed too peaceful for Lily's mood of suspense and alarm. She stood still in the moonlight, which seemed to make her figure luminous with her white bare feet and pale face. "Tell me!" she cried, "tell me! Marg'ret! Marg'ret! Where has she taken my baby? I want my baby—nothing more—nothing more."

"For the Lord's sake, mem!" said Katrin, "ye are shivering and trembling. Go back to your bed."

"Oh, my daurlin'!" cried the weeping Beenie. "Oh, my bonnie lamb, he's just away with his father in the geeg. Ye needna cry upon Marg'ret; she'll no hear you, for it's just her that's taken him away!"

"Oh, you born fool!" Katrin cried, supporting her young mistress with her arm.

But Lily twisted out of her hold. She turned upon Beenie, bringing her hands together wildly with a loud clap that startled all the silences about like the sudden report of a pistol, and then fell suddenly with a cry at their feet.

Since that moment she had not recovered consciousness. Both of them knew by the force of experience how dangerous a symptom in Lily's condition is the strong convulsive shivering which had seized her, and for the greater part of that dreadful night before Sir Robert's arrival they were both by her bedside striving with every kind of hot application to restore a natural temperature. But when they had partially succeeded in this, she still lay unconscious, sometimes agitated and disturbed, flinging herself about with her arms over her head, and once or twice repeating, what filled them with horror, the extraordinary clap together of her hands—sometimes quite still, and murmuring under her breath a continuous flow of inarticulate words, but never conscious of them or their ministrations, saying no word that had meaning in it. Sir Robert's arrival made a certain change, and left the weight of the nursing upon Beenie, Katrin, with her many additional labors, being unable to bear her share. They had already, however, had time for several consultations on the subject, which Sir Robert naturally disposed of with so much ease, but which to the two women was a much more serious matter—a doctor. Would not a doctor divine at once with his keen, educated eyes what had happened so recently? Would not he read as clearly as in a book what had been the beginning of Lily's illness? She lay helpless now, able to give them no assistance in disposing of her—she, so wilful by nature, who had always got her own way, so far, at least, as they were concerned. It filled them with awe to look at her lying unconscious, and to feel that her fate was in their hands. What were they to do? They were responsible for her life or death.

The doctor, when he came, listened with very small attention to Beenie's long and confused story, chiefly made up from things she had read and heard of the causes of Lily's illness. Whatever the causes were, the result was clear enough. She was in a high fever, her faculties all lost in that confusion of violent illness which takes away at once all consciousness of the present and all personal control. "Fever" was an impressive word in those days, more alarming in some senses, less so in others, than now. It was not mapped out and distinct, with its charts and its well-known rules. There was not, so far as I am aware, such a thing as a clinical thermometer known, at least not in ordinary practice; and the word "fever" meant something dangerously "catching," something before which nurses fled and friends retired in dismay—which is not to say that those who suffered from it were less sedulously guarded and taken care of by their own people then than now. The first idea of both Beenie and Katrin, however, was that it must be "catching," being fever, and Sir Robert, when he was informed, was not much wiser. "Fever—where could she have got it?" he said with a sudden imagination of some wretched beggar-woman with a sick child who might have given it to the young lady. "It is not a thing of that kind. You are thinking of scarlatina or maybe typhus. Nothing of that sort. It does not spring from infection. It is brain-fever," the medical man said. "Brain-fever!" said Sir Robert, indignant. "There was never anything of that kind in my family." He took it as a reproach, as if the Ramsays had ever been a race subject to disturbance in the brain!

But whatever they said, it mattered little to Lily. She lay on her bed for hours together moving her restless head to and fro, muttering inarticulate words, then pouring forth a stream of vague discourse, through which there gleamed occasionally a ray of meaning, a wild sudden demand, a flash of protest and expostulation. "Not that! not him!" she would sometimes say, "anything but him!" and the doctor, making out as much as that one day, believed that the poor girl had been refused her lover, and that it was the sudden arrival of the uncle, who was hostile to them, which had brought on or precipitated the trouble in her brain. Sometimes she would call for "Marg'ret, Marg'ret, Marg'ret!" in accents now of impatience, now of despair. And then he asked who Marg'ret was and why she did not come, or rather: "Which of you is Marg'ret?" to the confusion of the two women. "Oh, sir, neither her nor me," cried Beenie, "neither her nor me! but a woman that had something to do with her—in an ill moment." "Let her be sent for, then," he said peremptorily. Beenie and Katrin had a great deal to bear. Knowing every thing, they had to pretend they knew nothing, to shake their heads and wonder why the patient should utter words which were heartrending to them as betraying the dreadful persistence of that impression of misery in her mind which they knew so well. They gave themselves the comfort of exchanging a glance now and then, which was almost all the mutual consolation they had. For Katrin was very much occupied with the housekeeping and her work, and the necessity for satisfying her master and his guests, who, knowing nothing of Sir Robert's family, and never having seen his niece, did not propose to go away, as guests in other circumstances would have done. And Sir Robert was very far from desiring that they should go away. He was terrified to find himself here alone, without even Lily's company, and therefore said very little of her illness. What difference could it make to her, if she never saw them or heard of them, whether Sir Robert had company or not? So Katrin labored morning and night to feed with her best the party in the dining-room, and with very imperfect help at first to look after all the wants of the gentlemen, while Beenie, isolated in her mistress's room, nursed night and day the helpless, unconscious creature who required so little, yet needed so much care. Those were not the days of carefully regulated nursing, in which the most important matter of all is the preservation of the nurse's health and her meals and hours of taking exercise. It was an age when the household was sufficient for itself, and the domestic nurse devoted herself night and day to her charge, accepting all the risks and fatigue as a matter of course. Beenie had no help and wanted none. Sometimes for a moment's refreshment she would go down to the door, and breathe in a long draught of the fresh morning air, while Katrin stood by Lily's bed trying to elicit from her a look or sign of intelligence. But Beenie could not have remained absent from her young mistress had the wisest of nurses been there to take her place. "Na, na; I've ta'en care of her a' her days, and I'll take care of her till the end," Beenie said, when Katrin exhorted her to take a few minutes more of the outdoor freshness. "Hold your tongue, woman, with your ends!" cried Katrin—"a young thing like that with a' her life in her! She will see us baith out." "Oh, the Lord grant it!" cried Beenie, shaking her large head. "But how is she to live and face the truth and ken all that's happened if ever she comes to herself? She will just sit up in her bed, and clap her two hands together as she did yon dreadful night—and give up the ghost."

"God forgive him—for I canna!" said Katrin, with a deep-drawn breath.

"And Marg'ret! What do ye say to her, the deep designing woman, that had been planning it, nae doubt, all the time?"

"Marg'ret!" cried Katrin with disdain, with the gesture of throwing something too contemptible for consideration from her. But she added: "There is just this to be said: We could not have keepit the bairn. No possible, her so ill, and the doctor about the house, and a wee thing that bid to have had the air and could not be keepit silent, nor yet hid. Oh, mony's the thought I've had on that awful subject. It was the deed of a villain, Beenie! Maybe God will forgive him, but never me. And yet, being done, it's weel that it was done."

"Katrin!" cried Beenie in dismay.

But something, perhaps, in their low-toned but vehement conversation had caught some wandering and confused faculty not entirely overwhelmed in Lily's bosom. She began to call out their names again with a wild appeal, "Marg'ret, Marg'ret!" above all the others, flinging out her arms and rising up in her bed, as Beenie had described in her gloomy anticipations, as if to give up the ghost.

And in this way days and weeks passed away. Lily's fever seemed to have become a natural part of the life of the house. Robina seemed to herself unable to remember the time when she went to bed at night and got up again in the morning like other people, and had ordinary meals and went and came about the house. And all the incidents that had gone before became dim. If an answer had been demanded of her hurriedly, she could scarcely have ventured to affirm that any one was true: the marriage ceremony in the Manse parlor, the meetings of the young husband and wife, and above all the last tremendous event, which had seemed in its turn to be of more importance than anything else that ever occurred. They had all faded away into the background, while Lily, sometimes pale as a ghost, sometimes flushed with the agitation of fever, lay struggling between life and death. The doctor, an ordinary village doctor, knew little of such maladies. He was reduced by his practical ignorance to the passive position which is now so often adopted by the highest knowledge. He watched the patient with anxious and sympathetic eyes, naturally sorry for a creature so young, with her girlish beauty fading like a flower. He did not know what to do, and he wisely did nothing. He had made, as was natural, many attempts to find out how an attack so serious had been brought on. Had she received any great shock? Katrin and Beenie, looking at each other, had answered cautiously that maybe it might be so, but they could not tell. Had she suddenly heard any bad news? Oh, yes, poor thing, she had done that! very bad news that had just gone straight to her heart like the shot of a gun. "But, doctor, you'll say nothing to Sir Robert of that." The doctor drew his own conclusions and satisfied himself. No doubt the shock was the arrival of the old uncle. He had heard something of the young gentleman who was always coming and going, and that the two would make a bonnie couple if every thing went right, though this good-natured speech was accompanied by shakings of the head and prognostications of dreadful things that might happen if every thing went wrong. The doctor nodded his head and made up his mind that he had penetrated the affair. It would not even have shocked him to hear that it had gone the length of a secret marriage. Private marriages acknowledged late were not looked upon in Scotland with very severe eyes. Both law and custom excused them, though in such a case as Lily's it was strange that anything of the kind should occur.

But it becomes of very little importance, when such a malady has dragged along its weary course for weeks, to know what was the cause of it. The rapid cures which a promise of happiness works, in fiction at least, very seldom occur in life, and when the spiritual part of the patient becomes lost, as it were, in the hot running current of fevered blood, and the predominance of the agitated body is complete over all the commotions of the mind, it is vain to think of proposing remedies for the original wrong, even if that were possible. Sir Robert now and then paid a visit to his niece's room, short and unwilling, dictated solely by a sense of duty. He stood near the door and looked at her, tossing on her pillows, or lying as if dead in the apathy of exhaustion, with an uneasy sense, partly that he was himself badly used by Providence, partly that he might, perhaps, be partially himself to blame. He had left her here very lonely. Perhaps it was a mistake in judgment; but then he had been entirely ignorant of the circumstances, and how could it be said to be his fault? When she began to talk, he could not understand what she said— nor, indeed, could any one in the quickened and hurrying incoherence of the utterance—except the cry of Marg'ret, Marg'ret, Marg'ret! which still sometimes came with a passion that made it intelligible from her lips. "Who is Marg'ret?" he asked angrily. "I remember no person of that name." "Marg'ret! Marg'ret! Marg'ret!" cried Lily again, her confused mind caught by his repetition of the name. She flung herself toward the side of the bed which was nearest the door, opening her eyes wide, as if to see better, and adding, with a cry of ecstasy: "She has brought him back—she has brought him back!" Sir Robert hurried away with a thrill of alarm. Who was it that was to be brought back? Who was the Marg'ret for whom she cried night and day? Was it the mere delirium of her fever, or was something else—something real and unknown—hidden below?

CHAPTER XXXVI

Sir Robert had not at this time a happy life. His friends went away at last, having exhausted the little shootings of Dalrugas and finding that social amusement of any kind was not to be found there, besides the ever-present reason of "illness in the house" why they should not outstay the limits of their invitation. And no one else came. Why should they, considering how very little inducement he had to offer? This of itself was a hard confession for the proud old man to make, who, perhaps, had been tempted now and then to enhance at his club, or in his favorite society, those attractions of his little patrimony, which were so very different, as he remembered them, from what they were now. John Duff of Blackscaur made a call to say chiefly how sorry he was that he could show no civilities to his neighbor, having only come to a dismantled house for a few weeks' shooting, his wife being abroad. "I was glad to give a little sport to one of the young Lumsdens last year," he said. "I heard he was a friend of yours." "No friend of mine!" cried Sir Robert, suddenly recalled by the name to the original cause, which he had more than half forgotten, of Lily's banishment. "Ah!" cried John Duff indifferently, "it was a mistake, then. Of course I knew his father." This was the only social overture made to Sir Robert Ramsay, and it carried with it a sting, which gave him considerable uneasiness. "Would the fellow have the audacity to come after her here?" he asked himself. And he made up his mind wrathfully, when Lily was better, to enquire into this allusion. When Lily was better! But he was still more angry when any doubt was expressed on that subject. Katrin's tearful looks once or twice when the patient was worse he took as a personal affront. He would not believe that Providence, however hostile, could treat him so badly as that.

When he was in this lonely and unsatisfied state of mind, a letter came for him one day from the Manse, begging him in his charity to go and see the minister, who was unable to come to him. "Ah! old Blythe," Sir Robert said. He would not have thought very much of old Blythe in other days, but now he remembered, not without pleasure, the good stories the minister told, and the good company he was. "Will Rory last with me as far as the Manse?" he said to Dougal. "Rory, Sir Robert, he'll just last till the Day o' Judgment," said Dougal. "I have no occasion for him so far as that!" Sir Robert replied sharply; and he felt that it was not quite becoming his dignity to ride into Kinloch-Rugas mounted upon a Highland pony; but what can one do when there is no other way? The minister sat as usual in his great chair by the fire, which burned dully still, though the day was August. He said: "Come in, Sir Robert, come ben! I'm very glad to see you, though it is a long time since we met. You will, maybe, find the fire too much at this time of the year, but, you see, I'm a lameter that cannot move out of my chair, and I never find it warm enough for me."

"You should have a chair that you could move about and get into the sun now and then; that's the only thing that warms the blood—at our age."

"I am years older than you. I consider you a fine trim and trig elderly young man."

The minister laughed more cordially at this jest than Sir Robert did. He did not like the faintest suggestion of ridicule. It is true that he was trim and well dressed, an example of careful toilet and appearance beside the careless old heavy form in the easy chair. Mr. Blythe had long since ceased to care what his appearance was. Sir Robert was "very particular" and careful of every detail.

"And how are you liking your home-coming?" Mr. Blythe said. "It's a trial and a risk when you have been away all the best of your life. I'm doubting the auld tower looks but small to your eyes by what it did in the old days."

"Things are changed certainly," said Sir Robert a little stiffly, "especially among the old neighbors. There used to be plenty of society; now there seems none, or next to none."

"And that is true. The old folk are dead and gone; the young generation is changed: the lads go away and never come back, the lasses marry into strange houses. It's very true; but you are just very fortunate. Like me, you have a child to your old age; though you did not, like me, Sir Robert, take the trouble to provide her for yourself."

Sir Robert stared a little at this speech, and then said: "If you mean my niece Lily, Blythe, you probably know that she's very ill in bed, and a cause of great anxiety, not of comfort, to me."

"Ay, ay," said the minister, "we had heard something, but did not know it was so bad as that. But it will be a thing that will pass by; just some chill she has got out on the moor, or some other bit small matter. She has been very well and blooming, a fine young creature all the time we have had her here."

"I am by no means sure," said Sir Robert, with a cloud on his brow, "that I did not make a mistake in sending her here. I had no intention to send her into a desert. My mind was full of the old times, when we were cheerful enough, as you will remember, Blythe, whatever else we might be. There was not much money going—nor perhaps luxury—but there was plenty of company. However, I'm glad you have so good a report to give of her. She's neither well nor blooming, poor lassie, now."

The minister cleared his throat two or three times, as if he found it difficult to resume. "Sir Robert," he said, and then made a pause, "I am not a man that likes to interfere. I have as little liking for that part as you or any man could have—to be meddled with in what you will think your own affairs."

Sir Robert stiffened visibly, uplifting his throat in the stiff stock, which, in his easiest moment, seemed to hold him within risk of strangulation. "I fail to see," he said, "what there is in my affairs that would warrant interference from you or any man; but if you've got anything to say, say it out."

"I meddle with nobody," said the minister as proudly, "unless it is for the young of the flock. I can scarcely call you one of my flock, Sir Robert."

"A grewsome auld tup at the best, you'll be thinking," said Sir Robert, with a harsh laugh.

"Man!" said the minister, "at the least of it we are old friends. We know each other's mettle; if we quarrel, it'll do little good or harm to any body. And if you like to fling off in a fit, you must just do it. What I've got to say is just this: Women folk are hard to manage for them that are not used to them. I've not just come as well out of it as I would have liked myself; and that little thing up at Dalrugas is a tender bit creature. She has blossomed like the flowers when she has been let alone, and never lost heart, though she has had many a dull day. Do not cross the lassie above what she is able to bear. If you're still against the man she likes herself, for the love of God, Robert Ramsay, force no other upon her, as you hope to be saved!"

The old minister was considerably moved, but this did not perhaps express itself in the most dignified way. What with the fervor of his mind, and the heat of the fire, and the little unusual exertion, the perspiration stood in great drops on his brow.

"This is a very remarkable appeal, Blythe," said Sir Robert. "I force another man upon her! Granted there is one she likes herself, as you seem so sure—though I admit nothing of my own knowledge—am I a man to force a husband down any woman's throat?"

"I will beg your pardon humbly if I'm wrong," said Mr. Blythe, subdued, wiping the moisture from his face, "but if you think a moment, you will see that appearances are against you. We heard of your arriving in a hurry with a young gentleman in your train; and then there came the news Miss Lily was ill—she that had stood out summer and winter against that solitude and never uttered a word—that she should just droop the moment that it might have been thought better things were coming, and company and solace—Sir Robert, I ask you—"

"To believe that it was all out of terror of me!" cried Sir Robert, who had risen up and was pacing angrily about the room. "Upon my word, Blythe, you reckon on an old soldier's self-command above what is warranted! Me, her nearest relation, that have sheltered and protected her all her life—do you mean to insinuate that Lily is ill and has a brain-fever out of dread of me?"

"If you brought another man to her, knowing her wishes were a different way, and bid her take him or be turned out of your doors!"

Sir Robert was not a man who feared anything. He stood before the minister's very face, and swore an oath that would have blown the very roof off the house had Mr. Douglas, the assistant and successor, sat in that chair. Mr. Blythe was a man of robust nerves, yet it impressed even him. "I force a young man down a lassie's throat!" cried Sir Robert in great wrath, indignation, and furious derision. "Me make matches or mar them! Is't the decay of your faculties, Blythe, your old age, though you're not much older than I am, or what is it that makes you launch such an accusation at me?"

"There's nothing decayed about me but my legs," said the old minister with half a jest. "I'll beg your pardon heartily, Sir Robert, if it's not true."

"You deserve no explanations at my hands," said the other, "but I'll give them for the sake of old times. The young man was a chance acquaintance for a week's shooting. I'll perhaps never see him again, nor did he ever set eyes on Lily. And I have not exchanged a word with her since I came back. She knows me not—from you, or from Adam. Blythe, she is very ill, the poor lassie. She knows neither night nor day."

"Lord bless us!" said the minister, and then he put forth his large soft hand. "I beg your pardon," he said. "See how little a thing makes a big lie and slander when it's taken the wrong color. I was deceived, but I hope you'll forgive. In whose hands is she? what doctor? There's no great choice here."

"A man from the other side of the water," said Sir Robert in the old phraseology of the countryside. "Macalister, I think."

"Well, it's the best you can do here. Our man's a cleverer man, if you could ever be sure of finding him with his head clear. But Macalister is an honest fellow. I would not say but I would have a man from Edinburgh if it was me."

"Do you think so?" said Sir Robert.

"If it was my Eelen—Lord, it's no one, but half-a-dozen men I'd have from Edinburgh before I'd see her slip through my fingers. But there's nothing like your own very flesh and blood."

"I will write at once!" cried Sir Robert.

"I would send a man—the post's slow. I would send a man by the coach that leaves to-night; for an hour lost you might repent all the days of your life, Robert Ramsay," said the minister, once more grasping and holding fast in his large, limp, but not unvigorous hand the other old gentleman's firm and hard one. "Just bear with me for another word. If she's hanging between life and death—and you know not what may happen—and if there is a man in Edinburgh she would rather see than any doctor, for the love of God, man, don't do things by halves, but send for him, too."

"What the deevil do you mean with your 'man in Edinburgh'?" Sir Robert said, with a shout, drawing his hand forcibly away.

He rode home upon Rory, much discomfited and disturbed. It is scarcely too much to say that he had forgotten much, or almost all, about Ronald Lumsden in the long interval that had occurred, during which he was fully occupied with his own life, and indifferent to what took place elsewhere. He had sent Lily off to Dalrugas to free her from the assiduities of a young fellow who was not a proper match for her. That is how Sir Robert would have explained it; and he had never entertained a doubt that, what with the fickleness of youth and the cheerful company about, Lily had forgotten her unsuitable suitor long ago. But to have it even imagined, by the greatest old fool that ever was, that Lily's terror of being obliged by her uncle to accept another man had upset her very brain and brought on a deadly fever was too much for any man to bear. And old Blythe was not an old fool, though he had behaved like one. If he thought so, other people would think so, and he—Robert Ramsay, General, K. C. B., a man almost as well known as the Prince of Wales himself, a member of the best clubs, an authority on every social usage—he, the venerated of Edinburgh, the familiar of London—he would be branded, in a miserable hole in the country, with the character of a domestic tyrant, with the still more contemptible character of a match-maker, like any old woman! Sir Robert's rage and annoyance were increased by the consciousness that he was not himself cutting at all a dignified figure on the country road mounted upon Rory, for whom his legs were too long (though he was not a tall man) and his temper too short. Rory tossed his shaggy head to the winds, and did battle with his master, when the pace did not please him. He all but threw the old gentleman, who was famed for his horsemanship. And it was in the last phase of exasperation, having dismounted, and, with a blow of his light switch, sent Rory careering home to his stable riderless, that Sir Robert encountered the doctor returning from his morning's visit. Mr. Macalister's face was grave. He turned back at once, and eagerly, desiring, he said, a few minutes' conversation. "I cannot well speak to you with your people and those women always about."

"I am afraid, then," said Sir Robert, "you have something very serious to say."

"Maybe—and maybe not. In the first place there are indications this morning of a change—we will hope for the better. The pulse has fallen. There's been a little natural sleep. I would say in an ordinary subject, and with no complications, that perhaps, though we must not just speak so confidently at the first moment, the turn had taken place."

"I'm delighted to hear it!" cried Sir Robert. It was really so great a relief to him that he put out his hand in sudden cordiality. "I will never forget my obligations to you, Macalister. You have given me the greatest relief. When the turn has really come, there is nothing, I've always heard, but great care wanted—care and good food and good air."

"That was just what I wanted to speak to you about, Sir Robert," said the doctor, with one of those little unnecessary coughs that mean mischief. "Good air there is—she could not have better; and good food, for I've always heard your housekeeper is great on that; and good nursing—well, yon woman, that is, your niece's maid, Bauby or Beenie, or whatever they call her, is little more than a fool, but she's a good-hearted idiot, and sticks to what she's told—when there's nobody to tell her different. So we may say there's good care. But when that's said, though it's a great deal, every thing is not said."

"Ay," said Sir Robert, "and what may there be beyond that?" He had become suspicious after his experiences, though it did not seem possible that from such a quarter there should come any second attack.

"I'm very diffident," said the doctor in his strong Northern accent, with his ruddy, weather-beaten countenance cast down in his embarrassment, "of mentioning anything that's not what ye might call strictly professional, or taking advantage of a medical man's poseetion. But when a man has a bit tender creature to deal with, like a flower, and that has just come through a terrible illness, the grand thing to ask will be, Sir Robert, not if she has good food and good nursing, which is what is wanted in most cases, but just something far more hard to come by—if she's wanting to live—"

"Wanting to live!" cried Sir Robert. "What nonsense are you speaking? A girl of that age!"

"It's just precisely that age that fashes me. Older folk have got more used to it: living's a habit with the like of us. We just find we must go on, whatever happens; but a young lass is made up of fancies and veesions. She says to herself: 'I would like better a bonnie green turf in the kirkyard than all this fighting and striving,' and just fades away because she has no will to take things up again. I've seen cases like that before now."

"And what's my part in all this?" cried Sir Robert. "You come to me with your serious face, as if I had some hand in it. What can I do?"

"Well, Sir Robert," said the doctor, "that is what I cannot tell. I'm not instructed in your affairs—nor do I wish to be; but if there is anything in this young lady's road that crosses her sorely—the state of the brain that made this attack so dangerous evidently came from some mental shock—if it's within the bounds of possibility that you can give in to her, do so, Sir Robert. I am giving you a doctor's advice—not a private man's that has nothing ado with it. If you can give her her own way, which is dear to us all, and more especially to women folk, give it to her, Sir Robert! It will be her best medicine. Or if you cannot do that, let her think you will do it—let her think you will do it! It's lawful to deceive even in a case like this—to save her life."

"You are trying to make me think, doctor, that my niece has been pretending to be ill all this time in order to get her own way."

"You may think that if you like, Sir Robert. It's a pretending that has nearly cost you a funeral, and I will not say may not do so yet—but me, out of my own line, my knowledge is very imperfect. You know your own affairs best. But you cannot say I have not warned you of the consequences," Dr. Macalister said.

All the world seemed in a conspiracy against Sir Robert. He took off his hat formally to the doctor, who responded, somewhat overawed by such a solemn civility. What was it that this man, a stranger, supposed him to be doing to Lily? It was ridiculous, it was absurd! first old Blythe, and then the doctor. He had never done any harm to Lily; he had stopped a ridiculous love affair, a boy and girl business, with a young fellow who had not a penny. He did not mean his money to go to fit out another lot of long-legged Lumsdens, a name he could not bear. No, he had done no more than was his right, which he would do again to-morrow if necessary. But then in the meantime here was another question. Her life, a lassie's life! Nothing was ever more ridiculous: her life depending on what lad she married, a red-headed one, or a black-headed one, the silly thing! But nevertheless it seemed it was true. Here was the doctor, a serious man, and old Blythe, both in a story. Well, if she were dying for her lad, the foolish tawpy, he would have to see what could be done. To think of a Ramsay, the last of his race, following her passions like that! But it would be some influence from the other side, from the mother, James's wife, who, he had always heard, was not over-wise.

He was turning over these thoughts in his mind as he approached close to the house, when he was suddenly aware of some one flying out toward him with arms extended and a lock or two of red hair dropped out of all restraint and streaming in the wind. Beenie had waited and watched and lived half in a dream, never sleeping, scarcely eating, absorbed in that devotion which has no bounds, for the last six weeks. Her trim aspect, her careful neatness, her fresh and cheerful air, had faded in the air of the sick room. Combs do not hold nor pins attach after such a long vigil. She flew out, running wildly toward him with arms extended and hair streaming until, unable to stop herself, she fairly ran into the old gentleman's arms.

"Oh, Sir Robert," cried Beenie, gasping and trying to recover her breath, but too far gone for any apology, "she's come to herself! She's as weak as water, and white as death. But she's come to herself and she's askin' for you. She's crying upon you and no to be silenced. 'I am wanting Uncle Robert, I am wanting Uncle Robert!' No breath to speak, and no strength to utter a voice, but come to hersel', come to hersel'! And, oh! the Lord knows if it's for death or life, for none of us can tell!"

CHAPTER XXXVII

When Sir Robert went in somewhat reluctantly to Lily's room—for he was not accustomed to illness, and did not know what to do or say, or even how to look, in a sick room—he found her fully conscious, very white, very worn, her eyes looking twice their usual size and full of that wonderful translucent clearness which exhaustion gives. Her face, he did not know why, disposed the old gentleman to shed tears, though he was very far indeed from having any inclination that way in general. There was a smile upon it, a smile of wistful appeal to him, such a claim upon his sympathy and help as perhaps no other human creature had ever made before.

"Uncle!" she cried, holding out two thin hands which seemed whiter than the mass of white linen about her. "Uncle Robert! oh! are you there? I have been an ill bairn to you, Uncle Robert. I have not been faithful nor true. You sent me here for my good, and I've turned it to harm. But you're my only kin and my only friend, and all that I have in the world."

"Lily, my dear, compose yourself, my poor lassie. I am not blaming you: why should I blame you? When you were ill, what could you do but lie in your bed and be taken care of? Woman, have ye no sense? She is not fit yet to be troubled with visits; you might have seen that!"

"Oh, Sir Robert, and so I did! But how could I cross her when she just said without ceasing: 'I want my uncle. I want to see my uncle!' She was not to be crossed, the doctor said."

"It was not Beenie's fault." Lily stretched out her hands till they reached her uncle's, who stood by her bedside, yet as far off as he could, not to appear unkind. He was a little horrified by the touch of those hot hands. She threw herself half out of the bed to reach him, and caught his hard and bony old hand, so firm still and strong, between those white quivering fingers, almost fluid in their softness, which enveloped his with a sudden heat and atmosphere, so strange and unusual that he retreated still a step, though he could not withdraw his hand.

"Uncle Robert, you will not forsake me!" Lily cried. "I have only you now, I have only you. I have been ill to you, but, oh, be good to me! I am a very lonely woman. I have nobody. I have put my trust in—other things, and they have all failed me! I've had a long dream and now I've awakened. Uncle Robert, I have nobody but you in all the world!"

"Now, Lily, you must just compose yourself, my dear. Who thought of forsaking you? It is certain that you are my only near relation. Your father was my only brother. What would ail me at you? My poor lassie, just let yourself be covered up, and put your arms under the clothes and try if you cannot sleep a little. A good sleep would be the best thing for her, Robina, wouldn't you say? Compose yourself, compose yourself, my dear."

Lily still clung to his hand, though he tried so hard to withdraw it from her hold. "And I will be different," she said. "You will never need to complain of me more. My visions and my dreams they are all melted away, like the snow yon winter-time, when my head was just carried and I did not know what I was doing. Oh, I have been ill to you, ill to you! Eaten your bread and dwelt in your house and been a traitor to you. If they tell you, oh, Uncle Robert, do not believe I was so bad as that. I never meant it, I never intended— It was a great delusion, and it is me that has the worst to bear."

"Robina!" cried Sir Robert, "this will never do. What disjointed nonsense has the poor thing got into her head? She will be as bad as ever if you do not take care. No more of it, no more of it, Lily. You've been very ill; you must be quiet, and don't trouble your head about anything. As for your old uncle, he will stand by you, my poor lassie, whatever you may have done—not that I believe for a moment you have done anything." He was greatly relieved to get his hand free. He went so far as to cover her shoulders with the bedclothes, and to give a little pat upon the white counterpane. Poor little thing! Her head was not right yet. Great care must be taken of the poor lassie. He had heard they were fond of accusing themselves of all kinds of crimes after an attack of this sort.

"I suppose the doctor will be coming to-day?" he said to Beenie as he hastily withdrew toward the door.

"It's very near his hour, Sir Robert."

"That's well, that's very well! Keep her as quiet as you can, that's the great thing, and tell her from me that she is not to trouble her head about anything—about anything, mind," said Sir Robert with an emphasis which had no real meaning, though it awakened a hundred alarms in Beenie's mind. She thought he must have been told, he must have found out something of the history of these past months. But, indeed, the old gentleman knew nothing at all, and meant nothing but to express, more or less in the superlative, his conviction that poor Lily was still under the dominion of her delusions, and that it was her fever, not herself, which brought from her lips these incomprehensible confessions. He understood that it was often so in these cases; probably, if he had let her go on, she would have confessed to him that she had tried to murder—Dougal, say, or somebody else equally likely. The only thing was to keep her quiet, to impress upon her that she was not to trouble her head about anything, not about anything, in the strongest way in which that assurance could be put.

Lily lay quite still for a long time after Sir Robert had escaped from the room. She was very weak and easily exhausted, but happily the weakness of both body and brain dulled, except at intervals, the active sense of misery, and even the memory of those events which had ravaged her life. She was still quite quiet when the doctor came, and smiled at him with the faint smile of recovered consciousness and intelligence, though with scarcely a movement as she lay on her pillows, recovered, yet so prostrated in strength that she lay like one cast up by the waves, half dead, unable to struggle or even to lift a finger for her own help. A much puzzled man was the doctor, who had brought her successfully through this long and dreadful illness, but whose mind had been sorely exercised to account for many things which connected this malady with what had gone before. That he divined a great deal of what had gone before there was little doubt; but he had no light upon Lily's real position, and his heart was sore for a young creature, a lady, in such sore straits, and with probably a cloud hanging over her which would spoil her entire life. And he was a prudent man, and asked no questions which he was not compelled to ask. Had it been a village girl he would have formed his conclusions with less hesitation, and felt less deeply; but it was a very different matter with Sir Robert Ramsay's niece, who would be judged far more severely and lose much more than any village maiden was likely to do. Poor girl! he tried as best he could, like a good man as he was, to save her as much as possible even from the suggestion of any suspicion. "What has she been doing? You have allowed her to do too much," he said.

"She would see her uncle, doctor; she just insisted that she would see Sir Robert. If I had crossed her in that, would it no have been just as bad?"

The white face on the pillow smiled faintly and breathed, rather than said: "It was my fault."

"And he said she was not to trouble her head about ainy thing, not about ainy thing, doctor, and that was a comfort to her—she was so vexed, him coming for the first time to his ain house, and her no able to welcome him, nor do anything for him."

"That's a very small matter; she must think of that no more. What you have to do now, Miss Ramsay, is just to think of nothing, to trouble your head about nothing, as Sir Robert judiciously says; to take what you can in the way of nourishment, and to sleep as much as you can, and to think about nothing. I absolutely proheebit thinking," he said, bending over her with a smile. She was so touching a sight in her great weakness, and with even his uncertain perception of what was behind and before her, that the moisture came into the honest doctor's eyes.

Lily gave him another faint smile, and shook her head, if that little movement on the pillow could be called shaking her head, and then he gave Beenie her instructions, and with a perplexed mind proceeded to the interview with Sir Robert to which he had been summoned. He did not know what he would say to Sir Robert if his questions were of a penetrating kind. But Sir Robert's questions were not penetrating at all.

"She has been havering to me, poor lassie," said the old gentleman, "about being alone in the world and with nobody but me to look after her. It is true enough. We have no relations, either her or me, being the last of the family. But why should she think I would forsake her? And she says she has been an ill bairn to me, and other things that have just no sense in them. But that's a common thing, doctor? Is it not quite a common thing that people coming out of such an illness take fancies that they have done all sorts of harm?"

"The commonest thing in the world," said the doctor cheerfully. "Did she say she had stolen your gear, or broken into your strong-box?"

"There is no saying what she would have said if I had let her go on," said Sir Robert, with a laugh, "though, indeed, I was nearer crying than laughing to see her so reduced. But all that will come right in time?"

"It will all come right in time. She's weaker than I like to see, and you must send for me night or day, at any moment, if there is any increase of weakness. But I hope better things. Leave her to the women: they're very kind, and not so silly as might reasonably be expected. Don't go near her, if I might advise you, Sir Robert."

"Indeed, I will obey you there," said the old gentleman; "no fear of that. I can do her no good, poor thing, and why should I trouble both her and myself with useless visits? No, no, I will take care of that."

And the doctor went away anxious, but satisfied. If there was a story to tell, it was better that the poor girl should tell it at least when she was full mistress of herself—not now, betrayed by her weakness, when she might say what she would regret another time.

But Lily asked no more for Sir Robert. It was but the first impulse of her suddenly awakened mind. She relapsed into the weakness which was all the greater for that brief outburst, and lay for days conscious, and so far calm that she had no strength for agitation, often sleeping, seldom thinking, wrapped by nature in a dream of exhaustion, through which mere emotion could not pierce. And thus youth and the devoted attendance of her nurses brought her through at last. It was October when she first rose from her bed, an advance in recovery which the women were anxious to keep back as long as possible, while the doctor on the other hand pressed it anxiously. "She will lose all heart if she is kept like this, with no real sign of improvement," he said. "Get her up; if it's only for an hour, it will do her good."

"It will bring it all back," said Beenie in despair. She stopped herself next moment with a terrified glance at him; but he knew how to keep his own counsel. And he gave no further orders on this subject. Lily, however, was not to be restrained. When she was first led into the drawing-room, she went to the window and looked out long and with a steadfast look upon the moor. It had faded out of the glory of heather which had covered it everywhere when she last looked upon that scene. Nearly two months were over since that day, that wonderful day of fate. Lily looked out upon the brown heather, still with here and there a belated touch of color upon the end of the long stalks rustling with the brown husks of the withered bells. The rowan-trees gave here and there a gleam of scarlet or a touch of bright yellow in the scanty leaves, ragged with the wind, which were almost as bright as the berries. The intervals of turf were emerald green, beginning to shine with the damp of coming winter. The hills rose blue in the noonday warmth with that bloom upon them, like a breaking forth of some efflorescence responsive to the light, which comes in the still sunshine, disturbed by no flying breezes. Lily looked long upon the well-known landscape which she knew by heart in every variation, resisting with great resolution the endeavors of Beenie to draw her back from that perilous outlook.

"Oh, look nae mair, my bonnie leddy!" Beenie said. "You've seen it mair than enough, that awfu' moor!"

"What ails you at the moor, Robina?" Sir Robert said, coming briskly in. "You are welcome back, my dear; you are welcome back to common life. Don't stand and weary yourself; I will bring you a chair to the window. I'm glad, Lily, that you're fond of the moor."

Lily turned to him with the same overwhelming smile which had nearly made an end of Sir Robert before, which shone from her pale face and from her wide, lucid, liquid eyes, still so large and bright with weakness; but she did not wait for him to bring her a chair to the window. She tottered to one that had been placed for her near the fire, which, however bright the day, was always necessary at Dalrugas. "I am better here," she said. She looked so fragile seated there opposite to him that the old gentleman's heart was moved.

"My poor lassie! I would give something to see you as bright-faced and as light-footed as when you came here."

"Ah, that's so long ago," she said. "I was light-hearted, too, and perhaps light-headed then. I am not light in any way now, except, perhaps, in weight. It makes you very serious to live night and day and never change upon the moor."

"Do you think so, Lily? I'm sorry for that. I thought you were so fond of the moor. They told me you were out upon it when you were well, rambling and taking your pleasure all the day."

"Yes," she said, "it's always bonnie. The heather is grand in its time, and it's fine, too, in the gray days, when the hills are all wrapped in their gray plaids, and a kind of veil upon the moor. But it cannot answer, Uncle Robert, when you speak, or give you back a look or say a word."

"That's true, that's true, Lily. I was thinking only that it's a peaceful place, and quiet, where an old man like me can get his sleep in peace; though there's that Dougal creature with his pails and pony that is aye stirring by the skreigh of day."

"The pony was a great diversion," said Lily, "and Dougal, too, who was always very kind to me."

"Kind! It was his bounden duty, the least he could do. I would like to know how he would have stood before me if he had not been kind, and far more, to the only child of the old house!"

"Thank you, Uncle Robert," said Lily, "for saying so. They were all kind, and far more than kind. They have just been devoted to me, and thought of nothing but to make me happy. You will think of that—in case that anything should happen."

"Lily!" said Sir Robert with an angry tone, "I'm thinking you're both ungrateful and unkind yourself. God has spared you and brought you back out of a dreadful illness, and these two women have nursed you night and day, and though I could do little for you, having no experience that way, yet perhaps I've felt all the more. And here are you speaking of 'anything that might happen,' as if you had not just been delivered out of the jaws of death."

"Yes, I am very grateful," said Lily, holding out her thin hand, "to both them and you, Uncle Robert, and most of all to you, for it was out of your way indeed; but as for God, I am not sure that I am grateful to him, for he might have taken me out of all the trouble while he was at it, and that would have been the best for us all. But," she added, looking up suddenly with one of her old quick changes of feeling and countenance, "how should you think I meant dying? There are many, manythings that might happen besides that. I might go away, or you might send me away."

"I'll not do that, Lily."

"How do you know, Uncle Robert? You sent me away once before when you sent me here. You might do it again—or, what is more, I might ask you— Oh, Uncle Robert, let me go away a little, let me leave the sight of it, and the loneliness that has broken my heart!" Lily put her transparent hands together and looked at him with a pathetic entreaty in her face.

"Go away!" he said, startled, "as soon as I come here—the first time you come into the drawing-room to ask that!"

"It is true," said Lily, "it's ungrateful, oh, it's without heart, it's unkind, Uncle Robert, as you say; but only for a little while, till I get a little better. I will never get better here."

"This is a great disappointment to me," he said. "I thought I would have you, Lily, to keep me company. I thought you would be my companion and take care of me for a year or two. I am not likely at my age to trouble any body for very long," he added with a half-conscious appeal for sympathy.

"And so I will," said Lily; "I will be your companion. I will be at your side to do whatever you please—to read or to write, to walk or to talk. I will look for nothing else in this world, and I will never leave you, Uncle Robert, and there is my hand upon that. But I must be well first," she added rapidly. "And I will never get well here. Oh, let me go! If it was but for a week, for a fortnight, for two or three days. Is it not always said of ill folk that when they get better they must have a change? Let me have a change, Uncle Robert! I want to look out at something that is not the moor. Oh, how long, how long, if you will only think of it, I have been looking at nothing but the moor! I am tired, tired of the moor! Oh, I am wearied of it! I have liked it well, and I will come back and like it again. But for a little while, uncle, only for a little while, let me go away from the moor."

"Is it so long a time?" he said. "I was not aware you had been here so long a time. Why, it is not two years! If you think two years is a long time, Lily, wait till you know what life is, and that a year's but a moment when you look back upon it."

"It looks like a hundred years to me," she said, "and before I can look back as you do it will be a hundred years more. And how am I to bear them all without a break or a rest? If I were even like you, a soldier marching here and there, with your colors flying and your drums beating! but what has a woman to do but to sit and think and count the days? Uncle Robert," she said, putting her hand on his arm as he stood near her, with his back to the fire, "I'm not unwilling at all to die. I would never have minded if it had been so. I would have asked for nothing but a warm green turf from the moor, and maybe a bush of heather at my feet. But it has not ended like that, which would have been God's doing—only I will never get well unless I get away, unless I breathe other air; and if you refuse me, that will be your doing!" she cried with something of her old petulance and fire.

"Did the doctor say anything about this change?" Sir Robert asked Beenie, with a cloud upon his face.

"He said she was to be crossed in naething," Beenie replied.

CHAPTER XXXVIII

When it was settled that Lily was to have the change upon which she insisted, her health improved day by day, and with the increase of her strength, or perhaps as the real fountain-head and cause of her increased strength, her elasticity of spirit returned to her. By one of those strange gifts of temperament which triumph over every thing that humanity can encounter, this young creature, overwhelmed by so many griefs—a deserted wife, a mother whose child had been torn from her, her secret life so full of incidents and emotion ending all at once in a blank—became in the added grace of her weakness and of the spirit and courage which overcame it as sweet a companion to her old uncle, as full of variety and freshness, as the heart could desire. He, indeed, had never known such company before. She had been younger by an age when she left him in Edinburgh, less developed, half a child, at least in his eyes, and he had been surrounded by company and cronies of his own of a very different character. But now, in this lonely spot where there was nobody, Lily, rising from her sick-bed, with her eyes still large in their white sockets, her hands still transparent, her touch and her step still tremulous with weakness, became his diversion, his delight, making the long lonely days short, and even the rain supportable when it swept against the narrow windows, and intensified the brightness of the fireside and the pleasant talk, or even, when there was no talk, the sense of companionship within. Sometimes Lily would fall asleep in the afternoon or at the falling of the day, unawares, in the feebleness of her convalescence, and perhaps these were the moments in which most of all the old man of the world felt completely what this companionship was. He would lay down his paper or his book and look at her—the light of the fire playing on her face, giving it a faint touch of rose, and dissimulating the deep shadows under the eyes—feeling to his heart that most intimate confidence and trust in him, the reliance, almost unconscious, of a child, the utter dependence and weakness which could put up no barriers of the conventional, nor stop to think what would be agreeable: these things found out secret crevices in Sir Robert's armor of which neither he nor any one else had dreamed. The water stood in his eyes as he looked at her, saying "Poor lassie, poor little lassie!" secretly in his heart. She was as good company then, though she did not know it, as when she started from her brief sleep and exerted herself to make him talk, to make him laugh, to feel himself the most interesting of raconteurs and delightful of companions. Many people had flattered Sir Robert in his day—he had been important enough in much of his life for that—but he had never found flattery so sweet as Lily's demands upon the stores of his long experience, her questions upon his history, her interest in what he told her. It was not only that she was herself such a companion as he had not dreamed of, but that he never had been aware before what excellent company he was himself. He almost grudged to see her growing stronger, though he rejoiced in it from the bottom of his old world-worn heart.

"And so you are going to leave me, Lily—you've settled, that Robina woman and you—and you're off in two days seeking adventures?"

"Yes, uncle—in two days; but only for a little while."

"Without a thought of an old man left desolate—upon the edge of the moor."

"Yes, with a thought that is very pleasant—that there's somebody there wanting me back"—she paused a moment with a faint sigh and added: "and that I am coming back to in a little while. And then, as for the moor, it is full of diversion. You're never lonely watching the clouds and the shadows and all the changes: I have had much experience of it, Uncle Robert—two years, that were sometimes long, long."

"I never knew," said Sir Robert, a little abashed, "how lonely it was, Lily, and that all the old neighbors were gone. I pictured you surrounded with young folk, and as merry as the day was long."

"It was not exactly that," she said, with a smile; and then her face changed, as it did from moment to moment, like the moor which she loved, yet hated—shadows flying over it as swift, as sudden, and as deep. "But it's all past, and why should we think more of it? When I come back, Uncle Robert, we'll be cheery, you and me together by the fireside all the winter through, and never ask whether there are neighbors or not—or other folk in the world."

"I would not go so far as that," said the old gentleman. "We'll get the world to come to us, Lily, a small bit at a time. But you have never told me where you are going when you leave me here."

"To Edinburgh," she said.

"To Edinburgh! I thought you had consulted with the doctor, and were going to the seaside, or to the Bridge of Allan, or some of the places where invalids go."

"Uncle," said Lily, "I have been two years upon the moor, and in all that time I have not got a new gown, nor a bonnet, nor anything whatsoever. Oh, yes, we will go to the sea, or the Bridge of Allan, or to some place. But we are not fit to be seen, neither Beenie nor me. You do not take these things into consideration. You think, when I speak to you like a rational creature, that I am above the wants of my kind; but rational or not, a woman must always have some clothes to wear!"

Sir Robert laughed and clapped his hands. "Bravo, Lily!" he cried. "You cannot do better, my dear, than own you're just a woman and are as fond of your finery as the rest. By all means, then, go to Edinburgh and fit yourself out; but do not stay there, go out to Portobello, if you do not care to go farther, or a little more to the West, where it's milder, and you will get a warm blink before the winter weather sets in. And that reminds me that you will want money, Lily."

"A good deal of money, Uncle Robert," she said, with a smile. "You know I have had none for two years."

It was with a sensation of shame that he heard her allusions to those two years, and perhaps Lily was aware of it. She wanted money, she wanted freedom, and that her steps should not be watched nor her movements constrained. And the old gentleman was startled and humiliated when he realized that his heiress, his only relation, his brother's child, had been banished to this wilderness without a shilling in her pocket or a friend to help her. He could not imagine how he could have forgotten so completely her existence or her claims upon him and right to his support. He was glad to wipe that recollection from his own mind as well as hers by his liberality now. And Lily received from him an order upon his "man of business" in Edinburgh for an amount which seemed to her almost fabulous—for she knew nothing of money, had never had any, nor required it, although when she retired to her room with that piece of paper in her hand which meant so much, the reflection of what might have happened and what she could have done had she only at any time during these two years possessed as much, or half as much, came upon her with almost a convulsive sense of opportunities lost. She flung herself upon Beenie's shoulder when she reached the safe shelter of her room, where it was no longer necessary to keep herself up and make a smile for her uncle. "Oh, Beenie!" she cried, "if he had given me the half of that before, or the quarter! how every thing might have been changed."

"Oh, mem, my bonnie leddy," cried Beenie, who never now addressed her mistress as Miss Lily, "it's little, little that siller can do!"

Anger flashed in Lily's eyes. "It could just have done every thing!" she said. "Do you think I would have been put off and off if I could have put my hand in my pocket and taken the coach and gone, you and me, to see to every thing ourselves? Oh! many a time I have wished for it, and longed for it—but what could we do, you and me, and nothing, nothing to take us there? Oh, never say siller can do little! It might have spared us all that's happened—think! all that's happened! I might be thinking now as I thought yon New Year's time in the snow. I might be as sure and as full of trust. I might never have learned what it was to deceive and to be deceived. I might never have been a desolate woman without man or bairn—without my little bairn, my little baby!"

"Oh, my darlin' leddy! but you'll get him again, you'll get him again!" cried Beenie, with streaming eyes.

"I hope in God I shall," said Lily, tearless, lifting her eyes and clasping her hands. "I hope in God I shall, or else that he'll let me just lay down my head and die!"

"He has raised you up from the very grave," said Beenie. "We had nae hope, Katrin and me; we had nae hope at all. Here she is hersel' that will tell you. There was ae night—oh, come Katrin, come and bear me out—when you and me just stood over her, and kissed the bonnie white face on the white pillow, and wrung each other's hands, and said: 'If the baby's lost and her reason gane, God bless her, she'll be better away.'"

"Whisht with your nonsense," said Katrin; "that's a' past, and now we have nae such thoughts in our heads. But what will you do, my dear leddy, my bonnie leddy? Will ye bring him back here? A fine thriving bairn like yon you canna hide him. The first day, the first night, and the secret would be parish news. I was frichtened out of my wits the first days for Dougal, who is not a pushing man, to do him justice, or one that asks questions; but with Sir Robert in the house, oh, mem, my bonnie dear, what will ye do?"

"I have never wanted to make any secret, Katrin," Lily said.

"I ken that; but there will be an awfu' deal to tell when once you begin. And the bairn he is an awfu' startling thing to begin with. Do ye no think an auld gentleman like Sir Robert had better be prepared for it? It would give him a shock. It might even hairm him in his health. I would take counsel about it. Oh, I would take counsel! Do naething in a hurry, not to scandalize the country, nor to give our auld maister a fright that might do him harm."

"To scandalize the country!" said Lily, pale with anger. "Oh! to think it's me, me that she says that to! Do you think it is better to deceive every-body and be always a lie whatever way you turn?"

"Mem," said Katrin, "my dear, you'll excuse me; I must just say the truth. It's an awfu' thing to deceive, as you say, and well I ken it was never your wyte. But the worst of it is that when you begin you cannot end. You just have to go on. I'm no saying one thing or another. It's no my business, if it wasna that I just think more of you than one mortal creature should think of another. Oh! just take thought and take counsel! The maister is an old man. You've beguiled him with your winsome ways just as you've beguiled us a'. Can I see a thing wrong you do, whatever it is? And yet I have a glimmerin' o' sense between whiles. If he's looking for you back to be his bonnie Lily and his companion, and syne sees you come in with a bairn in your arms and another man's name, what will the auld man do? Oh, mem, the dear bairn, God bless him, and grant that you may soon have him in your airms! But if you hold by the auld gentleman and his life and comfort, for God's sake take thought! for that is in it, too."

"There is nothing, nothing," cried Lily, "that should keep a mother from her bairn! You are a kind woman, Katrin, but you've never had a bairn. When once I get him here, how can I ever give him up again?" she said, straining her arms to her breast as if the child was within them. Beenie wept behind her mistress's shoulder, overwhelmed with sympathy, but Katrin shook her head.

"When you see Mr. Lumsden there, and go over it all—"

Lily's face became instantly as if the windows of her mind had been closed up. Her lips straightened, her eyes became blank. She said nothing, but turned away, not looking at either of them nor saying a word.

"And it was no me breathed his name or as much as thought upon him," Beenie said a little later in an aggrieved tone, when she had rejoined Katrin down stairs.

"It was me that breathed his name, and I'll do it again till some heed is paid to what I say. We should maybe have refused yon day to be his witnesses. But being sae, Beenie, the burden is on you and me as well as on him. They should have owned each other and spoke the truth from that day. But now that it has all gone so far and no a whisper risen, and the countryside just as innocent as if they were two bairns playing, oh, I wouldna now just burst it all upon the auld man's head! He's no an ill auld man. He's provided for her all her life; he is very muckle taken up with her now, maybe in a selfish way, for he's feeling his age and his mainy infirmities, and he's wanting a companion. But, oh! I would not burst it on him now! He could never abide her man, and, to tell the truth, Beenie, I'm not that fond of him mysel', and she, poor thing, has had a fearfu' opening to her eyes. How could ye have the bairn here and no the father? Could she say to her uncle: 'I was very silly about him once and married him, and now I canna abide him'? Oh, no! that is what she will never say."

"And I hope she'll never think it either," Beenie said.

"Beenie," said the other solemnly, "you are a real innocent if such a thing ever was."

"No more than yoursel'," said Beenie, indignant; but she had to return to her mistress, and further discussion could not be held on this question.

They went away on the second morning, which was a little frosty, though bright. The establishment had widened out by this time. Sir Robert was not a man to be driven to kirk or market in the little geeg, drawn at his wilful pleasure by Rory, which had answered all Lily's purposes. There was now a phaeton and a brougham, and three or four horses accommodated tant bien que mal in the old stables, which had to be cleared of much rubbish and Dougal's accumulations of years before they were in a state to receive their costly inmates. It was in the brougham that Lily, wrapped up in every kind of shawl and comforter, drove with her maid to Kinloch-Rugas to take the coach, where the best places had been reserved for them. Beenie's pride in this journey exceeded the anxiety with which her mind was full, in respect to her mistress's health in the first place, and the many issues of their journey. But it was not a "pride" which met with much sympathy from her dear friends and fellow-servants. Dougal for his part stood out in the stable-yard carefully isolated from all possible connection with the new grooms and the new horses, though neither was he without a thrill of pride in the distinction of a kind of part-proprietorship with Sir Robert in these dazzling articles. He kept apart, however, with an air of conscious superiority to such innovations. "I wish ye a good journey," he said; "maybe it'll be warmer this fine morning in a shut-up carriage, but, Lord! I would rather have Rory and the little geeg than all the coaches in England!"

Lily was thrilling with nervous excitement, scarcely able to contain herself, but she made an effort to give a word and a smile to the whilom arbiter of all the movements of Dalrugas. "I would rather have you and Rory in the summer weather," she said. "If it is a warm day when I come back, you will come for me, Dougal."

"Na, mem, no me; we're no grand enough now to carry leddies: which I wouldna care much for, for leddies, as ye ken, are whiles fantastic and put awfu' burdens on a beast—but just because his spirit is broken with trailing peats from the hill, and visitors' boxes from the toun. They're sensitive creatures, pownies. I just begin to appreciate the black powny's feelings now I see the effect upon my ain."

"He shall drive me when I come back," said Lily, waving her hand as the brougham flashed away, the coats of the horses shining in the frosty sunshine, and the carriage panels sending back reflections. It was certainly more comfortable than the geeg. But the light went out of Lily's face as they left Dalrugas behind. The little color in her cheeks disappeared. She leaned back in her corner and once more pressed her arms against her breast. "Oh, shall I find him? shall I find him?" she cried.

"You'll do that—wherefore should you no do that?" said Beenie encouragingly.

"He'll be grown so big we will not know him, Beenie, and he will not know his mother; that woman Margaret that took him away will have all his smiles—she will be the first face that he sees, now that he's old enough to notice. Oh, my little bairn! my little bairn!"

"A bairn that is two months auld takes but little notice, mem," said Beenie, strong in her practical knowledge. "You need not fash your head about that. They may smile, but if ye were to ask me the very truth, I wouldna hide from you that what they ca' smiling is just in my opinion the—"

"If you say that word, I will kill you!" cried Lily. She laughed and then she cried in her excitement. "How will I contain myself? how will I keep quiet and face the world, and the folk in the world, and every-body about, till the moment comes—oh, the moment, Beenie!—when I will get my baby into my arms?"

"Eh, mem! but you must not make yoursel' sae awfu' sure about that," said Beenie. "We might not find them just at first—or he might have a little touch of the cauld, or maybe the thrush in his wee mouth, or measles, or something. You must not make yourself so awfu' sure."

"He is ill!" cried Lily, seizing her in a fierce grip. "He is ill, oh, you false, false woman, and you have never said a word to me!"

"There is naething ill about him; he is just thriving like the flowers. But I canna bide when folk are so terrible sure. It seems as if you were tempting God."

"It's you that are tempting me—to believe in nothing, neither Him nor women's word. But what would make a woman deceive a baby's mother about her own child? A man might do it, that knows nothing about what that means; but a woman never would do it, Beenie—a woman that has been about little babies and their mothers all her days?"

"No, mem, I never thought it," said Beenie in dutiful response.

At the coach, where they were received with all the greater honor on account of Sir Robert's brougham, and the beautiful prancing horses, Helen Blythe met them. "They would not let me come to see you," she said. "It's long, long, since I've seen you, Lily, and worn and white you've grown—but just as bonnie as ever: there comes up the color just as it used to do—but you must look stronger when you come back."

"I am going away for that," Lily said.

"And it is just the wisest thing she could do," said the doctor, who had come also to see her off. "And stay away as long as you can, Miss Ramsay, and just divert yourself a little. You have great need of diversion after that long time at the old Tower."

"She is not one that is much heeding diversion," said Helen, looking at her affectionately.

"We're all needing it whether we're heeding it or no," said the doctor. "And if you will take my advice, you will just take a little pleasure to yourself, as you would take physic if I ordered it. Good-by, Miss Ramsay, and mind what I say."

"He's maybe right," said Helen; "they say he's a clever man. I know little about diversion. But, oh! I would like to see you happy, Lily—that would be better than all the physic in the world."

"Perhaps I will bring it back with me," said Lily, with a smile.

CHAPTER XXXIX

It was not with a very easy mind that Ronald Lumsden had executed the great coup which had, so far as Lily was concerned, such disastrous consequences. He had been deeply perplexed from the moment of the baby's birth, nay, before that, as to what his future action was to be. It had been apparent to him from the first that the child could not remain at Dalrugas. Much had been ventured, much had been done, to all appearance successfully enough. No scandal had been raised in the countryside by his own frequent visits. What might be whispered in the cottages no one knew; but, apart from such a possibility, nothing that could be called public, no rumor of the least importance, had arisen. Every thing was safe up to that point. And he was not much concerned even had there been any subdued scandal floating about. At any moment, should any crisis arise, Lily could be justified and set right. What could it matter, indeed, if any trouble of a moment should arise? He was not indifferent to his wife's good name. He considered himself as the best guardian of that, the best judge as to how and when it should be defended. He had (he thought) the reins in his hands, the command of all the circumstances. If he should ever see the moment come when the credit of his future family should be seriously threatened, and the position of Lily become an affair of vital importance, he was prepared to make any sacrifice. The moment it became serious enough for that he was ready to act; but in the meantime it was his to fight the battle out to the last step, and to defend her rights as her uncle's heir, and to secure the fortune for her behalf and his own. He regarded the situation largely as from the point of view of a governor and supreme authority. As long as the circumstances could be managed, the world's opinion suppressed or kept in abeyance, and the one substantial and important object kept safe, what did a little imaginary annoyance matter, or Lily's fantastic girlish notions about a house of her own, and a public appearance on her husband's arm, wearing her wedding ring and calling herself Mrs. Lumsden? He liked her the better for desiring all that, so far as it meant a desire to be always with him; otherwise the mere promotion of being known as a married lady was silly and a piece of vanity, which did not merit a thought on the part of the arbiter of her affairs. All the little by-play about the house which could not be got till the term, etc., had been a jest to him, though it had been so serious to Lily. He had never for a moment intended that she should have that house. To keep her quiet, to keep her contented, Ronald did not stint at such a small matter as a lie. Between lovers, between married people, there must be such things. If a man intends to keep at the head of affairs, and yet to keep the woman, who has no experience and knows nothing of the world, satisfied and happy, of course there must be little fictions made up and fables told. Lily would be the first to justify them when the necessity was over, when the money was secured and their final state arrived at—a dignified life together, with every thing handsome about them. He had no compunctions, therefore, about the original steps. It might have been more prudent, perhaps, if they had not married at all, if they had waited till Sir Robert died and Lily was free, in the course of nature, to give her hand and her fortune where she pleased. That, no doubt, was a rash thing to do, but the wisest of men commit such imprudences. And, with the exception of that, Ronald approved generally of his own behavior. He did not find anything to object to in his conduct of the matter altogether.

But the baby put everything out. The prospect, indeed, occupied Lily and kept her quiet and reasonable for a long time, but the moment he knew what was coming a new care came into Lumsden's mind. A baby is not a thing to be hid. It was certain that nothing would induce Lily to part with it, or to be reasonable any longer. She would throw away the result of all his precautions, of all his careful arrangements, of his self-denial and thought, in a moment, for the sake of this little thing, which could neither repay her nor know what she was doing it for. Many an hour's reflection, night and day, had he given to this subject without seeing any way out of it. With all his powers and gifts of persuasion he had not ventured even to hint to Lily the idea of sending away the child. Courage is a great thing, but sometimes it is not enough to face a situation of the simplest character. He could not do it. After the child arrived, when the inconveniences of keeping it there became apparent, he had thought it might perhaps be easier; and many times he had attempted to arrange how this could be done, but never had succeeded in putting it into words. To do him justice, it was he who had sought out and chosen with the utmost care the nurse Marg'ret, in whose hands both mother and child would be safe, and he looked forward with that vague and foolish hope in some indefinite help to come which the wisest of men, when their combinations fail, still believe in, like the most foolish; perhaps some suggestion might come from herself, who could tell? some sense of the trouble and inconvenience arising in Lily's own mind might assist him in disposing of the little intruder. Why do babies thrust themselves into the world so determinedly where they are not wanted? Why resist the most eager calls and welcomes where they are? This confusing question was no joke to Ronald. It made him hate this meddling baby, though he was not without a young father's sense of pride and satisfaction, too.

He had instructed Marg'ret fully beforehand in the part she might be called upon to play, though he could not tell her either how or when he would accomplish the purpose which had gradually grown upon him as a necessity. In these circumstances, while he yet pondered and turned every thing over in his mind, failing as yet to perceive any way in which it could be accomplished, the suddenness of Sir Robert's coming, which he learned by accident, was like sudden light in the most profound darkness. Here was the necessity made ready to his hands. Lily could not doubt, could not waver; whatever might happen afterward, it was quite clear Sir Robert could not be greeted on his first arrival by the voice of an infant—an infant which had no business to be there, and whose presence would have to be accounted for on the very threshold, without any preliminary explanation—in the face, too, of his friends whom he brought with him, revealing all the secrets of his house. This was a chance which made Ronald himself, with all his coolness, shiver. And Lily, still in her weakness, not half recovered—what might the effect be upon her? It might kill her, he decided; for her own sake, in her own defence, not a moment was to be lost. The reader knows how he flashed into his wife's room in haste, but not able even then, in face of Lily's perfect calm, and utter inability to conceive the real difficulty of the situation, to suggest it to her, accomplished his design, secretly leaving her—not even then with any unkind intention, very sorry for her, but not seeing any other way in which it was to be done—to discover her loss and bear it as she might. He was anything but happy as he drove away with the traitor woman by his side and the baby hidden in its voluminous wrappings. Marg'ret was not such a traitor either as she seemed. She had been made to believe that, though no parting was to be permitted to agitate the young mother, Lily, too, was aware, and had consented to this proceeding. "The poor little lassie, the poor wee thing!" Marg'ret had said, even while wrapping up the baby for its journey; and she had slipped out into the darkness and waited at the corner for the geeg with a heavy heart.

It startled Lumsden very much that no wail of distress, no indignant outcry, came from Lily on discovering her loss. These were not the days of frequent communications. People had not yet acquired the habit of constant correspondence. They were accustomed to wait for news, with no swift possibility of a telegram or even a penny post to make them impatient; not, perhaps, that they would have grudged—certainly not that Ronald would have grudged—the eightpence which was then, I think, the price of the conveyance of a letter from one end of Scotland to the other, but that they had not acquired the custom of frequent writing. When no protest, no remonstrance, no passionate outcry, reached him for a week or two after the event, Lumsden became exceedingly alarmed. He said to himself at first that it was a relief, that Lily herself recognized the necessity and had yielded to it; but he did not really believe this, and as the days went on, genuine anxiety and terror were in his mind. Had it killed her? Had his Lily, in her weakness, bowed her head and died of this outrage? the worst, he now felt in every fibre of his being, to which a woman could be subjected. He wrote, enclosing his letter to Beenie; then he wrote to Beenie herself, entreating her to send him a line, a word. But Lily was unconscious of everything, and Beenie of all that did not concern her mistress, when these letters arrived. They were not even opened until Lily was convalescent, and then Beenie by her mistress's orders, in her large sprawling handwriting, and with many tears, replied briefly to the three or four anxious demands for news which had arrived one after the other. Beenie wrote:

"SIR: My mistress has been at the point of death with what they call a brain-fever. It has lasted the longest and been the fiercest that ever the doctor saw. She is coming round now—the Lord be praised—but very slow. She has but one thought—you will know well what that is—and will never rest till she has got satisfaction, night or day.

"I am, sir,

"Your obedient servant,

"ROBINA RUTHERFORD.

"P. S.—I was to tell you the last part, for it is not from me."

There was not much satisfaction to be got from this letter, and, indeed, his mind got little relief from anything, and the time of Lily's illness was a time of mental trouble for the husband, which was not, perhaps, more easy to bear. Had he lost her altogether? It seemed like that, though he could not think it possible that the child at least should be allowed to drop, or that the fever could have made her forget, which it was evident she had not done in his own case. The courts had begun again, and Lumsden was more occupied than he had ever been in his life. He made one furtive visit to Kinloch-Rugas, where he heard something of Lily's state, and engaged Helen Blythe to communicate with him anything that reached her ears. But no one was allowed to see her in her illness, and this gave him small satisfaction. He did not dare to go near the house, which Sir Robert guarded more effectually than a squadron of soldiers. There was nothing for him to do but to wait. The unusual rush of occupation which came upon him with the beginning of the session had a certain irony in it, that irony which is so often apparent in life. Was he about to become a successful man now that the chief thing which made life valuable was slipping out of his grasp? He went about his business briskly, and rose to the claims of his business and profession, so that he began to be mentioned in the Parliament House and among his contemporaries, and even by elder men of still more importance, who said of him that young Lumsden, old Pontalloch's son, though he had hung fire at first, was now beginning at last to come to the front. Was it possible that this was coming to him, this exhilarating tide of success, just at the moment when Lily, who would have stood by him in evil fortune and never failed him, had dropped away from his side? To do him justice, he had never thought of success, of wealth, of prosperity, without her to share it. And he did not understand it now. He could not understand how even a woman, however ignorant or unreasonable by nature, could be so narrow as not to see that all he had done had been for the best. The last step, no doubt, might be allowed to be hard upon her, but what else was possible? Could she for a moment have entertained the idea of keeping the child—a baby that cried and made a noise, and could not be hid—at Dalrugas? Even if there had been no word of Sir Robert, it still would have been impossible; and he had done no more than he had a right to do. He had considered, and considered most carefully—he did himself but justice in this—what as her head and guardian it was best for him to do. It was his duty as well as his right; and the responsibility being upon him as the husband, and not upon her as the wife, he had done it. Was it possible that Lily—a creature full of intelligence on other matters, who even now and then picked up a thing quicker than he did himself—should not have sense enough and judgment enough to see this? But these thoughts, though they mingled with all he did, and accompanied him night and day, did not make things any better. The fact that she had taken no notice of him all this time, that she had not written to him even to upbraid him, that she had not even asked him for news of the child, was very heavy on Lumsden's mind—almost, I had said, upon his heart, for he still had a heart, notwithstanding all that had come and gone. Perhaps it might have relieved him a little had he known that news had been obtained of the child, though not through him. Marg'ret—who, though she had been unfaithful to the young mother, to whom at the same time she had been so kind, certainly had a heart, which smote her much as being a party to a proceeding which became more and more doubtful the more she thought of it—had written twice to Beenie, altogether superior to the question of the eightpence to pay, to assure her of the baby's health. He was well, he was thriving, his mother would not know him he had grown so big and strong, and Marg'ret hoped that ere long she would put him, just a perfect beauty, into his mother's arms. These queer missives, sealed with a wafer and a thimble, had been better than all the eloquent letters in the world to Lily. When those from Ronald, full of excellent reason and all the philosophy that could be brought to bear on the circumstances, were given to her on her recovery, they had but made her wound more bitter and her resentment more warm; but the nurse's letters had given her strength. They had made her able to charm and please her uncle; they had enabled her to face life again and fight her way back to a certain degree of health; they had sustained her in her journey, and this first set out upon the world to manage her own affairs, which was as novel to her as if she had been fifteen, instead of twenty-five. They wanted only one thing—they had no address. The postmark was Edinburgh, but Edinburgh was (to these inexperienced women) a very wide word.

What Lily had intended to do when she had found out Marg'ret and recovered her child—as she was so confident of doing—I cannot tell. She did not herself know. This was the first step to be taken: every thing else came a world behind. Whether she was to carry the baby back in her arms, to beard Sir Robert with it and make her explanation—though with the conviction that she would then be turned from the door of her only home forever—or whether she intended, having escaped, to do what always seems so easy and natural to a girl's imagination: to fly away somewhere and hide herself with her child, and be fed by the ravens, like the prophet—she herself did not know and I cannot tell. The only thing certain was that she thought of the little house among the Edinburgh roofs—that house which could only be got at the term, and which it now made her heart sick to think of—no more. Had she found the door open for her and every thing ready Lily would have turned her back on that open door. She could not endure the thought of it; she could not even think of the time when it would have been paradise to her, the realization of her dearest hopes. In the depths of her injured soul she would have desired to find her child without even making her presence known to her husband. She had no desire even to see him again—he seemed to have alienated her too completely for any repentance. And up to this moment, her mind being altogether occupied by her child, none of those relentings toward those whom we have loved and who have wronged us, which make the heart bleed, had come upon Lily. She thought of nothing but her child, her child! to have him again in her arms, to possess him again, the one thing in the world that was entirely her own, altogether her own. The fact that this was not so, that the child was not and never could be entirely her own, did not disturb Lily's mind. Had she been reminded of it she would not have believed. She thought, as every young mother thinks in the wonderful closeness of that new relation and the sense of all it has cost her, that to this at least there could be no contradiction and no doubt—that her baby was hers, hers! and that no one in the world had the right to him that she had. It was for him that she hurried, as much as any one could hurry in these days, to Edinburgh, grudging every moment of delay—the time of changing the horses, which she felt inclined to get out and do herself, so slow, so slow was every-body concerned; the time for refreshments, as if one wanted to eat and drink when one was hastening to recover one's child. But however slow a journey is the end of it comes at last. It was a comfort to Lily that she knew where to go to—to the house of a very decent woman, known to Beenie, who kept lodgings, and where she could be quite quiet, out of the way of her former friends. But they arrived only in the evening, and there was another long night to be gone through before anything could be done.

CHAPTER XL

Robina had become more and more anxious and uneasy as they approached Edinburgh. She did not seem to share the anxious elation with which her mistress hailed the well-known features of the country, and recognized the Castle on its rock, and the high line of houses against the sky. Lily was in a state of feverish excitement, but it was mingled with so many hopes and anticipations that even her anxiety was a kind of happiness. "To-morrow! to-morrow!" she said to herself. Beenie listened with much solemnity to this happy tone of certainty. She would have liked to moralize, and bid her mistress modify her too great confidence. As the moment approached when it should be justified Beenie's mind became more and more perturbed. It was she who had been instrumental in bringing Marg'ret from Edinburgh, pretending, indeed, that the woman was her cousin, and she had till now taken it for granted, as Lily had done, without any doubt in her mind, that where Marg'ret had been found once she would be found again. But as the hour came nearer Beenie's confidence in this became much shaken. If he wanted to hide the child from his mother—a course which Beenie acknowledged to herself would be the wisest one, for how could the baby and Sir Robert ever live under the same roof?—would he have allowed the nurse to settle there, where her address was known and she could be found in a moment? Beenie's intellect was not quick, but she did not think this was probable. She was not accustomed to secrecy or to the tricks of concealment: they had not even occurred to her till now; but when she realized that she was to be her mistress's guide on the next morning to the house where Lily had persuaded herself she was certain to find her child, her heart sank to her boots, and there was no more strength left in her. "And what if we dinna find her there? and wherefore should we find her there?" Beenie asked herself. It stood to reason, as she saw now, that Lumsden would never have permitted her to remain. Why had she not thought of it before? Why had she come on such a fool's errand, to plunge her mistress only into deeper and deeper disappointment? Beenie did not sleep all night, though Lily slept, in her great fatigue, like a child. Beenie was terrified of the morning, and of the visit which she now felt sure would be in vain. Oh, why had she not seen it before? He must have known that the mother would not give up her child without an attempt to recover him ("Though what we are to do with him, poor wee man, when we get him!" Beenie said to herself), and he would never have left the baby where it could be found at once, and all his precautions made an end of. Beenie saw now, enlightened by terror, that this plan must have been in Lumsden's head all the time, though Sir Robert's sudden arrival gave the opportunity for carrying it out. She saw now that after all that had been done to keep the secret he was not likely to allow it to be thrown to the winds by the presence of the child at Dalrugas if he could help it. She divined this under the influence of her own alarm and anxiety. And would he let the woman bide there in a kent place where Lily could lay her hands upon the child whenever she pleased, night or day? Oh, no, no, no! he would never do that, was the refrain that ran through Beenie's mind all the night. She had thought how delightful it would be to hear the clocks striking and the bells ringing after the deep, deep silence of the moor. But this satisfaction was denied her, for all the bells and the clocks seemed to upbraid her for her foolishness. "Sae likely! Sae likely!" one of them seemed to say in every chime. "Cheating himself! Cheating himself!" said another. And was there not yet one, heavier than the rest—St. Giles himself for anything she could tell—which seemed to echo out: "You fool, Beenie! You fool, Beenie!" over all the listening town?

"Oh, my bonnie leddy!" said Beenie, when Lily, all flushed and eager with anticipation, took her place in the old-fashioned hackney coach that was to take them to Marg'ret's abode. This was in a narrow street, or rather close, leading off the Canongate—one of those places hidden behind the great houses which lead to tranquil little spots of retirement, and openings into the fresh air and green braes, which no stranger could believe possible. "Oh, my bonnie leddy, dinna, dinna be so terrible sure! I've been thinking a' the way—what if she should have flitted? There was nae address to her letter. She may have flitted to another house. She may be away at other work."

"What! and leave my baby!" cried Lily, "when she said in her letter he was all her occupation, as well as all her pleasure! I almost forgave her what she's done to me for saying that."

"And so she did," said Beenie doubtfully. "Oh, I'm no saying a word against Marg'ret—she would be faithfu' to her trust. But she might flit to another house for a' that. In Edinburgh the folk are aye flittin'. I canna tell what possesses them. Me—I would bide where I was well off; I would never think of making a change just for change's sake. But that is what they're aye doing here."

"Have you heard anything, Beenie?" cried Lily, turning pale. She had been so sure that the cup of joy was within reach, that the thirsting of her heart would be at once satisfied, that she felt as if a disappointment would be more than she could bear.

"Oh, mem," cried Beenie, producing a bottle of salts from her capacious pocket, "dinna let down your heart! I have heard naething. I was just speaking of a common fact that every-body kens. And if she had flitted, they would maybe ken where she had gone. Oh, ay, they would certainly ken where she has gone—a woman and a bairn canna disappear leaving no sign. It's not like a single person, that might just be off and away, and nobody the wiser, mem! I am maybe just speaking nonsense, and we'll see her at her door in a moment, with our bonnie boy in her airms."

Beenie, however, had succeeded better than she had hoped. She had conveyed to her mistress that sickening of the heart which, from the most ancient days of humanity, has been the consequence of hope deferred. The light went out of Lily's eyes. She leaned back in her corner, closing them upon a world which had suddenly grown black and void. She did not lose consciousness, being far too strongly bound to life by hope and despair and pain to let the thread drop even for a moment; but Beenie thought she had fainted, and, heartstruck with what seemed to her her own work, produced out of the reticule she carried a whole magazine of remedies—precious eau-de-Cologne, which was no common thing in those days, and vinegar with a sharp, aromatic scent, more used then than now, and even as the last resort a small bottle of whiskey, which she tried hard, though with a hand that trembled, to administer in a teaspoon. Lily had strength enough to push her away, and, in self-defence, opened her eyes again, seeing grayly once more the firmament, and the high houses on either side, and the dull day from which all light seemed to have gone. It was she, however, who sprang out of the coach when it stopped at the entrance to the close. Every-body knows what the Canongate of Edinburgh is—one of the most noble streets, yet without question the most squalid and spoiled of any street in Europe, with beautiful stately old houses standing sadly among the hideous growths of yesterday, and evil smells and evil noises enough to sicken every visitor and to shame every man who has anything to do with such a careless and wicked sacrifice of the city's pride and ornament.[A] But even in the midst of this disgraceful debasement there remain beyond the screen of the great old houses glimpses of the outlets which the old citizens provided for themselves—old court-yards, even old gardens, old houses secure within their little enclosures where the air is still pure and the sky is still visible. Lily's heart rose a little as she came out of the narrow entrance of the close into one of these unexpected openings. If he were here, he would be well. She could see the green beyond and the high slopes of Salisbury Crags. There was something in the vision of greenness, in the noble heights flung up against the sky, which restored her confidence.

But it was perhaps well that Beenie had spoken even so little adroitly on the way, for, indeed, Marg'ret was not found at her old address. She had never gone back there, they were told, since the time when she was called away in the summer to attend a lady in the North. She had not, indeed, been expected back. She had given up her rooms on going away, and removed her little furniture, and the rooms had been relet at once to a member of the same profession, who hoped to be sometimes mistaken for Marg'ret, a person of high reputation in her own line. The landlady knew nothing of the baby she had now to take care of nor where she was. The furniture? Oh, yes, she could find out where the furniture had been taken, but Marg'ret herself, she felt sure, had never come back. She was maybe with the lady still—the lady in the North. She was so much thought upon that whiles they would keep her, if the baby were delicate, for months and months. She had a wonderful way with babies, the woman said. (At this Lily, who had been leaning heavily on her attendant's arm, with her pale face hidden under her veil, and all her courage gone, began to gather a little spirit and looked up again.) Oh, just a wonderful way! They just throve wi' her like flowers in May. What she did different from ither folk there was not one could tell: if it was the way she handled them, or the way she fed them, or the pittin' on o' their claithes, with fykes and fancies that a puir buddy with the man's meat to get and the house to keep clean had no time for. But the fack was just this, that there was nobody like Marg'ret Bland for little bairns. They were just a different thing a'thegither when they were in her hands.

As this little harangue went on Lily's feeble figure hanging on Beenie's arm straightened itself by degrees. She put up her veil and beamed upon the homely woman, who showed evident signs that she had little time, as she said, to keep herself tidy for one thing. Lily was not discouraged by so small a matter. She said, holding out her hand: "Then you would leave a baby in her hands and have no fear?"

"Eh, my bonnie leddy," cried the woman, with a half shriek, wiping her hands upon her apron before she ventured to touch the lady's glove, "I would trust Marg'ret Bland maist to bring them back from the deid."

"We must find her, that is all," said Lily, as they turned away, Beenie trembling and miserable, with subdued sniffs coming from under her deep bonnet. Her mistress, in the petulance which neither anxiety nor trouble could quench, gave her "a shake" with her arm, which still leaned upon hers, though Lily for the moment was the more vigorous of the two. "We must find her, that is all! She must be clever indeed if she can hide herself in Edinburgh and you and me not find her, Beenie! We must search every street till we find her!" Lily cried. The color had come back to her cheeks and the light to her eyes. That blessed assurance that, wherever Marg'ret might be, the baby was safe, doubly safe in her skilled and experienced hands, was to the young mother like wine. The horror of the disappointment seemed to be disguised, almost to pass away, in that unpremeditated testimony. If it was for to-morrow rather than for to-day so long as he was so safe, so well, so assured against all harm, as that! "We have only to find her," Lily said, dragging Beenie back to the hackney coach, in which they immediately drove to the place where Marg'ret, now to be spoken of as Mistress Bland, had been supposed to place her furniture. But this was no more than a warehouse, where the person in charge allowed disdainfully that twa-three auld sticks o' furniture in that name were in his charge, but knew nothing more of the wumman than just that they were hers, and that that was her name. Lily, however, was not discouraged. She drove about all day in her hackney coach, catching at every clue. She went to the hospitals, where Mrs. Bland was known but supposed to be still with the lady in the North who had secured her services in the summer.

"If you know where she's to be heard of," one of the matrons said, "I will be too thankful, for there is another place waiting for her or somebody like her."

"And is she such a good nurse as that?" cried Lily, glowing with eagerness all in a moment, though her face had relapsed into pallor and anxiety.

"She is one of the best nurses we have; and especially happy with delicate children," the matron answered with some astonishment. And she tapped Beenie on the shoulder and said an indignant word in her ear. "Woman!" she said, "are you mad to let your mistress wander about like this, when it's well to be seen she's just out of her bed, and in my opinion not long past her time?"

"My mistress," said Beenie, with a gasp, "is just a young lady—in from the country."

"Just you get her back as fast as you can," said the experienced woman, "or you'll have her worse than ever on your hands again."

But this was what Beenie could not do. She had to follow Lily's impetuous lead on many a wild-goose-chase and hopeless expedition here and there from one place to another during the rest of the day; and when they returned to their lodgings, worn out and cast down, in the evening, it was still the mistress who had the most strength and spirit left. "There is only one thing to do now," she said, while Beenie placed her on the hard sofa beside the fire, and endeavored to induce her to rest. Her face was very pale and her eyes very bright, with a faint redness round the eyelids accentuating the absence of color. "There is one thing to do. Mr. Lumsden"—she paused a little after the name, as if it made her other words more difficult or exhausted her breath—"will have come back now to his lodging. You know where that is as well as I do. You will go and tell him that he is to come to me here."

"Mem!" cried Beenie in great perturbation.

"Did you think," said Lily, very clear, in a high, scornful tone, "that I would come to Edinburgh and not see my husband? Is it not my duty to see my husband? You will go to him at once!"

"It is no that," cried Beenie; "I thought you would see him first of all. He's your man, oh! my dear, dear lassie—you're married upon him never to be parted till death comes atween you. I would have had you see him first of a', and weel ye ken that; but now when you're wearied out body and mind, and nae satisfaction in your heart, and every thing that is atween ye worse and worse by reason of muckle pondering and dwelling on it—oh, mem, my dear, no to-night, no to-night! You have a sharp tongue, though you never mean it, and he is a gentleman that is not used to be crossed and has aye had his ain way. Oh, mem, he's a masterful man, though he's never been but sweet as sugar to you. Try to take a sleep and rest, and wait for the morn. The morn is aye a new day."

"I am glad," said Lily, with shining eyes, "that you think I have a sharp tongue, Beenie; and you may be sure, if ever I meant it in my life, I will mean it now. But I will not discuss Mr. Lumsden with you or any one. You will just go to him—"

"Mem, let me speak once, if I'm never to say a word again!" cried Beenie. "That your heart should be sore to see the dear bairn, to take him back into your airms, oh, that I can weel understand. So is mine, though I'm far, far from being what you are to him, and no to be named in the same breath. But, mem, oh, my dear leddy, my bonnie Miss Lily! if I may just say that once again, what will ye do with him when you have him? Oh, let me speak—just this once. You canna, canna take him to that auld gentleman at hame; you canna do it. He has maybe not been much to you in the years that are past, but he's awfu' fond of you now. He looks to you to make him a home, to be the comfort of his old age. Oh! I'm no saying he deserves it at your hands. But what do the best of us deserve? We just get what we dinna deserve from God the first, and sometimes from a tender he'rt here below. And he is an auld man and frail; he has maybe no long to live. Will you tell him a' that long story, how we've deceived him and the whole world, and about your marriage, and about the birth, and a' in his house, that he meant for such different things?"

"Beenie," said Lily, "stop, or you will kill me. If I have deceived him so long, it was with no will of mine. Oh, God knows, if none of you know, with no will of mine, nor yet intention! Is that not the more reason that I should deceive him no longer? He may turn me away. What will that matter? We will be poor creatures the two of us, you and me, if we cannot help ourselves and the darling bairn."

"But it will maitter to him," said Beenie steadily, "the poor auld gentleman in that lonely house. He's been a kind of a father to you, if no so tender a father as might have been. I'm no saying you should have deceived him, but that's done, and it canna be undone. If you tell him now, it will maybe kill him at the hinder end, and whether that will be better you must just think for yoursel', for I have said all that I'm caring to say."

Lily had covered her face with her hands, and there was a moment of silence, unbroken save by a sob from Beenie, who naturally, having spoken forth her soul, was now crying as if her heart would break.

"Beenie," said Lily, all at once looking up, "you will go to Mr. Lumsden, who will be now at his lodgings dressing, I would not wonder, to go out to dinner—that is what is most likely—and tell him I am here. I would not wish to make him lose his engagement if he has one; you can say that."

"Oh, mem!" murmured Beenie under her breath.

"But when it suits with his convenience, I would like to see him, to ask him a question or two. Go now, go," she said impatiently, "or you will be too late."

Weeping, Beenie went forth to do her mistress's behest. Weeping, she put on her big bonnet, with a veil over it, of a kind of Spanish lace with huge flowers, which was the fashion of the day, and which allowed here and there a patch of her tearful countenance to appear, blocking out the rest. She found some difficulty in gaining admittance to Ronald, who was, his landlady informed her, "dressing to go out to his dinner," as Lily had foretold, and it was in the full glory of evening dress that he came forth upon her after she had fought her way to his sitting-room, and had waited some time for his appearance. He was very much startled by the sight of her, and came up taking her hand, demanding: "Lily—how is my Lily?" with an energy and anxiety which partly quenched Beenie's unreasonable exasperation at the sight of his dress.

"She is here, sir, and wishful to see you," said Beenie, "when it's convenient to you."

"Lily here—where? What do you mean? Convenient! Do you mean she is at the door?"

"It is not likely, sir," cried Beenie with indignant disgust.

"What do you mean, woman? Lily who, you wrote to me, was just recovered from a nearly fatal illness!"

"And that's true. Her blood would have been on the head of them that brought it on her if it had not been for the mercy of God."

"Where is she?" cried Lumsden, seizing his hat.

"She said," said Beenie with much intensity: "'He will most likely be going out to his dinner. I will not have him break his engagement for me!'"

"I think," he cried, "that you mean to drive me mad! Where is she? Does any one know she is here?"

"It is known she is here," said Beenie sententiously, "to get change of air, as is thought, after her long, long illness; but, in fack, to look for her dear little bairn, which is the object in her ain mind, my poor bonnie leddy. And, oh, sir! if ye ken where the baby is, as ye must ken, having taken the responsibility upon your hands, for we canna find him, we canna find him! and it will just break her heart and she will die!"

"Here—and looking for the child without consulting me!" he said, with an exclamation of anger and astonishment. He flung on a coat rapidly, and, almost thrusting Beenie out of the room before him, hurried her away. A few more questions put to her as they hastened along the streets showed him exactly the state of the case. It was no running away. Lily had not come to him to throw herself upon his mercy, to be owned and established and have her child restored to her in the legitimate way. Had it been so it would have been very difficult to reject her, to silence her prayer and send her back, without losing hold upon her altogether. Had he lost hold upon her altogether without that? He was very much alarmed, but yet he felt that the situation was less impossible than if she had come to demand her place at his side and public acknowledgment. She did not want him—she wanted her baby; and what without him could she do with her baby? how produce it, how account for it? Ronald began to feel more at his ease, to feel himself again master of the situation as he hurried Beenie, who was very tired and wretched, and scarcely able to keep up with him, to Lily's refuge. Let no one suppose for a moment that he meant to disown her, that any dishonor was in his thoughts. In the last resort, if nothing else was to be done, Ronald had no intention but to stand faithfully by his wife. He had not, indeed, any power of doing otherwise; for were there not Mr. Blythe and the two witnesses and the marriage lines against him? But, as a matter of fact, he never thought of that, although he breathed more freely when he knew no such claim was intended, and felt once again that the helm was in his own hands.

But in the meantime how to meet Lily was occupation enough for his thoughts. He walked along the darkling streets, with the wind in his face and a whirlwind of thought in his mind. How was he to meet her—what was he to say to her? It was an interview on which might depend the whole after-course of his life.

CHAPTER XLI

It was a very little, homely lodging in which Lily was, the little parlor of an old-fashioned poor little house, intended at its best to receive an Edinburgh lawyer's clerk, or perhaps a poor minister or teacher, on his promotion. Ronald had never seen his wife in such surroundings. He gave a cry of surprise and dismay as he pushed open the door. How often had she said that she would share any poverty with him, and yet it hurt him to see her here, out of her natural sphere, like a princess banished into a sordid world of privation and ugliness. At the sound of his voice Lily sprang up from the slippery black hair-cloth sofa on which she had been reposing. He thought at first it was to meet him as of old with open arms and heart to heart, but of this she showed no sign, nor even when he rushed forward to take her into his arms did she make any movement. She had seated herself on the sofa again, drawing back in an attitude of repulsion which could not be mistaken. "Lily!" he cried, "Lily! Is this the way you receive me? Have you nothing to say to me?"

"Oh, yes, I have a great deal to say to you. Give Mr. Lumsden a chair, Beenie. It is as I thought; you were going out to dinner," said Lily, with a gleam of exasperation at the sight of his evening dress, which was of course wholly unreasonable. "Why should you have broken your engagement for me?"

"You know well I would break any engagement for you," he said. "You must know all that I have suffered during the past two months, unable to see you, even to hear of you, and not a word, not a word from yourself all that time."

"What hindered you coming to see me?" she asked. "What prevented you? If I had died, as seemed likely, it could have done you no harm in the world, for with me every hope of Uncle Robert's money, which is what has been my destruction, would have fallen to the ground."

"Lily, you never will understand! I did go to Kinloch-Rugas. I was once under your windows, but got no satisfaction. A man has to be silent and endure where a woman cries out. I did what I could to—"

"That is enough," said Lily, waving her hand. "Between you and me there need be no more talking. I sent for you for one thing, to ask you one question—where is my baby? You took him out of my arms; bring him back again to me, and then there may be ground to speak."

"He is my baby as well as yours, Lily. I have the responsibility of the family. I did what I felt to be best both for him and you."

"What was best?" she cried. "Are you a god to judge what is best? But I will not argue with you. Give me my baby back! His mother's arms—that is his natural place! Give me back my child, and then, perhaps, I may hear you speak."

He had thought this matter over as he came along with the rapidity of highly stimulated thought, and a sudden great necessity for decision; he had thought of it often before, looking at the subject from every point of view. To give her back the baby was to ruin every thing for which he had fought. He had not deprived himself of the company of a wife he loved, he said to himself, for a small motive; not for nothing had he encountered all the difficulties of the position in the past, and all her reproaches, tacit and expressed. Her very look at him had often been very hard to bear, and yet he paused now before making his last stroke. Once more, like lightning, the question passed through his mind, what other way was there? Was there any other way in which her mind could be satisfied and her foolish search made an end of? Could he in any other way secure her return to her home, and the carrying out to the end of his scheme? But on the other hand would she ever forgive him for what he must now do? He had not more than a moment to carry on that controversy, to make his final decision. And she was looking at him all the time: Lily's eyes, which so often had smiled upon him, so often followed him with tenderness and met him with the sudden flash of love and delight, were fixed upon him steadily now, shaded by curved brows, regarding him sternly without indulgence, without wavering or softening. He was no longer to Lily covered with the glamour of love. She saw him as he was, nay, worse than he was, with a look that took no account of his real feeling toward herself, or of what was in fact a perverted desire to do the best, as he saw it, for her as well as for himself. Would these eyes ever soften, whatever he might do or say? Would she ever forgive him even now?

"Lily," he said with an effort, overcoming the dryness of his throat, trying still to gain a little time. "I am your husband, I am your natural head and guide; it is my part to judge what is wisest, what is the best thing for you. I am older than you, I am more experienced in the world. I know what can be done, and what cannot be done. Whatever you may wish and whatever you may say, it is for me to judge what is the best."

It is not often that a woman hears an uncompromising statement of this kind with patience, and Lily was little likely to have done so in her natural condition of mind, but at present she had no thought but one. "I have told you," she cried, "that you can speak after, and that I will hear. But in the meantime bring me back my little baby. I ask nothing but that, I've no mind for reasoning now. Give me back my baby, my little bairn; that's all I am asking. My baby, my baby! Ronald, if ever in your life you had a kind thought of me, a thought that was not all interest and money, and for the love of God, if ever you knew that, give me back my baby! and then," she cried with a gasp—"then we can talk!"

His mind was made up now; there was nothing else for it. His face assumed an air of the deepest gravity; that was not difficult, for, indeed, his situation was grave enough. He put out his hand and laid it upon hers for a moment. "Lily," he said, "I've been endeavoring to put off this blow. It was perhaps foolish, but I thought you would feel it less were you kept in ignorance than if all your hopes were cut off. Fain, fain would I bring back your baby and lay him in your arms again! You think I am a harsh man with no softness for a mother and a child, but you are mistaken, Lily. All that I am worth in this world I would give to bring him back. But there is but one hand that could do that."

She raised herself up with a start, flinging off his hand, which again had touched hers. "What do you mean? What do you mean?" she cried, with wild staring eyes, eyes that seemed to be bursting from her head. She had been leaning back on the hard sofa in her weakness. Now she sat upright, her hands raised before her as if to push off some dreadful fate.

"You know what I mean, Lily," he said, looking at her with a determined steadiness of gaze. "What is the life of an infant like that? It is like a new-lighted candle that every breath can blow out. Oh! blame me, blame me; I will not say a word. Tell me it was the night journey, the plunge into the cold, after the warm bosom of his mother. I thought it was the only thing I could do, but I will not say a word if you tell me I was to blame. Anyhow, whosever blame it was, the baby, poor little thing—"

"You mean he is dead!" said Lily, with a great cry.

He thought she had fainted: they all were in the way of thinking she had fainted when all her life went from her, except pain, which is the strongest life of all. Every thing was black before Lily's eyes; her heart leaped with a wild movement and then seemed to die and become still in her breast; her lips dropped apart, as if the last breath had passed there with that cry. Ronald thought she had fainted for the first moment, and then he thought she had died. He sprang up with anguish in his heart; he had done it, braving all the risks, knowing her weakness, yet Beenie, rushing in at the sound of Lily's cry, with all her battery of remedies, forgave him whatever he might have done at the sight of his face. "I have killed her! I have killed her!" he cried; "it is my fault!"

"Oh, sir, you should mind how weak she is!" cried Beenie, bringing forth her essences, her salts, her aromatic vinegar. Their words came faintly to Lily's brain. She struggled up again from the sofa, on which she had fallen back, beating the air with her hands, as if to find and clutch at something that would give her strength. "My baby is dead!" she cried, stumbling over the words. "My baby, my baby is dead, my baby is dead!" It seemed as if the wail had become mechanical in the completeness of her downfall and misery, body and soul.

"Oh, sir!" cried Beenie again. She looked at him once more with another light in her eyes. She was but a simple woman, but to such there comes at times a kind of divination. But Ronald's look was fixed upon Lily, his eyes were touched with moisture, the deepest pain was in his face. Could it be that a man could look like that and yet lie?

"Say nothing to her!" she cried almost with authority; "let her get her breath. But tell you me, sir, when was it that this came about? I heard you tell her to blame you if she pleased. What for were you to blame? Tell me that I may explain after. Mr. Lumsden, she has a right to ken. When did it happen and what was the cause? For all so little as a bairn is, it's no without a cause when the darlings die."

"You take too much upon you, Beenie," he said. "You have no right to demand explanations. And yet, why should not I give them?" he said, with a tone of resignation. "I fear the poor little thing never got the better of that night journey. What could I do? I could not stay there to face Sir Robert on his first arrival. I could not leave Lily to bear the brunt. I had but little time to think, but what was there else to do? I felt even that to snatch him away at a stroke would be better for her than a lingering parting with him, and the anticipation of it. There was every cause. Beenie, you're a reasonable woman."

"I will not say, sir," said Beenie, "that it was without reason; me and Katrin have said as much as that between ourselves, seeing a' that had gone before."

"Seeing all that had gone before," Ronald repeated with readiness. "But Providence," he added, "turns all our wisest plans sometimes to nought. I know nothing about children—"

"But Marg'ret kent weel about children!"

"Yes, she was perhaps the more to blame, if any one is to blame. Anyhow, the poor little thing—I can't explain it, you should see her, she would tell you—caught cold or something. How could I send you word when she was so ill? I would have kept it from her now, at least till she was stronger and better able to bear it."

"It would, maybe, have been better," Beenie said, with a brevity that surprised Ronald and made him slightly uneasy. The woman did not break forth into lamentations, as he had expected, but that might be for Lily's sake, who, lying back again upon the white pillow which Beenie had placed behind her head, with the effect of making her almost transparent countenance, with its faint but deepened lines, look more fragile than ever, was coming gradually to herself. Tears were slowly welling forth under her closed eyelids, but she was very still. Whether she was listening, or whether she was absorbed in her own sorrow and careless of what was going on, he could not tell. Anyhow, it was a relief to him that she was silent, and that the woman who was her closest attendant and confidant was so easily satisfied. He began to question her anxiously as to where Lily should go for her convalescence now that her object in coming there was so sadly ended. Portobello, Bridge of Allan, wherever it was, he would go at once and look for rooms. He would come when she was settled and spend as much time as possible with her. He took the whole matter at once into his own hands. And it was with a sensation of relief that he concluded after all this was said that he could now go away. "You will do well to get her to bed and give her a sleeping-draught if you have one," he said, bending over Lily with a most anxious and tender countenance as she lay, still with her eyes closed, against the pillow. It was not how he had expected her to take this dreadful news which he had brought: he had expected a passion of grief, almost raving; he had expected violent weeping, a storm of lamentation. He had, on the contrary, got through very easily; the tears even had ceased to hang upon Lily's closed eyelids. He bent down over her and kissed her tenderly on the forehead. She shrank from the touch, indeed, but yet he felt that he must expect so much as that.

"There is but one thing, sir," said Beenie: "the woman Marg'ret, that does not seem to me to be such a grand nurse as we heard she was—you say we should see her and she would tell us a'. And that is just what I'm wanting, to see her, if you could tell me where to find her."

"I tell you! How should I know?" he said. "She will be in the same place where we found her before, I suppose."

"No, sir, she is not there."

"Then she will have gone off to nurse somebody else. That's her way of living, isn't it? No, I can tell you nothing about her. You may suppose the sight of her was not very pleasant to me after— But she is a well-known person. You will find no difficulty in finding her out."

"If that's your real opinion, Mr. Lumsden—"

"Of course it is my opinion. I will take a run to the Bridge of Allan to-morrow, and in the evening I will bring you word."

With this, and with careful steps, not to disturb Lily, but yet with an uneasy soul and no certainty that he had succeeded in his bold stroke, Lumsden went away, Beenie respectfully accompanying him to the door. But when it was closed upon him, Beenie, though no light-footed girl, flew up the stairs, and rushing into the room with her hands outstretched, was met by Lily, who fell upon her maid's shoulder, both of them saying together: "It is not true! it's no true!"

"The Lord forgive him!" said Beenie. "And, oh, I hope you'll be able to do it, but no me! I'm not a good woman, I'm just a wild Highlander, and I could have put a pistol to his head as he stood there!"

"I can forgive him easier," said Lily, with the tears now coming freely, "than if it had been true. Oh, Beenie! if it had been true!"

"Whisht, whisht, my darling leddy! but no, my dear, just greet your fill. Eh, mem, how little a man kens! They're so grand with their wisdom, and never to think that a woman would send a scart of a pen whatever to let us ken the dear lamb was well. I've often heard the ministers say that the deevil's no half as clever as he seems, and now I believe it this day. But you'll just go to your bed and I'll give you the draught, as he said, for this has been an awfu' day."

"Yes, I'll go, to be strong for to-morrow," said Lily, and then she turned back and caught Beenie again, throwing her arms round her. "But first," she cried, "we'll give God thanks on our bended knees that my baby is safe. Oh, if it had been true!"

They both felt the baby's life to be more certain and more assured because his father had sworn he was dead, and they knew that was not true.

Next morning they were both up betimes and had changed their lodging early, going not to Portobello nor to the Bridge of Allan, but to a village on the seaside, very obscure and little thought of, where, late as the season was, they could still spend a week or two without being remarked; and when she had settled her mistress there, Beenie went back to Edinburgh to search again and again through every corner that could be thought of, where Marg'ret might be heard of, but in vain.

They went again next day, and every day, together, and I think traversed Edinburgh almost street by street on a quest so hopeless that both had given it up in their heart before either breathed a word of her despair. Then they did what seemed even to Lily (and still more to Beenie) a most terrible and unparalleled thing to do, and to which she had great difficulty in bringing her mind. This was to apply to the police on the subject, what we should call putting it into the hands of the detectives. Perhaps even now there are innocent persons to whom the idea of "sending the police after" an innocent wanderer still seems a dreadful thing to do. And these were days in which the idea of the detective was little developed and still less understood. They are not always still the most successful of functionaries, but they have at least become heroes of the popular imagination, and a certain class of fiction is full of the wonderful deeds they have succeeded in doing, when all things were arranged to their hand. I do not know that there was a single individual of the order at that time in Edinburgh under the present title and conditions, but the thing must have existed more or less always; and when, with many hesitations and much trouble of mind, Lily made her appeal to the ingenuity of the police service to find the missing woman, it was with a little flutter of hope that she saw Margaret Bland's name and description taken down. Beenie would not even be present when this was done. She lifted up her testimony, declaring that nothing would induce her to send the police after a decent honest woman that had never done any body any harm. "Oh, mem, you may say what you like," Beenie cried. "She has had no ill intention. Send the pollisman after Anither if you will. It wasna her contrivancy, it wasna her contrivancy! I would sooner die myself than harry a woman to her ruin and take away her good name!" This had been the peroration with which Beenie had broken away, slamming the door in the face of the official who came to take Miss Ramsay's orders. Lily was very unhappy and deeply depressed. She had no one to stand by her. "It is for no harm. You will understand she is to come to no harm. Her address only—that is all I want," she cried. "We'll put it," said the man, writing down his notes in his little book, "that it will be something to her advantage. That or a creeminal chairge is the only way of dealing with yon kind of folk."

"Yes, yes—let it be something to her advantage," Lily cried. "And it will," she said, "it will! it will be more to her advantage than anything she has ever known. You will take care that she is not frightened, not harmed in any way, not in any way!"

"How should it harm an innocent person, if this person is an innocent person?" the functionary said, and left Lily trembling for what she had done, and unable to bear the eye of Beenie, who would scarcely for a whole day after forgive her mistress. They themselves lived in terror of being found, perhaps, in their turn, hunted down by the pollis, Beenie cried—"for if you can do it for her, mem, what for no him that has nae scruples for you?" Lily in her heart trembled too at this thought. It seemed to her that if such means were set in action against herself she would die of misery and shame.

Ten days later she returned to Dalrugas, a little stronger, for her youth and vigor, and the distraction of her thoughts, even though so painfully, from all preoccupation with herself, had given her elastic vitality its chance of recovery: but a changed and saddened woman, never again to be the Lily of the past. Her husband had not sought her, at least had not found her, nor had she wished him to do so; but yet that he should not have penetrated so very easy a mystery seemed to prove to her that he had not wished to do so, and, despite of all that had come and gone, that was a very different matter. Lily's heart was as heavy as a woman's heart could be as she went home. The whole secret of her existence, the mystery in which she had been wrapped, which she had felt to be so guilty a secret, and a mystery so oppressive, seemed now to be about to melt away, leaving her for her life long a false and empty husk of being, an appearance and no reality. All this tremendous wave of existence seemed to have passed over her head and to be gone, leaving her, as she was, Lily Ramsay, her uncle's companion, the daughter of the desolate house, and no more, neither wife nor mother, nothing but a false pretence, a pitiful ghost, the fictitious image of something that she was not, and never again could be.

CHAPTER XLII

It was not without much thought that Lumsden decided to leave his wife unmolested when she fled from him. It did not cost him much trouble to discover where she had gone, and he watched her proceedings and those of Beenie carefully, and had little difficulty in discovering what their object was. But he had foreseen all that and taken his precautions, and he had no doubt as to the result. With Lily's absolute inexperience, and the few facilities which existed at that period, a very simple amount of care would have been enough to baffle her. But he had taken a great deal of care. Margaret Bland and her charge were out of the reach of any researches made in Scotland, and his mind was quite easy as to the chances of further investigation, for Scotland was very much more separated from the rest of the world in those days than it is now. I do not say that it did not cost him a pang to know that Lily herself was within reach and to refrain from seeing her, from saying a word further to excuse or explain, and from making at least an endeavor to recover her confidence. But he had gone too far now for excuses and expedients, and he felt that it was wiser to refrain from every thing of the kind until the moment came when, in the course of nature, he would be liberated from all restrictions and be able to go to her and claim her freely, without fear of interference. If he could do so, bringing a great joy and surprise in his hand, he felt that he was more likely to be received and forgiven than if he were able only to establish a reconciliation upon the old basis of concealment and clandestine meetings, which now, indeed, would be impossible. He thought that absence would draw her heart toward him, and that in the silence she would make his excuses to herself better than he could do; and what would not a man merit who would bring back to a mother, who had mourned for him as dead, her living child? He said over to himself, being a man of literary taste, some verses of Southey's, who was more thought of then as a poet than now:

"When the fond mother meets on high
The babe she lost in infancy."

Would not all be forgiven for the sake of that? But then came in the question, had they believed him? Had they not believed him? Had there been some channel of which he knew nothing by which they had procured information in respect to the child? This was the one doubtful matter which would be enough to crush all his most careful schemes. But he could not see how it was possible they could have obtained any information. That Margaret Bland should have written did not occur to him. Persons of her class did not write letters daily then as they do now; and he thought he had secured her devotion wholly to himself, and made it quite clear to her that for his wife's sake this was the only thing that could be done. Margaret had understood him completely. She was a person of superior intelligence. She was an admirable nurse and devoted to the baby. But she was quite unaware at first that the arrangement made with her was unknown to Lily, nor had she known that in writing to Robina she had transgressed her contract with the child's father. It was her duty to be silent now, she was informed, in order to avoid all danger of a correspondence that might be discovered; but nothing even now had been said to Margaret which could have made her feel herself in the wrong, or led her to confess what she had done. Thus the one thing which would have made him see how fatally he had risked all his possibilities was concealed from Lumsden. He could still honestly, or almost honestly, persuade himself that, though what he had done might be cruel for the moment, it was, in reality, the best thing for Lily. Nothing else would have satisfied her, nothing less. She would never have had a moment's peace had she understood that her child might be found. She would have thought nothing of any sacrifice involved. Her inheritance would have been of no value to her in comparison with the possession of her baby. She was capable of making every thing known to her uncle at any moment if by this means she could have secured the child. He had not ceased to love her, nor to entertain for her the admiration, mingled with indulgence, which makes a young woman's faults almost more attractive than her virtues to her lover. It would be like Lily to do all that; it was like Lily to give him all that trouble about the house which he never intended to get for her, but which it cost him so many fictions, so much exercise of ingenuity, to satisfy her about. There were very pardonable points in that foolishness. The desire to be with him, to identify her life altogether with his, was sweet: he loved her the better for it, though, as the wiser of the two, he knew that it was impracticable, and that it must be firmly, but gently, denied to her. And to desire to have her baby was very natural and very sweet, too. What prettier thing could there be than a young mother with her child? But there were more serious things in the world than those indulgences of natural affection, which are in themselves so blameless and so sweet, and this, in her own best interests, he, her husband, her natural head and guide, was forced to deny her, too.

I do not think that Lily was aware of the tenor of these reasonings. She made very little allowance for her husband; at no time had she been disposed to allow that in these matters, which were of such great importance in her life, he knew best. He had deceived her first of all, and then he had made her a reluctant accomplice in deceiving others. Nature, truth, honor, honesty, had all been from the beginning on her side, and she had thought Ronald as little wise as he was right in setting them all at defiance for the preservation of a secret which ought never to have been made a secret at all. She had endured it all when there was only herself in question, but from the moment in which there was hope of the baby Lily had felt with a leap of the heart that here was the solution of the problem, and that every thing must now be made open to the light of day. It may be supposed that when, after all this dreadful episode, she returned alone, like, yet so unlike, the Lily Ramsay who was sent to Dalrugas two years before into banishment with Robina, her maid, the whole matter was turned over and over in her mind with all those dreadful visions of past chances, steps which, if taken, might have changed every thing, which are the stings of such a review. To Lily, as she pondered, there seemed so many things she might have done. She might have resisted the marriage first of all. She might have refused to be married in secrecy, in a corner—the very minister, she had always felt sure, though he had been kind, disapproving of her all the time; but then (she excused herself) she had not foreseen that the marriage was to be kept a secret: it was only, she had understood, an expedient to secure quietness and speed without preliminaries that would have called the attention of the whole parish. And then, when she followed her own story to that time after Whit-Sunday, when she had expected her husband to secure the house, which could not, he swore, be obtained till the term, Lily now saw that she should have taken the matter into her own hand, that she should have permitted no more playing with the question, that, whether he liked it or not, she should have insisted on having some home and shelter of her own. Especially before the birth of her baby should she have insisted upon this. She clasped her hands with impatience and a sense of bitter failure as she thought it all over. She ought not to have allowed herself to be silenced or hindered. Her child should have been born in her own house, where he could have been welcomed and rejoiced over, not hidden away. She cried out in her solitude, with that clasp of her hands, that it was all her fault, her own fault, that she was responsible for the child above all, and that it was she who should have done this had not only her husband, but all the powers of the earth gone against it. Then Lily reflected, with the impulse of self-defence, that she had no money, and did not know how to get any, and that it would have been hard, very hard for her, without her present enlightenment, to have gone against Ronald, to have flown in his face and thwarted him so completely in a matter upon which he had so firmly made up his mind. Oh, what a difference there was between the Lily of that time—hesitating, miserable to yield and yet unable to resist, not knowing how to take a great step on her own authority, to oppose her husband and all the lesser chain of circumstances, the unconscious influence even of the women who held her with a softer bond of watchfulness and affection—and this Lily now, braced to any effort, having withdrawn and separated herself from him and from every other restraint of influence, as she thought, standing alone against all the world, deeply disenchanted, and considering every pretence of love and happiness as false and deceitful. Had it been now how little would she have hesitated! But was not this the bitterness of life: that it was then only she could have acted effectually, and not now?

She settled down to the winter at Dalrugas with these thoughts. She was Miss Ramsay, the daughter and the mistress of the house. She did not know and did not care what was thought of her in the countryside. If stories were told of the gentleman who had come so often from Edinburgh, but now came no longer, Lily heard none of them. Some faltering questions from Helen Blythe, who, instinctively, though she did not know why, never referred to Ronald in presence of Sir Robert, were all the indications she ever had that his disappearance was commented on, and Lily did not care who spoke of Ronald, or how or where their secret might be betrayed; and this indifference delivered her from many doubts and questionings. She had no objection that any body should tell in detail the whole thing to Sir Robert. She held her head very proudly above all terrors of being found out. She was afraid of nothing now. Every thing, she thought, had happened that could happen. She was separated from her husband, not by any formality, not by any such motive as had kept the secret hitherto, but by a great gulf fixed, which Lily felt it was impossible should ever be bridged over. He had wronged her as surely never woman had been wronged before, lied to her, made her herself a lie, deprived her—last and greatest wrong of all—of her child. Oh, how much time, leisure, quiet, she had to think over and over all these thoughts, to persuade herself that happiness and truth were mere words, and that nothing but falsehood flourished in this world! Gradually she sank into silence on the subject even to Beenie. Her life-history, over, as it seemed, at twenty-five, dropped out of knowledge as if it had never been. She received no letters. Ronald, indeed, continued to write at intervals for some time, addressing his letters boldly to Miss Ramsay, but she never replied to them, and by degrees they ceased. She heard nothing at all from the outside world. She heard nothing of her child. They had concluded between them, Robina and she, that if "anything happened" to the child, Margaret would be restrained by no man, but would let his mother know in any case. This was all the sustenance upon which Lily lived. Her enquiries far and near had come to nothing. The harmless detectives of the old-fashioned Edinburgh police had not succeeded in tracking the fugitive. They had no news of Margaret to send. They had never found out anything about her, except what all the world knew. By one thread, and one only, Lily clung to life, and that was her vague faith in Margaret, notwithstanding all things, that the child's life was safe as long as she made no sign.

Sir Robert found himself very comfortable in Dalrugas during that winter. He had no idea he could have been so comfortable in the old lonely place on the edge of the moor. It was wonderful how possible it was to live without amusement—nay, to feel thankful that he was no longer burdened with amusement and with the thought of what he was to do with himself and how he was to find a little distraction season after season. When a man is over seventy, the care of these things is perhaps more trouble than the advantage is worth when secured; but so long as he is in the old habitual round it is difficult to learn this. He had thought that he detested monotony, but now it appeared that he rather liked monotony— the comfort of getting up with the certainty that he had no trouble before him, no change to think of, no decision to make—to read his newspaper, to read his book, to take his walk or his drive. Sir Robert's horses and carriages very much enlarged his sphere and modified its loneliness. A longish drive now brought him to a neighbor's house, and introduced Lily to the ladies of the county, who made explanations to her and regrets not to have made her acquaintance before. And callers became, if not numerous, yet occasional, thus adding something to the little round of Sir Robert's distractions. An old gentleman or two in the distant neighborhood who had known him as a boy would come occasionally with the ladies, or a younger one, whose father had known him. And there were occasional dinner-parties, though these occurred but seldom. Sir Robert liked them all, but at bottom was more than contented when the clouds hung low and the rain or snow fell and put it out of the question that he should be disturbed at all. He liked Lily's talk best of all, or her silence, when they sat together by the fireside, where comfort and quiet reigned. He had not been such a good man in his life that he deserved any such halcyon time at its end, or to feel so virtuous, so satisfied, so peaceful as he did. But the sun shines and the rain falls alike on the just and the unjust, and he had, by good fortune, the art to take advantage of the good things which Providence sent him. Lily played a game of piquette with him, "not so very badly," he said with happy condescension, and was in time advanced to chess; but there showed signs of beating her instructor, which made Sir Robert think chess was a little too much for his head. In moments of weakness they even came down to simple draughts, and thus got through the long evenings which the old gentleman had so much feared, but which now were the happiest part of the day.

"I am told you have been here for a long time, Miss Ramsay," Lady Dalzell said, who was the great lady of the neighborhood: "how was it we never knew? We are here, of course, only for a short time in the year, but long enough to have driven over to Dalrugas had we known."

"I have been here," said Lily, "for two years—but how it is my neighbors have not known I cannot tell. I could scarcely send round a fiery cross to say that a small person of no great account had arrived at her uncle's house."

"I should have thought Sir Robert would have written or made some provision. Do you really mean that you have been without a chaperon, without protection?"

"Even as you see me," said Lily, with a laugh.

"And nothing ever happened," said the great lady, "to make you feel uncomfortable?"

Did she look at Lily with some meaning in her eyes? Did she mean nothing? Who could tell? There might have been a whole world of sous-entendus in what Lady Dalzell said, or there might be nothing at all. Lily met her gaze with perhaps a little more directness than was necessary, but she did not change color.

"There was no raid made upon the house," said Lily. "I never was in any danger that I know of. There was Dougal, who would have fought for me to the death—perhaps, or, at all events, till some one came to help him. And I had two women who took only too much care of me."

"Ah, it was not perils of that kind I was thinking of," said Lady Dalzell, shaking her head.

"I am sorry," said Lily—"or perhaps I should rather be glad—that I don't know what perils your ladyship was thinking of."

Then the young lady of the party, Lady Dalzell's daughter, interposed, and began to talk of the approaching Christmas and the entertainments to be given in the neighborhood. "If we had only known, we should have had you to the ball," she said. "We had not one last New Year, but the year before, and you were here then."

"Yes, I was here then."

"It was the year of that dreadful snow-storm. How lonely it must have been for you, shut up for that long fortnight. Mamma, imagine! Miss Ramsay was here all alone the year of the snow-storm, shut up in Dalrugas—and we had our ball and all sorts of things."

"I hope Miss Ramsay had some friends or something to amuse her," said Lady Dalzell.

"I had Helen Blythe from the Manse up to tea," cried Lily, with a little burst of laughter, which did not seem out of place in the violent contrast which was thus implied, though she felt it herself almost like a confession. The two ladies looked at her strangely, she thought, and hastened to change the subject. Did they look at her strangely? Did they think of her at all? Or was it the thought of their own shortcomings in respect to this lonely girl, who was Sir Robert's niece and heiress, which made a shade upon their brows? They invited her to the ball, which was to happen this year, with much demonstration of friendliness. Not to tire Sir Robert, she and her uncle were asked to go a day or two before this important festivity and join the home party, and Miss Dalzell conveyed to Miss Ramsay the delightful intelligence that there would be "plenty of partners"—all the county, and the officers from Perth, and a large party from Edinburgh. The girl spoke of all these preparations with sparkling eyes.

"Well, Lily," said Sir Robert, when the visitors were gone, "this will be something for you: you will have one ball at least." He did not much relish the prospect for himself, but he was grateful, and felt that he must face it for her.

"I don't feel so much enchanted as I ought," said Lily. "Would it disappoint you much, uncle, if I wrote to say we could not go?"

"Disappoint me, my dear! But you must go, for you would like it, Lily. Every girl of your age likes a ball."

"My age, Uncle Robert! Do you know I am five-and-twenty? I would rather sit alone all night and sew, though I am not very fond of sewing. Unless you want to dance and flirt and behave yourself as gentlemen of your age ought not to do, I think we'll stay at home and play piquette. I am going to no ball," cried Lily, her patience breaking down for the moment, "not now, nor ever. I—to a ball! after all these years!"

"Lily," said Sir Robert, with a disturbed look, "I have expressed my regret that you should have had such a lonely life, but it hurts me, my dear, to hear you express yourself with such bitterness about those years; there were but two of them, after all."

"That is true," she said, recovering herself quickly, "but when one has a great deal of time to think, one changes one's mind about a great manythings, especially balls."

"That is true, too," he said, "so long as you are not bitter about it, as I sometimes fear you are inclined to be, my dear."

"Not bitter at all," she cried, with a smile that quivered a little on her lip. She got up and stood at the window, with her back to him, looking out upon the moor. The clouds were hanging low, almost touching the hills, the sky so heavy that it seemed to be closing down, in one deep tone of gray, upon the dumb, unresisting earth. "I hope," said Lily, "that they will get home before the snow comes down." She stood there for some time looking out upon that scene, which had seen so much. "It was the year of that dreadful snow-storm," the girl had said. And the ball to which they had asked her was on the anniversary of her wedding day.

CHAPTER XLIII

It did not snow that year: the weather was mild and wet. There was not the exhilaration, the mystery, the clear-breathing chill, of the snow, the great gorgeous sunsets over the purple hills. But the little world was closed in with opaque walls of cloud; the sky low, as if you could almost touch it; the hills absent from the landscape, replaced by banks of watery mist, indefinite, meaning nothing; and all life shut up within the enclosure, where there was shelter to be had, and warmth, if nothing else. It was thus that the anniversary of Lily's honeymoon passed by. Her mind was like the sky, covered by heavy mists, falling low, as if there were no longer earth and heaven, but only a land of darkness and of despair between. Behind these mists all her existence had disappeared. Her child, perhaps, was there, her husband was there, the woman she might have been was there, so was the old Lily, the girl full of laughter and flying thoughts, full of quick resolutions and plans and infinite hope. The woman who stood by the window was a woman whom Lily scarcely knew, who did what she had to do mechanically, whether it was ordering Sir Robert's dinner, or playing piquette with him, or gazing, gazing out of that window before he came down stairs. She gazed, but she looked for no one upon the distant road; her gaze meant nothing, any more than her life did. She had no hope of anything, scarcely, she thought to herself, any desire left. A ball! to go to a ball! which her uncle thought every one of her age must wish to do. He had been going out to dinner that night; most likely he was going to balls also, about the New Year time, when there were so many in Edinburgh. He could not well get out of it, he would probably say to himself. At the New Year time! the New Year!

That season passed over, and so did many more. Miss Ramsay of Dalrugas became almost well known in the county. She went nowhere, being very much devoted, every-body said, to her old uncle, and perhaps a little bitter at being tied to him, never able to do anything to please herself; for it was only natural to suppose it would please her better to see her friends, to see the world, to have her share of the amusements that were going, than to sit over the fire with that old man. "I must say that she is goodness itself to him," Lady Dalzell said; "now at least, whatever she may have been." These words fired the imagination of her company, who were eager to know what Miss Ramsay might have been in the past, but Lady Dalzell was very discreet, all the more that she knew nothing and was unprovided with any story to tell. "Whatever she may have done, she is not the least what she used to be when she was a girl in Edinburgh," she said. And every-body was disposed to believe that Lady Dalzell referred to the recollections of her own youth, when she was herself a girl in Edinburgh, and Miss Ramsay of Dalrugas perhaps a little younger and something of a contemporary. There was nobody who did not add on ten years at least to Lily's age.

The little population at Dalrugas itself almost felt the same. To them, too, it seemed that ten years and more had suddenly been added to their young mistress's age. They themselves had departed to an incredible distance from her or she from them. To think how they had surrounded her with their almost protecting and familiar love so short a time before, watching every movement, feeling every variation of feeling in her, knowing all her secrets, giving her their most zealous guardianship, and that now they should be pushed so far away—the servants of the house, to receive their orders, but all silence between them, every thing that had been ignored, not a word said. It was Katrin who felt it most, having been aware all the time that she herself had much more to do in the matter, and was a more responsible person, than Beenie, who often would have been very little fitted to meet any such emergencies as had occurred, but who was now the best off, receiving from time to time a scrap of confidence, perhaps, at least the chance of close attendance, while Katrin had to be thinking of her dinner, and of all that was wanted in the enlarged and much more troublesome household. Lily never looked at Katrin, even, as if there had been anything more intimate between them than the ordinary relations of mistress and servant. Had she forgotten how Katrin had stood by her, all she had seen, all she had known? Sometimes Katrin asked herself, with indignation and a sense of injured affection, what Lily, with more reason, asked herself, too: had these scenes ever existed but in imagination? had it been all a dream? Sometimes as she came down stairs with her orders for the day, and with a full heart, swelling with disappointment after some little implied appeal to the past, of which Lily had taken no notice, Katrin had hard work to keep from crying, which would, she felt, be an eternal disgrace to her "afore thae strange women"—the maids, who now took the work of the house from her shoulders, and enforced the bondage of the conventional upon her life. Katrin felt this as deeply as if she had been the most high-minded of visionaries. Nowadays she had always to "behave herself," always to be upon her p's and q's. She could not even fly out upon Dougal, which sometimes might have been a consolation, lest these strange women should exchange looks, and say to each other how little dignified for Sir Robert's housekeeper this person was. Dougal, indeed, in the emergency, was the only one who gave her a rough support. He would say, with a jerk of his thumb over his shoulder in the direction of the stairs: "She's no just hersel' the noo. Ye should ken that better than me; but ye make nae allowance. I would like to get her out some day for a ride upon the powny, and maybe she would open her heart."

"To you!" Katrin said, with a sort of shriek, pushing him from her, the strange women for once being out of the way.

"She might do waur," said Dougal, pushing his bonnet to his other ear. "But, my faith! if I ever lay my hand on that birky frae Edinburgh, him or me shall ken the reason!" he cried, bending his shaggy brows, and swinging his clenched fist through the air.

"You're a bonnie person to interfere in my mistress's affairs," Katrin cried, "your pownies and you! If she's mair distant and mair grand, it's just what's becoming, and the house full of gentlemen and ladies, no to speak o' thae strange women, that are at a person's tails, spying every movement, day and night. For gudeness' sake, gang away and let me be quit of ye, man! If you come in on the top o' a' to take up ony moment's peace I have, I will just gang clean out of the sma' sense that's left me, and pison ye all in your broth!" cried Katrin, with flashing eyes.

Dougal withdrew to the place in which he was most at home in the altered house, Rory's stable, where he and his favorite rubbed their shaggy heads together in mutual consolation. Rory, too, had fallen from his high estate. Never now did he carry the young lady of the house (which, truth to tell, was not an honor he had ever appreciated much), never convey a guest to the coach or the market. Rory went to the hill for peat; he was ridden into the town, helter-skelter, by a reckless young groom, for the letters; instead of the gentleman of the stable, with the black pony under him to do all the rough work, it was he who had become, as it were, the black pony, the pony-of-all-work of the establishment. Yet what things he had known! What scenes he had seen! There was a consciousness of it all, and a choking, no doubt, of honest merit undervalued in his throat, too, as he rubbed his nose against Dougal's shoulder. He had been even "further ben" than Dougal in the secrets of the life that was past.

And Lily did not console Katrin, said nothing to Robina, did not even attempt to save the pony from his hard fate. She was as hard as Fate herself, wrapped up as in robes of ice or stone, smiling as if from a pinnacle of chill unconsciousness upon all those spectators of her past existence, the conspirators who had helped out every contrivance, the accomplices. And yet it was not the rage which sometimes silently devoured her which separated her from her humble friends. She was angry with them, as with all the world, and herself most of all. But sometimes her heart yearned, too, for a kind word, for a look from eyes which knew all that had been and was no more. But I think she dared not let it be seen, lest the flood-doors, once opened, should give forth the whole tide and could never close again.

When all this came to an end, I do not think Lily was aware how long it had been: if it had been two years or three years, I believe she never quite knew; the dates, indeed, established the course of time, but when did she think of dates, as the monotonous seasons followed each other, day by night, and summer by winter, and meal by meal? Routine was very strong in Sir Robert's house, where every hour was measured, and every repast as punctual as clockwork, and there was nothing which happened to-day which did not happen to-morrow, and would so continue, unwavering, unending, till time was over. Such a routine makes one forget that time will ever be over: it looks as if it might go on forever, as if no breach were possible, still less any conclusion; and yet, in the course of time, the conclusion must always come at last.

One of these winters was a bad one for the old folk; something ungenial was in the air. It was not actually that the temperature was much lower than usual, but the cold lasted long, without breaks or any intervals of rest: always cold, always gray, with no gleams in the sky. The babies felt it first, and then the old people; every-body had bronchitis, for influenza was not in those days. There was coughing in every cottage, and by degrees the old fathers and mothers began to disappear. There were not enough of them to startle people in the newspapers as with any record of an epidemic, but only the old people who were ripe for falling, and wanted only a puff of wind to blow them away like the last leaves on a tree, felt that puff, and dropped noiselessly, their time being come. It began to appear of more decided importance when Mr. Blythe was known to be very ill, not in his usual quiet chronic manner, but with bronchitis, too, like all the rest. There had not been very much intercourse between Dalrugas and the Manse since Sir Robert's arrival. He had been eager to see the old minister, who was almost the only relic of the friends of his youth, and they had found a great deal to say to each other on the first and even on the second visit. But Sir Robert liked his visitors to come to him, and Mr. Blythe was incapable of moving from his chair, so that their intercourse gradually lessened even in the first year, and in the second came almost to nothing at all. There was an embarrassment, too, between the two old gentlemen. Mr. Blythe felt it, and would stop short even in the midst of one of his best stories, struck by some sudden suggestion, and grow portentously grave, just where the laugh came in. Sometimes he would look round at Lily, half angry, half enquiring. He could not be at ease with his old friend when so great a secret lay between them, and though Sir Robert knew nothing about any secret, nor even suspected the existence of such a thing, he yet felt also that there was something on Blythe's mind. "What is it he wants to speak to me about?" he would say to Lily. "I am certain there is something. Is it about his girl? He should be able to leave his girl pretty well off, or at least to provide for her according to her station. Does he want me to take the charge of his girl?" "Helen will want nobody to take care of her," said Lily. "Then what is it he has on his mind?" Sir Robert asked, but got no reply. Thus it was that their intercourse had been checked. And there was a cloud between Lily and Helen, who was deeply troubled in her mind by the complete disappearance of Lumsden from the scene. There were manythings about him, and her friend's connection with him, that had disturbed Helen in the past. She had not known how to account for many circumstances in the story: his constant reappearance, the mystery of an intercourse which never came to anything further, yet never slackened, had troubled her sorely. She had not asked, nor wished to hear, any explanation which might be, in however small a degree, derogatory to Lily. She would rather bear the pain of doubt than the worse pain of knowing that her doubts were justified. And there were a host of minor circumstances which had added to her confusion and trouble just before Sir Robert's arrival, when Lily had, as she thought, withdrawn from her society, and even made pretexts not to see her, to Helen's astonishment and dismay. And then there came Lily's illness, and Ronald's anxious visit, and then—nothing more: a curtain falling, as it were, on the whole confused drama; an end, which was no end. Ronald's name had never been mentioned since; he had never been seen in the country; he had gone out of Lily's life, so far as appeared, totally without reason given or word said. And Helen had not continued to question Lily, whom she, like every-body else, found to be so much changed by her illness. There was something in the face which had been so sweet and almost child-like a little time before which now stopped expansion. Helen looked into it wistfully, and was silent. And thus the veil which had fallen between the two old men came down still more darkly between the other two, and the intercourse had grown less and less, until, in the cold wintry weather of this miserable season, it had almost died away.

But it was a great shock to hear, one gray, dull morning when every thing seemed more miserable than ever, the sky more heavy, the frost more bitter, that the minister had died in the night. This news came to them with the letters and the early rolls, for which every morning now a groom rode into Kinloch-Rugas upon the humiliated Rory. The minister dead! Sir Robert was more impressed by it than could have been imagined possible. "Old Blythe!" he said to himself, with a shock which paled his own ruddy countenance. Why should he have died? The routine of his life was as fixed and certain as that of Sir Robert himself. There seemed no necessity that it should ever be broken. He was part of the landscape, like one of the hills, like the gray steeple of his church, a landmark, a thing not to be removed. Yet he was removed, and Mr. Douglas, the assistant and successor, was now minister of Kinloch-Rugas. In a little while the place which had known him so long would know him no more. Sir Robert ate very little breakfast that morning; he had himself a bad cold which he could not shake off; he got up and walked about the room, almost with excitement. "Old Blythe!" he repeated, and began to recall audibly to himself, or at least only half to Lily, the time when old Blythe was young, as young as other folk, and a very cheery fellow and a good companion and no nonsense about him. And now he was dead! It was probably the fault of that dashed drunken doctor, who fortunately was not Sir Robert's doctor, who had let him die. Lily on her part was scarcely less moved. Dead! The man who had held so prominent a place in that dream, who had never forgotten it, in whose eyes she had read her own history, at least so far as he knew it, the last time she met his look, with so living a question in them, too, almost demanding, was that secret never to be told? ready to insist, to say: "Then I must tell it if you will not!" She had read all that in his look the last time she had seen him, and in her soul had trembled. And now he was dead and could never say a word. She had a vague sense, too, that she had one less now among the few people who would stand by her. But she wanted no one to stand by her, she was in no trouble. The mystery of her existence would never now be revealed.

"I think I ought to go and see Helen, uncle," she said.

"Certainly, certainly!" he cried, more eager than she was. "Order the brougham at once, and be sure you take plenty of wraps. Is there anything we could send? Think, my dear: is there anything I could do? I would like—to show every respect."

He made a movement as if he would go to the escritoire in which he kept his money; for checks were not, or at least were not for individual purposes, in those days.

"Uncle," she said, "they are not poor people; you cannot send money—they are like ourselves."

"Let me tell you," he said, with a little irritation, "that there are many families even like ourselves, as you say, which the Blythes are not, who would be very thankful for a timely present at such a moment. But, however— Is there nothing you can take—no cordial, or a little of the port, or—or anything?"

"Helen wants nothing, uncle—but perhaps a kind word."

"Helen! Ah, that's true: the auld man's gone that would have known the good of it. Well, tell her at least that if I can be of any use to her— I always thought," he cried, with a little evident but quickly suppressed emotion, "that he had something he wanted to say to me, something that was on his mind."

How little he thought what it was that the old minister had on his mind! and how well Lily knew!

Helen was very calm, almost calmer than Lily was, when they met in the old parlor where the great chair was already set against the wall. "You are not to cry, Lily. He was very clear in his mind, though sore wearied in his body. He was glad at the last to get away. He said: 'I've had my time here, and no a bad time either, the Lord be praised for all his mercies, and I'll maybe find a wee place to creep into that She will have keepit for me: not a minister,' he said, oh, Lily! 'but maybe a doorkeeper in the house of the Lord.' Is that not all we could wish for, that his mind should have been like that?" said Helen, with eyes too clear for tears. She was arranging every thing in her quiet way, requiring no help, quite worn out with watching, but incapable of rest until all that was needful had been done. The darkened room where so much had happened, isolated now from the common day by the shutting out of the light, seemed like a sort of funereal, monumental chamber in all its homely shabbiness, a gray and colorless vault, not for him who had gone out of it, but for the ghosts and phantoms of all that had taken place there. Lily's heart was more oppressed by the gray detachment of that room, in which her own life had been decided, than either by the serene death above or the serene sorrow by her side.

When she got back, Sir Robert, very fretful, was sitting over the fire. He was hoarse and coughing, and more impatient than she had seen him. "If it goes on like this, I'll not stay here," he said, "not another week, let them say what they like! Four weeks of frost, a measured month, and as much more in that bitter sky. No. I will not stay; and, however attached you are to the place, you'll come with me, Lily. Yes, you'll come with me! We'll take up my old travelling carriage and we'll get away to the South, if I were but free of this confounded cold!"

"We must take care of you, uncle. You must let us take care of you, and your cold will soon go."

"You think so?" he said eagerly. "I thought you would think so. I never was a man for catching cold. I never had a bronchitis in my life; that's not my danger. If that doctor man would but come, for I thought it as well to send for him?"

He looked up at her with an enquiring look. He was anxious to be approved in what he had done. "It was the only thing to do," she said, and he was as glad she thought so as if she had been the mistress of his actions.

But by the evening Sir Robert was very ill. He fought very hard for his life. He was several years over seventy, and there did not seem much in life to retain him. But nevertheless he fought hard for it, and was very unwilling to let it go. He made several rallies from sheer strength of will, it appeared. But in the end the old soldier had to yield, as we must all do. The long frost lasted, the bitter winds blew, no softening came to the weather or to Fate. Sir Robert died not long after the old minister had been laid in the grave. It was a dreadful year for the old folk, every-body said; they fell like the leaves in October before every wind.

CHAPTER XLIV

I do not think that Lily in the least realized what had happened to her when her uncle died. She grieved for him with a very natural, not excessive, sorrow, as a daughter grieves for an old father whose life she is aware cannot be long prolonged. He was more to her than it was to be expected he could have been. These two years of constant intercourse, and a good deal of kindness, which could scarcely be called unselfish, yet was more genuine on that very account, had brought them into real relationship with each other; and Lily, who never had known what family ties were, had come to regard the careless Uncle Robert of her youth, to whom she had been a troublesome appendage, as he was to her the representative of a quite unaffectionate authority, as a father, who, indeed, made many demands, but made them with a confidence and trust in her good feeling which were quite natural and quite irresistible, calling forth in her the qualities to which that appeal was made. Sir Robert had all unawares served Lily, though it was his coming which was the cause of the great catastrophe in her life. She did not blame him for that—it was inevitable; in one way or other it must have come—but she was grateful to him for having laid hands upon her, so to speak, in the failure of all things, and given her duties and a necessity for living. And now she was sorry for him, as a daughter for a father, let us say a married daughter, with interests of her own, for a father who had been all that was natural to her, but no more.

She was a little dazed and confused, however, with the rapidity of the catastrophe, the week's close nursing, the fatigue, the profound feeling which death, especially with those to whom his presence is new, inevitably calls forth; and very much subdued and sorrowful in her mind, feeling the vacancy, the silence, the departure of the well-known figure, which had given a second fictitious life to this now doubly deserted place. And it did not occur to Lily to think how her own position was affected, or what change had taken place in her life. She was not an incapable woman, whom the management of her own affairs would have frightened or over-burdened, but she never had possessed any affairs, never had the command of any money, never arranged, except as she was told, where or how she had to live. Until her uncle had given her, when she went to Edinburgh, the sum which to her inexperience was fabulous, and which she had spent chiefly in her vain search after her child, she had never had any money at all. She did not even think of it in this new change of affairs, nor of what her future fate in that respect was to be.

This indifference was not shared by the household, or at least by those two important members of it Katrin and Robina, who had been most attentive and careful of Sir Robert in his illness, but who, after he was dead, having little tie of any kind to the old gentleman, who had been a good enough master and no more, dropped him as much as it was possible to drop the idea of one who lay solemnly dead in the house, the centre of all its occupations still, though he could influence them no more. "What will happen now?" they said to each other, putting their heads together, when the "strange women," subdued by "a death in the house," were occupied with their special businesses, and Sir Robert's man, his occupation gone, had retired to his chamber, feeling himself in want of rest and refreshment after the labors of nursing, which he had not undergone. "What will happen noo?" said Katrin. "And what will we do with her?" Beenie said, shaking her large head. "I'll tell you," said Katrin, "the first thing that will happen: Before we ken where we are we'll hae him here!"

"No, no," said Beenie; "no, no! I am not expecting that."

"You may expect what ye like, but that is what will happen. He will come in just as he used to do, with a fib about the cauld of the Hielands, and a word about the steps that are so worn and no safe. Woman, he has the ball at his fit now. Do you no ken when a man's wife comes into her siller it's to him it goes? She will have every thing, and well he kens that, and it's just the reason of all that has come and gone."

"He'll never daur," said Beenie, "after leaving her so long to herself, and after a' that's come and gone, as you say."

"It's none of his fault leaving her to hersel'. He has written to her and written to her, for I've seen the letters mysel'; and if she has taken no notice, it is her wyte, and not his. She will have a grand fortune, a' auld Sir Robert's money, and this place, that is the home o' them all."

"I never thought so much of this place. She'll not bide here. Her and me will be away as soon as ever it's decent, I will assure you o' that, to seek the bairn over a' the world."

"You'll never find him," said Katrin.

"Ay, will we! Naebody to say her nay, and siller in her pouch, and the world before her. We'll find him if he were at its other end!"

"Ye'll never find him without the father of him!" cried Katrin, becoming excited in her opposition.

"That swore he was dead!" cried Beenie, flushing, too, with fight and indignation, "that stood up to my face, me that kent better, and threepit that the bairn was dead! And her that was his mother sitting by, her bonnie face covered in her hands!"

"Woman!" cried Katrin, "would you keep up dispeace in a house for anything a man may have said or threepit? I'm for peace, whatever it costs. What is a house that's divided against itsel'? Scripture will tell ye that. Even if a man is an ill man, if he belongs to ye, it's better to have him than to want him. It's mair decent. Once you've plighted him your word, ye must just pit up with him for good report or evil report. If the father's in one place and the mother's in another, how are ye to bring up a bairn? And a' just for a lie the man has told when he was in desperation, and for taking away the bairn when we couldna have keepit him, when it was as clear as daylight something had to be done. Losh! Dougal might tear the hair out o' my head, or the claes frae my back, he would be my man still."

"Seeing he is little like to do either the one thing or the other, it's easy speaking," Beenie said.

Lily did not come so far as this in her thoughts till a day or two had passed, and then there came upon her, as Beenie had divined, the sudden impulse, which nevertheless had been lying dormant in her mind all this time, to get up and go at once in pursuit of her baby. All the people she had employed, all the schemes she had tried, had come to nothing. At first her ignorant efforts had been balked by that very ignorance itself, by not knowing what to do or whom to trust, and then by distance and time and agents who were not very much in earnest. To look for a great criminal—that was a thing which might waken all the natural detective qualities even before detectives were. But to look for a baby, with no glory, no notoriety, whatever might be one's success! Lily saw all this now with the wisdom that even a very little practical experience gives. But his mother—that would be a very different matter. His mother would find him wheresoever he was hidden. And after the first day of consternation, of confusion and fatigue, this resolution flashed upon her, as it had done at times through all the miserable months that were past. She had been obliged to crush it then, but now there was no occasion to crush it any longer. She was free; no one had any right to stop her; she was necessary to nobody, bound to nobody. So she thought, rejecting vehemently in her mind the idea of her husband, who had robbed her, who had lied to her, but who should not restrain her now, let the law say what it would. Lily did not even know how much the property of her husband she was. Even in the old bad times it was only when evil days came that the women learned this. The majority of them, let us hope, went to their graves without ever knowing it, except in a jibe, which was to the address of all women. She did not think of it. Ronald had robbed her, had lied to her, and was separated from her forever; but that he would even now attempt to control her did not enter into Lily's mind. He was a gentleman, though these were not the acts of a gentleman. She did not fear him nor suspect him of any common offence against her. He had been guilty of these crimes—that was the only word to use for them—but to herself, Lily, he could do nothing. She had so much confidence in him still. Nor, indeed (she thought at first), would he have anything to do with it. He would know nothing; she would go after her child at once, as was natural, his mother's right. And he surely would not be the man to interfere.

Then as she began to wait, to feel herself waiting, every nerve tingling and excitement rising in her veins every hour, in the enforced silence of the shadowed house, until the funeral should set her free, Lily came to life altogether, she could not tell how, in a moment, waking as if from the past, the ice, the paralysis that had bound her. She had lived with her uncle these two years, and she had not lived at all. She had not known even what was the passage of time. Her existence had been mechanical, and all her days alike, the winter in one fashion, the summer in another. The child, the thought of the child, had been a thread which kept her to life; otherwise there had been nothing. But now, when that thought of the child became active and an inspiration, her whole soul suddenly came to life again. It was as when the world has been hid by the darkness of night, and we seem to stand detached, the only point of consciousness with nothing round us, till between two openings of the eyelids there comes into being again a universe that had been hidden, the sky, the soil, the household walls, all in a moment visible in that dawn which is scarcely light, which is vision, which recreates and restores all that we knew of. To Lily there came a change like that. She closed her eyes in the wintry blackness of the night, and when she opened them, every thing had come back to her. It was not that she had forgotten: it was all there all the time; but her heart had been benumbed, and darkness had covered the face of the earth. It was not the light or warmth of the sunrise that came upon her; it was that revelation of the earliest dawn that makes the hidden things visible, and fills in once more the mountains and the moors, the earth and the sky.

It was with a shock that she saw it all again. She had been wrapped in a false show, every thing vanity and delusion about her—Miss Ramsay, a name that was hers no longer; but in reality she was Ronald Lumsden's wife, the mother of a child, a woman with other duties, other rights. And he was there, facing her, filling up the world. In her benumbed state he had been almost invisible; so much of life as she had clung to the idea of the baby. When he appeared to her, it was as a ghost from which she shrank, from which every instinct turned her away. But now he stood there, as he had stood all the time, looking her in the face. Had he been doing so all these years? or had she been invisible to him as he to her? She was seized with a great trembling as she asked herself that question. Had he been watching her through the dark as through the light, keeping his eye upon her, waiting? She shuddered, but all her faculties became vivid, living, at this touch. And then there were other questions to ask: What would he do? Failing that, more intimate still, what would she do, Lily, herself? What, now that she was free, alone, with no bond upon her, what should she do? This question shook her very being. She could go on no longer with her life of lies: what should she do?

Sir Robert's man of business came from Edinburgh as soon as the news reached him. He told her that she was, as she had a right to be, her uncle's sole heir, there being no other relation near enough to be taken into consideration at all. Should she tell him at once what her real position was? It was a painful thing for Lily to do, and until she was able to set out upon that search for her child, which was still her first object, she had a superstitious feeling that something might happen, something that would detain or delay her, if she told her secret at once. She had arranged to go away on the morning after the funeral. That day, before Mr. Wallace left Dalrugas, she resolved that she would tell him, and, through him, all who were there. Her heart beat very loud at the thought. To keep it so long, and then in a moment give it up to the discussion of all the world! To reveal—was it her shame? Oh, shame, indeed, to have deceived every one, her uncle, every creature who knew her. But yet not shame, not shame, in any other way. Much surprised was Mr. John Wallace, W. S., Sir Robert's man of business, to find how indifferent Miss Ramsay was as to the value and extent of the property her uncle had left her. She said "Yes," to all his statements, sometimes interrogatively, sometimes in simple assent; but he saw that she did not take them in, that the figures had no meaning for her. Her mind was otherwise absorbed. She was thinking of something. When he asked her, not without a recollection of things he had heard, as he said to himself, "long ago," when Sir Robert's niece had been sent off to the wilds out of some young birky's way, whether there was any one whom she would like specially summoned for the funeral, Lily looked up at him with a quick, almost terrified glance, and said: "No, no!" She had, he felt, certainly something on her mind. I don't know whether, in those days, the existence of a private and hidden story was more common than now: there were always facilities for such things in Scotland in the nature of the marriage laws, and many anxious incidents happened in families. A man acknowledging a secret wife, of whose existence nobody had known, was common enough. But a young lady was different. At all events there could be no doubt that this young lady had something on her mind.

The arrangements were all made in a style befitting Sir Robert's dignity. The persons employed came from Edinburgh with a solemn hearse and black horses, and all the gloomiest paraphernalia of death. A great company gathered from the country all about. They had begun to arrive, and a number of carriages were already waiting round to show the respect of his neighbors for the old gentleman, of whom they had actually known so little. The few farmers who were his tenants on the estate, which included so little land of a profitable kind among the moors (not yet profitable) and the mountains, waited outside in their rough gigs, but several of the gentlemen had gathered in the drawing-room, where cake and wine were laid out upon a table, and Mr. Douglas, now the minister of Kinloch-Rugas, stood separate, a little from the rest, prepared to "give the prayer." The Church of Scotland knew no burial service in those days other than the prayer which preceded the carrying forth of the coffin. Two ladies had driven over, with their husbands, to stay with Lily when the procession left the house. They did not know very much of her, but they were sorry for her in her loneliness. The appearance of a woman at a funeral was an unknown thing in those days in Scotland, and never thought of. This little cluster of black dresses was in a corner of the room, in the faint light of the shadowed windows, Lily's pale face, tremulous with an agitation which was not grief, forming the point of highest light in the sombre room, among the high-colored rural countenances. She meant to tell them on their return.

It was at this moment, in the preliminary pause, when Mr. Douglas, standing out in the centre of the room, was about to lift his hand as the signal for the prayer—about to begin—that a rapid step became audible, coming up the stairs, stumbling a little on the uppermost steps as most people did. It was nothing wonderful that some one should be a little late, yet there was something in the step which made even the most careless member of the company look round. Lily, absorbed in her thoughts, was startled by the sound, she could not tell why. She moved her head a little, and it so happened that the gentlemen standing about by an instinctive movement stepped aside from between her and the door, so as to leave room for the entrance of the new-comer. He was heard to quicken his pace, as if fearing to be too late, and the minister stood with his hand raised, waiting till the interruption should be over and the tardy guest had appeared.

Then the door opened quickly, and Ronald Lumsden came in. He was in full panoply of mourning, according to the Scotch habit, his hat, which was in his hand, covered with crape, his sleeves with white "weepers," his appearance that of chief mourner. "I am not too late?" he said, as he came in. Who was he? Some of those present did not know. Was he some unacknowledged son, turning up at the last moment to turn away the inheritance? Mr. Wallace stepped out a little to meet him, in consternation. Suddenly it flashed through his memory that this was the young fellow out of whose way Lily Ramsay had been sent by her uncle. He knew Lumsden well enough. He made a sign to him to be silent, pointing to the minister, who stood interrupted, ready to begin.

"I see," said Ronald in the proper whisper, with a nod of his head; and then he stepped straight up, through the little lane made for him, to where Lily sat, like an image of stone, her lips parted with a quick, fluttering breath. He took her hand and held it in his, standing by her side. "Pardon me that I come so late," he said, "I was out of town; but I am still in time. Mr. Wallace, I will take my place after the coffin as the representative of my wife." This was said rapidly, but calmly, in the complete self-possession of a man who knows he is master of the situation. There was scarcely a pause, the astonished company had scarcely time to look into each other's face, when the proceedings went on. The minister's voice arose, with that peculiar cadence which is in the sound of prayer. The men stood still, arrested in their excitement, shuffling with their feet, covering their faces with one hand so long as they could keep up that difficult position. But this was all unlike a funeral prayer. The atmosphere had suddenly become full of excitement, the pulsations quickened in every wrist.

Lily remained in her chair; she did not rise. It was one of the points of decorum that a woman should not be able to stand on such an occasion. The two ladies, all one quiver of curiosity, stood behind her, and Ronald by her side, holding her hand. He did not give it up, though she had tried to withdraw it, but stood close by her, holding his hat, with its long streamers of crape, in his other hand, his head drooped a little, and his eyes cast down in reverential sympathy. To describe what was in her mind would be impossible. Her heart had given one wild leap, as if it would have choked her, and then a sort of calm of death had succeeded. He held her hand, pressing it softly from time to time. He gave no sign but this of any other feeling but the proper respectful attention, while she sat paralyzed. And then came the stir—the movement. He let her hand drop, and, bending over her, touched her forehead with his lips; and then he made a sign to the astonished men about, even to Mr. Wallace, who had been, up to this moment, the chief authority, to precede him. There was a sort of a gasp in the astonished assembly, but every one obeyed Ronald's courteous gesture. There was nothing presumptuous, nothing of the upstart, in it: it was the calm and dignified confidence of the master of the house. He was the last to leave the room, which he did with another pressure of Lily's hand, and a glance to the ladies behind, which said as distinctly as words: "Take care of my wife." And he was the first in the procession, placing himself at once behind the coffin. The burying-ground was not far away; it was one of those lonely places among the hills, with a little chapel in ruins, a relic of an older form of faith, within its gray walls, which are so pathetic and so solemn. The long line of men walking two and two made a great show in their black procession, their feet ringing upon the hard frost-bound road. But Ronald walked alone, in front, as if he had been Sir Robert's son. And his heart was full of a steady and sober elation. It had been a hard fight, but he had conquered. Though he was not a son, but an enemy, he was, as he had always intended, Sir Robert's heir.

CHAPTER XLV

"But this is all very strange and requires explanation. I do not doubt in the least what you say, but it requires explanation," Mr. Wallace said.

Only a few of the gentlemen returned with him to the house. Two of them were the husbands of the two ladies who had been with Lily, and who now, with each a volume in her face, joined the surprised and curious men. Lily, too, had come back to the room. It was now that she had intended to make her statement, and it had become unnecessary. She was saved something, and yet there was worse before her than if this had not been saved.

"There is no explanation we are not ready to give," said Ronald calmly. "We were married four years ago, in the Manse of Kinloch-Rugas, by Mr. Douglas's predecessor, dead, I am sorry to hear, the other day. My wife has the lines, which she will give you. Two witnesses of the marriage are in the house. Every thing is in perfect order and ready for any examination. The reason of the secrecy we were obliged to keep up was the objection of Sir Robert, whom we have just laid with every respect in his grave."

"With every respect!" Mr. Wallace said with emphasis, and there was a murmur of agreement from the company round.

"These are my words—with every respect. One may respect a man and yet fail to sacrifice one's own happiness entirely to him. My wife and I were in accord as to saving Sir Robert anything that might vex him in his old age."

Here Lily raised her head as if about to speak, but said nothing by a second thought, or perhaps by inability to utter anything in the midst of the flow of his address.

"It is unnecessary to say what it has cost us to keep up this, but we have done it at every risk. Our duty now is changed, and it is as necessary to make our position clearly understood as it was before to keep it private to ourselves. I would not allow Mrs. Lumsden to take this avowal upon herself, as I am sure she would have done had I not been here, or to encounter the fatigue of the day alone. I have preferred to look like an intruder, as I fear some of the gentlemen here must have thought me."

"No intruder," said one. "No, no, to be sure, no intruder," said another. "Not," said a third, "if this extraordinary story is true."

"That's the whole question," said Mr. Wallace. "My client knew nothing of it. He left his money to his niece as to a single woman. The lady has always been known as Miss Ramsay. How are we to know it is true?"

"You know me, however," said Ronald, with a smile: "Ronald Lumsden, advocate, son of John, of that name, of Pontalloch. I think I have taken fees from you before now, Mr. Wallace. It is not very likely I should tell you such a lie as that in the lady's face."

"Miss Ramsay," said Mr. Wallace—"Lord! if I knew what to call the lady!—madam, is this true?"

"It is true that I have deceived my uncle and every one who knew me. It has been heavy, heavy on my conscience, and a shame in my heart. I can look no one in the face!" cried Lily. "I meant to confess it to you to-day, as he says. Yes, it is true!"

Though the house was still the house of death, according to all etiquette, and the blinds not yet drawn up from the windows, Mr. Wallace, W. S., uttered, in spite of himself, a low whistle of astonishment. And then he coughed, and drew himself up that nobody should suspect him of such an impropriety.

"This is a strange case, a very strange case! These gentlemen must understand that I had no inkling of it when I invited them here to-day."

"What would it have mattered what inkling you had, Wallace?" said one of the most important of the strangers. "We cannot change what is done. Perhaps, indeed, there's no occasion. It is a dreary moment for congratulations, Mrs.—Mrs. Lumsden, or I would wish you joy with a good heart."

"You will let me thank you on my wife's account," said Ronald. "As you say, it's a dreary moment—and we have had a dreary time of it; but that I hope is all over now."

"Over by the death of the poor gentleman that suspected nothing; that has treated his niece like his own child," said Mr. Wallace. "It is not a pretty thing, nor is it a pleasant consideration. I hope you will not think I am meaning anything unkind to you, Miss Lily—I beg your pardon, the other name sticks in my throat. It was not with any thought of this that my old friend left all his money to his niece; and we are met here to mourn his death, not to give thanks with these young people that it's over. He was a good friend to me, gentlemen. You'll excuse me; it sticks in my throat—it sticks in my throat!"

"The feeling is very natural, and I'm sure we're all with you, Wallace; but, as I was saying, what's done cannot be undone," said the first gentleman again.

"And no doubt it is a painful thing for the young people," said another charitably, "to have to tell it at this moment, and to have it received in such a spirit. No doubt they would rather have put it off to another season. It's honest of them, I will say for one, not to put it off."

"And there's the will, I suppose, to read," said another, "and the days are short. My presence is certainly not indispensable, and I think I must be getting home."

"You will not take it unkind, Mrs. Lumsden, if we all say the same. It's enough to give the horses their deaths, standing about in the cold."

"There's no difficulty about the will," said Mr. Wallace. "It is just leaving all to her, and no question about it. Scarcely anything more but a legacy or two to the servants. He was a thoughtful man for all that were kind to him. You can see the will when you please at my office, and the business can be put into your hands, Lumsden, when you please. I suppose you're not intending to remain here?"

"That is as my wife pleases," said Ronald. "In that respect I can have no will but hers."

And then they all stood for a moment, in the natural awkwardness of such a breaking up. No will read; nothing to make a natural point of conclusion. The ladies came to the rescue, as was their part. One of them, touched by pity, took Lily into her arms, and spoke tenderly in her ear.

"My dear, you must not blame yourself beyond measure," she said. "You were very good to the old man. I have thought for a long time you had something on your mind. But if you had been his daughter ten times over, and had a conscience void of offence, you could not have been a better bairn to the old man."

"Thank you for saying so," said Lily. "I will remember you said it as long as I live."

"Hoot!" said the kind woman, "you will soon be thinking of other things. I will come back soon to see you, and you must just try to forgive yourself, my dear." She paused a moment, and Lily divined that she would have said, "and him," but these words did not come.

"We will all come back—and bring our good wishes—another day," said this lady's husband, and then they all shook hands with her, with at least a show of cordiality, the half-dozen men feeling to Lily like a crowd, the other lady saying nothing to her but a half-whispered good-by. Ronald elaborately shook hands with them all, with a little demonstration again as of the master of the house. He went to the door with them, seeing them off, enquiring about their carriages. He was perfectly good-mannered, courteous, friendly, but showing a familiarity with the place, warning the strangers of the dark corners, and especially of that worn step at the top of the stairs, which was positively dangerous, Ronald said, and must be seen to at once, and with an assumption of the position of the man of the house which did not please the country neighbors. He was too well acquainted with every thing, too pat with all their names, overdoing his part.

"Oh, Miss Lily, Miss Lily," cried old Wallace, who had not called her by that name since she was a child, "how could you deceive him? a man that trusted in you with all his heart!"

"Nobody can blame me," said Lily drearily, "as I blame myself."

"You would never have had his money had he known. The will's all right, and nobody can contest it, but that siller would burn my fingers if it were me. I would have no enjoyment in it. I would think it a fortune dearly bought."

"The money—was I thinking about the money?" Lily cried, with a touch of scorn which brought back its natural tone to her voice.

"No, I dare swear you were not," said the old gentleman; "but if not you, there were others. It's never a good thing to play with money: either it sticks to your fingers and defiles you, or it's like a canker on your good name. He's away to his account, that maybe had something to answer for. He should have given you your choice—your lad or my siller. He should have put it into words. He should have given you your choice."

"He did," said Lily, almost under her breath.

"He did! I'm glad to hear it—it was honest of him—and you—thought it better to have them both. I understand now. It was maybe wise, but not what I would have expected of you."

Lily had not a word to say; she had hidden her face in her hands.

"Mr. Wallace," said Ronald, coming back, "I cannot have my wife questioned in my absence about things for which, at the utmost, she is only partially to blame. I am here to answer for her, and myself, too."

"You will have enough to do with yourself. Did you think, sir, you were to come and let off a surprise on us all, and claim Sir Robert's money, and receive his inheritance, and never a word said?"

"If it eases your mind, say as many words as you like!" cried Ronald cheerfully; "they will not hurt either Lily or me—precious balms that do not break the head!"

"I would just like, my young sir, to punish ye well for your mockery of the Holy Scriptures, if not of me!"

"The punishment is not in your hand," said Lily, uncovering her pale face. "We are not clear of it, nor ever will be; it will last as long as our lives."

"I can well believe that," said old Wallace. He put up the papers with which the table was strewn into his bag. "You can come to me in my office when you like, Mr. Lumsden, and I will show you every thing. It's unnecessary that you and me should go over it here," he said, snapping the bag upon them, almost with vehemence. "She's badly hurt enough; there is no occasion for turning the knife in the wound. I will leave you to make it up within yourselves," he said.

Once more Ronald accompanied the departing guest down stairs. He called Mr. Wallace's clerk; he helped Mr. Wallace to mount into the geeg which awaited him. No master of a house could have been more attentive, more careful of his guest. He wrought the old gentleman up to such a pitch of exasperation that he almost swore—a thing which occurred to him only in the greatest emergencies; and that it was all he could do to prevent himself from using his whip upon the broad shoulders of the interloper who was thus speeding the parting guests. But the exigencies of the coach, which he had to get at Kinloch-Rugas at a certain hour, prevented much further delay. And Ronald stood and watched the departure of the angry man of business in the Kinloch-Rugas geeg with a sensation of relief. Was it relief? He was glad to get rid of him, no doubt, and of all the consternation and disapproval with which his appearance had been greeted. No one now had any right to say a word—the first and greatest ordeal was over. But yet there remained something behind which made Ronald's nerves tingle; all that was outside had passed away. He had now to confront alone an antagonist still more alarming: his Lily, whom he loved in spite of every thing, whose image had filled this gray old place with sweetness, who had always, up to their last meeting, been sweet to him, sweeter than words could say—his first and only sweetheart, his love, his wife. Now all the strangers were gone the matter was between him and her alone. And Ronald, though he was so sensible and so strong, was, for the first time, afraid.

He came upstairs slowly, collecting himself for what was before him; not without a pause at the top to examine again that defective step, which he had so often remarked upon, which now must be seen to at once. He had accomplished all he had hoped. Sir Robert had not even kept him long waiting. Two years was not a very long time to wait; two years in comparison with the lifetime that lay before Lily and himself was nothing. They were young, and with this foundation of Sir Robert's fortune every thing was at their feet: all that his profession could give, all its prizes and honors, all that was best in life—the ease of never having to think or scheme about money, the unspeakable freedom and exemption from petty cares which that insures. To do him justice, he did not think of the money itself. He thought that now, whether he was successful or unsuccessful, Lily was safe—that she would have no struggle to undergo, no discomfort—while, at the same time, he was very sure now that he would be successful, that every thing was possible to him. A modest fortune to begin with, enough to keep the wife and family comfortable, whatever happens, and to free him from every thought but how to make the best of himself and his powers—was not that the utmost that a man could desire, the best foundation? He went back to his Lily, saying all this to himself, but he could not get his heart up to the height of that elation which had possessed him when he had put on his weepers and his crape for Sir Robert. He had not quite recognized the drawbacks then. Half of them—oh, more than half of them—had been got over. There only remained Lily: Lily, his wife, who loved him, for whom he had in store the most delightful of surprises, to whom he could show now, fully and freely, without fear of any man, how much he loved her, whose future life he should care for in every detail, letting her feel the want of nothing; oh, far better than that—the possession of every thing that heart of woman could desire.

She was sitting as he had left her, in a large chair drawn out almost into the centre of the room—a sort of chair of state, where she, as the object of all sympathy, had been surrounded by her compassionate friends. It chilled him a little to see her there. She wanted that encirclement the ladies behind her, supporting her, the surrounding of sympathetic faces. Now that position meant only isolation, separation; it gave the aspect of one alone in the world. He went up to her, making a little use of this as a man skilled in taking advantage of every incident, and took her hand. "Lily, my darling, let me put you in another place. Here is the chair you used to sit in. Come, it will be more like yourself."

"I am very well where I am," she said.

There was the chair beside the fire where she had once been used to sit. How suggestive these dumb things, these mere articles of furniture, are when they have once taken the impress of our mortal moods and ways! It had been pushed by chance, by the movement of many people in the room, into the very position which Lily had occupied so often, with her lover, her husband, hanging over her or close beside her, in all the closeness of their first union, when the snow had built its dazzling drifts on every road, and shut them out from all the world. To both their minds there came for a moment the thought of that, the sensation of the chill fresh air, the white silence, the brilliance of the sun upon the sparkling crystals. But it was a hard and bitter frost that enveloped them now—black skies and earth alike, every sound ringing harshly through. Lily sat unmoving. She looked at him with what seemed a stern calm. She seemed to herself to have suffered all that could be suffered in so short a space of time, the shame of her story all laid bare—her story, which had so different an aspect now, no longer the story of a true, if foolish and imprudent, love, but of calculation, of fraud, of a long, bold, ably planned deception for the sake of money. Her neighbors did not, indeed, think so of her, or speak so of her, as they jogged along the frost-bound roads, talking of nothing but this strange incident; but she thought they were doing so, and her heart was seared and burned up with shame.

He drew a chair near to her and laid his hand upon hers. "Lily!" he said.

She did not move; the touch of his hand made her start, but did not affect her otherwise. "There is no need for that," she said, somehow with an air as if she scorned even to withdraw her hand, which was so cold and irresponsive. She added with a long-drawn breath: "You can tell me what you want—now that you have got what you want. It is all that need be said between you and me."

"Lily," he said, lifting her hand, which was like a piece of ice, and holding it between his, "what I want is you. What is anything I can get or wish for without you?"

She withdrew her hand with a little force. "All that," she said, "is over and past. Why should so sensible a man as you are try to keep up what is ended, or to go on speaking a language which is—which has lost its meaning? You and I are not what we were; I at least am not what I was."

"You are my wife, Lily."

"Yes, the more's the pity—the more's the pity!" she cried.

"That's not what I should ever have expected from you. You are angry, Lily, and I confess there are things which I have done—in haste, or on the spur of the moment, or considering our joint interests perhaps more, my dear, than your feelings—"

"It would be well," cried Lily with some of her old animation, "to decide which it was—a hasty impulse, as you say, on the spur of the moment, or our joint interests, which I deny for one! I never for a day was for anything but honesty and openness, and no interest of mine was in it. But at least make up your mind. It was either in your haste or it was your calculation—it could not be both."

"I did not think you would ever bring logic against me," he said.

"Because I was an ignorant girl—and so I was, believing every thing you said, so manythings that turned out one after another to be untrue: that you were to take me home at once as soon as the snow was over; that you were to get a house at Whit-Sunday, at Martinmas, and then at another Whit-Sunday, and then—" Lily had allowed herself to run on, having once begun to speak, as women are apt to do. She stopped herself now with an effort. "Of these things words can be said, but of what remains there are no words to speak. I will not try! I will not try! You have trampled on my heart and my soul and my life to your own end—my uncle's money, my poor uncle that believed me, every word I said! And now I ask, what do you want more? Let me know it, and if I can, I will do it."

"Do you know," he cried, suddenly grasping her hand again with an almost fierce clutch, "that you can do nothing but what I permit? You are my wife, you have nothing, your uncle's money or any other, but what I give you. You're not your own to do what you like with yourself, as you seem to think, but mine to do what I like, and nothing else. If we're to play at that, Lily, you must know that the strong hand is with me!"

"So it appears," she said, with a fierce smile, looking at her fingers, crushed together, with the blood all pressed out of them, as he dropped her hand. His threat, his defiance, did not enter into her mind in all its force. Even in those days such a bondage of one reasonable creature to another was at first impossible to conceive. And Ronald was quick to change his tone. Of all things in the world the last he wanted was to enter into the enjoyment of Sir Robert's fortune without his wife.

"Lily," he said, "Heaven knows it is far from my wish to be tyrannical to you. There is no happiness for me in this world without you. If you can do without me, I cannot do without you. Am I saying I am without fault? No, no! I've done wrong, I've done manythings wrong. But not beyond forgiveness, Lily— surely not that? What I did I thought was for the best. If I had thought you would not understand me, would not make allowance for me—but I believed you would trust me as I trusted you. Anyway, Lily, forgive me. We're bound till death us part. Forgive me; a man can say no more than that."

He was sincere enough at least now. And Lily's heart was torn with that mingling of attraction and strong repulsion which is the worst of all such unnatural separations. She said at last: "I am going away to-morrow, Beenie and me. I had it settled before. You will not stop that. If you will give your help, I will be thankful. Nothing in this world, you or any other, can come between me and that! If it is a living bairn, or if it is a green grave—" Lily stopped, her voice choked, unable to say a word more.

CHAPTER XLVI

Lily was no more visible that day. She retired to her room, having, indeed, much need of repose, and to be alone and think over all that had passed. He said a great deal more to her than is here recorded; but Lily's powers of comprehension were exhausted, or she did not listen, or her mind was so much absorbed in her own projects that she was not aware what he said. His presence produced an agitation in her mind which was indescribable. At first the sense that he was there, the mere sight of him, after all that had come and gone, was intolerable to her. But after a while this changed; his voice became again familiar to her ears, his presence recalled a hundred and a hundred recollections. This was the man whom she had chosen from all the world, whose coming had made this lonely house bright, who had changed her lonely life and every thing in it, who was hers, her love, her husband, the one man in the world to Lily. There was no such man living, she said to herself sternly, as the Ronald of her dreams; but yet this was the being who bore his name, who bore his semblance, who spoke to her in a voice which had tones such as no other voice had, and made her heart beat in spite of herself. This was Ronald—not her Ronald, but Ronald himself—the man who had deceived her and made her a deceiver, who had robbed her of her child in her weakness, when she could not go after him, and swore to her a lie that the child was dead. All that was true; but it is not much of a love which dies with the discovery that the object of it is unworthy. She had thought it had done so; all things had seemed easy to her so far as he was concerned. But now Lily discovered that life was not so easy as that. The sound of his voice, that so familiar voice which had said so much to her, had gone through all these delusions like a knife. Was he to blame that she had made a hero of him, that she had endowed him with qualities he did not possess? This was Ronald, the real man, and there was between him and her the bond of all bonds, that which can never be broken. And she saw confusedly that there had been no false pretences on his part, that he had been the same throughout, if it had not been that her eyes were blinded and she saw her own imagination only. The same man; she did not do him the injustice to think that he had been a cheat throughout, that he had not loved her. It was not so simple as that either; but he had determined with that force which some men have that she should not lose her fortune. Already her heart, excusing him, put it that way; and he had, through all obstacles, carried out this determination. Was it her part to blame him? and even if that were her part, was it the part of a woman never to forgive?

I do not say that these were voluntarily Lily's thoughts; but she had become, as she had never been before, the field of battle where a combat raged in which she herself seemed to have comparatively little part. When the one side had made its fiery assault, then the other came in. There rose up in her with all these meltings and softenings a revulsion of her whole being against Ronald, the man who had made her lie. Into what strange thing had he turned her life for all these years? A false thing, full of concealments, secrets, terrors of discovery. He had led her on from lie to lie, and then when the climax of all came, there had been no mercy, no relenting, no remorse in his breast. He had torn her child from her without care for him or for her, risking the lives of both, and leaving in the bosom of the outraged mother a wound which could never be healed. She felt it now as fresh as when she awakened from her illness and came to life again by means of the pain—even now, when perhaps, perhaps that wrong was to be put right and her child given back to her. If he were in her arms now, it would still be there. Such a blow as that was never to be got over; and it had been inflicted for what? For no high motive of martyrdom—for the money, the horrible money, which now, at the cost of so many lies and outrages of nature, had fallen into his hands.

Oh, no, no! things are not so easy in this world between human creatures made of such strange elements as those of which it has pleased the Master of all things to compound us. It is not all straightforward: love—or else not love, perhaps hate. Love was on every side, the heart crying out toward another that was its mate, and at the same time an insupportable repugnance, revulsion, turning away. He was all that she had in the world; all protection, companionship, support, that was possible to her was in him; and yet her heart sickened at him, turning away, feeling the great gulf fixed which was between them. This great conflict within deadened Lily to all that was going on outside. She was too much occupied with the struggle even to see, much less feel, the state of affairs round her. What she did herself she did mechanically, carrying on what she had intended beforehand, with the waning strength of that impulse which had originated in her before this battle began. She remembered still what she had resolved to do then, and did it dully, without much consciousness. She had made up her mind to go off at once upon her search. Had anything occurred to prevent her doing this? She could not tell, but she went on in so different a way, carrying out her resolution. She counted her money, which was all hers now, about which she could have no scruples. There was some of the housekeeping money, which still she herself felt was her uncle's, intrusted to her, but which certainly, when she came to think of it, was her own now, and some which Sir Robert had given her, about which there could be no question. It seemed a large sum of money to her inexperience—if only she knew where to go, and what to do!

Robina was packing, or appearing to pack—a piece of work which ought to have been done before now. Lily reproved her for being so late, but not with any energy. The things outside of her were but half realized, she was so busy within. Beenie was in a curious state, not good for much. She wept into the box over which she stooped, dropping tears on her mistress's linen when she did not succeed in intercepting them with her apron. But though she wept all the time, she sometimes broke into a laugh under her breath, and then sobbed. It was evident that she had no heart for her packing. She put in the most incongruous things and then took them out again, and would rise up stealthily from her knees when Lily's back was turned, and run to the window, coming back again with a hasty "Naething, naething, mem!" when her mistress remarked this, and asked what she wanted. Down stairs—but Lily did not see it, nor would have remarked it had she seen—Katrin stood at the open door. She had her hand curved over her eyes, though there was no sunshine to prevent her from seeing clearly anything that might appear on the long, dark, frost-bound road. Half the morning, to the neglect of every thing within, Katrin stood looking out. It was a curious thing for the responsible housekeeper of the house— the cook, with her lunch and her dinner on her mind—to do; and so the other servants said to themselves, watching her with great curiosity. Were there any more "ferlies" coming, or what was it that Katrin was expecting from the town?

Of these things Lily took no notice. She went into the drawing-room ready for her journey, conscious that she must see her husband before she left the house, but with a great failing of heart and strength, wishing only to get away, to be alone, to go on with the terrible struggle in her thoughts. There was no one there when she went in, and it was a relief to her. She sat down to recover her strength, to recover her breath. She had told him that she was going, and so far as she could remember he had made no opposition. She had appealed to him to help her, but so far as she knew he had not attempted to do so. It was not yet quite time to go, and Beenie was behindhand, as she always was. Lily was glad, if the word could be used at all in respect to her feelings at this moment, of the little quiet, the time to breathe.

There was, however, some strange commotion going on in the house—a sound outside of cries and laughter, a loud note of Beenie's voice in the adjacent room, and then the rush of her heavy footsteps downstairs. There arose in Lily's mind a vague wonder at the evanescence of all impressions in the women's minds. They had all wept plentifully the day before at the funeral, and spoken with sickly stifled voices, as if they had been not only sorrowful, but bowed down with trouble. And now there was Beenie, loud with a shriek of what sounded like joy, and Katrin's voice rising over a little babel of confused sound, in exclamations and outcries of delight. What could have changed their tone so suddenly? But Lily asked herself the question very vaguely, having no attention to give to them. The only external thing that could have thoroughly roused her would have been her husband's step, and the thrill of being face to face with him again.

It was not long before the sound of approaching footsteps made her heart leap into the wildest agitation again. The noise had gone on down stairs, the cries of delight, the sound of sobbing, and for one moment something—a small brief note which made Lily start even in her self-absorption. But she had not heeded more than that one quick heart-beat of surprise. Was that at last Ronald's step coming quickly up the winding stair? She clasped her hands firmly together, and wound herself up as best she could for this meeting, the interview which would perhaps be their last. Her eyes were fixed upon the door. She was conscious of sitting there rigidly, like a figure of stone, though her being was full of every kind of agitation. And then there was a pause. He had not come in. Why did he not come in?

Finally the door was slowly opened, but at first no one appeared. Then there was a whisper and another sound—a sound that went through and through the listening, waiting, agitated woman, who seemed to have no power to move, and then—

There came in something white into the room, a little speck upon the darkness of the walls and carpet— low down, white, with something like a rose above the whiteness. This was what Lily saw: her eyes were dim and every thing was confused about her. Then the speck moved forward slowly with tottering, uncertain movements, the whiteness and the rose wavering. There came a great cry in Lily's heart, but she uttered not a word; a terror, lest any movement of hers should dispel the vision, took possession of her. She rose up noiselessly, and then, not knowing what she did, dropped upon her knees. The little creature paused, and Lily, in her semi-conscious state, became aware of the blackness of her own figure in her mourning, and the great bonnet and veil that covered her head. Noiselessly she undid the strings and threw them behind her, scarcely breathing in her suspense. The child moved again toward her, relieved, too, by the removal of that blackness, and Lily put out her arms. How can I tell what followed? She could not, nor ever knew. The child did not shriek or cry, as by all rules he should have done. He rolled and wavered, the rose growing distinct into a little face, with a final rush into his mother's arms. And for a moment, an hour—how long was it?—Lily felt and knew nothing but that again she had her baby in her arms—her baby, that had been snatched from her unconscious, that came back to her with infantile perceptions, smiles, love in its face! She had her baby in her arms, not shrinking from her, as she had figured him to herself a hundred times, but putting up his little hands to her face, pleased with her, not discomposed with her kisses, putting his soft cheek against hers; the one was as soft as the other, and as the warm blood rose in Lily's veins and the light came to her eyes and the joy to her heart, as softly, warmly tinted, too, one rose against another. She forgot herself and all about her—time and space, and all her resolutions and her struggle and strain with herself, and her mourning and her wrongs. Other people came into the room and stood round, women crying, laughing, unable to do anything but exclaim and sob in their delight. But Lily took no notice. She had her child against her heart, and her heart was healed. She could not think where all the pain had gone. Her breath came free and soft, her life sat lightly on her, her cares were over. She wanted to know nothing, see nothing, hear nothing more.

But this could not be. In another minute Ronald came into the room quickly, no doubt full of anxiety, but full also of the energy of a man who has the command of the situation and means to settle it in every way, not unkindly, but yet authoritatively. With a word he dispersed the women, stopping their outcries, which had been a sort of accompaniment to the song of content that was in Lily's heart, and then he came quickly forward and put his arm round the group of the mother and child. He pressed them to him and kissed them, first his wife and then the baby, who sat on her knee. "Now all is well," he said; "my Lily, all is well! Every thing is forgiven and forgotten, and you and me are to begin again!"

Then Lily came suddenly back out of her rapture. She came back to the life to which he called her, in which he had played so strange a part. How her heart had melted toward him when he was not there! To be Ronald had seemed to her by moments to be every thing. But now that he was here, kneeling before her, his child on her knee, his arms around her, his kiss on her cheek, there rose up between them a wall as of iron, something which it seemed impossible should ever give way, a repulsion stronger than her own will, stronger than herself. She made an involuntary movement to free herself. And her face changed, the rose-hues went out of it, the light from her eyes. All well! How could all be well? Two years, during which this child had been growing into consciousness in another house, with other care, with neither father nor mother; and she left widowed and bereft, to play a lying part and be another creature—not what she was! And all for money, money—nothing better! And now the money was won by all those lies and deceptions, now all was to be well?

"Let me be," she said hoarsely, "let me be! A little rest, I want a rest. I am not equal to any more."

He got up to his feet, repulsed and angry. "You do not think what I am equal to," he said, "or hesitate to inflict on me what punishment, what cruelty, you please! And yet every thing that has been done was done in your own interests, and who but you will get the good of it all?"

"My interests?" Lily cried.

And then there came an unexpected interruption. The baby, for all so young as he was, became aware of the change of aspect of things around him. His little roselip began to quiver, and then he set up a lamentable cry which, to the inexperienced heart of Lily, was far more dreadful than ever was the cry of a child. As she tried to soothe him there appeared in the doorway Margaret Bland, the woman who had taken him away. And Lily gave a cry like that of her child, and clung to the baby, who, for his small part, struggled to get to his nurse, the only familiar figure to him in all this strange place. "Not you," cried Lily, "not that woman who stole him from me! Beenie! not you, not you!"

"And yet, mem," said Margaret, "it is me that has been father and mother and all to him when none of you came near. And the darling is fond o' me and me of him like my own flesh and blood."

"Beenie, Beenie!" cried Lily, wild with terror, as the child slid and struggled out of her arms. "Katrin, Katrin! oh, don't leave her, not for a moment—don't let her take him away!"

Once more the cloud of women appeared at the door, all the maids of the house delighted over the child, and Beenie in the front, seizing Margaret by the skirts as she gathered up the child in her arms. "Na, na, she'll no take him an inch out o' my sight!" Beenie cried.

Lily stood up trembling, breathless, confronting her husband as this little tumult swept away. A passion of terror had succeeded her rapture of love and content; and yet there was a compunction in it and almost a touch of shame. That chorus of excited women did not add to the dignity of her position. He had not said anything, but was walking up and down the room in impatience and annoyance. "Who do you think would take him from you now?" he cried in his exasperation, adding fuel to the fire.

Oh, not now! There were no interests to be involved now; the money was safe, for which all these hideous plans had been laid. If this was meant to soothe, it was an ill-chosen word. And for a moment these two people stood on the edge of one of those angry recriminations which aggravate every quarrel and take all dignity and all reason from the breach. Ronald perceived his mistake even before Lily could take any advantage of it, had she been disposed so to do.

"Lily," he said, "your life and mine have to be decided now. There is neither credit nor comfort in the position of deadly opposition which you have taken up. I may have sinned against you. I told you what was not true about the child, I acknowledge that. I should not have pretended he was dead. I saw my mistake as soon as I had committed it, but it was as ineffectual as it was wrong. You did not believe me for a minute, therefore I did no harm. The rest was all inevitable; it could not be helped. Enough has been said on that subject. But all necessity for these expedients is over now. Every thing is plain sailing before us; we have the best prospects for our life. I can promise that no woman will have a better husband than you will find me. You have a beautiful healthy child who takes to you as if you had never been parted from him for a day. We have a good house to step into—"

"What house?" she cried, surprised.

"Oh, not the garret you were so keen about," he answered, a smile creeping about the corners of his mouth, "a house worthy of you, fit for you—the house in George Square!"

"Uncle Robert's house!" she cried, almost with a shriek.

"Yes," he said, "to which you are the rightful heir, as you are to his money. They are both very safe, I assure you, in my hands."

"You are," she said breathlessly, "the proprietor—now?"

"Through you, my bonnie Lily; but there is no mistake or deception about that," he said, with a short laugh; "they are very safe in my hands."

No man could be less conscious than Ronald, though he was a man full of ability and understanding, of the effect of these words of his triumph upon his wife's mind. He thought he was setting before her in the strongest way the advantages there were for her, and both, in agreement and peaceful accord, and how prejudicial to her own position and comfort anything else would be. He was perhaps a little carried away by his success. Even the experiment of this morning—how thoroughly successful it had been! The child might have been frightened and turned away from the unknown mother: instead of this, by a providential dispensation, he had gone to her without hesitation and behaved himself angelically. How any woman in her senses could resist all the inducements that lay before her, all the excellent reasons there were to accept the present and ignore the past—in which nothing had been done that was not for her interest—he could not tell. He began to be impatient with such folly, and to think it might be well to let her have a glimpse of what, if she rejected this better part, lay on the other side.

Lily had seated herself once more in her chair; it was the great chair she had occupied when the funeral party assembled, and gave her something of the aspect of a judge. She had lost altogether the color and brightness that had come into her face. She was very pale, and the blackness of her mourning made this more visible. And, she sat silent, oh, not convinced, as he hoped—far from that—but struck dumb, not knowing what to say.

At this moment, however, there was another interruption, and the little figure of Helen Blythe, covered, too, with crape and mourning, but with a natural glow and subdued brightness as always upon her morning face, appeared at the door.

CHAPTER XLVII

Helen was in all her crape, and yet her upper garment was not "deep," like that of a woman in her first woe. It was a cloak which suggested travelling rather than any formality. And it appeared that the bright countenance with which she came in was one of sympathy for Lily, rather than of any cheerfulness of her own. She came forward holding out both her hands, having first deposited her umbrella against the wall. "I am glad, glad," she said, "of all this that I hear of you, Lily: that you have got your husband to take care of you, and, it appears, a delightful bairn. I knew there was something more than ordinary between you two," she said, stopping to shake hands with Ronald in his turn. "And vexed, vexed was I to see that Mr. Lumsden disappeared when old Sir Robert came. It must have been a dreadful trial to you, my poor Lily. But I never knew it had gone so far. Married in my own parlor, by my dear father, and not a word to me—Lily, it was not kind!"

Lily had no reply to make to this. It carried her away into a region so far distant, so dim, like a fairy-tale.

"But my dear father," said Helen, "had little confidence in my discretion, and he might think it better I should know nothing, in case I should betray myself—and you. Oh, how hard it must have been many a time to keep your secret; and when your child came, poor Lily, poor Lily! But I do not yet understand about the bonnie bairn. They tell me he is a darlin'. But did he come to you in a present, as we used to think the babies did when we were children, or by what witchcraft did you manage all that, Lily, my dear?"

"And where did you hear this story that you have on your fingers' ends?" said Ronald, interrupting these troublesome questions.

"Well," said Helen, half offended, "if I have it on my fingers' ends, it is that I take so much interest in Lily and all that concerns her—and you, too," she added, fearing that what she had said might sound severe. "You forget that there were two years when we saw you often, and then two years that we saw you not at all; and often and often my father would ask about you. 'Where is that young Mr. Lumsden?' 'Have you no word of that young Mr. Lumsden?' He was very much taken up about you, and why you did not come back, nor any word of you. To be sure, he had his reasons for that, knowing more than the like of me."

"Those very reasons should have shown him how I could not come back!" said Ronald sharply. "But you have not told me where it was you got this story, which few know."

"Well—not to do her any harm if you think she should have been more discreet—it was Katrin that told me. She is a kind, good, honest woman. She was just out of herself with joy at the coming of the dear bairn. You will let me see him, Lily?"

"You look as if you were going on a journey. Oh, Helen, where are you going?" cried Lily, glad to interrupt the questions, and to give herself also a moment's time to breathe.

"Yes, I am going on a journey," Helen said, steadfastly looking her friend in the face. Her eyes were clear; her color, as usual, softly bright, not paled by the crape, or by her genuine, but not excessive, grief. She had mourned for her father as truly as she had nursed him, but not without an acknowledgment that he had lived out his life and departed in the course of nature. By this time, though but ten days of common life had succeeded the excitement and commotion of Mr. Blythe's funeral, at which the whole countryside had attended, Helen had returned to the ordinary of existence, and to the necessity of arranging her own life, upon which there was now no bond. The plea of the assistant and successor (now minister) of Kinloch-Rugas that there should be no breach in it at all, that she should accept his love and remain in the house where she was born as his wife, had not moved her mind for a moment. She had shaken her head quietly, but very decisively, sorry to hurt him or any creature, yet fully knowing her own mind; and, in so far as she could do so in the village, Helen had made her preparations. She had a little land and a little money, the one in the hands of a trustworthy tenant, the other very carefully, very safely, invested by her father with the infinite precautions of a man to whom his little fortune was a very great matter, affecting the very course of the spheres. Helen had boldly, with indeed an unspeakable hardihood, notwithstanding the horror and remonstrances of the man of business, taken immediate steps to withdraw her money and get it into her possession. All this was done very quietly, very quickly, and, by good luck, favorably enough. And then she made arrangements for her venture, the great voyage into the unknown.

"Yes," she said, "I am going on a journey. You will perhaps guess where—or if not where, for I am not just clear on that point myself, you will at least know with what end. I have nothing to keep me back now"—a little moisture came into Helen's eyes, but that did not affect her steady, small voice—"and only him in the world that needs me. I am going to Alick, Lily. You will tell me it's rash, as every-body does, and maybe it is rash. If he has wearied at the last and given up all thoughts of me, I will never blame him; but that I cannot think, and it is borne in on my mind that he has more need of me than ever. So I am just taking my foot in my hand and going to him," she said, looking at Lily, with a smile.

"Helen! oh, you will not do that! Go to him, to you know not where, to circumstances you are quite, quite ignorant of? Oh, Helen, you will not do that!"

"Indeed, and that will I," said Helen, with the same calm and steady smile. "I am feared for nothing, but maybe that he might hear the news and start to come to me before I could get to him."

"That is enough!" cried Lily. "Oh, wait till he comes; send for him! Rather anything than go all that weary way across the sea alone."

"I am feared for nothing," Helen said, still smiling, "and who would meddle with me? I am not so very bonnie, and I am not so very young. I am just as safe, or safer, than half the women in the world that have to do things the other half do not understand."

"Like myself, you think," Lily said; and it was on her lips to add: "If you succeed no better than me!" But the bondage of life was upon her, and of the pride and the decorum of life. Ronald had taken no part in this conversation, but he was there all the time, standing against the window, looking out. He was very impatient that his conversation with his wife, so important in every way, should be interrupted. His own affairs were so full in his mind, as was natural, that any enforced pause in the discussion of them appeared to him as if the course of the world had been stopped. And this country girl's insignificant little story, perfectly wild and foolish as it was, that it should take precedence of his own at so great a crisis! He turned round at last and said in a voice thrilling with impatience: "I hope, as Lily does, that you will do nothing rash, Miss Blythe. We have a great deal to do ourselves with our own arrangements."

"And I am keeping Lily from you? You will excuse me," cried Helen, wounded, "but I am going to do something very rash, as you say, and I may never come back; and I cannot leave a friend like Lily, and one my father was proud of, and thought upon on his death-bed, and one that knows where I am going and why, without a word. There is perhaps nobody but Lily in the world that knows what I mean, and what I am doing, and my reasons for it," Helen said. She took her friend's hands once more into her own. "But I will not keep you from him, Lily, when no doubt you have so much to say."

"You shall not go," said Lily, with something of her old petulance, "till you have seen what I have to show you, and till you have told me every thing there is to tell. Oil, my baby, my little bairn, my little flower! I could be angry that you have put him out of my head for a moment. Come, come, and see him now."

Ronald paced up and down the room when he was left alone; his impatience was not, perhaps, without some excuse. He was very anxious to come to some ground of agreement with Lily, some basis upon which their life could be built. He had hoped much from the great coup of the morning, from the bringing back of the child, which he had intended to do himself, taking advantage of the first thrill of emotion, and identifying himself, its father, with the infant restored to her arms; but the women, with their folly, had spoiled that moment for him, and lost him the best of the opportunity, and now there was another woman thrusting her foolish story into the midst of that crisis in his life. Ronald was out of heart and out of temper. He began to see, as he had never done before, the difficulties that seemed to close up his path. He had feared, and yet not feared, the tempest of reproaches which no doubt Lily would pour upon him. He did not know her any better than this, but expected what the conventional woman would do in a book, or a malicious story, from his wife; and he had expected that there would be a great quarrel, a heaping up of every grievance, and then tears, and then reconciliation, as in every story of the kind that had ever been told. But even if she could resist the sight of him and of his pleading, Ronald felt a certainty that Lily could not resist the return of her child; for this she would forgive every thing. This link that held them together was one that never could be broken. He had calculated every thing with the greatest care, but he had not thought it necessary to go beyond that. When she had her child in her arms, Lily, he felt sure, would return to his, and no cloud should ever come between them more.

But now this delusion was over. She had not showered reproaches upon him. She had not done anything he expected her to do. The dreadful, the astounding revelation that had been made to him was that this was not Lily any longer. It was another woman, older, graver, shaped by life and experience, without faith, with a mind too clear, with eyes too penetrating. Would she ever turn to him otherwise than with that look, which seemed to espy a new pretence, a new deception, in every thing he said? Ronald still loved his wife; he would have given a great deal, almost, perhaps, the half of Sir Robert's fortune, to have his Lily back again as she had been; but he began now for the first time to feel that it would be necessary to give up that vision, to arrange his life on another footing. If she would but consent at least to fulfil the decorums of life, to remain under his roof, to be the mistress of his house, not to flaunt in the face of the world the division between these two who had made a love-marriage, who had not been able to keep apart when every thing was against their union, and now were rent asunder when every thing was in its favor! What ridicule would be poured upon him! What talk and discussion there would be! His mind flashed forward to a vision of himself alone in Sir Robert's great house in George Square, and Lily probably here at Dalrugas with her child. Sir Robert's house was his, and Sir Robert's fortune was his. Except what he chose to give her, out of this much desired fortune—for which, indeed, it was he who had planned and suffered, not she—she had no right to anything. There was so much natural justice in Ronald Lumsden's mind that he did not like this, though, as it was the law, and he a lawyer, it cost him less than it might have done another man; but he meant to make the strongest and most effective use of it all the same. He meant to show her that she was entirely dependent upon him—she and her child; that she had nothing and no rights except what he chose to allow her: and that it was her interest and that of her child (whom, besides, he could take from her were he so minded) to keep on affectionate terms with him.

This, though it gave him a certain angry satisfaction, was a very different thing, it must be allowed, from what he had dreamed. He had thought of recovering Lily as she was in the freshness of her love and faith before even the first stroke of that disappointment about the house, the garret in Edinburgh, upon which her hopes had been fixed: full of brightness and variety, a companion of whom one never would or could tire, whose faith in him would make up for any failure of appreciation on the part of the rest of the world, nay, make an end of that—for would not such a faith have inspired him to believe in himself, to be all she believed him to be? Did he live a hundred years, and she by his side, Ronald now knew that he would never have that faith again. And the absence of it would be more than a mere negative: it would inspire him the wrong way, and make him in himself less and less worthy—a man of calculations and schemes—all that she most objected to, but of which he felt the principle in himself. It is not to be supposed that he himself called, or permitted himself to imagine, these calculations base. He thought them reasonable, sagacious, wise, the only way of getting on in the world. They had succeeded perfectly in the present instance. He was conscious, with a sort of pride, that he had thus fairly gained Sir Robert's fortune, which he had set before him as an object so long ago. He had won it, as it were, with his bow and his spear, and it was such a gain to a young man as was unspeakable, helping him in every way, not only in present comfort, but in importance, in his profession, in the opinion of the solicitors, who had always more confidence in a man who had money of his own. Ah, yes, he had won in this struggle—but then something cold clutched at his heart. He was a young man still, and he loved his wife—he wanted her and happiness along with all those other possessions; but when he won Sir Robert's money, he had lost Lily. Was this so? Must he consent that this should be so? Were they separated forever by the thing that ought to unite them? He said to himself: "No, no!" but in his heart he felt that cold shadow closing over him. They might be together as of old—more than of old—each other's constant companions. But Lily would never be to him what she had been; they would be two, living side by side, unconsciously or consciously criticising each other, spying upon each other. They would no more be one!

To meet this, when one had expected the flush and assurance of success, has of all things in the world the most embittering and exasperating effect upon the mind. Ronald had looked for trouble with Lily— the ordinary kind of trouble, a quarrel, perhaps à outrance, involving many painful scenes—but he had never thought of the real effect of his conduct upon her mind, the tremendous revulsion of her feelings, the complete change of his aspect in her eyes, and of that which she presented to him. A moment of disgust with every thing—with himself, with her, with his success and all that it could produce— succeeded the other changes of feeling. It is not unnatural at such a moment to wish to do harm to somebody, to throw off something of that sense of the intolerable that is in one's own mind upon another. And Ronald bethought himself of what Helen Blythe had said, her complete acquaintance with the story which had been so carefully concealed from her, and her confession that she had it from Katrin. A wave of wrath went over him. Katrin had been in the secret from the beginning, not by any desire of his, but because the circumstances rendered it inevitable that she should be so, and nothing could be done without her complicity. He said to himself that he had never liked her, nor her surly brute of a husband, who had looked at him with so much suspicion on many of his visits here. They thought themselves privileged persons, no doubt; faithful servants, who had been of use, to whom on that account every thing was to be forgiven; who would be in his own absence, as they had been in Sir Robert's, a sort of master and mistress to Dalrugas, recounting to every-body, and to the child when he grew up, the history of his parents' marriage, entertaining all the country neighbors with it—an intolerable suggestion. With them at least short work could be made. He rang the bell hastily and desired that Katrin should be sent to him at once, she and her husband, and awaited their appearance impatiently, forming sharp phrases in his mind to say to them, with the full purpose of pouring on their heads the full volume of his wrath.

Katrin received that summons without surprise. She had thought it likely that something would be said to her of gratitude for her faithful service, and for her care of Lily; perhaps a little present given, which Katrin did not want, but yet would have prized and guarded among her chief treasures. She called in Dougal from the stable, and hastily brushed the straws and dust from his rough coat. "But they ken you're aye among the beasts!" she said. She herself put on a spotless white apron, and tied the strings of her cap, which in the heat of the kitchen were often flying loose. Dougal followed her, with no such look of pleasure on his face. To him Ronald was still "that birky from Edinburgh," whose visits and absences, and all the mystery of his appearance and disappearance, had so often upset the house and wrought Miss Lily woe. The wish that he could just have got his two hands on him had not died out of his mind, and it was bitter to Dougal to feel that this man was to be henceforth his master, even though he believed he was about to receive nothing but compliments and gratification from his hand. Ronald was still walking up and down the room when the pair—Katrin with her most smiling and genial looks—appeared at the door.

"Oh, you are there!" he said hastily with a tone of careless disdain. "I wished to speak to you at once to let you know what I have settled, that you may have time to make your own arrangements. There are likely to be many changes in the house—and the way of living altered altogether. I think it best to tell you that, after Whit-Sunday, Mrs. Lumsden will have no further occasion for your services."

He had not found it so easy as he thought, in face of Katrin's changing face, which clouded a little with surprise and disappointment at his first words, then rose into flushed amazement, and then to consternation. "Sir!" she cried, when he paused, aghast, and without another word to say.

"I kent it would be that way," Dougal muttered, behind her, in the opening of the door.

"Well!" said Ronald sharply, "have you anything to say against it? I am aware you have for a long time considered this house your own, but that was simply because of the negligence of the master. That time is over, and it is in new hands. You will understand, though it is not the usual time for speaking, that I give you lawful notice to leave before the Whit-Sunday term in this current year."

"Sir," said Katrin again, "I'm thinking I canna rightly trust to my ears. Are you meaning to send me—me and Dougal, Sir Robert's auld servants, and Miss Lily's faithful servants—away? and take our places from us that we've held this twenty year? I think I maun be bewitched, for I canna believe my ears!"

"Let us have no more words on the subject," said Ronald; "arguing will make it no better. You are Sir Robert's old servants, no doubt, but Sir Robert is dead and buried; and how far you were faithful servants to him—after all that I know of my own experience—the less said of that the better, it seems to me."

"Dougal," said Katrin, with a gasp, "haud me, that I dinna burst! He is meaning the way we've behaved to him!"

"And he has good reason!" said Dougal, his shaggy brows meeting each other over two fiery sparks of red eyes. "'Od, if I had had my will, many's the time, I would have kickit him out o' the house!"

Dougal's words were but as a muttering—the growl of a tempest—but the two people blocking the door, meeting him with sudden astonishment and a quick-rising fury of indignation which matched his own, wrought Ronald's passion to a climax; he seized up his hat, which was on the table, and pushed past them, sending the solid figures to right and left. "That's enough. I have nothing more to say to you!" he said.

It was Katrin that caught him by the arm. "Maister Lumsden," she said, "ye'll just satisfy me first! Is it because of what we did for you—takin' ye in, makin' ye maister and mair, keepin' your secret, helpin' a' your plans—that you're now turnin' us out of our daily bread, out o' our hame, out o' your doors?"

"Cheating your master in every particular," said Ronald, "as you will me, no doubt, whenever you have a chance. Yes; that is one of my reasons. What did you say?"

He raised the cane in his hand. The movement was involuntary, as if to strike at the excited and threatening countenance of Dougal behind. They were huddled in a little crowd on the top of the winding stair. Ronald had turned round, on his way out, at Katrin's appeal, and stood with his back to the stair, close upon the upper step. "What did you say?" he cried again sharply. Dougal's utterances were never clear. He said something again, in which "Go-d!" was the only articulate word, and made a large step forward, thrusting his wife violently out of the way.

It all happened in a moment, before they could draw breath. Roland, it is to be supposed, made a hasty, involuntary step backward before this threatening, furious figure, with his arm still lifted, and the cane in it ready to strike, but lost his footing, and thus plunged headforemost down the deep well of the spiral stair.

CHAPTER XLVIII

Lily was very reluctant to let Helen go. She kept her on pretence of the child, who had to be exhibited and adored. A great event annihilates time. It seemed already to Lily that the infant had never been out of her arms, that he had always found his natural refuge pressed close to her, with his little head against her breast. She had at first, with natural but unreasonable feeling, ordered Margaret out of her sight, she who had been the instrument of so much suffering to her; but the woman had defended herself with justice. "It is me that have done every thing for him all this time," she said. "It is me that have trained him up to look for his mammaw. Eh, it would have been easy to train the darlin' to look to nobody but me in the world; but I have just made it his daily thought that he was to come to his mammaw, and summer and winter and night and day I have thought of nothing but that bairn." Lily had yielded to that appeal, and Beenie had already made Margaret welcome. They sat in the little outer room, already established in all the old habits of their life, sitting opposite to each other, with their needle-work, and all its little paraphernalia of workboxes and reels of thread, brought out as if there had never been any interruption of their life, and the faint, half-whispered sound of their conversation making a subdued accompaniment; while Lily, with her child on her knee, pausing every moment to talk to him, to admire him, to respond to the countless little baby appeals to her attention, appeared to Helen an image of that perfect happiness which is more completely associated to women with the possession of a child than with any other circumstance in the world. Helen did not know, except in the vaguest manner, of anything that lay below. She divined that there might be grievances between the two who had been so long parted. But Helen herself would have forgiven Ronald on the first demand. His sins would have been to her simply sins, to be forgiven, not a character with which her own was in the most painful opposition. She would have entered into no such question. Lily detained her as long as possible, enquiring into all her purposes, which it was far too late to attempt to shake. Helen, in her rustic simplicity and complete ignorance of the world, was going to America, to its most distant and rudest part, the unsettled and dubious regions of the West, the backwoods, as they were then called, which might have been in another planet for anything this innocent Pilgrim knew of them, and, indeed, at that time, unless to those who had made it a special study, those outskirts of civilization were known scarcely to any. "There will aye be conveyances of some kind. I can ride upon a horse if it comes to that," Helen said, with her tranquil smile. "And no doubt he will come to meet me, which will make it all easy."

"And that is the whole of your confidence!" cried Lily.

"No, no! my confidence is in God, that knows every thing; and, Lily, you should bless his name that has brought you out of all your trouble, and given you that darlin', God bless him, and a good man to stand by you, and your settled home. Oh, if I can but get Alick to come back, to settle, to work my bittie of land, and live an honest, quiet life like our forbears"—the tears stood for a moment in Helen's eyes— "but I will think of you, a happy woman, my bonnie Lily, and it will keep my heart."

What a strangely different apprehension of her own position was in Lily's heart as she sat alone when Helen had gone. The baby had gone to sleep and had been laid on the bed, and she began to pace slowly about in her room, as Ronald was doing so near to her, with a heavy heart, notwithstanding her joy, wondering and questioning with herself what the life was to be that lay before her. A settled home, a good man to stand by her, a lovely child. What more could woman want in this world? The crisis could not continue as it was now; some ground of possibility must be come to, some foundation on which to build their future life. To think of accompanying her husband to Edinburgh, taking possession of her uncle's house, establishing herself in it, he the master of every thing, made her heart sick. If they had stolen his money from old Sir Robert, it would have been less dreadful than thus to take every thing from him, in defiance of all his wishes, as soon as he was dead, when he could assert his own will no more. If she could remain where she was, Lily felt that she could bear it better. But this was only one part of the question before her which had to be settled. She—who had become Ronald's wife in the fervor and enthusiasm of a foolish young love, who had lived on his coming, on the hope of his return, on the dream of that complete and perfect union before God and man in which nobody could shame them or throw a shadow on their honor—to find herself now, after being betrayed and deceived and outraged, her heart torn out of her breast, her child out of her arms, the truth out of her life, in the position of the happy woman, her home assured, her husband by her side, her child in her arms—to be called upon to thank God for it, to take up her existence as if no cloud had covered it, and face the world with a smiling face, forgetting all that interval of misery and deprivation and falsehood! Her steps became quicker and quicker as the tide of her thoughts rose. Amid all the surroundings, which were those of perfect peace—the child asleep in its cradle, the soft undertones of the attendant women—yet all that passion and agony within!

But Lily knew this could not be. Dreadful reason and necessity faced her like two dumb images of fate. Some way of living had to be found, some foundation on which to build the new, changed, disenchanted life. She had no desire to shame Ronald in the sight of his friends, to make her indignation, her disappointment, the property of the world. There would be critics enough to judge him and his schemes to secure Sir Robert's money. It was hers, in the loyalty of a wife, to take her share of the burden, to let it be believed, at least, that all had been done with her consent; and obnoxious as this was to Lily, she forced her mind to it as a thing that had to be. That was, however, an outside matter; the worst of the question was within: how were they to live together side by side, to share all the trivialities of life, to watch over together the growth of their child, to decide together all the questions of existence, like two who were one, who were all in all to each other—these two who were so far and so fatally apart? But Lily did not disguise from herself that this must be done. She calmed herself down with a strong exertion of her will, and prepared herself to meet her husband, to discuss with him, as far as was possible, the future conditions of their life.

She had turned to leave her room in order to join Ronald and proceed to this discussion when the silence of the house was suddenly disturbed by a shriek of horror and dismay: no little cry, but one that pierced the silence like a knife, sharp, sudden, terrible, followed by a voice, in disjointed sentences, declaiming, praying, crying out like a prophet or a madman. The two women came rushing to Lily from the outer room, struck with terror. What was it? Who was it that was speaking? The voice was not known to any of them; the sound of the broken words, loud, as if close to their ears, gradually becoming intelligible, yet without any meaning they could understand, drove them wild with terror. "What is it?" they all cried. Was it some madman who had broken into the house? Lily cast a glance—the mother's first idea—to see that all was safe with the child, and then hastened through the empty drawing-room, where she expected to find Ronald. The door was open, and through the doorway there appeared a tragic, awful figure, a woman with her hands sometimes lifted to her head, sometimes wildly flung into the air, her voice growing hoarser, giving forth in terrible succession those broken sentences, in wild prayer, exhortation, invective, it was impossible to say which. Some locks of her hair, disturbed by the motion of her hands, hung loose on her forehead, her eyes were wildly enlarged and staring, her lips loose and swollen with the torrent of passionate sound. For a moment Lily stood fixed, terrified, thinking it a stranger, some one she had never seen before, and the first words were like those of a prayer.

"Lord hae mercy! Lord hae mercy! Swear ye didna lay a finger on him, no a finger! Swear ye didna touch him, man! Oh, the bonnie lad! oh, the bonnie lad!" Then a shriek again, as from something she saw. "Tak' him up gently, tak' him softly! his head, his head! tak' care of his head! Oh, the bonnie lad, the bonnie lad! Lord hae mercy, mercy! Say ye didna lay a finger on him! Swear ye didna touch him! Oh, his head, his head, it's his head! Oh, men, lift him like a bairn! Lord hae mercy, hae mercy! Say ye didna lay a finger on him! Oh, the bonnie lad, the bonnie lad!" The wild figure clasped its hands, watching intently something going on below, which now became audible to the terrified watchers also—sounds of men's footsteps, of hurried shuffling and struggling, audible through the broken shrieks and outcries of the woman at the top of the stairs.

"Who is it?" cried Lily, breathless with terror, falling back upon her attendants behind her.

"Katrin, Katrin, Katrin!" cried Beenie, carried away by the wild contagion of the moment; "she's gone mad, she's gone out of her senses! Mem, come back to your ain room; come back, this is nae place for you!"

Katrin! was it Katrin, this wild figure? Lily darted out and caught her by the arm.

"Katrin! what has happened? Is it you that have been crying so? Katrin, whatever it is, compose yourself. Come and tell me what has happened! Is it Dougal? What is it? We will do every thing, every thing that is possible."

Katrin turned her changed countenance upon her mistress; her swollen lips hanging apart ceased their utterance with a gasp. She looked wildly down the stairs, then, putting her hands upon Lily's shoulders, pushed her back into the room, signing to Robina behind. "Keep her away, keep her—" she seemed to them to say, making wild motions with her hands to the rooms beyond. Her words were too indistinct to be understood, but her gestures were clear enough.

"Oh, mem," cried Beenie, "it will be something that's no for your eyes! For mercy's sake, bide here and let me gang and see!"

"Whatever has happened, it is for me to see to it," said Lily. And then, disengaging herself from them, she said, for the first time very gravely and calmly: "My husband must have gone out. Go and look for him. Whatever has happened, it is he who ought to be here."

She got down stairs in time to see the stumbling, staggering figures of the men carrying him into the library. But it was not till some time afterward that Lily had any suspicion what it was. She thought it was Dougal, who had met with some dreadful accident. She had the calmness in this belief to send off at once for a doctor in two different directions; and, having been begged by her uncle's valet not to go into the room till the doctor came, obeyed him without alarm, and went out to the door to look for Ronald. It was strange he should have gone out at this moment, but how could he know that anything would be wanted to make his presence indispensable? Most likely he was angry with her for keeping him waiting, for talking to Helen Blythe when there were things so much more important in hand. She went out to the door to look for him, not without a sense that to have him to refer to in such an emergency was something good, nor without the thought that it would please him to see her looking out for him over the moor.

Ronald never spoke again. If his death was not instantaneous in point of fact, it was so virtually, for he never recovered consciousness. He had fallen with great force down the stairs from the worn upper step, which had failed his foot as he made that recoil backward from Dougal's threatening advance—the step of which he had so often spoken in half derision, half seriousness, as a danger for any old man. Neither he nor any one else could have supposed it was a danger for Ronald, so young, so full of energy and strength. And many were the reflections, it need not be said, upon the vicissitudes of life and the fate of the young man, just after long waiting come into possession of all that was best in life—fortune and happiness, and all the rest. The story was told all over the country, from one house to another, and in Edinburgh, where he was so well known. To have waited so long for the happiness of his life and then not to enjoy it for a week, to be seized by those grim fangs of fate in the moment of his victory, in the first hour of his joy! The papers were not as bold in those days as now. The fashion of personalities had not come in unless when something very scandalous, concealed under initials, was to be had. But there was nothing scandalous in Ronald Lumsden's story.

In the enquiry that followed there was at first an attempt to suggest that Dougal, who was shown to have been always in opposition to him, and sometimes to have uttered half threats of what he would do if he could get his hands on that birky from Edinburgh, was instrumental in causing his death. And poor Katrin, changed into an old woman, with gray hair that would not be kept in order under her white cap, and lips that hung apart and could scarcely utter a word clearly, was examined before the procurator, especially as to what she meant by the words which she had been heard by all in the house to repeat as she stood screaming at the head of the stairs: "Swear you never lifted a finger upon him!" Were these directions she was giving to her husband in case of any future investigation? or was she adjuring him to satisfy her, to let her know the truth? But Katrin was in no condition to explain to any one, much less to the procurator in his court, what she had meant. But there was no proof against Dougal, and every evidence of truth in his story; and any doubt that might subsist in the minds of persons apt to doubt every thing, and to believe the worst in every case, died away into silence after a while. It is possible that the possibility harmed him, though, as he retained his place and trust in Dalrugas, even that was of no great consequence; but Katrin never was, as the country folk said, "her own woman" again. She never could get out of her eyes the horror of that sudden fall backward, the sound against the stone wall, on the stone steps. In the middle of the night, years after, she would wake the house, calling upon her husband, with pathetic cries, to swear he never laid a finger on him. This made their lives miserable, though they did not deserve it; for Katrin knew at the bottom of her heart, as Dougal knew—but having said it once, would not repeat—that he laid no finger on Ronald, nor ever, save in the emptiest of words, meant him any harm.

Lily was lost for a time in a horror and grief of which compunction was the sharpest part. Her heart-recoil from her husband, her sense of the impossibility of life by his side, her revulsion against him, overwhelmed her now more bitterly, more terribly, than the poignant recollections of happiness past which overwhelm many mourners. The only thing that gave her a little comfort in those heavy depths was the remembrance of the moment when, all unknowing that he could never again come to her, she had gone out to look for Ronald over the moor. There might have been comfort to her after a while in that moor, which had been the confidant of so many of her thoughts of him; but to go up and down, in all the common uses of life, the stairs upon which he died was impossible. She felt a compunction the more to leave the scene of all the happier days, the broken life which yet was often so sweet, which had been the beginning of all. It seemed almost an offence against him to leave a place so connected with his image, but still it was impossible to remain. There was a little mark upon the wall which made them all shudder. And Lily was terrified when her baby was carried up or down those stairs: the surest foot might stumble where he had stumbled, and it is not true that the catastrophes of life do not repeat themselves. Life is all a series of repetitions; and why not that as well as a more common thing?

It was this above all things else that made her leave the house of her fathers, the place where her tragedy had been played out, from its heedless beginning to its dreadful, unthought-of end. It was not so common then as now for the wrecked persons of existence to betake themselves over the world to the places where the sun shines brightest and the skies are most blue; but still, when the wars were all well over, it was done by many, and the young widow, with her beautiful child, and her two women attendants, was met with by many people who knew, or were told by those who knew, her strange story and pitied her with all their hearts. They pitied her for other sufferings than those which were really hers. Those that were attributed to her were common enough and belong to the course of nature; the others were different, but perhaps not less true. But it cannot be denied either that as there was a certain relief even in the first shock of Lily's grief, a sense of deliverance from difficulties beyond her power to solve, so there was a rising of her heart from its oppression, a rebound of nature and life not too long delayed. Her child made every thing easy to her, and made, all the more for coming back to her so suddenly, a new beginning of life. And that life was not unhappy, and had many interests in it notwithstanding the fiery ordeal with which it began.

Helen Blythe came back to Kinloch-Rugas within the year, bringing her husband with her. He was not, perhaps, reformed and made a new man of, as he vowed he would be in her hands. Perhaps, except in moments of exaltation, she had not expected that. But she did what she had soberly declared to be the mission of many women—she "pulled him through." They settled upon her little property and farmed it more or less well, more or less ill, according as Alick could be kept "steady," and Helen's patience. Two children came, both more or less pathetically careful, from their birth, of their father; and the household, though it bore a checkered existence, was happy on the whole. When Helen saw the Manse under the chill celibate rule of the new minister, she was very sorry for him, but entertained no regrets; and when, later in life, he married, the preciseness of the new establishment moved her to many a quiet laugh, and the private conviction, never broken, that, in her own troubled existence, always at full strain, with her "wild" Alick but partially reformed, and the many roughnesses of the farmer's life, her ambitions for her boy, and her comfort in her girl, she was better off than in her old sphere. She did not make her husband perfect, but she "pulled him through." Perhaps, had she taken the reins of that wild spirit into her hands at first, she might have made him all that could have been wished; but as it was she gave him a possible life, a standing-ground when he had been sinking in the waves, a habitation and a name.

Lily came back to the North to establish herself in a house more modern and comfortable, and less heavy with associations, than Dalrugas, some years after these events, and there was much friendship between her and the old minister's daughter, who had been so closely woven with the most critical moments of her life. They were different in every possible respect, but above all in their view of existence. Helen had her serene faith in her own influence and power to shape the other lives which she felt to be in her charge, to support her always. But to Lily there seemed no power in herself to affect others at all. She, so much more vivacious, stronger, to all appearance of higher intelligence, had been helpless in her own existence, able for no potent action, swept by the movements of others into one fated path, loved, yet incapable of influencing any who loved her. She was now a great deal better off, her life a great deal brighter, with all manner of good things within her reach, than Helen, on her little bit of land, pushing her rough husband, with as few detours as possible, along the path of life, and smiling over her hard task. Lily was a wealthy woman, with a delightful boy, and all those openings of new hope and interest before her in him which give a woman perhaps a more vivid happiness than anything strictly her own. But the one mother trembled a little, while the other looked forward serenely to an unbroken tranquil course of college prizes and bursaries, and at the end a good manse, and perhaps a popular position for her son. What should Lily have for hers? She had much greater things to hope for. Would it be hers to stand vaguely in the way of Fate, to put out ineffectual hands, to feel the other currents of life as before sweep her away? Or could she ever stand smiling, like simple Helen, holding the helm, directing the course, conscious of power to defeat all harm and guide toward all good? But that only the course of the years could show.

Margaret Oliphant – A Short Biography

Margaret Oliphant Wilson was born on April 4th, 1828 to Francis W. Wilson, a clerk, and Margaret Oliphant, at Wallyford, near Musselburgh, East Lothian.

She spent her childhood at Lasswade, near Dalkeith, Glasgow before moving to Liverpool.

Her youth was spent in establishing a writing style so much so that, in 1849, she had her first novel published: Passages in the Life of Mrs. Margaret Maitland based on the Scottish Free Church movement. It met with some success and was a good start to her career.

Two years later, in 1851, her third book Caleb Field was published. It was also now that she met the publisher William Blackwood in Edinburgh and was asked to contribute to his well-received Blackwood's Magazine. It was to be a lifelong endeavor. Over the course of the relationship she would have well over 100 articles published.

In May 1852, Margaret married her cousin, Frank Wilson Oliphant, at Birkenhead, and they settled at Harrington Square, Camden, London. He was an artist working primarily in stained glass. With the marriage she became Margaret Oliphant Wilson Oliphant.

Their marriage produced six children but three tragically died in infancy.

When her husband developed signs of the dreaded consumption (tuberculosis) they moved, on the advice of doctors, to warmer climes. In January 1859 it was to Florence, and then to Rome where, sadly, he died.

Margaret was naturally devastated but was also now left without support and only her income from her writing. She returned to England and took up the task of supporting her three remaining children by her literary activity.

By now she was being published both as an established novelist and regularly in Blackwood's Magazine, amongst several others. Her incredible and prolific work rate increased both her commercial reputation and the size of her reading audience.

Against this her domestic life continued to be tragic, full of sorrow and disappointment.

In January 1864 her only remaining daughter, Maggie, died and was buried in her father's grave in Rome. Her brother, who had emigrated to Canada, was shortly afterwards involved in financial ruin. Margaret generously offered a home to him and his children, adding another demand to her already heavy responsibilities.

In 1866 she settled at Windsor to be closer to her sons, who were being educated at near-by Eton School. That year, her second cousin, Annie Louisa Walker, came to live with her as a companion-housekeeper. Windsor was now to be her home for the rest of her life.

Her literary career for three decades was one of constant delivery and success. Whether she wrote historical works or across several genres in fiction: domestic realism, historical, romance or supernatural she was successful.

For more than thirty years she pursued a varied literary career but family life continued to bring problems.

The literary ambitions she wished for her sons were unfulfilled. Cyril Francis, the eldest, died in 1890, leaving a Life of Alfred de Musset, which was later incorporated in his mother's Foreign Classics for English Readers. The younger, Francis, who she nicknamed 'Cecco', collaborated with her in the Victorian Age of English Literature and won a position at the British Museum, but was rejected by Sir Andrew Clark, a famous physician. Cecco died in 1894.

With the last of her children now lost to her, she had but little further interest in life. Her health steadily and inexorably declined.

Margaret Oliphant Wilson Oliphant died at the age of 69 in Wimbledon on 20th June 1897. She is buried in Eton beside her sons.

At her death, Margaret was still working on Annals of a Publishing House, a record of Blackwood's Magazine with which she had enjoyed such a successful relationship.

Her Autobiography and Letters, which present a thoughtful picture of her domestic anxieties, was published in 1899. Only parts were written with a wider audience in mind: she had originally intended the Autobiography for her son, but he died before she could finish it.

Opinions on Oliphant's work are split, with some critics seeing her as a 'domestic novelist', while others recognize her work as influential and important to the Victorian literature canon. Critical reception from her contemporaries is also divided. John Skelton took the view that Oliphant wrote too much and too quickly. Writing a Blackwood's article called 'A Little Chat About Mrs. Oliphant', he asked, "Had Mrs. Oliphant concentrated her powers, what might she not have done? We might have had another Charlotte Brontë or another George Eliot." However not all of the contemporary reception was negative. The esteemed M. R. James admired Oliphant's supernatural fiction, concluding that "the religious ghost story, as it may be called, was never done better than by Mrs. Oliphant in 'The Open Door' and 'A Beleaguered City'. Mary Butts lavished praise on Oliphant's ghost story 'The Library Window', describing it as "one masterpiece of sober loveliness".

More modern critics of Oliphant's work include Virginia Woolf, who asked in 'Three Guineas' whether Oliphant's autobiography does not lead the reader "to deplore the fact that Mrs. Oliphant sold her brain, her very admirable brain, prostituted her culture and enslaved her intellectual liberty in order that she might earn her living and educate her children."

Whatever the merits of their cases Margaret Oliphant has been shamefully neglected in modern years. She is now becoming more widely recognised as a leading writer of her day.

Margaret Oliphant – A Concise Bibliography

A canon of more than 120 works, including novels, travel books, histories, and volumes of literary criticism.

Novels
Margaret Maitland (1849)
Merkland (1850)

Caleb Field (1851)
John Drayton (1851)
Adam Graeme (1852)
The Melvilles (1852)
Katie Stewart (1852)
Harry Muir (1853)
Ailieford (1853)
The Quiet Heart (1854)
Magdalen Hepburn (1854)
Zaidee (1855)
Lilliesleaf (1855)
Christian Melville (1855)
The Athelings (1857)
The Days of My Life (1857)
Orphans (1858)
The Laird of Norlaw (1858)
Agnes Hopetoun's Schools and Holidays (1859)
Lucy Crofton (1860)
The House on the Moor (1861)
The Last of the Mortimers (1862)
Heart and Cross (1863)
Salem Chapel (1863)
The Rector (1863)
Doctor's Family (1863)
The Perpetual Curate (1864)
Miss Marjoribanks (1866)
Phoebe Junior (1876)
A Son of the Soil (1865)
Agnes (1866)
Madonna Mary (1867)
Brownlows (1868)
The Minister's Wife (1869)
The Three Brothers (1870)
John: A Love Story (1870)
Squire Arden (1871)
At his Gates (1872)
Ombra (1872
May (1873)
Innocent (1873)
The Story of Valentine and His Brother (1875)
A Rose in June (1874)
For Love and Life (1874)
Whiteladies (1875)
An Odd Couple (1875)
The Curate in Charge (1876)
Carità (1877)
Young Musgrave (1877)
Mrs. Arthur (1877)

The Primrose Path (1878)
Within the Precincts (1879)
The Fugitives (1879)
A Beleaguered City (1879)
The Greatest Heiress in England (1880)
He That Will Not When He May (1880)
In Trust (1881)
Harry Joscelyn (1881)
Lady Jane (1882)
A Little Pilgrim in the Unseen (1882)
The Lady Lindores (1883)
Sir Tom (1883)
Hester (1883)
It Was a Lover and his Lass (1883)
The Lady's Walk (1883)
The Wizard's Son (1884)
Madam (1884)
The Prodigals and Their Inheritance (1885)
Oliver's Bride (1885)
A Country Gentleman and His Family (1886)
A House Divided Against Itself (1886)
Effie Ogilvie (1886)
A Poor Gentleman (1886)
The Son of His Father (1886)
Joyce (1888)
Cousin Mary (1888)
The Land of Darkness (1888)
Lady Car (1889)
Kirsteen (1890)
The Mystery of Mrs. Biencarrow (1890)
Sons and Daughters (1890)
The Railway Man and His Children (1891)
The Heir Presumptive and the Heir Apparent (1891)
The Marriage of Elinor (1891)
Janet (1891)
The Cuckoo in the Nest (1892)
Diana Trelawny (1892)
The Sorceress (1893)
A House in Bloomsbury (1894)
Sir Robert's Fortune (1894)
Who Was Lost and is Found (1894)
Lady William (1894)
Two Strangers (1895)
Old Mr. Tredgold (1895)
The Unjust Steward (1896)
The Ways of Life (1897)

Short stories

Neighbours on the Green (1889)
A Widow's Tale and Other Stories (1898)
That Little Cutty (1898)
The Open Door (1918)

Selected Articles

Mary Russel Mitford (Blackwood's Magazine, Vol. 75, 1854)
Evelin and Pepys (Blackwood's Magazine, Vol. 76, 1854)
The Holy Land (Blackwood's Magazine, Vol. 76, 1854)
Mr. Thackeray and his Novels (Blackwood's Magazine, Vol. 77, 1855)
Bulwer (Blackwood's Magazine, Vol. 77, 1855)
Charles Dickens (Blackwood's Magazine, Vol. 77, 1855)
Modern Novelists—Great and Small (Blackwood's Magazine, Vol. 77, 1855)
Modern Light Literature: Poetry (Blackwood's Magazine, Vol. 79, 1856)
Religion in Common Life (Blackwood's Magazine, Vol. 79, 1856)
Sydney Smith (Blackwood's Magazine, Vol. 79, 1856)
The Laws Concerning Women (Blackwood's Magazine, Vol. 79, 1856)
The Art of Caviling (Blackwood's Magazine, Vol. 80, 1856)
Béranger (Blackwood's Magazine, Vol. 83, 1858)
The Condition of Women (Blackwood's Magazine, Vol. 83, 1858)
The Missionary Explorer (Blackwood's Magazine, Vol. 83, 1858)
Religious Memoirs (Blackwood's Magazine, Vol. 83, 1858)
Social Science (Blackwood's Magazine, Vol. 88, 1860)
Scotland and her Accusers (Blackwood's Magazine, Vol. 90, 1861)
The Chronicles of Carlingford (Blackwood's Magazine 1862–1865)
Girolamo Savonarola (Blackwood's Magazine, Vol. 93, 1863)
The Life of Jesus (Blackwood's Magazine, Vol. 96, 1864)
Giacomo Leopardi (Blackwood's Magazine, Vol. 98, 1865)
The Great Unrepresented (Blackwood's Magazine, Vol. 100, 1866)
Mill on the Subjection of Women (The Edinburgh Review, Vol. 130, 1869)
The Opium-Eater (Blackwood's Magazine, Vol. 122, 1877)
Russian and Nihilism in the Novels of I. Tourgeniéf (Blackwood's Magazine, Vol. 127, 1880)
School and College (Blackwood's Magazine, Vol. 128, 1880)
The Grievances of Women (Fraser's Magazine, New Series, Vol. 21, 1880)
Mrs. Carlyle (The Contemporary Review, Vol. 43, May 1883)
The Ethics of Biography (The Contemporary Review, July 1883)
Victor Hugo (The Contemporary Review, Vol. 48, July/December 1885)
A Venetian Dynasty (The Contemporary Review, Vol. 50, August 1886)
Laurence Oliphant (Blackwood's Magazine, Vol. 145, 1889)
Tennyson (Blackwood's Magazine, Vol. 152, 1892)
Addison, the Humorist (Century Magazine, Vol. 48, 1894)
The Anti-Marriage League (Blackwood's Magazine, Vol. 159, 1896)

Biographies

Edward Irving (1862)

Francis of Assisi (1871)
Count de Montalembert (1872)
Dante (1877)
Cervantes (1880)
Life of Sheridan in the English Men of Letters series (1883)
John Tulloch (1888)
Laurence Oliphant (1892)

Historical & Critical Works
Historical Sketches of the Reign of George II (1869)
The Makers of Florence (1876)
A Literary History of England from 1760 to 1825 (1882)
The Makers of Venice (1887)
Royal Edinburgh (1890)
Jerusalem (1891)
The Makers of Modern Rome (1895)
William Blackwood and his Sons (1897)
The Sisters Brontë. In: Women Novelists of Queen Victoria's Reign (1897)